Reviews on

Hard P.

#1 in the Detective Inspector Todd "Ratso" Holtom series

"Douglas Stewart has done a great job and has created in Detective Ratso a character who is quick-witted, clever and a worthy addition to the action thriller genre."

"This book engenders the same get-to-the-end compulsion for the reader as does a Harlan Coburn crime suspense or a Simon Kernick or Mark Billingham police novel… the prose is easy to read and the plot is enthralling."

"Couldn't stop reading, this was worth 5 stars."

"Fantastic read, great characters, gripping storyline. Definitely want to read more adventures from Ratso. Roaring success Mr Stewart!"

"I read a lot of thrillers and Hard Place is high up on my list of favourites."

"Each chapter leaves you eager to continue reading. This was the first of Stewart's novels I have read but I will definitely read more."

"It is as if the author has inside knowledge of these characters and places; their portrayal is simple, effective and truly insightful."

"Wow! What a page turner! I can't wait for the next release. A definite five-star from me!

Praise for Douglas Stewart's Previous Books

"A clever blend of villainy"

—*Sunday Times, London*

"Stewart's writing is fast-moving and laced with that natural British sarcasm that comes so effortlessly. Tough to put down"

—*Richard Marcus – Author and Gambling Expert*

"Do read this superb novel"

—*Sunday Independent*

"He makes us think but entertains us"

—*Evening Telegraph*

"So hard to put down"

—*A1 Crime*

Hard Place

DOUGLAS STEWART

©

#1 in the Detective Inspector Todd "Ratso" Holtom series.

Website: www.DouglasStewartBooks.com
Facebook: www.facebook.com/DouglasstewartBooks
Email: Doug@douglasstewartbooks.com

1

West London

The slender figure slowed his pace as he approached 22 Westbrook Drive. The suburban street was empty; he was alone. Or so it appeared. Outside the line of 1930s semi-detached houses was the usual array of ageing Fords, beat-up Honda saloons and tradesmen's vans. Most of the front lawns had been converted to concrete for off-street parking.

When he had sussed out the neighbourhood, he reckoned nosy owners snooped on their neighbours, watching out for deliverymen taking advantage of that randy bit at number 19. Anything to break the humdrum monotony of life in this suburban backwater. But no lace curtains would twitch now. Not at gone 2:30 a.m. The good folk of Westbrook Drive were asleep.

But Erlis Bardici in number 22 was not good. Not even nearly.

The midnight visitor knew Bardici was evil, a killer and enforcer for a drug baron's empire. Not someone to mess with—not if you fancied retiring to sun and sangria in Spain. Or even slippers by the fire in South London.

As the small figure paused outside number 20, he saw a light glowing next door. Keeping close to a hedge, he peered cautiously at the thick curtains in the downstairs front room, lit from within. *Damned night owl!* On the positive side, there it was, his target for the night: the Range Rover parked on what had once been the small grass lawn at number 22.

Still crouching in his all-black gear in the lee of the hedge, he pulled latex gloves onto his slim fingers. From his pocket, he produced a small radio bug, the size of a fly. He wasn't nervous. Certainly not scared. As a veteran of undercover work in Northern Ireland at the height of the Troubles, his talents had been sharpened to the finest point. Back then, operating from his base outside Belfast, the gadgetry had been cruder, nothing as sophisticated as this little marvel, which would track the Range Rover. Since then, he had worked in Bosnia, Pakistan, Colombia, West Africa, freelancing wherever someone would pay for his experience and expertise. And not always on the side of the angels though that part of his life he kept tight and close. But there was no room for complacency. Not with Erlis Bardici.

Tonight, he was flying solo—breaking with police protocol, all that health and safety crap. Except that the crap was there to protect *his* health and safety. *To hell with that!* Desperation at assistant commissioner level had warranted breach of protocol. He was a deniable—in copper jargon, a *snout* or *chis*—a *covert human intelligence source*. For the Met to run him *off the books* was rare and risky. It meant *putting bollocks on the line*, as Ratso, his DI pal, had confided. Not that Ratso would have called him a chis. To Detective Inspector Todd "Ratso" Holtom, he was a *snout* or a *friendly*, a talent for hire when needs must.

When doing a job by the book, he'd have team support, including a couple of uniforms to distract, reassure, or mislead a suspicious householder. After the last snafu, he'd told the Met where to shove the team. *If you want the job done, I'm going in alone. No more relying on coppers too young to shave.* But flying solo was different. Get caught? *No soft landing. You're on your own, son.* Denials all round. He knew the rules. Say nothing. Go quietly. Take your licks. Even jail.

He had been selected for special duties because of his anonymous appearance, his slender form and his height at only five feet seven. Back then, he'd always acted alone. Teams were only as good as the weakest link, *so sod 'em*. The last operation had been screwed up by a pimply faced copper more suited to reading comics than covering someone's arse at dead of night.

He glanced again at the lighted window. There was no sign of movement—just the faint sound of a late-night movie. He took in the peeling paintwork around the front door. All quiet. Time to go.

He advanced a few paces until all that stood between him and the front door was a few feet of concrete. Inwardly, he cursed the manufacturers of modern cars. Gone were the days when the wide expanses of metal offered innumerable places to fix a device. Nevertheless, he knew what he was doing, knew the point where the tracker could be concealed.

With a sudden darting movement, he ducked down behind the silver of the Range Rover's boot. In a couple of nimble movements, he was flat on the ground, slithering snake-like under the chassis. It was a moment he always loved—savouring the smell of the tyres, the fuel, the exhaust and the dried mud under the wheel guards. It took him back – different places, same smells.

He wriggled toward the front suspension and the place where the magnet would work. Starting tomorrow, every journey would be tracked, every destination plotted. He pressed his heels into the concrete, seeking leverage. He felt good about it. With any luck, the tracker would bring down Erlis Bardici, perhaps to a suitably brutal end. God knows the Albanian bastard had dished out enough stuff for too long.

He ran his gloved hand under the chassis, seeking the small spot he wanted. He knew every inch of the vehicle's underside. Knew it even better than he knew Charlene's underside…and he had savoured *that* often enough.

Somewhere in the distance, he heard the siren of an emergency vehicle but it faded away. As he lay on his back, wriggling the last inches, the street was lit by a passing car. He held his breath, wondering if it would stop at the only house where the occupant was still awake. It did not. But moments later, in the silence of Westbrook Drive, the front door of number 22 opened with a sound like the crack of a rifle. The concrete surrounding the car was illuminated.

He heard footsteps. Slow. Deliberate. Cautious. Then he saw the feet. Heavy-duty CAT boots in brown. A less-experienced operative would have panicked.

Not Neil. Not Neil, a veteran of undercover in Ireland, Bosnia, Iraq. He lay still, his breathing soft and measured.

Surely the man just wanted some fresh air? Or as fresh as it gets so close to the Heathrow flight path.

From the corner of his eye, he saw the feet move toward the driver's door. *My God! If he's going for a drive, then I'm stuffed.* But no. The feet kept moving, toward the boot. They moved out of sight. Then they stopped.

"Come out!" The English was heavily accented. No surprise there. He knew the man was Albanian.

Shit! Had he been spotted? Worse still, had someone shopped him? A copper turned by the Albanians? The last snafu had been put down to sodding luck. And now…a second time?

"Come out." The guttural, throaty tone was heavy with menace.

He started to slither back but not before he had planted the tiny device, leaving the second in his pocket to be found.

2

Clapham, South London

Todd "Ratso" Holtom walked briskly along Glebeside Lane, his MP3 beating out a U2 number. *And I still haven't found what I'm looking for.* Bono's rasping voice brought out the soulfulness that he so obviously felt. Ratso agreed with every word, every sentiment. In his personal life, he knew what he wanted. *Simple pleasures*— supporting Fulham, playing or watching cricket and doing his bit with patients at the Spinal Injuries Unit at Stoke Mandeville Hospital in Buckinghamshire.

That was the easy part.

It was in his life as a detective inspector that he hadn't found what he was looking for.

Boris Zandro. Just the Albanian's name made his footsteps pound harder, his determination more intense. He trod the London pavements most days and as often as possible. It showed in his tall, lean but muscled frame, his long legs filling his jeans to good effect.

Boris Zandro. I'm coming to get you. Because it's you *I'm looking for.*

Ratso's eyes were alert, the eyes of a skilled police officer well used to working on surveillance or undercover. Not that he was undercover now. He was glad to be out of that scene. Too much hassle—changing cars, work locations, number plates, IDs. *Living a lie.*

The morning rush-hour traffic threaded its way toward the Red Zone of Central London. He glanced at the procession. *Good morning, lemmings.* For him, getting to work was quality time. Ratso spurned a car, preferring to grab a Tube and walk a couple of miles. He could read the movie revues, do a crossword, or study the cricket scores while his Blackberry and iPhone were neutered by the tunnels. It was also a good opportunity to anticipate the day ahead—the morning briefings; the reports of last night's events; joshing with his Scottish sergeant about the Rangers' heavy defeat *at home*. Plan the next moves in the long struggle against the *untouchable* Boris Zandro.

But that was the best and worst of life as an officer in SCD7—part of the Specialist Crime Directorate tackling *Serious and Organised Crime*. SCD7 was today's name. With the Tory-Liberal Democrat coalition now bedded in, who knew what it would be called next week or even tomorrow. Someone had said it might be SCO7 - OCC (Organised Crime Command). *Really rolls off the tongue, that does.* Everything was changing and not necessarily for the better. He mentally shrugged off the alphabet soup. Whatever they called it, in his mind, his role was twenty-four-seven. And sad git that he was, he liked that. *Loved* it, maybe. *Married to the job.* That was what Clara, his last long-suffering lover had said before she quit. But she was wrong. It was worse than that—or better. SCD7 made all the demands of a rampant mistress, dominating every waking moment. Even sleep was no escape. *In your dreams* took on a whole new meaning after you'd faced an Albanian with a machine gun, been battered with an iron bar by two Nigerian dope peddlers or fought off an attacker flailing a Samurai sword that threatened to slice you like salami.

The drug barons. Like Boris Zandro. Zandro with his rumoured huge deal, his swan song, maybe.

The barons were always there, sticking up two fingers at PC Plod. They had no need to laugh up their sleeves. They were above that. Massively rich, careful, cunning and invariably detached from the daily routine of distributing Class A to the masses, Zandro was a seeming pillar of society. When he was not jetting off on his Gulfstream or cruising aboard his eighty-million-pound yacht, Zandro lived in his mansion in North London.

Even now, as Bono moved on to "Where the Streets Have no Name," Todd Holtom's knuckles clenched and his firm jaw jutted forward as the smug face of Boris Zandro taunted him, grinning like a giant toad. *Can't get me, you cop wankers. You can prove nothing.*

Yet Ratso wouldn't give up his job, not for anything - not even because of the stench in the Cauldron at the end of a hot, sweaty day. This was the nickname for the room where too many detectives sat in cramped basement conditions. A solitary plug-in air freshener struggled to cope, while two electric fans shifted the dust between the stacked files and empty pizza cartons.

Last night had been upbeat. Erlis Bardici's Range Rover was about to be bugged. *Was that just last night? It seemed an age ago.* The bloody iPhone on his bedside table vibrating, intruding on his *quality time* with Nadine. Pissed her off something rotten. The young Swiss waitress had been the latest to hope for equal billing with his job. No chance. She'd had enough of cancelled plans, of him disappearing without warning. But Neil's text coming in when they were *at it* was too much. *Coitus interruptus*, the legal boys called it. Or was it *in flagrante delicto*? Maybe *both*. Damned iPhone.

As he'd paid for her taxi, she hadn't actually said, *Piss off, Todd, get a life* but her glacial eyes had delivered the unspoken message.

Whatever. Ratso Holtom adjusted his padded leather bomber jacket against the stiff northeasterly and quickened his pace.

The message had been important though. Operation Clam was moving again. Little Neil Shalford, a great mate and piss artist, had sent a text confirming he had just parked close to Westbrook Drive. *Operation Clam! Getting Zandro* was moving again. The Albanian had seen off the previous attempt to nail him a few years before. But now Assistant Commissioner Wensley Hughes had approved Neil going solo. High risk. Rare, maybe even unique. The uniqueness had been born from desperation to get the device planted; Operation Clam had been going nowhere.

Little Neil Shalford…his great mate with the sharp wit and an ego as big as Belfast. No team. No backup. One man trespassing beneath the car of a sadistic killer. Little Neil. Alone and bollock naked if he were caught. Then would follow the spin, the lies and cover-up. He stopped for a friendly word with a dosser and slipped a quid into his upturned cap before hurrying on, his mind tormented by thoughts of Neil. Was he alive or dead?

3

Hampstead, North London
Around the time Ratso Holtom had been leading Nadine out of the kebab house on King Street in Hammersmith, Boris Zandro was only a few miles away in distance but light-years away in circumstances.

   His palatial North London home was all white with a massive portico and pillars; the upstairs rooms commanded extensive views over the Heath and the mansion boasted twelve bedrooms and garaging for six. Tonight, as he did regularly, Zandro was entertaining guests for dinner. As he looked down the table at the assembled company, he came close to despising the lot of them. He had no interest in them as people. To him, they were a useful part of his sugar-coated public image. The parties helped him appear in gossip columns for all the right reasons. His patronage of the arts and charitable works were other shields. He feigned interest in the bores he met over canapés at Royal Academy functions or in Mayfair's private galleries. He struggled to stay awake at the Royal Opera House. But the cultured image and generous donations were invaluable. Sometimes while quaffing champagne on these occasions he could exchange an urgent message with a lieutenant.

Tonight's eclectic mix was typical and included a Conservative cabinet minister, a Spurs footballer, a svelte TV presenter, a hedge fund manager and the chair of the local arts group. He always selected the invitees but it was his second wife, Sophia who handled the details. The guests soaked up the Grand Cru pampering but better still for them was rubbing shoulders with other celebrities or persons with the power that money or politics delivered. The politicians welcomed his support for party funds while never questioning the spin: that Boris Zandro had made his millions from a serious stake in an African iron-ore discovery. With the ten-bagger gains, he had ploughed that windfall into an oil exploration company that had struck it big in Uganda. End of story. But as he spooned up some Grand Marnier soufflé he fought not to frown as his thoughts drifted to the balls-aching delays at the shipyard. That Lance Ruthven guy had screwed things up big time.

After emigrating from Albania in the early 1980s, Zandro had opened a small travel agency near Wembley. Long hours, hard work and living frugally had enabled him to rent more shops around the North London fringe. Some of the cash he had invested in small drug deals—low profile but with tidy profits. Gradually, with ever bigger deals, he had distanced himself from the sharp end. In quiet moments, Zandro knew he had been lucky. Back then, the Met Police had poor technology, weak laws and money-laundering was as easy as dropping by a Jersey bank with a suitcase crammed with cash. Now, cleaning money was tougher, much, much tougher. As he pretended to listen to Mandy, the woman prattling away on his left, he was rehearsing methods and contacts to shift the millions for his current deal. Twenty years ago, investing the profits of cocaine, cannabis and heroin into iron ore shares had been a doddle. "Just changing one commodity for another," he had joked to himself at the time—not that his stockbrokers knew or cared about *source of funds* back then.

His gaze wandered to the portrait of himself in a regal posture, his hands clasped. It was a far cry from the ragged-arsed urchin who had played in the narrow streets of Tirana. Quite deliberately, his clothes this evening were the very ones in the portrait. The Russian artist had captured his cultivated look of intense sincerity. The eyes showed warmth and the artist had even made his lips seem less mean by emphasising the thick greying moustache that dominated his upper lip. With his plentiful, swept black hair turning slightly grey, he looked patrician - like a prime minister or captain of industry.

But without my street-smart cunning? My tenacity. For sure, I'd still be a market trader, selling fruit and vegetables in the poorest part of Tirana. He finished the last morsel of dessert, almost licking the plate, a habit from those days when his empty stomach had rumbled. *No. Nothing— and certainly not the Metropolitan Police—will stop this deal. But .... Oh God!* He turned to his neighbour with a forced smile as Mandy, the footballer's WAG interrupted his line of thought wanting to share the latest episode of *I'm a Celebrity*.

Down the table, Sophia looked stunning, head cocked, her beautiful teeth sparkling. She was twenty-six years Zandro's junior and reckoned that at fifty-four, it was time for him to relax on the yacht or, as he saw it, to fool around with as many young women as he could. But retirement was not yet an option. Sophia knew nothing of his plans for the biggest drug deal ever into Europe but with the aggro in the Bahamas and from

Kabul, he sometimes wondered whether the deal was worth the bother. Absent-mindedly, he nodded towards Mandy but more because he was thinking of well-placed friends, especially in the Home Office. Befriending a Scotland Yard Commander and a former Home Secretary had been useful. Now the cops were picking off the small guys and targeting the Hogan crowd from south London. It was good being below the radar for a change.

The first Mrs Zandro, from peasant stock in Albania, had been a millstone, out of her depth in North London. She would have been happier shouting abuse in a Tirana fish market than making conversation with an American hedge-fund manager. Though he tried to see her right in a friendly divorce settlement, her greedy lawyer pushed too far and Mrs Dafina Zandro had mysteriously fallen overboard from the deck of his yacht, the *Tirana Queen* while cruising the Greek Islands. Boris himself had been thousands of miles away and had suitably grieved at her tragic death.

He stifled a yawn. *Dear God! This Mandy woman is asking me something.* "Sorry, you were asking how far Albania was?" He saw her nod. "Under three hours by air."

"Oh! I thought it was sort of close by—just up the M1."

"You must be confusing it with St Albans, my dear."

"Oh, blimey! So it's foreign like? Do they like speak English there?"

He gave her a thirty-second geography lesson but even that was beyond her attention span. Zandro turned away to the blue-rinse wife of the Tory party grandee on his right. She too was heavy going but worth it because of her loose tongue and her husband's recent role as foreign secretary. He could learn so much from boastful politicians and their wives without even asking any questions: they all loved to yak on after a few glasses of Petrus or Romanée Conti. *Especially* the wives.

But his top henchmen on whom his empire depended, his two lieutenants, would never grace Wisteria Lodge. *Sup with a long spoon.* Wasn't that an expression he'd picked up from Baroness Chestercorn? What in hell's name was happening in the shipyard? It was screwing up everything. Maybe it was job for Bardici. His hammer could sort out the shipyard, no sweat. As his mobile vibrated in his pocket, he knew it was urgent and excused himself, promising to be back a few moments. But he had no intention of speaking on the phone. The vibration was all the message he needed to know what to do next.

4

Clapham, South London

Only a couple hundred metres and Ratso would be there. Perhaps they had information. Neil's last text had been at 2 a.m.—five hours ago. Since then, zilch. Neil had gone to ground. Silent as the grave. Ratso dodged round the back of a red Routemaster, knowing Neil would have loved the gallows humour. It came with the territory. *No disrespect, mate.*

He saw the block ahead, saw his unlit office window on the first floor. The building gave no hint it was a police station: no blue lamp or grimy red brickwork. It *was* brick shithouse ugly but without the bricks. It was a conflation of concrete slabs and identical, grimy windows about twenty metres off the busy road near Clapham Common. The automatic red-and-white barrier was no real giveaway either. Plenty of office blocks now had that type of precaution to prevent illegal parking.

As he gazed up at his tiny office, he reckoned passers-by would assume the five-storey block housed several hundred civil servants. It was easy to imagine grey men in grey suits or patterned pullovers pushing paper and pencils around their plastic teacups till it was time to rush for the exit. It was the sort of building where you expected to find clerks sorting Incapacity Claims or debating whether ladders should have a warning on the top rung that read *STOP HERE*. Ratso's pet hate, one of many, was the Nanny State getting in the way of common sense. Damned Health and Safety officials! Effing human rights campaigners. Brussels bureaucrats! Pinko liberal judges, mindless social workers and brain-dead jurors.

Yeah, put like that I've a few pet hates.

But he loved his work. Loved every minute. Hated every minute. Didn't mean he loved his boss: DCI Arthur Tennant, that complacent time-server. He doubted *anybody* in *any* job loved their boss unless nookie was involved and that was usually lust and not love. As he turned off the music and slipped the MP3 into his jacket pocket, he knew he could never ever respect Arthur Tennant. He'd often wondered how that clown won a transfer to the elite Serious and Organised Crime team. *Probably covered a superior's arse after a botched job.*

He crossed the car park, a touch of drizzle falling on the anonymous staff cars that filled one or two of the bays. The good stuff used by his team for surveillance or for OPs was round the back, pool cars for every occasion: a dented Ford for Merton High Street or a dark red BMW for cruising in leafy Hampstead. His hands clenched unwittingly as he thought again of Tennant. Tennant, *the master of the soft option. Lazy bastard Tennant. Take-no-chance Tennant. Play-it-by-the-book Tennant. Count-the-days-till-retirement Tennant.* That was why Neil's little trip last night had to go up to the assistant commissioner at Scotland Yard. It was off balance-sheet work, outside Tennant's comfort zone.

If it went wrong, no shit would stick to Arthur bloody Tennant. Tennant, the nit-picker, the fault-finder whose main hobbies were picking his nose while picking winners at Wimbledon dog track.

Forget sodding Tennant. The runt'll be gone soon. Early retirement if he can fix it.

But if bugging Bardici had gone wrong, would the shit stick to Todd Ratso Holtom?

Perhaps.

His jaw tightened as he entered the building, its familiar smells the welcome mat for another day. The harsh austerity of the place got to him, wrapping around him like wet mist on Dartmoor. Now he had to face the unthinkable, the uncertainty that had dogged him since dawn. Neil must have run into a problem. But then, Neil had always been unpredictable.

"Morning, sir," the uniformed security officer called as Ratso breezed through the ugly glassed reception area. In their functional zone, the two security personnel could watch the surrounds on closed-circuit monitors. *Functional. Yeah. That just about described it. Effing dysfunctional sometimes.*

Think of the positives. Arresting those Jamaican Yardies and that West African lot. Watching them being taken down, their eyes filled with hate and menace. But now the Albanian thugs were his daily diet. He'd spent hours on the web learning about them and their country. He'd romp it on that TV programme. *Welcome to Mastermind, Mr Holtom. And your special subject is Albanian crime in the UK. Right, you have two minutes... starting now.*

Two minutes? He could answer questions for two hours—and then some.

He swung into the featureless yellow corridor leading to his office. *I'd go a storm on Mastermind. But the general knowledge questions? Questions about ballet, longest bleedin' rivers, works of Picasso, Jung's theory, or similar crap? Forget it, mate! Now, if it was how many wickets Jim Laker took in the Fourth Test at Old Trafford in 1956, or did Fulham ever win the FA Cup—now you're talking.*

He switched on his office light. Barely bigger than a shoebox, it wasn't difficult to light every corner. *Two's company, three's a squash.* His small personal whiteboard no longer displayed a map of Albania, the secretive, dangerous Mediterranean enclave. He had returned from Tirana couple of months back, lucky not to come back in a box.

Back in the eighties, Albania had exported too many of its worst to the UK. Albanian families had abandoned the hot summers in Tirana and headed to London in droves. Ever since, day by day, their power and control of the drug scene became stronger. The toughest and most ruthless had risen by fear and intimidation to become the bosses. Bastards like Boris Zandro had grown tax-free rich. It was cat-and-mouse stuff. Ratso knew every one of them from old files and the well-collated material on the database, even shirt size and name of their favourite tailors—but making something stick? That was the challenge.

These thugs had been destroying British families for profit—dividing parents from kids, undermining and abusing the inherent values of decent folk. Destroying kids like Freddie, his brother's son. Last seen alive snivelling in a doorway off the Edgware Road. Later found dead in a bus shelter on the Kilburn High Road two weeks back. Aged just nineteen.

Destroyed by a drug cartel, probably Zandro's.

At a Home Office briefing, he'd learned how the Albanians had brought heroin, cocaine and pills into City bars, London discos, clubs and hangouts at every level of society. From that base, with mounting brutality, they had won turf wars, extending their power through the nation's arteries till their evil was everywhere. Places better known for genteel respectability like Canterbury, Chester, Tavistock and Tunbridge Wells, had fallen into their clutches. Nowhere was immune. And it wasn't just drugs. Ratso flung his jacket onto a visitor's chair and scowled as he considered how these gangsters had muscled their way into every criminal racket: brothels, sex trafficking, cigarette smuggling, counterfeiting, immigration and arms dealing. Murder and torture were weapons of choice for Erlis Bardici as he kept the foot soldiers in line.

The great British public still remembered the Krays, the Richardson gang or talked in pubs about killers like Fred West but few were aware of the fierce grip of the Albanians. Now, they dominated the length and breadth of the British Isles.

The Yardies? The Krays? The Richardsons? Pussycats compared to this lot. These Albanians had started a nationwide war. And the bastards were winning.

As a detective inspector fronting operations, there was little time for fear—during the day, anyway. But nights were different. In quiet moments, he relived running for his life through the narrow alleys of Tirana, the machine gun firing, bullets ricocheting off the walls, his weary legs screaming for relief. Hiding beneath a truck. Heart pounding, the black night his only friend.

Every day was about joining the dots. He knew Erlis Bardici was the enforcer, a murderer at least twelve times over. He knew Zandro and his cousins but there were still big gaps, the missing dots between Zandro and the engine room of the trafficking empire. Putting them all away would be beyond pleasure. It was even beyond obsession. It was a way of life. He owed it to Freddie—mouth open, emaciated, filthy T-shirt and no shoes - found next to the fast-food cartons in a stinking bus shelter. Wasted to a frazzle by drugs and starvation.

Futile, really. You nail the Zandro gang. You even jail Boris Zandro. Cut off one head, there'll be another tomorrow. Relentless. Bring down Zandro and another clone would move in. The Drug King is dead. Long live the Drug King.

But Boris Zandro, I'm coming anyway. Operation Clam is gathering speed. I'm coming to get you, Boris, if it's the last thing I do.

As he was about to ease into his seat, he saw a yellow Post-It pinned to his computer screen. It was Jock Strang's writing. *See me, boss. Urgent.* Without even booting up the computer, he edged back round his desk and headed downstairs to the Cauldron.

When he saw the machine, he debated whether to risk a cup of coffee. Had the pipes been cleaned recently? Probably not. He decided to leave it. An espresso at Café Nero across the road was a better option. And maybe a toasted panini. He'd skipped breakfast, eager to get to base as soon as Nadine's taxi sped off to Dollis Hill.

As he passed the men's bog, the solid bulk of Detective Sergeant Tosh Watson emerged, as it often did. Ratso reckoned Tosh must have had the weakest, smallest bladder ever to come off the production line. His face was well-shaven as far as his well-trimmed goatee, while the top of his head was a burr cut with a number-one blade, a dark veneer of growth covering most of it. Watson was not obese, though the way he put away fast food, he deserved to be. But he *was* overweight, decidedly so for someone aged early thirties. Keeping fit was not his style - he rarely lifted anything heavier than a pint glass or a dart. "If you were paid for pissing against a wall, you'd be a rich man, Tosh, retired probably."

Ratso was rewarded with a nod and a forced grin. Tosh had heard it before, lots of times. But he usually reacted with a quip or jibe of his own. Not today. It was a bad sign. Ratso tapped in the code and entered the Cauldron.

One look at the faces staring at him from around the central bank of desks and he knew Neil Shalford was dead. But of the two or three officers gathered, only his two trusted sergeants knew the truth; the rest would only know that a *drinking mate* of Ratso's had probably been murdered. On a need-to-know basis, only Ratso, Tosh Watson and Jock Strang were aware of the plan. After the right balls-up following Health and Safety rules last time, it had been Jock Strang who suggested Neil work off the books.

Ratso trusted Neil to the nth degree, even though he was sometimes paid by drug gangs for snooping on rivals. But the Irishman's chameleon quality, fitting in with whoever paid, was his strength. He picked up the gossip, knew where the hard guys hung out and so had eventually agreed to become Ratso's snout. Better still, he knew Erlis Bardici well enough to despise him. More than once, he had told Ratso that *the cocksucker baboon made his flesh creep.*

On a needs must basis, Ratso had taken Jock's idea to the AC. Ratso had felt sure he'd get the yes. When he had been detective chief superintendent, Wensley Hughes' had been seen off by Zandro and the taste of defeat was still bitter years later. The AC had agreed but his pointed warning had made Ratso's scrotum shrink as if he'd been doused in freezing water.

"I feel pretty relaxed about that, sir," Ratso had deluded himself, desperate for *anything* that might achieve the big break. But now the AC's words rang fresh in his ears as he saw the worried look on Strang's face.

"Morning, boss. Let's use your room," volunteered the Scot, nodding for Tosh to follow.

In his late forties and ten years older than Ratso, Strang's gruff voice evoked images of meat pies, the Ibrox terracing,

Irn-Bru and whisky chasers. He had the frame of a Gorbals copper—around five foot nine but every inch packed with hard experience from Glasgow's violent underbelly. His physique shouted *I take no shit*. Of the three, Ratso was the tallest and fittest and for Jock, losing a few pounds round his midriff would have been an improvement. "It's no the whisky or the fish suppers, boss," he would often protest. "It's ma knees. Cartilage damage playing fitba." Ratso had bought the explanation. Cricket had played hell with his own joints.

"A report in ten minutes ago. There's a body. Small park, top of the Fulham Palace Road. Hammersmith." The trio were crammed into Ratso's airless office.

It was Jock Strang who broke the news. Ratso looked into Jock's eyes, burning now with anger, his cheeks reddened from late nights and booze. Somewhere along the way, something had happened to leave Jock's right eye lower than his left. Jock had never volunteered an explanation and nobody seemed inclined to ask. The dour, unhealthy face beneath iron-grey hair cropped short matched his voice.

"A body? Hammersmith? Happens all the time," Ratso deliberately exaggerated. He was perched on the edge of his desk and swung a long leg as if he had no cares. "Nasty area at night."

"Tossed over the railings into Frank Banfield Park. Naked. Small build. Aged about fifty. Nearly bald. Tattoo on his left buttock."

Ratso said nothing.

"*Widna* be needing nail polish for Christmas."

Ratso rose slowly to his full height, couldn't take the news sitting down.

"Nor condoms, neither."

Shit! Tortured! That bastard Bardici. What had Neil revealed?

Ratso nodded but said nothing as he weighed the implications. "We'd better take a look. Pick me up outside Nero's. It's going to be a long morning."

5

Washington, DC
3:15 a.m. Lance Ruthven was awake instantly. He silenced the alarm and climbed out of the double bed that he shared with nobody. After wrapping himself in a silk dressing gown with a dragon motif, he glided down the narrow corridor to the kitchen where he fired up the coffeemaker on the black marble countertop. He saw the flip-top lying on the table and moved toward it. He resisted momentarily but then flicked open the pack. As he waited for the Costa Rican dark roast, he lit up and stood by the window looking down onto Dumbarton Street, conveniently close to M Street and a pleasant walk to the State Department where he worked.

Unlike New York, a couple hundred miles farther north, Washington, DC, was a city that slept. Of course, down Pennsylvania Avenue, government buildings would be buzzing with activity, as would some of the big law firms. But midweek, this was not a party town. Washington took itself seriously. Running the world *was* serious. Life-and-death decisions were taken in the few square miles that he could almost see from his window. The lives of soldiers and citizens globally depended on the *perceived* knowledge and wisdom of the politicians, military figures, spooks and government servants who ran DC. Sure, he could imagine the occasional senator or other party animals being tossed into cabs from the K Street Lounge or the Good Guys Club on Wisconsin. But mostly, it was early to bed and early to rise.

But not 3:15 a.m. early.

He checked his Cartier Santos watch, a little luxury he had picked up on the Rue du Rhone in Geneva while attending a top-secret meeting during the Iraq War. Times had changed; Afghanistan now filled his working day. Kabul, Kandahar and the integrity of the Green Zone were the agenda at 2201 C Street NW. He poured a coffee and stubbed out the cigarette. On the table lay his Blackberry and a neat silver pay-as-you-go cellphone. He checked the time again, picked up the phone and dialled.

Seven thousand miles away, the phone rang in a magnificent turreted *poppy palace* in the Sherpur district of Kabul. An urbane man with a round O of a mouth adjusted his glasses, waved an aide from the room and answered the call. He felt at ease, totally secure with over thirty-five guards patrolling his ten acres day and night.

"How's it going?" Ruthven asked.

"Usual diplomatic crap. I'm meeting a British delegation shortly." The speaker sighed at the tediousness of it all. The Afghan's voice was guttural but his English was heavily American East Coast. Not surprising. Until fifteen years before, Adnan Shirafi had been at Harvard Business School following private schooling in New Hampshire. His top-class education had taught him everything…and nothing. Certainly nothing that had enabled him to become the pivotal figure controlling and exporting over 80% of the world's heroin.

As a cousin to Afghanistan's new president, he had a comfortable impression he was above the law. The US and British governments knew of Shirafi and his drug empire but were powerless to expose him. Helmand Province was Shirafi's fiefdom, the area that produced the endless supply of poppies. He could turn the Help Button on or off at a whim. He could fix elections—and had. He could stir up the local tribesmen for good or ill. He played Downing Street and the White House as easily as Sir Elton John played the piano.

The governments were neutered. Helmand was critical in the war against the Taliban and had already cost countless British and US casualties. Top brass in the Pentagon and the MoD in London had convinced the politicians that to win the war in Helmand, Shirafi was a better friend than a foe.

Shirafi stretched out on the chaise longue and popped a date into his small mouth, then wiped his thick black moustache with a chubby hand. "There's still shit flying after those leaks from your State Department."

"Wikileaks? Here too, believe me!" Ruthven hopped nervously from foot to foot. "Funny thing about the truth. *Knowing* folk are saying things behind your back, sure, that hurts…but hell, it hurts a darned sight more when they're in confidential memos that become front-page news around the fucking globe." Lance Ruthven leaned back against the wall as he thought of the State Department's disparaging comments about Adnan Shirafi. He coughed nervously. "But, er…nothing's changed, huh?"

"Everything's good to go." Shirafi paused to sip his herbal tea. "GB? All ready?"

"I'm flying down there." Ruthven's imagination took him to the shipyard at Freeport on Grand Bahamas, where the refit work was continuing. Or should be.

"So can I confirm February, January even to our guys?"

Even these few mundane words made Ruthven flinch. Was it something in his old pal's tone? Ruthven and Shirafi usually enjoyed easy banter, dating back to shared days and long nights at Harvard. But somehow this was different. Ruthven licked his lips as he assessed the edginess in his friend's voice.

"Give me till March." Ruthven heard a grunt followed by an overlong silence.

"You made the wrong choice. I said to use that yard in NS. Those bums down in GB are too damned lazy. We're running behind. It's giving me a heap of shit."

Ruthven felt queasy as his stomach churned. It was true. He *had* persuaded Shirafi to send the vessel south to the sun rather than north to the cold of Nova Scotia. The quoted price had been cheaper but for the American, that had not been the clincher. Unsaid had been exchanging the penetrating chill of a Washington winter for guaranteed warmth, rum-based drinks and steel bands. That hidden agenda had now come back to bite him in the ass. *Time to get off the phone.*

"Same time Monday, then?" There was hesitance in the American's voice.

"Agreed." Shirafi paused and Ruthven was unsure whether the call was over. "You'll meet a guy there."

Ruthven fell silent for a long beat as he weighed up the implications. "Whoa! Whoa, hold on! But our deal—we agreed…"

"Change of plans." Shirafi's dark brown eyes narrowed and had Ruthven been with him, he'd have spotted the lie in the slyness of the man's features. "London put him in. Beyond my control."

Ruthven's blood ran hot with anger and then cold with fear before he spoke. "Our deal! Nobody was to know of me, or of my role. Just you." He sensed he sounded too wheedling, so he sharpened his tone. "Take a hike!"

"London insists. Their patience is exhausted. Another deadline missed could screw up everything. As well as…"

"I'm not going. *Nobody* must know who I am. Let this other guy do it." But even as he said it, Lance Ruthven could see he was being shortsighted.

"Relax, my old friend." The tone was intended to be reassuring but Lance had sat in too many diplomatic meetings to be fooled. "With your other ID," the speaker paused "you can be confident he won't know…"

Shirafi meant his false passport. Ruthven shook his head. "No way am I letting anybody know a goddamned thing. Not *any* name."

"You quitting, then…*my friend?*" Again the innocuous words seemed full of menace, a hard edge Ruthven had never heard personally before. He hesitated in his reply. He paced the room, phone to his ear. He fought for what to say. *A guy in my position. Hell, I'm a senior trusted government servant in the State Department. Me, mixing with some lowlife London drug dealer?*

Shirafi's voice intruded. "I asked if you're quitting."

Ruthven faltered. "No…but." Shirafi had never come across like this in Boston. He knew he should tell Shirafi to shove it right up his hairy asshole. "We had a deal."

"So sue me." Shirafi laughed mockingly, then realised he had gone too far and softened. "Look, my friend, I'm sore about this too. But London? Big customers. They talk. Even *I* jump. Trust me. I had no choice."

But at that moment Ruthven knew he couldn't trust Shirafi anymore. "Cut me a bigger slice for the added risk."

"Excuse me? Five million bucks for what you had to do is pretty damned good already."

Ruthven gripped the phone tighter. He had no illusions; there was one good reason to quit and five million bad ones to continue. In daydreams, he'd spent the millions time and again—a condo on Grand Cayman, global travel, five-star hotels and still a shitload to invest. He had almost felt the sand between his toes, had swayed gently on the double hammock with that cute-assed attorney from H Street. Now, as he imagined losing the chance of massaging her breasts with Australian Gold suntan lotion, he was hooked. "You're right. I'll go." He almost choked on the words.

"Good. You'll get the guy's name through the usual channel. It won't be his real one, naturally." There was another long pause as Shirafi awaited a reaction.

Ruthven felt sick, lightheaded. "I'll call you on Monday" was all he could get out. He cut the call and sagged like a falling sack deep into his red recliner. For a moment as it wrapped around him, he felt cocooned but seconds later the stark horror of what he had done overwhelmed him. Whom was he meeting? A scumbag with a criminal record? Undoubtedly a right bastard being sent in to scare the crap out of the slob who ran the shipyard. *But now I'm risking everything. Big time.* What had been a low-risk role, a real secret, was spiralling out of control. He clasped his head, one hand over each ear. There was no turning back now.

He rose from the chair and grabbed a bottle of bourbon. After pouring a generous slug into his half-cold coffee, he sank back into the chair and downed the lot in a couple of gulps.

He closed his eyes, his right cheek twitching, his fingers beating on the leather as he fought to make sense of the sinister turn of events. Adnan Shirafi had a point: the damned shipyard workers *were* idle, happiest when *taking their ease* listening to rappers and hip-hop on their ghetto blasters. The refit *was* three months behind schedule and he feared still more delays. Maybe he had swallowed too much bullshit. Perhaps he *had* been too polite, accepting flimsy excuses. But a deal was a deal. No way was anyone else to know of his role. Now he had been screwed by his oldest and dearest friend. He reached for a cigarette as if that would somehow clear his confusion. *All those years of friendship suddenly meaningless.* All that remained was the Afghan's lies echoing round his head.

No way. No way would Shirafi be dictated to by *anyone*, whether in London, Berlin, or Chicago.

Ruthven sat motionless, finally crushing his cigarette into the onyx ashtray. He hated these damned middle-of-the-night calls. He would never sleep now. He poured another bourbon, lit his third cigarette and blew a perfect ring. *Forget Freeport!* This morning at nine, he was meeting Secretary of State Karl Weissner about the next Kabul trip. Top secret. *If anything was secret anymore.* Wikileaks probably knew the agenda better than he did.

A couple of years back, he would have gotten a buzz working with a top politician. No more. As assistant secretary to the number three in the State Department hierarchy, Lance Ruthven knew he had peaked. Now, he was bored as hell. He had reached a ceiling. Not glass; more like concrete. He had worked his way up the ranks, *a safe pair of hands.* But he was going no higher, not now.

Age forty come April. Just a time-server. Game over.

He poured another coffee and reached for a cookie. It had all been so neat. An old pal from Harvard days. Regular visits to Kabul. The perfect cover for a small job on the side. *Monitor the refit, that's all, Lance. Easy. No sweat.* Or so it had seemed. He ran his hand through the thinning waves that rolled back from his pale forehead. His slate grey eyes closed as the torment raged. His normally untroubled face was twitching again, a muscle in his cheek working double-time.

No honour among thieves.

Pop had always said that. *Right as usual, old man.* And now Lance Argentis Ruthven was sinking into the clutches of London's criminal underworld. If he knew, Pop would crap his pants.

Forget it. Think of the money! Think of that young attorney. Amber Yardley. Age 31. Born Summerlin, Las Vegas. Patent law specialist. Outside interests, snorkelling and sailing. Amber, lying on a water bed with him near Seven-Mile Beach. Naked. Eager.

He was aroused just by the thought, went to his laptop and clicked open her photo on the law firm's website. His hand drifted down beneath his dressing gown as he gazed into the softness of her brown eyes.

He couldn't wait to meet her.

6

South London

"So what do we know, Tosh?" Ratso turned to Detective Sergeant Watson, who was driving them westward to Hammersmith. But it was Jock Strang, the never-lost-for-words Scot, who chirped up from the back seat.

"Neil went in. No more contact. The body was found at 0645." For Jock, this summary was brief but the atmosphere was sombre. Neil had been known to them all, a drinking mucker on the occasional bender.

Ratso was unimpressed. "You must know more."

It was Tosh who joined in. "He lived around Kingston."

"I know that," Ratso snapped, irritated at the lack of information. He looked at Watson's profile, the narrow nose, the aggressive head. Even in another fourteen years, he would never match Jock for effectiveness. But Ratso liked the stolid worthiness of the man. "Wolsey Drive. That's where he lived, with Charlene."

"Tasty little raver, she was and all," Tosh grinned, taking his eyes off for the road to look at his boss. "Remember that night up West when she was wearing that pussy-pelmet and…"

"I remember but I'm in no mood for memory lane. Not with Neil dead. Not with our big chance screwed up again. Not with my bollocks about to be chewed."

Strang leaned over from the rear seat. He knew the boss was hurting. "That time of night, Neil must have gone there in his Honda Civic."

"Good thinking! It was blue. We need to find it. He usually parked about ten minutes away from a job."

"The widow? Who's going to speak to her? You?"

Ratso stared down at the Thames as they crossed Putney Bridge and then joined the slow-moving traffic waiting to filter up the New King's Road or continue through to Hammersmith. "I'll visit her, of course but..." His voice trailed away as a jumble of thoughts intervened. "They weren't married, y'know. Neil reckoned twice was two times too often."

"They were close, though?"

Ratso looked disinterested. "Hard to say. It was a convenient relationship. Each got something from it." He thought of Charlene and wondered how he would break the news. She was feisty, alright—strong features, a slightly sharp nose with melting green eyes like a colleen from County Cork. But Ratso knew they were eyes that wandered. "She grew up in Cheriton, not far from the entrance to the Channel Tunnel. She would be, oh, about thirty-one now. No kids. No commitments except their timeshare in Marbella." Ratso was unsure how long they had been an item—*going at it like stoats in a sack* to use Neil's description. "She was fond of Neil, for sure. But committed? I'd pass on that one."

Ratso could tell that Tosh Watson was watching his every reaction, so he had been picking his words with care. He found himself rehearsing some lines for meeting Charlene. *A good man.*

Mixed in difficult circles. Didn't deserve this. But Ratso knew he would have to be careful. To Charlene, Ratso was just Neil's friend who happened to be a copper. No way did Charlene know what Neil did in his long, strange hours.

"Tricky, eh boss? I mean. He's dead because of you."

Ratso did not need Jock's reminder and sat in silence, staring at the church at the northern end of the bridge.

"You reckon he'd have spilled the truth? I mean Erlis Bardici..." Tosh ended the uncomfortable silence but only created a different one.

At last Ratso spoke. "Neil was a mercenary, open for hire to all comers, good or bad But he was a great mate and a true pro. My money? He fed Bardici the bullshit we planned."

"You know this place he was found, boss?" enquired Tosh as he swerved around an ambulance waiting to turn into Charing Cross Hospital. "Frank Banfield Park?"

"Not my stamping ground. I live the other side of Hammersmith Broadway. The posh side." His listeners might have laughed in different circumstances. "It's on the left, about four hundred yards. Used to be pretty much waste ground till about three years back. Park anywhere now." Tosh turned off the Fulham Palace Road into a small side street and stopped.

"Anything from Neil's bug?"

Strang shook his head. "The wee gadget says the vehicle never moved. That...or the bug was never fixed."

"Or Bardici found it."

"Or it was found," echoed Strang, offering round peppermints.

"If it *is* Neil, we know who killed him—more or less—and we know why. We're ahead of the curve." His eyes fixed each of his sergeants in turn. "We keep it that way, understood? Just to ourselves. Arresting Erlis Bardici now would kill Operation Clam. Deader than Neil. And that," he gripped Strang's arm, "must not happen."

Tosh had declined a peppermint and instead was gnawing at a Mars bar. "If it is Neil, what's Plan B? Bug Bardici again?"

"Plan B is to save my arse."

Jock slapped Ratso's back. "That would be Plan A, boss." All three laughed for the first time that morning.

In the two years, eight months spent working together, a bond of mutual respect had developed between them. Though Ratso was unquestionably the boss, the relationships were more than business. A friendship had developed built on respect and a common zeal to bang up the Zandro gang.

As they clambered out of the car into the grey misery of the London morning, Ratso thought again how different the sergeants were in every way. Their value came from dedication, solid instincts and experience but Tosh had all the subtlety of a naked light bulb. "Like my new jacket?" Tosh looked across at the listeners as they were walking along the side of the park. "North Face."

Ratso shrugged. "If that's his North Face, Jock, I'd hate to see the South."

"Don't go there boss," Jock replied with a toothy grin. "You reckon he's up for climbing the Eiger? North Face and all?"

"With that stomach, Tosh couldn't climb a ladder, let alone a sodding Swiss mountain."

"Ye're right. The Eiger would crumble under his weight!"

"Jealous, eh! Just 'cos I'm as warm as toast in this. It's bloody freezing this morning."

"Look." Ratso pointed ahead. "That's Chancellor's Road." They could now see where the junction with the Fulham Palace

Road had been blocked. Two constables stood in front of the blue-and-white cordon beside the flashing blue lights of three patrol cars. Ratso pushed between about ten onlookers with as many dogs and turned to his sergeants. "Forget the textbook, right? This is delicate with a capital D. No room for snafus. I can feel suspension and the AC breathing down my neck already." He marked two nods.

Tosh Watson cleared his throat. "Reckon the MIT boys will be here yet?"

Ratso looked at his no-frills steel watch with its navy blue face. "Yeah. Trying to overcome the snafus made by the local boys with their size-tens everywhere they didn't ought to have been."

The sardonic tone suited the moment. He paused and then turned to face them, slate grey eyes piercing in his rugged face. The wind ruffled the wavy brown hair that was combed forward in a Caesar style with the sides flopping over his ears, something he had long ago decided was a fashion statement worth making. His lugs were scarcely his best feature. Women seemed to prefer his eyes, wide set beneath hooded eyelids; his nose that was prominent without being beaky; and the designer stubble on his cheeks. He had a mouth that rarely smiled above his firm but narrowing jawline. The overall impression was imperious—something he had found worked to his advantage. He rarely shouted, ranted, or snapped to command respect. There was no need; a withering look got the message across.

His two sergeants looked at him, awaiting instruction. All three understood they were in dangerous territory. "On no account admit we know the stiff or from where or why. Leave the lies to me."

He approached one of the constables at the ribbon and showed his ID. "Morning. D.I. Holtom, SCD7 and these are two of my team, Sergeants Watson and Strang." He saw the slightly raised eyebrow as the youngster realised that SCD7 was taking an interest, three times over. Ratso's tone was friendly enough. "Who's in charge?"

The constable licked his lips nervously. "DCI Caldwell, sir." He turned and pointed to a dapper figure about seventy metres down the road, where a white tent was being erected behind the park railings. The officer was waving his arms in every direction as he addressed about eight uniformed officers and three plainclothes.

With a curt nod, Ratso headed off. Strang and Watson ducked under the line and joined the broad-shouldered figure of their boss as he pulled up his collar against the wind blowing raw from the Thames. "Anyone know Caldwell?"

It was Tosh who responded. "He's smart. Ambitious. And he won't much like us being here."

They joined the group getting instructions. It was a moment or two before Caldwell acknowledged their arrival. "Yes?"

"I'm Detective Inspector Todd Holtom. These are Sergeants Watson and Strang. SCD7."

Ratso saw a barrier go up behind Caldwell's rather piggy eyes. Ratso looked him up and down, took in the highly polished loafers, the razor-sharp trousers beneath a shortie coat that was expensively cut. The yellow silk tie over a paler yellow shirt. *He must be smart to be a DCI at his age. That or he's older than he looks.*

"SCD7, eh?" Caldwell obviously hoped for a response. Ratso said nothing. "What's SCD's interest?" His tone was a mix between curious and miffed.

"None yet. But the preliminary description fitted someone who...was a person of interest. I thought we'd take a look." With difficulty, Ratso offered his smile. Usually the set of his face transmitted aloofness, as if he were looking at an evil world from a position not far removed from God's side. "No witnesses yet? Nobody see anything suspicious?"

"Nothing yet. And there's no papers, driving licence. Except for one black trainer, the guy's bollock-naked. Reckon you can ID him?"

Ratso shrugged. He peered over to the tented area. "What do we know?"

"*I* know," emphasised Caldwell "that the body was probably dumped during the night and before 5:45 a.m. A passer-by who works at the Water Board down the road saw a trainer on the pavement. Then he saw the body."

"Tipped over the railings?"

"Into those shrubs. Yes."

Ratso looked up and down Chancellor's Road. The other side was lined with about thirty gentrified terraced properties. Most had lights on. "Before 5:45, eh? Not too many folk round here munching muesli at that time."

"Door-to-door is underway."

"Just another gangland killing then, sir?" Strang's Glaswegian rasp was world-weary. His face and voice showed that he had seen it all, the bad years busting Glasgow gangs like the Tongs and Parkhead Rebels.

Caldwell was not impressed. "*Every* murder is important." Strang looked away. "Get togged up and you can take a look. A positive ID would be a good start." As Caldwell turned away to do whatever he thought more important, the light drizzle turned to sleet.

Ratso didn't give a fig for Caldwell's sniffy tone and quickly got kitted up in his white suit. "Sooner I'm in that tent the better," he muttered through the railings to a wizened face who seemed to be in charge of the forensic team. His look was intense. "Can you manage scrambled egg on toast for three in there?" The man ignored the remark, simply saying his name was Bahim Prasad and yes, they could take a look at the body.

As the sleet intensified, Ratso enjoyed watching Watson struggle to get his suit over his generous arse. "You're such an apple, duckie," Ratso said in a camp voice.

"Just as well it was dry till they got the tent up," Watson panted as his backside wiggled frantically. "This weather won't help the Sherlock Holmes lot with their specimen bags."

Ratso shrugged. "I doubt they'll get much by the body. Just a quick heave-ho over the railing." He watched as Watson's struggle continued. "No more burger and fries for you."

"Bollocks! Even Ronnie Corbett would struggle with this suit."

Ratso turned to watch as photos were taken of the shoe, still lying where it had been spotted by the passer-by. It was black, small, well-worn and probably a Reebok. He had seen Neil wearing it just eighteen hours before. He headed to the park entrance and then doubled back to the tent, which was now lit up by a couple of powerful spots.

Lying in a contorted position was a naked man, half on his side, half facing up. The remaining black shoe and sock on his left foot seemed incongruous. Ratso knew at once this was not the crime scene. He was pretty sure that was somewhere eight miles further west.

Ratso could feel Caldwell's suspicion. Like a poker player, he was watching for tells. But Ratso played possum, crouching down, looking at the face, the open mouth, the well-kept teeth and bloodied fingers. No question it was Neil. He had known at once. Mention of the tattoo on the buttock had been damning.

When had he seen it before? Oh yes! That night at the Wheat Sheaf! With the party going well, Neil had leaped onto the bar, lowered his jeans and waggled his bum to the assembled group of friends.

Now here it was again: the cobra coiled and ready to strike. As the sleet spattered noisily on the tent, Caldwell, Ratso and the two sergeants took in the small black menace of the cobra's eyes. Ratso looked at his friend, end to end, from the thinning hair to his dainty feet. The victim's frame was near anorexic— so mighty in life, now so feeble in death. Ratso had always said Neil's physique was perfect for clambering through windows or placing bugs in roof voids.

"He'd fit that white suit ye're wearing, Tosh," muttered Strang. "Could do with it and all," he added. "Catch his death out here in weather like this." Ratso suppressed a smirk as he glanced sideways at Caldwell. *Piss artists* was written contemptuously over Caldwell's face as he chewed his lip.

Ratso's eyes took in the blue nylon cord that had finally throttled the life from Neil. "You can get that cord just about anywhere," he murmured to nobody in particular. But as quickly, like the others, his eyes turned to the todger, or what little remained of it.

"Jewish circumcision ceremony gone wrong?" Strang's irreverence would never change. The Scot spotted a frosty glare and more lip chewing from Caldwell but his superior said nothing. Fifteen years working the tenements on Glasgow's south side had given Strang a rhino's hide, unless Celtic had beaten his beloved Rangers.

Ratso turned to the Indian scientist who knelt by the body. "Did you find it? The todger?"

Before Prasad could respond, Caldwell pointed to a polythene bag. Ratso picked up the small bag. Neil's manhood lay clearly visible, a flaccid, docile dwarf of a thing.

Ratso stared at it. It was hard to imagine that this little pink bud had given so much pleasure to so many. Over a few beers, listening to Neil's tales of his services to women round Belfast, Birmingham and South London, Ratso had often laughed till the early hours. Tall, small, young, old, fat or thin; lying down, knee-tremblers, in a cupboard, down an alley, husband in the next room—Neil was your man. But no more. Now this slightly bloodied relic, barely larger than an acorn, was all that remained of the mighty swordsman's weapon.

Prasad looked up. "It fell from his mouth."

Nobody spoke. Perhaps even Jock Strang felt humbled at what had happened to a good bloke who had died in their cause. An uncomfortable silence hung for a long moment as his attention turned to Neil's right hand, where every nail was missing. Ratso for one was praying to a God in whom he did not believe that he would never, *ever* have to suffer like this.

The other hand, with surprisingly long slender fingers, had four nails missing. *Had that been the pain threshold? Had number nine been the moment when Neil had suffered enough and revealed what he had been doing? But then what had he told Bardici before he was throttled?* Ratso looked across to Tosh Watson and Strang in turn and shook his head.

"Well?" Caldwell was impatient.

Ratso deliberately decided to piss him off. *Jealous of those shiny expensive loafers, am I?* More suited for a tea dance at the Waldorf than for a sodding wet morning in Hammersmith. The DCI obviously spent his wad in the likes of Baron Jon's boutique in Westfield rather than pissing cash against a wall Friday nights. He looked the younger man up and down with something close to insolence, wondering how he would have coped in Tirana. *For sure, you wouldn't catch Caldwell rummaging for boxer shorts in a T.K.Maxx dump bin.* At last he responded as if he were doing

Caldwell a huge favour. "Get me a photo sent over, can you? And his measurements. Todger apart."

He was rewarded with a scowl. "You do or don't recognise him?"

"Very familiar but not the guy we were…I dunno whether to say…hoping or expecting. Not the guy we wanted to see on a slab." Ratso stood up and turned to his sergeants. "Not anybody you wanted to see, is it?" On seeing the shaken heads, he turned to face the yellow shirt and tie. "We'll leave you to it. We'll be pretty much dropping out. Nothing for us here. Let us know if you get an ID."

Caldwell examined his manicured nails. "You, too." The words were innocuous but Ratso could tell Caldwell was probing and edgy. But there was no going back now. The die was cast. Ratso's conspiracy to obstruct the police investigation had started. He imagined himself down the Bailey, courtesy of Caldwell. *But I acted in the greater good, M'Lud.* He could imagine it now…the judge looking across at the Witness Box. *"Setting yourself up above the law, are you, Inspector Holtom? You should take heed of Lord Denning's admonition to the attorney-general—'Be you never so high, the law is above you.'"* The thought was uncomfortable.

With a come-along nod, Ratso turned briskly and left the shelter of the tent. The sleet slapped his half-shaved cheeks. He knew there would be more and worse slaps to come. And then he saw Watson and the sight cheered him.

"C'mon, Tosh. Get your white kit off. I need a good laugh."

7

West London

Tosh Watson had spotted Neil's navy blue Honda Civic as Strang checked his iPad. "Bardici hasn't moved. Our silent friend's still at 22 Westbrook Drive."

Ratso was flicking through web pages to find Cricinfo.com. "That's assuming..."

Tosh Watson blew warmth into his hands. "So drive by number 22, boss?"

"I'll go on foot. Alone." Ratso was talking autopilot as he checked his Blackberry for the overnight cricket news from the Second Test in Adelaide. He grunted with satisfaction as he saw England were 297 for 2. One day, he was going to follow the team to India, Australia and the West Indies, watch every match—enjoy the heat, sink some local brews and see England stuff the opposition. This time of year, early December, his passion for cricket had to make do with TV highlights or sometimes watching live till long after midnight. But last night, with Nadine there, turning on the TV would have been impolite...and physically impossible given what he was doing with his hands at the time.

"Cricket! Grown men ponsing about in white trousers. Game for woofters," said the Scot's voice from the rear seat. "Ham and Egg ties; naff striped blazers and stupid straw hats. Gimme the Ibrox terraces any day. Real people. Real men."

"You Scots. Blinkered from a game that really is beautiful." He paused while Watson accelerated past a truck on the Great West Road. "Fact is, cricket's too difficult for you to appreciate."

Jock Strang was about to reply when Ratso took a call from base.

"Holtom." His head nodded occasionally as a dismembered voice let rip. Apart from the occasional *yes* or *but*, it was a one-sided conversation. Ratso caught Watson's glance and winked. Only when it was over did Ratso find his tongue. "Arse-covering time for our friend Arthur."

"Tennant? He'll still be Snow White whenever the shit hits the fan. Always is," complained Strang.

Ratso laughed his agreement. "More like one of the dwarves. Dopey. Or maybe Grumpy." The three men savoured the comparison. "You can guess: Tennant had just taken a call from *upstairs*. That's a better laxative than prunes, that is."

Watson laughed, coarse but infectious. "Yeah. He was probably sitting on the bog when he phoned you. What'd he say?"

"Warned me not to screw up any more than I have already."

"Nice one. Didn't he approve Neil going in solo?"

Ratso shook his head. "That bleeder? Didn't want to soil his hands."

"Or crap his pants." Strang leaned forward against his seatbelt. He tapped his watch. "I could sink a wee one," he volunteered.

Watson looked enthused. "You're on. The Chequers on Twickenham High Street does a good pie-and-pint deal. Suit you, boss?"

Ratso checked the time, thought of his trim waistline and looked at Tosh whose stomach was rubbing against the foot of the steering wheel. He had no plans to turn into a fattie any time soon. "You two get stuck in. I'll head over to Westbrook Drive."

After dropping off the two eating machines outside the dreary ochre-painted pub, Ratso headed to the anonymous array of suburban streets between Isleworth and Hounslow. In a variety of vehicles, he had driven past Bardici's rented property several times over the past couple of months. But today he wanted to take it nice and slow, hoping somehow to get the feel of what had happened just hours before. He parked up and checked the iPad that Jock had left on the passenger seat. *Still no sign of the Range Rover moving.* In theory, it should not be there; typically at this time of day, Bardici would be out on his *errands*, dropping by the money-changers. If his information was right, Bardici's boys laundered money through dozens of these outlets.

He cursed the weather as the sleet slapped his face. He pulled on his Fulham FC beanie and entered Ali's Corner Emporium. From a diminutive Pakistani, he bought soup, canned spaghetti and mineral water to carry in a plastic bag as he walked past number 22. He caught his fragmented reflection in the rain-spattered glass door of the shop. In a Britain now littered with home-grown fat slobs, scruffs and immigrants from all quarters of the globe, it was becoming increasingly hard not to look like a plainclothes copper, especially when he was over six feet and super fit. But the low beanie, the slouch, the hunched shoulders and the plastic carrier were a help. He set off up Westbrook Drive, keeping on the opposite side to number 22, still feeling as exposed as a pimple on a stripper's bum.

There it was. Number 22. The downstairs curtains were drawn but the upstairs ones were both open. There were no lights on and the place looked deserted, unless someone was in the kitchen at the rear. More importantly, the Range Rover was still there. So maybe Neil had managed to plant the bug.

Ratso had been eighteen years in the force and he still got that weird feeling that somehow just by staring hard enough, evil places like number 22 would give up their dark secrets. For a second, he imagined Neil's naked body strapped to a chair as Bardici approached with pliers and wire cutters. He could almost see the smirk on Bardici's swarthy features.

He shuddered, wishing the job was not such a bitch. Maybe there would be evidence of the murder but it was pretty damned unlikely. The Albanian was too bloody smart for that.

He rounded the bend farther along and had just passed a broken fence at number 89 when he saw a couple approaching on the other side. It was not Bardici; the man was too short and his shoulders too narrow. Definitely younger than Bardici, who was forty next year–14 June to be precise. The man was mid-thirties, the woman rather less. A nondescript couple probably heading for Ali's Corner Emporium or perhaps walking home from the bus stop on the main road. They were talking, that much he could tell from the man's arm waving and her intent look. But only at the last moment could he hear some words. "*Nuk e di.*"

Ratso's blood pumped faster, his heart suddenly pounding overdrive. *Nuk e di.* He didn't know much Albanian but *nuk e di* was a phrase he'd picked up in Tirana, meaning *I don't know*. He'd gone masquerading as one of the Hogan gang. Several locals he had chatted with had used it when asked about Boris Zandro. *Nuk e di. I don't know.* Lying bastards but scared shitless that just one careless word would bring Zandro's gang down on them.

He continued walking, debating what to do. *Is Westbrook Drive an Albanian enclave?* He didn't think so. He'd smelled curry from several properties, had seen Asian kids peering at him from the occasional window. He crossed the street and pretended to post a letter from his carrier bag at the corner box. Then he turned round to walk back past number 22, picking up his pace. As he rounded the bend, he saw the taillights appear on the Range Rover and in a couple of swift movements it had gone, heading steadily in the other direction. Of the Albanian couple, there was no sign. He had no choice but to blow cover by checking the iPad. He got the map on screen and was at once rewarded. Neil *had* planted the bug, his dying act. *Good on yer, Neil!*

Ratso fought the urge to run back to his car. There was no rush, no need to panic. The bug would help him. He reached the car pool Mazda and used the covert radio channel to speak to Jock Strang on the secure encrypted wavelength. "Our friend is singing and I'm following. Get someone to pick you up immediate. Then call me again."

"Barrr-deecchee?" The sergeant's accent always seemed even more Glaswegian on the phone.

"An Albanian couple. Heading…" He paused to check. "West toward the A30."

"Nae bother, boss. I'll phone *the noo* and then we can finish our game. I need double-top to win."

Ratso smiled as he accelerated away, watching the blink on the small screen as the target vehicle moved steadily west and slightly north on the A30. He reckoned he was about two, maybe three miles behind and keeping pace well.

His thoughts turned to Neil and getting the word on the street. What would he say? *Got it!* Neil had been working for the Hogan twins, thug brothers who ran the south London drug scene. All hell would break loose. It could get nasty. Or nice, depending on your standpoint.

8

Grand Bahama Island
After the short hop from Fort Lauderdale, Lance Ruthven's Bahamasair flight touched down at Grand Bahama International. Now his long, slim legs were stretched out sideways in the back of the taxi heading for the Marlin Hotel. He wore a heavy black moustache—fake, unfortunately, as he'd shaved his own when he fell in love with Amber, believing somehow his smooth skin gave him a more refined look. His brow puckered at his unsettling train of thoughts: the unknown Brit, the CEO taking the piss about *unforeseen problems*. He knew the ship owners were being gouged but then the shipyard had the company by the balls. Confidentiality was crucial and Lamon Wilson, the wily CEO knew it.

No more taking that crap, Ruthven had vowed on the flight. *This time I'm standing firm* but one wrong word to the Brit and his own true ID could come out, ending his career. The Brit was called Mujo Zevi, or at least that was his cover. Ruthven's knuckles whitened as he gripped the seat. What type of Brit would give himself such a name? His mood darkened even more and his feet scuffed the carpet. He looked out at the palm trees swaying in the late afternoon breeze and the pastel pinks and greens of the buildings. Usually this was paradise. Today it felt like paradise lost.

Get real, Lance. Show this Mujo Zevi you can kick ass and soon you'll be pocketing five million greenbacks. Goodbye, DC. But not before persuading Amber that Lance Ruthven was the man of her dreams.

Amber Yardley! Just the name, the thought of her made his groin ache. He had watched her for hours, followed her to her condo seven miles from Downtown, watched her buying perfume in Nordstrom, lusted over a Victoria's Secret lace bra and panties he had bought but never given her. Twice he had hung around outside Amber's condo till late into the night to make sure that she lived alone.

Of course, Amber had not been the first woman to catch his eye. There had been others before her—others he had followed home to Great Falls or to Arlington or DuPont Circle. But not one of them had excited him as she did.

The lurch of the taxi over a pothole brought him back to the moment, a couple of stray dogs yapping and leaping along the unkempt verge. He watched some kids playing with a hoop made from an old bike wheel. Not an iPad, iPhone, or MP3 player in sight. It was another world compared to the teenage kids strutting down Georgetown's M Street, diving in and out of the bars and hangouts, irritating him with their endless whooping and high-fives.

But then he remembered he too was no longer Lance Ruthven. Right now, he was Hank Kurtner, from Detroit, Michigan; he had no shackles – just the immediate prospect of picking up Cassie, that hooker in the Red Poppy bar. The confrontations with the limey and at the shipyard would come later.

He sighed. He was used to diplomacy, where lies were silky smooth and nasty spats avoided by doublespeak. But the time for diplomacy had gone. If he faced the truth, it had *long* gone. The CEO had played him for a fool.

The taxi bumped and lurched into Jolly Roger Drive and he took in the familiar sights from his previous visits. At last, the icy grip of Washington seemed blissfully distant. Each trip, he stayed at a different beach hotel, anxious to avoid anybody shouting *Welcome back, Mr Kurtner*.

Earlier that morning, his breakfast meeting at State had ended in good time for him to catch the 10:30 a.m. flight from National to Fort Lauderdale. Among his colleagues, the word was Lance was long-weekending again at the Hilton Beach Resort in Fort Lauderdale—*poor-man's snowbirding*, as he called it. The Hilton was large enough to be anonymous, right on the beach and yet not far from the airport. The price was consistent with his lifestyle but as he had no intention of staying in the suite, he resented every last dime it cost him.

After checking in, he always stripped off his charcoal grey suit with white shirt and formal club tie and hung them neatly in the closet. A faded lime windsurfer T-shirt, Bermuda shorts and Nike Swoosh sandals completed the dress change. He moved quickly, familiar with the routine, following a pattern he had practised on previous trips. He pulled back the bedding, disturbed the sheets and then completed the makeover from Lance to Hank Kurtner.

From the false bottom of his Gladstone bag, he removed the Kurtner passport and driving licence and donned a dark brown wig, parted on the left. It hid his ears and hung overlong at the back too, changing the shape of his head. He put pads in his cheeks and stuck on the generous black moustache. The tinted shades completed the change. He looked younger and fatter than moments before. In the room safe, he left his driving licence, Amex card and the world of Lance Ruthven. After a final check, he exited the hotel, walking with a slight limp—something he always did as Kurtner—his few spare clothes in a small rucksack hung low on his back. He told the car jockey he was going to the Ritz-Carlton but after climbing into a taxi told the driver he was short of time and to go direct to the airport instead.

That had been just under two hours before, a thought confirmed with a glance at his watch as his Grand Bahamas taxi pulled up to the pale pink colonnades of the Marlin Hotel. It was 5:20 p.m. and the sun was setting.

But it would rise in the morning and before then…*ah yes, before then!* A shower, aftershave and off to the Red Poppy bar.

9

Oxfordshire, England

As he turned off the M40 to head north into rural Buckinghamshire, Ratso knew the area quite well – this was the route he often used when visiting the patients at Stoke Mandeville Hospital. For two years now, he had made a point of working with the staff to identify half-a-dozen suitable wheelchair patients to join him for a day at Lord's or at Fulham FC's ground at Craven Cottage. Afterwards he would treat them to a steak dinner at a pub near the hospital.

He found it emotional to go into the National Spinal Injuries Centre. If it was a privilege enough to walk in, it felt even more so to be able to walk out. Seeing so many people with their lives blighted by permanent paralysis brought back memories that at times he preferred to forget. He had first been to the world-famous hospital at the age of six, grappling to understand why his mother cried so much after every visit. It took him months to understand that his father was never again going to walk, run or play games with him. One single mistake and his dad's lumbar spine had been fractured. Life could be cruel and now if he could cheer up the patients as they battled to come to terms with a lifestyle they had never expected, then he was delighted to be of help. *Only a few more weeks till the day at Craven Cottage and then Lord's in May.* The thought cheered him as he puzzled over where the Range-Rover was headed.

He called his sergeants. "This is getting like a Sunday afternoon outing. They'll be stopping for a cuppa and Mr. Kipling's cakes in a Lay-By at this rate."

"Where are you, guv?" It was Tosh Watson.

"Leafy Bucks! Wait one! To be precise, I have just left the M40 at Junction Six and am heading for Chinnor. They're about a mile ahead. Where are you?"

Ratso heard muttering. "Near Windsor."

"Windsor? What the hell are you doing near there? Lost your map? Or lost your marbles?"

"Tea with Her Majesty…and the dawgs." Strang, seated beside Tosh, heard the snort of irritation. "Sorry, boss! Pile-up on the M25. It's closed, so we're proceeding toward the A404. We'll hit the M40 at High Wycombe."

"Well, if you want to join us for some exceedingly fine cakes, you'd better look sharp because…hello. They've turned right. Up a lane leading to…or called Kingston Hill. See it?" After only a brief silence, Strang confirmed. Ratso looked at the narrow winding track on the moving map. "Remember that Chris Rea song—'The Road to Hell'?" He almost smiled as the Scot broke into song. "Well he could've been thinking of this road. More like a bleeding track. It goes effin' here, there and nowhere. Doubles back east to God knows where." Ratso accelerated to close the gap now. "Maybe I was right about them having a picnic."

"Window-steamers, are they? Bit of hanky-panky on the back seat?"

"Maybe. But I'd say it was husband and wife. Bell me in ten." Ratso saw the signpost to Kingston, single track. He turned in slowly and headed more or less east uphill. Then the blip on his screen stopped. It was somewhere up ahead. But maybe not on the road. Close though. "Two sugars in mine and an Angel Slice," he muttered as he sensed a wasted trip.

Blocking the road, he pulled up before reaching the target. He'd hoped the couple would lead him to a rendezvous. Maybe there was a meet up there. Someone who had arrived before. He had hoped for new faces or another car to photo, or even to spot cash or drugs changing hands. *But out here?* Anything was possible, from sighting discarded panties to a couple sitting on a fallen branch enjoying mugs of tea. After a quick call to the sergeants, he cruised slowly up the rest of the hill between the banks and tall hedges. If anybody came the other way, *someone* would have to do a load of reversing.

But nobody came. He drove cautiously, all the while watching the stationary blip on the iPad. Just beyond the crest of the hill, the road kinked and as he rounded it, he saw another vehicle, perhaps a BMW or Audi saloon but just its rear view as it accelerated away far too fast for the road. The blip had not moved and he was almost upon it. The speeding car disappeared round a bend and was gone. He was now just eighty metres from the blip but of the Range Rover there was no sign.

10

West London

Even without the lingering execution of the mystery man during the night before, Erlis Bardici would have been heading for Heathrow. He had never planned to use the Range Rover to get there but the night's events had made prudence doubly necessary. Since dragging the scrawny figure feet first from under the vehicle, he had not been near it. Gagged and bound, his prisoner had been shifted within minutes into his cousin's grey van. They had taken him the few miles to a safe house, an apartment in Sheen. At the time, he had not believed the man's denials of placing a bug. That's when the nail-pulling had commenced. But perhaps the little man had been telling the truth. This morning, with daylight, he had found a neat little device lying on the hard standing close to the driver's door.

The discovery had been troubling—not because he had perhaps needlessly tortured the bastard but because it left him uncertain what to do next. The Range Rover only had 7,000 on the clock but he had nobody trustworthy to discover if another bug had been planted. Not with certainty. Not the type of certainty he needed. And no way was he driving it anywhere. Hell, there could even be an explosive device under there. Not likely but could he be sure? Not with the Hogans looking for trouble. Over his breakfast of cold meats and cheese with green tea, he weighed it all up. It was only money, a lot of money but he could buy a replacement. *I could buy an effing fleet if I wanted.* No way could he risk being tracked by whoever had sent the little man. No way was he going to risk being blown up by a bomb. As he poured a second cup, his mind was clear: *I'm not stepping into that damned thing.*

Now as the taxi headed for Terminal Five, he could relax and relive the man's wriggles against the belts that had held him secure to the chair. His face broke into a smile as he recalled those screams through the gag, the man's face puce with effort, his cheeks dripping in sweat, his eyes wide open with something between defiance and fear.

Credit to the bastard, it took nine nails before he cracked. *My name's Robbie Bracewell*, he'd said but Bardici hadn't believed him. No matter. The real name would be in the papers shortly. Whoever he was, the runt had admitted to working for those Hogan bastards from Tooting. Dan and Jerry Hogan had started supplying coke and pills to the bars and clubs round Mitcham, Morden and towards Croydon and the message he had received from the Big Man was the Hogans had to be stopped. Killed. ASAP.

But getting both Hogans together so far had been impossible. The feelers were out. But had they bugged him as the little guy had said? It made sense. The ninth finger he had twisted slowly as he pulled the nail until all three bones, the distal, middle and proximal phalanges, were all broken, causing mind-blowing pain. But it had been effective. After careful thought over breakfast, he had selected a pay-as-you-go phone from over a dozen that he owned and constantly discarded. He rang a different cousin, in Chiswick and gave clear instructions on what he had to do.

Such thoughts left his mind as Bardici presented his passport at the British Airways desk at Terminal Five with his ID of Mujo Zevi from the Albanian-speaking coastal resort of Ulcinj in Montenegro. His papers, for a short vacation in Florida, were checked and accepted with no hesitation despite the fact that his burly frame and height of over six feet gave him an air of danger if not actual menace, even when smiling. But the small beard and tinted contacts changed his eye colour and helped create a perfect match for his false ID. The premature iron grey in his hair was now luxurious black to complete the look.

As he accepted the offer of champagne and nuts in the Lounge, he thought ahead to his meeting in Freeport with Lance Ruthven. Of course the man would be using the name Hank Kurtner but Bardici had been well briefed by his superior, one of the lieutenants used by the Big Boss. He knew every last detail about the American. The rendezvous he had chosen was the car park of the Pink Flamingo Calypso Bar, a few miles east of Freeport. From an Internet café just round the corner and with help from Google Maps, Bardici had judged the bar to be suitably anonymous and unlikely to be busy early in the evening before the steel band arrived.

Now, as he reclined in his Club World seat, he was looking forward to the fixing the devious shit who ran the shipyard. It wouldn't be as pleasurable as slicing off the Irishman's manhood with the long-handled shears. But then… yes, wasn't it Rod Stewart who had proclaimed that *the first cut is the deepest?* He smiled wolfishly. *Not when I'm involved, Rod. Every cut is deep.*

11

Oxfordshire, England

Ratso was a mere twenty metres from the Range Rover when he saw it, or rather, guessed where it was. The afternoon sky was rapidly filling with thick black smoke rising from an unmade track just to his left. He cruised forward, windows down and was hit by the pungent smell of acrid fumes at the same moment he heard the roar of a fire. A second later he saw the Range Rover engulfed in flames. Whether it had gone down with its occupants, it was already too late to tell. Petrol had obviously been thrown generously over the bodywork as well as inside before it had been fired. Roaring flames leapt skyward between the trees in the clearing and the air was already darkening with a spreading black cloud. From his own car, he took a series of photos showing the registration number but with the intensity of the fire he went no closer, taking no chances.

Ratso knew that some smartasses reckoned fuel tanks don't explode but the whole team had only recently watched the footage of a Los Angeles firefighter being blasted from close range while battling a blazing green saloon when the tank let rip.

Somehow, the poor sod had survived. If the couple were inside the Range Rover, frankly he didn't give a stuff. More likely they had been chauffeured away in the speeding saloon. He started to accelerate after it but then changed his mind. He was never going to catch it.

He phoned Watson. It was Jock Strang who answered.

"Not a picnic after all, Jock. More of a barbeque. Tosh could grill his burgers a treat."

"Torched it, did they?" The Scot heard Ratso's grunted yes. "Ye got them?"

"No. Probably whisked away in a Beamer saloon - a Three Series. Or maybe an Audi." He checked the map on screen. "My guess—and it is a guess—is they must somehow be getting back to the M40. No, wait one. The A40 first. This piddling little lane eventually winds to it. Where are you?"

"Tosh is chatting to the Duke about the rising price of deer-stalker hats. Hang on, guv, I'm checking." Strang ran his finger along the routes. "Shit and buggerrr-ation!"

"Spilt tea on the corgis, have you?"

"We're too far north. We're just turning off the M40 at Stokenchurch."

"You'll still spot them. Take the A40 doubling back to London. The lane from Kingston Hill joins it after about a mile. Look out for a saloon with either one or three occupants. Probably two males, one female heading for London…but it might go your way. Get the number."

"Intercept?"

"No. Follow if you can. Get intel unit back at base to check the number. Get me a forensic team out here. A pickup truck for the remains. I'm staying put so nobody corrupts the scene."

"Take care, boss."

"Keep me posted."

Ratso reversed a few metres and stopped, blocking the road. The Range Rover, almost unrecognisable now, was engulfed by a raging roar of red, yellow, gold and black. Still keeping well clear, he got out and studied the tyre tracks on the verge. They could have been caused by one vehicle passing another but hopefully had been left by the saloon parked in the soggy mud and grass. He looked at the muddy track down which the car was blazing. There were footprints everywhere—plenty for the forensic boys to play with but they wouldn't make it for another hour. At least the sleet had stopped, leaving just the icy wind that whipped over the crest of the Chiltern Hills.

He settled back to wait, wondering whether his sergeants had been too late. He grabbed his phone. There was much to do; cancelling his cricket nets for this evening, for starters. He felt pissed off about that, missing the banter and the pint afterward. He'd been looking forward to bowling to the new young Aussie who had played Grade Cricket in Melbourne. And he had to fix a meet with Lefty Denholm. And talk to Charlene—once Caldwell had sent a young PC to break the news. But first, it had to be Wensley Hughes.

Though the assistant commissioner had a supercilious look, with a face like an inquisitive and whiskerless gerbil, Ratso liked him. He'd been tagged as a copper's copper. He'd had the bottle to approve Operation Clam as a totally clandestine venture.

Wensley Hughes had abandoned his stack of dog-eared files in disgust, convinced that *someone*—someone high up and well placed—had been leaking to Zandro. Confidential reports to the Home Office were insecure. *A piss-poor bucket full of leaks* had been his dismissive description of the Home Secretary of the day.

So now, as an AC, Wensley Hughes remained supportive but Neil's murder could be the tipping point. Would Hughes hold his nerve? He was less bothered about Arthur Tennant. True, that shit would carp, sneer and look smug in that *I told you so* sort of way. Always the first to be in his running shoes if any shit was flying. Just the thought of him made Ratso's toes curl. Slowly he dialled the AC. Would he be hung out to dry? The odds were good. For a thin, gaunt figure, rather frail-looking with waxy skin, the assistant commissioner had the balls of a stallion and the courage of a lion

12

Freeport, Grand Bahama Island

Erlis Bardici's short hop from Miami to Freeport touched down at gone 10 p.m. local time after delays due to *operational difficulties*—not words the Albanian enjoyed hearing. He hated flying in small planes and *operational difficulties* conjured up unwelcome images of drunken pilots screwing the cabin crew in an airport hotel, cracks in the wings, leaking fuel pipes, or faulty avionics. Especially in small planes, he always felt uneasy and his blue shirt showed nervous sweat as he exited, carrying his seersucker jacket over his shoulder and striding toward Immigration. But for the breeze, the night air would have been warm but any sense of a subtropical paradise was lost in the roar of turboprop engines and the smell of aviation fuel.

He picked up a battered Suzuki Vitara with a dodgy 77,000 on the clock. No point checking for dents in the dimly lit rental zone, as every side had been bumped or scraped on countless occasions. He quite liked that. Nobody could later try to pin a damage claim on him, as had once happened with a rental in Paris.

Though he had learned the direct route to his hotel, on leaving the airport he drove in the other direction. During the flight he had changed his plans. Now he was heading for the Pink Flamingo. According to the map, it was a doddle. But he quickly found that maps take no account of reality. A road closure from a burst water pipe, for starters. The badly signed diversion threw him completely, so that the twenty-minute journey took him over an hour through parts of Freeport he had no wish ever to see again.

Funny, he thought as at last he re-joined a better road, how environment changes everything. In what he had come to regard as *his* manor of West London, nothing and nobody scared him. He walked tall, felt good. There was nothing he could not control or fix with a couple of calls. But here, driving through the slums of Freeport, he felt strangely ill at ease, his hands clammy, his eyes watchful at every small junction as he anticipated armed black men, built like oak trees. But nothing happened. Without a rope, gun, or knife at hand, he felt naked but no way could he have risked carrying anything through airport security. Not these days.

The interior light was broken, just like the wing mirror. He could not check the map but he guessed the Pink Flamingo could only be another mile or two along the main highway and then down a track toward the beach. Traffic was moderate, mainly old vans, open 4x4s and Japanese saloons batting around with young people, four to a car, listening to the blast of rock or reggae, heading to bars or clubs for a night of boozy laughter. Moments later, he saw a faded wooden sign with an arrow and an image of a flamingo standing on one leg. He swung the wheel into the turning. The little 4x4 lurched alarmingly through a deep pothole but Bardici grunted with satisfaction at having arrived without having to ask the way.

The unmade track was four hundred metres long before it ended in a bare earth car park with room for perhaps sixty vehicles. He lost count at thirty but still felt confident from the web revues that this was only a late-night dive, one for the night owls and that in the early evening tomorrow the place would be deserted. It would be a good place to bring the CEO, plenty intimidating enough if the guy played it tough. He wound down the window and smelled what might have been chicken being grilled on charcoal in a shack out of sight beyond the pines. Google's aerial views had not lied. It was a perfect spot for tomorrow's chat with the American.

For a hungry second or two, he was tempted to sink a local beer and devour chicken and fries to the thump of reggae, the music being carried by the cool breeze. For a lingering moment, his hand even gripped the grubby door handle. But no. Best get to the hotel. He crunched the vehicle into gear and cruised slowly back to the highway.

His hotel was only about three miles back and by midnight, he had downed a couple of large Grey Goose vodkas and a shrimp kebab as he prepared for the day ahead. Next to his guide book was his shopping list. It was not long. Buying decorated conch shells or a ceramic toothpick holder for his ageing mother did not feature.

As Bardici slipped the list into his hip pocket, Lamon Wilson, the CEO of the shipyard was scribbling figures on a notepad, dreaming up a scenario to screw that wimp Kurtner. Less than a mile away, the American was entering his hotel with Cassie, the eighteen-year-old daughter of a port worker. For $270, she was his for the night.

Bardici ordered another vodka, as he made his plans, a quiet smile playing on his lips

13

Clapham, South London
It was only a short walk from base round the corner to the Indian store on Balham Rise. Though the peak rush hour had long ended, traffic heading out of London was still heavy and tailing back at the traffic lights at the Glebeside Lane junction. Ratso wondered if he had seen the same lemmings that morning. *Probably.* Everyone, except too many clock-watching civil servants, now had to work harder, longer days and all wait longer till retirement.

He looked at the occasional driver, their faces resigned to another night getting back too late to see the kids before bedtime. Vans, cars, Chelsea tractors, the drivers stressed out and anxious to get home. He had huge sympathy for them—most of them were decent folk trying to pay off their credit cards and mortgages at the end of the month while the minority but a pretty damned powerful one, was plotting, dealing, stealing and killing. Paying no taxes, either. Hard men, outside the system.

One thing was for sure–there was no recession in the crime industry. More villains would be starting careers now as job opportunities disappeared. It was sad but inevitable, he concluded as he swung into a tiny shop and grabbed a bottle of Chardonnay from the chiller. Everybody was sinking in the same damned boat called *Recession*. He didn't buy all this *hate the bankers* stuff. Politicians and Eurocrats could have intervened any time to kill the excess. *Politicians and Eurocrats!* Just the thought of them swilling vintage wine in overpriced Michelin-starred restaurants in Brussels made him scowl. In the real world, real people like him were trading down with less to spend and scouring the shelves for the cheapest plonk from convenience stores.

Armed with South African Chardonnay, Ratso breezed into the unlicensed Balti Gem restaurant just along the road. He was pleased to find a free table with a good view of the door. He liked to sit where nobody was behind him and he could scope the room. Jock Strang was yet to arrive, so Ratso ordered poppadoms and a fiery chutney dip strong enough to blow the bollocks off a donkey. It was his regular choice after a long day. He flicked through the messages he had grabbed from his desk and sorted the clutter that had accumulated during his afternoon in the Chilterns.

Twenty minutes later the Scot's bulk filled the door, With a pleased look of recognition, Strang advanced, rubbing his hands warm as he did so. He slumped into the chair rather than sat down and Ratso knew at once that all was not well. "Jock. Don't blame yourself about the missing out on the target. He was really shifting when I saw him. The bastard must have been well gone before you were close." Even as he spoke, Ratso realised he had lost his audience.

"It's no that, boss."

"Give! What's up?" Ratso pushed across the poppadoms. Strang declined the chutney with a rueful grin but then turned stony-faced again. "He didn't make it."

Ratso was thrown. Who hadn't made it? Who'd been dying and had now lost the battle?

"Gordy."

Ratso was in synch now. Jock's young son Gordy had been spotted by the Glasgow Rangers as a likely talent, a future star to follow in the footsteps of legends like Jim Baxter, John Greig and Ally McCoist. Ratso knew that his sergeant lived his life through the boy, especially since his ex had run off with another man—a Celtic supporter, to twist the knife.

Ratso fought for the right things to say, then simply shook his head and leaned across to pat Jock's sleeve. "Aye," Strang continued. "But for the injury, he'd have made the reserves this season, maybe even have got on the bench. Now, they're no keeping him on." Ratso thought the sergeant was going to destroy his hard man image by shedding a tear. Certainly he bit his lip, eyes lowered. "His knee's unstable and he's lost a yard."

"Life's a bitch." Ratso waved the hovering waiter away. "More physio, maybe?"

Strang shook his head. "The Club have been just great despite their financial problems. They've tried everything. His knee winna stand ninety minutes, let alone a season. Like Brian Clough. Busted outta the game."

"Except Cloughie got some great goals till his injury."

"The lad's heartbroken. Fitba was his life."

Ratso played with his cutlery, debating what to do or say. He needed Jock as Operation Clam moved into overdrive but there was no choice. "Gordy needs you. Take some time. Get back to Glasgow for a few days."

Jock produced a bottle from the depths of his black windcheater. Ratso saw the quadruple measure of whisky poured with an unsteady hand.

"You're not driving, are you?"

Strang laughed at last. "I'll be too pissed to walk."

The tiny waiter, all smiles and teeth, was still hovering too close for Ratso's liking. "C'mon, let's order."

Jock went first. "Naan bread, rice and a medium lamb balti. Spinach. The non-stick-in-yer-teeth type." The waiter looked confused but then turned to Ratso, who followed up with a hot Rogon josh chicken curry, easy on the rice and plenty of green salad. The waiter disappeared. "I'll take the bus," Strang continued. "And boss, yer offer? Ye're right. The boy needs me. I'm due a few days anyroads."

Ratso fell silent as he thought of England cricket captain Michael Vaughan: knee injury, premature end to a golden career. Simon Jones. Syd Lawrence. The list of cricketers with devastating injuries was endless. "Sport can be cruel. But I bet the hardest thing is life without it. That's why Gordy needs you."

Jock nodded agreement but his voice was emotional, scratchy as he moved on. "Change of subject, eh boss? What happened with the AC? Or Arthur Tennant?"

"Tennant?" Ratso laughed mockingly. "Never saw him. Long gone to the ten-pin bowling. Lazy sod. Part-time bleeding job he does."

"Ten-pin? I thought he had a bad back? That so-called injury last year?"

Ratso laughed, head thrown back. "It only hurts if he's working."

"Just wait, boss. He'll play the injury game, get in a claim for a work injury and early retirement."

"You mean like lifting a heavy file on a Monday morning?"

Strang laughed. "Aye, right enough! Nae bad, is it? Early retirement with injury compensation and a full pension. I've seen it before! Plenty like him in Glasgow."

"I thought Scots cops were all like Rebus and Taggart."

"Only me." Jock sank his Bells and poured another. "And Wensley Hughes?"

"Said he was working till midnight. And I believe him." He sipped the wine, unimpressed. "I should stick to red. Even with Indian." He grinned and thumped the table. "We go on. We've still got his backing."

"There's more?"

"I'll meet Neil's woman in the morning." He gave a sly look, eyes narrowed. "One of my snouts phoned the Yard. Told them he'd heard on the radio about the body at Hammersmith. Said he was due to meet a pal called Neil Shalford who hadn't turned up. Reckoned you could set your clock by him."

"So your guy ID'd him?"

Ratso grinned. "*And* he's putting it about that Neil did jobs for the Hogan brothers."

"Nice one. And yer snout, let's call him Lefty Denholm for convenience." Strand knew he had hit a bull's-eye. "He's safe? Won't be, er, indiscreet?"

Ratso flinched when Lefty's name was used. He thought nobody knew the identity of this snout who hung out around the fag end of Wandsworth. But Strang himself had his own sources, built over the years working the area. "Lefty? Nah! It wasn't him." He sounded convincing but Jock was not taken in. "My snout's as tight as a newt's arsehole."

"And Charlene? How's she going to be?"

"Cut up, I guess."

"Bit like her man, then." Jock growled across the steaming food that had now arrived. "Sorry, boss. I know you liked Neil. Charlene too."

Ratso did a double take, sensing innuendo.

"Did she no miss him when he didna come back?"

"Nah! She wouldn't have worried. Will-o-the-wisp she called him. He reckoned she never asked. He never volunteered."

"She got anyone? I mean company for tonight?"

"Brother on an oil rig somewhere. Sister might have driven up from Folkestone."

"She must be in some state. Ye should see her tonight."

Ratso put down his fork. He frowned, knowing he had already debated this and had put off a decision. "You're right, Jock. I could grab a train from the Junction. Then walk. Do me good." He refilled with Chardonnay to the brim. The second glass always slipped away quicker. He was about to continue when he had a thought and dialled a number. "Hi, Ranji! Todd Holtom here, SCD7. Remember me? That job in Merton? Right. Any reports of stolen vehicles today? Yeah, I know. Silly question! Silver Range Rover. Hounslow way. Anything?" He continued forking fiery chicken pieces into his mouth as he held on. At last he nodded and scribbled on his pad. Then he laughed. "Call me psychic. Thanks!"

"Our pal Bar-deechi reported it stolen, did he?"

Ratso played thoughtfully with his glass, twirling it round in a manner that would have made wine buffs flinch. "No. Not Bardici. A guy called Klodian Skela. He's a cousin. Skela reported it stolen around 5 p.m."

"That Bardeechi bastard! Setting up an insurance claim for a stolen vehicle." He paused to look sadly at his nearly empty whisky bottle. "Know this Skela guy?"

Ratso shook his head. "Tosh checked out the name once, remember? Nothing. We never followed up. Check him out in the morning before you go. He claimed he was picking up the car to take it for service."

"At 5 p.m.? Bollocks! So where is Bardici, then?"

Ratso shrugged. "Tell you this for free, though. Erlis Bardici must have been shit scared. You don't go torching a new Range Rover, a Christmas tree job and all."

Jock Strang nodded. "Bar-deechi thought it was a bomb?"

"Thought it *could* be a bomb," agreed Ratso as he called for the bill. "My shout. This is on me, Jock." He put down a ten and a twenty. "Here's our problem. Boris Zandro is King of the Shit Heap. We know Bardici but it's the bit in the middle we're missing: the lieutenants, his serious and I mean his fucking good top-class guys who run everything. The bug might have done that. If we ID them, Zandro's empire collapses. We can hoover up the runners, custodians, enforcers, moneymen once we've removed the bleeding chicken's head and shoulders."

"Maybe Skela will squeal."

Ratso shook his head dismissively. "Small fry. A gofer, my guess. He won't know how Zandro communicates with his lieutenants or how Bardici gets his instructions." Ratso stretched and yawned. "Beneath Zandro's lieutenants, there must be local distributors. We had that lead pointing to Crawley, somewhere near Gatwick Airport but it went cold. We know some small fry—the pushers who get caught now and then."

"Omerta. A wall of silence." Strang was all too familiar with that from time spent around the tenements and tower blocks around Glasgow's Castlemilk.

"Ten murders, maybe thirteen. All dealers, pushers. Tortured and dumped, almost certainly by Bardici. Keeps the rest in line. A loose word and they're dead meat."

"So the chain's broke in two spots: Zandro to his lieutenants and below them to the distributors." Strang saw the resigned nod of agreement.

Ratso turned to the waiter. "Keep the change." He looked toward the door and his eyes turned sad as an elderly woman struggled to push a man in a wheelchair through the narrow entrance. For a moment he was back to his childhood. He looked at the flock wallpaper to conceal his inner thoughts. "Klodian Skela was expendable. He was used to remove the car. If he and his woman's remains had been catapulted all round Hounslow, Bardici would have shrugged and moved on."

"The bastard." Strang slipped the nearly empty bottle into his fleecy coat.

Ratso stood up. "Klodian Skela had no idea why he was doing what he did. Just briefed to drive, torch and then report a theft."

"So it wouldna' get us any closer to Boris Zandro." He looked all of his forty-nine years as he struggled with the zip on his windcheater. The wrinkled, lined face, like a relief map of the Grampians, showed he had lived his life to the full. "But Bardici? Where's he? Why didn't he report the theft?"

Ratso had no idea. The man was unpredictable. "The truth or his cover story? *Listen, guv, I was away when it happened. Been staying wiv me aunt in Bexhill. Ask her.*"

"He speaks London English, then?" The Scot was unsure whether he was joking.

"Like the best of them.."

"Ye reckon he's lying low?"

Ratso's shrug said it all. "Life's a bitch." Ratso gripped the Scot's arm as they headed for the exit. "You know what bothers me? How was Neil caught?"

"Ye mean?" Jock's face showed his concern.

"Can't rule it out." Ratso looked grim. All the way back from the burned-out car, the thought had been troubling him. "I'd hate to think one of my lads had been turned by the Albanians." Jock looked at his clumpy black shoes before acknowledging the possibility. They both upped their collars against the wintry blast that was shifting empty cans and burger wrappers down the street. "We know the leak isn't coming through the Home Office. They're blindsided." Ratso's face showed his concern and not just because a few snowflakes were fluttering around them as they headed for the traffic lights. Ratso tugged Strang's sleeve in a sudden movement. "We need Klodian Skela's mobile."

"It'll be pay-as-ye-go."

"Maybe not. The big guys, they change phones more often than socks but this guy was expendable. Doing a relative a favour for a few quid. He phoned to report the vehicle stolen. We have a number. Check it out, can you?"

"I'm on compassionate leave."

Ratso playfully punched his bicep and rather wished he hadn't. He was about to enter the tube station when Strang turned to face him.

"There's something you need to know boss."

Ratso looked at him cautiously. "You sure I want to hear this?"

Strang looked at a young woman staggering drunkenly across the road, carrying what looked like a bottle of Smirnoff. "This afternoon. When we joined the A40."

"Chasing the Beamer, yes."

"Tosh needed a leak. Desperate. We had to stop. Lost a couple of minutes."

Ratso studied a discarded fag end, eyes fixed downward. At last he looked up and laughed. "Tosh and that bloody weak bladder of his." He clasped the sergeant's arm. "Thanks for telling me. Keep that away from Tennant. He's looking to shit on us from a great height."

14

Kingston-on-Thames

It was a long, miserable walk from Kingston Station to Wolsey Drive. The wind-driven, intermittent sleet and snow was a right bloody downer. It squelched from Ratso's shoes and streamed down his neck. The main road heading north to Richmond was busy enough to give him something to look at but otherwise the soulless surroundings of small shops, traffic lights and forgettable housing were dreary and not worthy of attention. Only the steady beat of Metallica kept his spirits up. Each step took him nearer to facing Charlene and sitting in a chair where Neil used to sit, holding a glass used by his old friend.

But Charlene must never discover that it was me who sent him to his death. And she'll get nothing. No widow's pension. No golden goodbye. Nothing. Just the press boys sniffing round about Neil's underworld contacts. All because of me.

No. All because of Boris Zandro.

It was twenty-five minutes before he was amongst the terraced homes of Wolsey Drive. Would she be alone or would her sister have arrived yet? Or a neighbour, perhaps? He swung open the familiar metal gate set in a wooden fence and walked slowly through the small, well-kept garden, the wintry grass looking lush in the light from the front room. He rang the bell and heard the familiar musical chime, which he had always regarded as naff.

He heard footsteps. "Who is it?" The fear and confusion was obvious.

"It's me. Todd."

"Ratso!" There was welcome in the voice and the door was quickly unlocked in three places. Without a word, he stepped inside and she fell into his arms, clinging to him, her body trembling as she stood on tiptoes to press her cheek to his. "Oh God, Ratso! Why, why? He didn't deserve..."

Ratso broke away as he back-heeled the door shut and then locked it. Charlene had obviously decided to look her best to go to the morgue. *Was she a stunner or what?* Her hair was as well coiffured as ever he'd seen it. Brown in colour, it was parted in the middle and hung either side of her face to near shoulder length. Her skin was slightly tanned and wrinkle-free. Her hair just hid the tops of her ears, which were each adorned with a dangly earring. The navy trouser-suit, figure-hugging over a simple white blouse, he had never seen before and he guessed she had selected it for the sombre occasion. Her makeup was immaculate, unspoiled by tears. Her eyes! Ratso had always regarded them as her most striking feature, green and of seemingly infinite depth.

For a moment they stood under the burgundy shade of the single hall light but then she clasped his hand and led him into the front room. Her hand was cold, deathly cold. The living room was silent, empty. The cosy room that used to echo with Neil's rasping Belfast accent felt unloved and unwelcoming.

"Thanks for coming, Ratso. There's nobody I'd rather have here at a time like this. You were so close." Charlene motioned him to a chair. "Oh, sorry. You're off duty, I suppose. A drink. Neil bought some single malt the other day. There's plenty..." Her voice faded away.

"I'll get one for both of us. You sit down."

But Charlene did not. Instead she followed him to the kitchen, standing close to him as he studied the array of bottles and selected a Macallan. "He loved his whiskies," she explained. "Well, I guess you knew that!" Her laugh was nervous and her voice quavered with each word. "The Macallan! I just knew you would choose that one. Neil was planning to share it with you." She bit her lip and wiped away a tear.

Ratso took two tumblers from the Formica-fronted cupboard and poured generously, then splashed in a drop of water. The kitchen light was bright but her beauty held as they chinked glasses. "To Neil."

Charlene nodded. "God rest his soul." They both swallowed a good mouthful before heading back to the comfort of the easy chairs. The room smelled of sandalwood from a candle burning on a small table.

As if reading his mind, Charlene volunteered that Neil had never told her much of what he did. "A dark horse," Ratso agreed. "He had skills learned in Ireland that had made him valuable."

"To the underworld." Her tone was bitter. "That's what some journalist said. He phoned just before you arrived." Charlene shifted uncomfortably and then tucked her feet under her on the chair across from him. Ratso was amazed at how the word he had put out through the snout had travelled so fast. *Had it reached Bardici...wherever he was?*

"Don't always believe the press." Ratso saw she was unconvinced. "Look, Neil was not known to us. No previous convictions."

"So who would…kill him?" For the first time Ratso noticed anger in her voice.

"Depends on what he was doing and who was paying him." Ratso liked the answer. It was matter-of-fact but he hesitated before continuing. "Taking one extreme…you know—knew Neil well enough. It might have been an angry husband."

Charlene took it in her stride. "He was a randy sod, all right." She shook her head ruefully but without any sign of irritation. "Morals of a tomcat. But," she hesitated, "we had…an understanding." She paused. "Don't ask, don't tell." She sank the whisky. "He always came back. Treated me like a princess. Kind. Good with money."

"You tamed him and all," Ratso agreed. "Neil and I—we go back over twelve years and he's never stuck with one person as long as you. You got the nearest to muzzling him." He rose from his chair and strolled round the small sitting room, studying a photo of Neil and Charlene laughing on the London Eye. It would have been a good night for a fire but the grate was empty, as was the coal scuttle. "Look, Charlene, if I'd ever thought he was part of some underworld mob, I'd have let our friendship cool. I'd have had no choice." The lie was essential and it came out easily.

"You said one extreme just now. What's the other, then?" Her stare was business-like and disbelieving.

"Not so extreme—corporate espionage. Ferreting for big companies involved in litigation or takeover bids. It pays well."

Charlene did not look convinced. She too stood up and in a sudden move clung to him. "I'd bet he was murdered by a hardened criminal. Are you on the case?"

Ratso wondered if anyone had hinted at what agonies Neil had suffered. He hoped not. "Not me. DCI Caldwell is in charge.

You haven't seen him yet?" He saw her shake her head. "You will. Who took you to the morgue?"

"A couple of youngsters. I don't remember the man's name, wasn't really concentrating on that. She was WPC Stella Tuson."

Ratso went to the kitchen to refill the glasses. On his return they sat down, this time next to each other on the sofa. "I'm not too good at the emotional stuff. I never have been. Even when my folks died. Tears and drama aren't my way. It's the Capricorn in me. Feet on the ground. Face facts. So let me ask. Financially—will you be okay? Neil had no index-linked pension or death-in-service benefits."

"It'll be hard." She twirled the tumbler between her slim fingers. "We got a bit put by in the bank."

"Mortgage?"

"No. Rented. My earnings cover that and a bit on top. Neil's money was the bunce. The *fun money*, he called it."

"Good, that's good." Ratso was captivated by her eyes as she watched him, their pale green drawing him in. "Never be too proud to ask for...y'know, a bit of help. Neil was a real mate. If he'd ever got to understand cricket, he'd have been the best. I took him to Lord's once." Ratso laughed. "He spent the entire day drinking Pimms in the bookmakers. Never saw a ball bowled."

"He loved hanging out with you guys."

"But watching cricket is about being together—debating tactics, arguing, complaining about the umpires, sinking a few while watching! I never saw him all day. And he got lucky! Won eighty quid on racing from Kempton. He said he'd had a great day, so I jokingly asked for his winnings to pay for his ticket. I never got it." He was rewarded with a smile.

"I'm glad you came, Ratso." She looked away, staring at a photo of Neil in a Hawaiian beach shirt and bright red shorts.

"Neil envied your dedication. One of the best, he reckoned. Always said if anything happened to him, you were the guy to turn to."

"I'm flattered."

"Course, I never expected…"

"Well no, of course not. You don't, do you?" Ratso stood up to leave.

"You're not going, are you?"

"I really only dropped by to see if I could help, to give you a shoulder to cry on. But you're doing just great."

"That's only 'cos you're here." She stood up and moved toward him, clasped his hand. "I don't want to be alone tonight. There's a spare bed. It's late. Anyway, for you heading for Hammersmith, this is not the best place to start."

Ratso felt a pleasing but untimely stirring down below as he had met her pleading look. Not for the first time, he imagined comforting her with a right good rogering, pounding hard into those slim hips, her body heaving and her groans deep. He had always envied Neil the luxury of sharing her body but he had quashed the thought as absurd.

"I'll have to be away early. And you shouldn't be alone. Your sister?"

"She's in Tenerife. She's flying back for the funeral."

"Neighbours?"

Charlene patted her thigh dismissively. "Nobody I'd really want here that much."

"Work colleagues? I mean, it's not just tonight."

"There's Sandra, I suppose. A right laugh she is but she's young, no life experience." She turned slightly and clasped her arms round his back. Her voice was suddenly hoarse, throaty and emotional. "Remember Princess Diana said that butler of hers was *her rock*. I can feel that about you. Steady and sensible."

"Dull and boring, eh? That's the Capricorn in me again! But I'll stay…if it helps."

She rested her head just below his shoulder and murmured thanks, clasping him to her so that Ratso was uncomfortably aware that his inner thoughts were all too evident. But if she noticed, there was no sign as she pulled back and said she would make up the spare bed and find the new electric razor she had only just bought as Neil's Christmas present. As she said the words, her voice cracked, her head and shoulders slumping back against the wall, making her look frail and very vulnerable. Ratso knew it was always the little things, the sudden flash of memory or chance word that could trigger deep-seated emotions. As she turned to leave, Ratso closed in behind her and stroked a tear away with his finger.

"It's okay. I'll be fine." She left the room and he heard her feet clattering up the wooden stairs.

Next morning, Ratso awoke only when Charlene stood beside him in her pale pink dressing gown over not a lot else. "You slept through the alarm." She smiled. "Here's some tea. You used to like it strong." He felt uncomfortably aware of her closeness as he lay naked under the duvet. Her breasts swayed gently as she placed the cup on the low bedside locker. He felt a wreck. The night had been too short, the previous day too long. He felt sure he looked a mess, his hair tousled and his face no doubt flabby, unshaven and misshapen from sleep.

She perched on the side of the bed as he leaned on one elbow. "You're going to work?" he enquired.

"No. I'll go to the undertakers in Kingston. I'm on compassionate. Open-ended."

"Sleep okay?"

She looked down at him and mouthed no. "But you did. I could hear you!"

"I was knackered after yesterday. You must think..."

She placed a finger on his lips. "Forget it. My head was buzzing. So many contradictions, regrets, uncertainties. You coming here just confused me even more." She stood up. "I'll go to the bathroom first. Finish your tea." She left him with an erection that was more than just morning piss-proud. He checked his watch. 0620. He was going to be later than usual and the lads would be sniggering about why.

It was nearly 0730 when he left the house, turning right toward Kingston Station. He had declined Charlene's offer of a lift, preferring to get in some exercise and catch up on the day's play in Adelaide as he walked. After giving her a lingering hug on the doorstep and insisting she phone anytime, he was gone, waving a cheery goodbye and blowing a final kiss. He watched her head droop as she closed the door and for a moment he had to resist the urge to return.

Slowly, he turned away and crossed Wolsey Drive. He never noticed a small black Rover saloon parked down the street with two men in the front seats.

15

Grand Bahama Island
Lance Ruthven's nervousness showed in the decision to have the taxi drop him off at the Pink Flamingo car park nearly forty minutes early. The dark Caribbean night surrounded him as he walked down the track with his Hank Kurtner limp. To either side of him was pine forest, lit every few metres by solar lights till he reached the pink shack just back from the water's edge.

Erlis Bardici had arrived even earlier but not because of nerves. He had things to do—things that prevented him going to the beach bar but which enabled him to see Kurtner arrive. Though it was Saturday evening, the car park was almost deserted. The main crowd would not arrive for a good while yet. There were just six vehicles parked randomly round the muddiness of the area following the afternoon cloudburst.

Ruthven entered the shack with tentative steps, uncertain whether the Brit might already be here. But the bar was empty except for one couple locked in a passionate embrace in a corner. In the coolness of the evening, the swish of the overhead fans seemed a waste of electricity as he ordered a mojito and watched the bartender mix the rum, mint and lime. The youngster seemed miffed to have his enjoyment of the Dallas Cowboys game interrupted. Ruthven declined a menu but volunteered he might eat later *when the joint had livened up.*

His thoughts were jumbled, reliving the night before with Cassie, who, despite her young age, seemed to have learned more than a few tricks of her profession. He wondered if Amber would be as inventive when he whisked her from Washington to his Caribbean retreat. But just as he was imagining Amber leaping astride him, his thoughts tumbled back to the meeting now only twenty minutes away. *Shouldn't take long,* he reasoned. *Explain to the limey about the delays and then reassure him that tomorrow we can both kick ass like it had never been invented.* And, with luck, later tonight he'd find another little beauty in here, all glistening black skin and thick lips.

He drained the last of the mojito, leaving just the ice and chopped mint in the large beaker. Moments later, he had dodged most of the puddles on the track and was in the large expanse of car park. It was precisely 8 p.m. He looked around for any sign of the stranger who was to signal his presence but there was only blackness. He wondered for a moment if the Brit would be a no-show but then he saw two flashes from the lights of a Suzuki parked toward the far edge of the area. He limped slowly toward it, regretting that his disguise made him look so feeble.

He was almost at the car when the window on the driver's side wound down. "Hank?"

"That's me," he responded, his voice strained and throaty.

"Jump in." The driver leaned across and flung open the passenger door and after a pause to try to see the man's features, the American clambered in. The limey did not sound very English.

Maybe a Pole with good but accented English. "I'm Mujo. You're right on time. I like that," Bardici enthused.

Lance Ruthven clattered the door shut and peered at the hulk next to him. "Hank Kurtner," he volunteered cautiously as he offered his hand but the driver looked away. "You don't fit my image of the typical Brit. Not the name, not the accent." He tried to sound casual but failed miserably.

"I was born in Montenegro. Part of former Yugoslavia. I've lived in London most of my life." He offered Ruthven a cigarette and they both lit up, giving each the chance to catch a flickering glance at the other. "So where are you staying? Close by?"

"The Marlin, not too far. Ten minutes on these roads. It's pretty darned good."

"Maybe I'll stay there if I ever have to come back. But enough of that. These black bastards here have been pissing all over you. Screwing up the entire plan. You and me, we're going to show them tomorrow. Lamon Wilson will never again screw anybody. You got me, don't you?" Bardici's laugh was chilling to the listener as the message sunk in."

Lance Ruthven wanted to protest but the man's tone discouraged any such action. He could envisage this limey giving the CEO a right hammering and blowing both their covers if the cops were called. "Right on. Excuses, excuses." He paused to take a deep drag. "But I sure gave them hell last trip--a final warning. Tomorrow it's time for balls on a plate."

"Good, good," murmured the listener. "I like your style, Hank. Now tell me everything—what work they've done, what you have seen so far. From the first visit till now." It was his turn to pause. "And I mean *everything*. Every detail. This ship is one long buggeration. Any more delay could kill the whole damned operation. And if that happened." In the darkened interior, Bardici stopped to run his finger across his throat.

Ruthven licked his lips. "It'll be just fine. You'll see." His voice sounded weak and simpering. "The refit could be over in…oh, maybe three weeks—to be safe, with Christmas and New Year, maybe five."

The listener said nothing till he had stubbed out his cigarette. "Is this some kind of joke? Too long. Way too long." He turned to the American and his shoulders blotted out the window behind him. "So…I want to know everything."

Ruthven smelled the garlic on the man's breath. He smiled with all the forced confidence of a comedian knowing he had lost his audience. "You know about the…"

Bardici interrupted at once. "Assume I know nothing."

"It'll take a while. Let's do this over a bite. The bar's pretty good down at the water."

The Albanian shook his head. "Too early for me. Later, let's have a beer or two."

It took the American over thirty-five minutes but Bardici was a good listener, rarely asking a question and if he did, it was sharply worded and to the point. As Ruthven recounted the history, using lines he had rehearsed on his flights, his confidence grew and he even managed to slip in some dry humour that was lost on his audience. A couple of cars arrived and the occupants headed noisily for the waterfront. Ruthven covered the smallest details of the work being undertaken and why the plans were behind. He concluded with items still outstanding and pen pictures of the key figures, especially Lamon Wilson. Bardici scribbled some costings but nothing more. Some young Americans arrived, already flying high on local rum but they quickly disappeared between the trees, whooping and shouting. Ruthven was just about done as they disappeared down the track to the sea.

After a final curt question or two about security at the shipyard, Bardici was satisfied that he had what he needed. "Okay, Hank. You want that drink?"

Ruthven's unease about the meeting taking place in the vehicle had dissipated and he was looking forward to building a team with the man—*team bonding*, in Washington speak. "Sounds like a plan," he replied as Bardici's hands fumbled in the dark. The Albanian muttered about dropping his cigarette lighter. Suddenly, his hand shot out in front of Ruthven's face to point into the trees.

"Hey! Over there." The voice was sharp, the tone guttural. "Look, in those trees! You tell anyone you was coming here? We're being watched."

"Me? Never told nobody." Ruthven turned his head sharply to get a better view through the passenger window toward the distant trees that ringed the car park. He saw nothing. Bardici leaned across to point and Ruthven twisted to his right, straining to see who was there. "I don't see nothing. I…"

Lance Ruthven got no further as Bardici's thin wire garrotte, nearly three feet long, dropped over his head and noosed his neck from front to rear. The Albanian tightened the wire, sensing it biting enjoyably deep into the long, thin neck. As the American's head started to slump amid a torrent of gurgling sounds, his arms flailing, his legs feebly kicking forward in the well of the vehicle, Bardici went in for the kill, pressing his thumbs on the carotid artery on each side of the neck. In seconds, all life had gone.

The Albanian smiled in satisfaction. It had been pleasing enough, though less exciting than torturing the bastard from beneath the Range Rover. He climbed out and, once sure there was nobody around, opened the passenger door and pulled out the lifeless body, disappearing with it into the tall forest of pines and cursing the occasional shrub that smacked across his face or impeded his progress. Twenty metres into the inky black surroundings, he recognized the outline of the grave he had dug earlier. The ground was heavy, clingy and wet from the earlier downpour.

After emptying the American's pockets, he pitched Lance Ruthven's corpse into the pit without ceremony. Fifteen sweaty minutes later, he had refilled the hole, covering it with branches and other vegetation so that the disturbed ground was scarcely evident. He was confident nobody would walk through there in the next fifty years. He bumped unevenly along the track back to the highway in Kurtner's baby Kia; wearing latex gloves, he headed for the Marlin, where he parked the car, leaving the keys in the ignition. Unseen, he slipped away and strolled along the beach to the next hotel where, after grabbing a beer, he took a taxi back to the Pink Flamingo. After the taxi had gone, he leaped into his Suzuki and headed back to the Marlin. The whole process was a bit roundabout but he was too much of a professional to mind.

Using the room key he had found in the victim's shorts, he stripped the American's room of a few odds and ends of clothing and the seven remaining condoms from the pack of twelve. There was no safe in the room but he found the passport in the name of Hank Kurtner and nearly six hundred dollars tucked into the waterproof section of a wash bag. He trousered the passport and cash but bundled everything else into Ruthven's rucksack.

It was nearly 11 p.m. local and not yet dawn in London when he breezed into the bar and ordered beer and conch fritters. The bill came and copying the signature on the American's passport, he signed for the refreshments as Hank Kurtner Room 262. Nobody in the crowded bar took any notice of him and he did not much care if they did.

Outside, he dumped the rucksack in the back of the Suzuki beside the shovel and headed north into the poorer part of town behind the docks. Sure enough, he found empty streets lined on both sides with small timber-built chalets, all in unloved, faded colours. On the occasional porch he could see a couple or small group chatting but otherwise the streets were remarkable only in their lack of human life. From inside many of the homes came laughter and the noise of reggae or TV programmes. Only the third street in, he spotted what he wanted: a builder's skip half full of junk, pushchairs, rubble, rotting wood and trash tipped in by countless passers-by.

He dumped the garrotte and the American's clothes, covering them with rubble, chucked the empty rucksack into another skip. The shovel he left leaning against a cement mixer as if forgotten by a road worker. He bet himself it would be gone within an hour of daylight.

All that remained was Kurtner's passport and the condoms. He would get rid of them in the morning before checking the American out of the hotel.

16

Clapham, South London

"Why's he called Ratso anyway?" enquired DC Erasmus Blyth, a new addition to the team, as they gathered in the cramped basement room. He was rewarded with the odd chuckle.

"Anyone know—besides me?" It was Jock Strang who spoke, clearing his desk in time to catch the afternoon flight to Glasgow.

"Cos he gets rat-arsed?" volunteered DC Giles Connors.

"Looks like a bleedin' rodent an all," suggested another.

"I'll tell ye." Jock leaned back on his chair, hands clasped behind his head. "Way back, when he was as green as you lot, he got locked in a cellar in a derelict building down Bermondsey way and with a young woman—constable."

"Bet he gave her one to pass the time."

"Nah. He'd have wanted paying. He never gives nothing away."

Recalling who had paid for dinner and who always bought his round, Jock knew that was not true but he let the repartee take its course with a smile. "It wisna funny at the time, I was told. Half the Met were looking for them. They were down there for nearly a week. Nothing to eat and just damp running down the walls for water. Some bastard had tricked them into entering to check for a body, then took their radios and phones at gunpoint."

"And locked them in?"

"Aye! Right enough." Jock stood up and walked round the listeners, who were all seated at the large group of desks that dominated the centre of the room. He saw the upturned heads and eyes following him as he slowly made his way between the stacks of yellowing papers, worn trainers, empty buckets of KFC and discarded riot gear. "He cornered a rat and as it jumped at his throat, he clobbered it with a piece of wood." Jock was enjoying himself. "He reckoned no England cricketer could have done better. On the fifth day, he killed another one...and this one, in desperation, he ate."

There was a stunned silence as everyone embraced the idea of eating uncooked rat.

"Even the arsehole?" DC Connors' grin was ear to ear.

"The bollocks is the best bit. So they say," suggested Nancy Petrie, a plump-faced detective constable with streaky blonde hair who enjoyed behaving and being treated as one of the boys.

"So there ye are," Jock concluded. "I'm told they were found on the sixth day."

"Mattrafact," added Tosh Watson, "I had dinner with Ratso last year in a posh French place up West and he asked for ratatouille. I thought he wanted bleedin' grilled rat. I didn't know it was some weird veggie dish, did I?"

The general laughter died as the door opened and the man himself appeared. Whether everybody was aware that he had spent the night at Charlene's, Ratso was unsure. Jock Strang was no gossip. But if Jock had been asked the right questions, Ratso knew he would be vulnerable.

"Morning, morning," he shouted needlessly above the sudden silence. He felt everybody was indeed watching him closer than usual. *Or am I being paranoid?* He rubbed his hands, his face showing excitement. "Heard the score from Adelaide?"

"Who cares?" The cry came from down the far end of the room.

"Aye but Rangers lost at Ibrox." Jock Strang looked as if he'd been hit by a truck.

"It's the haggis wotdunit, Jock," retorted Ratso. "You should support our cricketers. We're stuffing the Aussies something rotten." With his loping stride, he dodged through the clutter that surrounded every desk, every filing cabinet and filled every shelf or spare inch of floor. All eyes were on him as he studied the whiteboard, taking in the crisscross of leads, connections, contacts, photos.

Several lines on the board pointed to Erlis Bardici. Ratso's face puckered into a scowl as he took in Bardici's rounded visage, lined forehead, receding hairline and dark eyes set beneath prominent black eyebrows. He looked all of his late thirty years. But the lines on the board stopped there. Worse still, too many other lines, like the vague suggestion of a Crawley connection, came to dead ends where the investigation had run dry. "You've seen the paper today? "His question was accompanied by his eyes sweeping round as he flourished the freebie newspaper.

He saw a couple of nods but mainly blank faces.

"Trouble is you lot only read the Sports Section or Page 3 of the *Sun.*" He pulled a cutting from his pocket and pinned it to the board while reading it out. "The body found early yesterday in Hammersmith has been identified as Neil Shalford, aged 49. He lived in Kingston-on-Thames. Detective Chief Inspector Alex Caldwell, who is leading the investigation, refused to comment on suggestions that the victim was known in South London to have gangland connections. However, Caldwell did confirm that the victim had been murdered and that enquiries were continuing. An inquest will be opened shortly." He turned to the gathering. "Tosh? Jock? Comments?"

Jock sensed precisely what to say. "Gangland connections? That would be Dan and Jerry Hogan." Tosh moved his chair noisily as he nodded agreement. "But ye knew him well, boss. One gang taking it out on another?"

"Makes sense." Ratso looked thoughtful. "But sometimes, he was used as a snout." Ratso took care to avoid mentioning the actual job Neil had been doing. "Big question: was he murdered because someone out there discovered he was a snout, because something leaked?" He paused for a couple of beats. "Because *someone* leaked." If he expected to see anyone look away, lower their eyes, or look embarrassed, he was disappointed. Only Tosh and Jock had known and that had been only in desperation this past week. *Surely neither of them would have leaked or let anything slip to one of the younger DCs, who then leaked to gangland?* He let the topic drop as he continued. "Forensics are going over what's left of the Range Rover. Nothing yet." He sniffed dismissively. "Waste of time. Anything else, Jock?"

"The Beamer we, er, tried to catch was stolen and was traced and found in Kennington. Forensics are taking a look. Nothing on Klodian Skela. As you said, no record, nothing known. But we'll find him. I've several leads." The sergeant lifted a mug of strong brown tea. "What about getting a warrant to listen in? You said he used a regular line to report the vehicle stolen."

Ratso looked thoughtful. You could waste hours listening in to conversations more boring than BBC Radio Three. "Best used sparingly, Jock. Klodian's nothing—wet-fart territory. We'll be listening to his wife's shite about the price of cabbages or cheap flights from Luton to Tirana."

"So?" Jock and Tosh glanced at each other, waiting for the steer from the boss.

"Find and interview Skela. Scare the shit out of him. If it's the guy I saw, he's in a lose-lose position." He raised two fingers to emphasise the options, counting them off one by one. "We either do him for thieving, for reporting it stolen when he knew it was not, or he admits he drove it away and burned it. Whichever, we have his bollocks in our fist." Ratso's grin revealed his enthusiasm. "Jock, you'll be away but Tosh, you and me—we'll scare the bugger till his scrotum shrinks to the size of a prune."

Jock Strang laughed. "Easier to hold that way, boss. Give me an hour. I'll find him"

"Sightings of Erlis Bardici?"

Nancy Petrie was quick to respond. "Negative. Not seen in any of his usual haunts."

"Lying low, then. What about Zandro?"

"Zilch," replied Tosh. "Nothing unusual. Pub lunch in Hampstead. The cinema in Swiss Cottage with that bint of his and a dinner party at his house last night."

"A typical day, then." Ratso's tired face showed frustration at the lack of anything positive. "We gave up bugging Zandro yonks back, after that negative report from the listening boys in Sussex. He never uses that known mobile number except for crap routine calls."

"Unless he's using a code? Like if he says he's buying cheese, he's buying E's?" It was Nancy Petrie, her face and voice bright with enthusiasm.

Ratso turned away from the whiteboard and headed for the water dispenser to fill a small beaker. "Good thinking, Nancy but whatever code he's using would defy the Enigma machine." Ratso's brow furrowed as he ran his fingers through his wavy hair, as if that would provide inspiration instead of a couple of flakes of dandruff. "We need a new angle on Zandro. The bastard's in this up to his double chin."

He drained the water, lobbed the cup into a bin from three metres and loped toward the door, where he stopped.

"Any new ideas?" He saw blank and sheepish looks. "I want results. Not faces as empty as Old Mother Hubbard's cupboard." His tone was clipped, his pent-up frustration showing through. "Zandro's not Superman," he snapped. "There's a connect somewhere. Call this the Cauldron?" He glared round the packed room. "Cauldrons bubble! You should be brimming with ideas." He swivelled 360 degrees, taking in everyone, his eyes wide and burning with passion. "Look! Somehow Zandro's communicating with his lieutenants." He knew he was being unusually brusque but could not help himself. "Anybody remember Winnie-the-Pooh? When he had lost something, our Winnie looked everywhere without success but then the bear of little brain said something like, *We've looked everywhere it isn't. We must now look where it is.*"

He heard sniggers from the youngsters.

"No," Ratso barked. "This is not a fucking joke. He's making us look like a load of donkeys. Right?" He stomped between the desks until he reached the whiteboard again, banged it with his knuckles. "Not looking in the right places. Not doing the right things. If we've no breakthrough on him by next week, we'll need a brainstorming session. New ideas. Think right out of the box. Got it? We're missing something. Someone or some place is the link." He banged the board again for emphasis before heading for the exit.

The room was totally silent, the listeners taken aback by the rare sharpness of Ratso's tone. The youngsters on the team returned to their screens or paperwork, nobody saying a word.

Jock joined Ratso by the door. "There's something you need to know." The Scot kept his voice unusually low. "That DCI Caldwell phoned. Y'know—him of the yellow shirt and expensive loafers?"

"What did he want?"

"You're to see Arthur Tennant."

Ratso shrugged. He was not surprised. "Good of Arthur to drop by here occasionally. I'll go up now." As soon as the heavy-duty door had closed behind him, there was a spontaneous burst of laughter as someone asked if anyone had smelled a rat.

Ratso went up two flights of stairs, his black trainers silent on the worn lino. He knocked and then entered the office of the Detective Chief Inspector without waiting for consent. Tennant's office was larger than Ratso's but not by much. The room smelled of aniseed balls. Ratso had often wondered if Tennant had Pernod on tap somewhere under the cheap metal-framed desk. But knowing his boss, Tennant probably had an endless supply of aniseed balls that he never produced or offered around.

"Morning, Ratso." The words were innocuous enough but the listener felt the cold blast of trouble ahead. "Take a seat."

Ratso sat down and clasped his hands behind his head to show relaxation. "Morning, boss. I've just checked downstairs. There's nothing new."

If Tennant heard, it didn't show on his impassive face. His features never flickered, never showed the slightest reaction. His face was round with small dark brown eyes. *The man who put pug in pugnacious,* Ratso had often joked to Jock Strang in the

Nags Head. His head was shaven close so that his ears looked large, floppy, even grotesque. His teeth could have graced a zebra. The lines on his face were deeply etched so that he looked older than fifty-one. But above all, it was his hands that you always noticed, though they weren't particularly large, small, or even riddled with early arthritis. No. They were always in the frame because Tennant's hands were always moving—waving, chopping, calming, or pounding his desk somewhere between the phone and a photo of him being introduced to the Prince of Wales.

"Overslept?"

Bloody cheek coming from you, you lazy slob. Ratso's hackles rose. You could accuse him of most things but failing to put in the hours was not one of them. He said nothing, forcing his boss to continue.

"Trouble on the line from Hammersmith, perhaps?"

"Not so I noticed."

"Late night?"

Ratso shrugged, uncertain where this was leading.

"I received these. About forty minutes ago." Arthur Tennant slid his notebook to one side and revealed some photos. Ratso saw a solitary figure, back to the camera. Tennant shoved it across the near empty desk so that Ratso could pick it up; a quick glance showed it was a shot of him crossing Wolsey Drive yesterday evening. *Fucking shit! What the hell?* He fought to look disinterested, cool in the face of the enemy. Photo two showed him at Charlene's door. Photo three captured the warm welcome on the doorstep, Charlene on tiptoes. The rest were taken of his departure this morning—the friendly kiss, the tearful look on Charlene's face, him blowing a kiss from the road.

"Well?"

"Well nothing. I went to see the grieving woman, an old friend and I stayed the night. I guess that Beau Brummel character—er, DCI Caldwell—his lads must have seen me arrive as well as leave this morning."

"Don't piss me about. What the hell were you doing spending the night with the dead man's woman? Especially when she looks like she's got the hots for you." Then, in a familiar movement, he rammed a finger up his left nostril and explored hungrily. Ratso looked away with a loud sniff but Tennant, not one to feel embarrassed, continued with typical vigour.

"I was comforting her. She and Neil have been close friends for years."

"Is that what you call it. *Com…forting.*" His contempt was obvious as he withdrew his finger and inspected it carefully. "Emphasis on the *come*, I expect." He seemed to be enjoying Holtom's discomfort. "De-briefing her, were you?" He laughed again at his joke but this time it was Ratso who sat poker-faced before starting to ease himself out of the uncomfortable chair with the sagging bottom.

"I didn't come here to listen to this crap. If I want smutty jokes, I'll go to the Improv. Is that all, boss?"

"Sit down. I have questions." Both hands jabbed downward before he turned a page on his pad and Ratso saw the familiar lazy scrawl in biro. "You went to identify the body yesterday?"

"Correction. We went to see who it was."

"DCI Caldwell," he studied his notes "said you did not recognise the deceased." Ratso said nothing, raising Tennant's blood pressure a notch or two. "Well? You've just admitted you knew Neil Shalford"

"No secret, boss."

"Did you recognise him yesterday morning?"

"Yes."

"So why did you deny recognition?"

Ratso thought any moron from SCD7 could see why denial had been the only option. "I didn't deny recognition, *sir*." He added the final word as a measure of defiance.

"Oh? So you're challenging Caldwell, are you?"

"I've two witnesses. Yes."

"You mean *lie-my-arse-off–for-you* Sergeants Strang and Watson?"

"I mean two *reliable* witnesses who will recall my precise words. As should a yellow-shirted DCI, even if he's seeking promotion using shit-stirring garbage like this."

"So? What *did* you say?"

"Beau Brummel asked me *if I did or did not recognise him*." He pulled out his notebook written up after leaving the crime scene. "I replied, quote, 'Very familiar but not the guy we were…I dunno whether to say…hoping or expecting. Not the guy we *wanted* to see on a slab.'" Even as he repeated the words used, Ratso admired the cunning way he had danced on the head of a pin. But it had still obstructed the course of Caldwell's enquiries.

Tennant's hands stilled. His little eyes looked upward as if seeking a crib sheet on the ceiling. Ratso took the chance to pile in.

"You think I should have said, *Oh yes, Mr Brummel. We know this is Neil Shalford and we know who murdered him and why and where. Because he was working for SCD7 on an operation without backup that went pear-shaped.*"

Tennant's mouth dropped open as the facts clicked. Then a slight smile and look of relief took over, as he realised how bloody smart he had been passing the buck to the AC. "Well. Put like that."

"Is there any other way?"

"I'll have to say something to Caldwell."

"Tell him to get lost and that if he pokes his nose into SCD7's sensitive OPs again—or worse still, screws up thousands of hours of our work—I'll personally stuff his highly polished loafers right up his arse." Ratso stood up. "And warn him I shall enjoy it. As might he." He pointed at Tennant for emphasis. "And if he thinks I murdered Neil to carry on an affair with his widow, tell him to charge me." Ratso glared at Tennant. "And, sir, don't go near the truth either, otherwise I'll have Wensley Hughes after you from a great height. I wouldn't give a fag paper for your career after that. The AC put his head on the block when you hadn't the balls."

Tennant did not like problems, never had. His arms waved helplessly as he anticipated the difficult phone call ahead. Ratso was almost out of the door when he let rip again.

"Tell the git to stop concentrating on me and work on the Hogans. A witness yesterday linked them to Neil. Keep him out of my hair."

"But, er, er…you and what's-her-name? I mean, I see where Caldwell's coming from."

"You reckon I'd pull off the fingernails of an old mate? Cut off his todger and stuff it in his mouth? Do me a favour, sir." His voice had risen to a crescendo but now he turned quiet. "Me and Charlene? Yeah! She's a right little raver. 'Cos she's in mourning, she'd only let me give her one while wearing black stockings and suspenders. Trouble was I hadn't got a black condom, so I was scuppered."

In a trice, he was out of the door, leaving his boss to wonder where truth ended and fantasy began.

17

Chiswick, West London
Despite Jock Strang's confidence that he would locate Klodian Skela in an hour, it was another day before Ratso and Tosh Watson pulled up outside the apartment block just north of Chiswick High Road in West London. It had been Tosh who followed up a lead that several Albanian families lived as tenants in a rundown five-storey at the western end of Chiswick.

Ratso's check of the public records at the Land Registry had revealed that the landlord for the entire block was a Gibraltar company called Chewbeck Holdings Limited, registered in the offices of a Corporate Service Provider in Main Street, Gibraltar. The name of the lawyers involved was not a matter of public record but a phone call had revealed some unpublished information. The conveyancing when Chewbeck had purchased the block had been carried out by solicitors Ratso had never heard of called Arkwright, Fenwick and Stubbs, with offices in Lime Street in the heart of the City of London.

Ratso decided to start with Gibraltar. He knew that many respectable businesses operated from there for bona fide business reasons. In particular, large British bookmakers had taken the exit route to the Rock on accountants' advice. But Gibraltar had also been a hotbed of sharp-end business and had laundered money for years. As he logged onto Gibraltar's Companies House, he was immediately transported back to a wild night with the Gibraltar police a couple of years ago. Lifetime friendships had been formed during a raucous karaoke party followed by entertainment from some energetic lap dancers. With a wistful sigh, he returned to data mining and quickly found Chewbeck Holdings Limited.

The Gibraltar CSP was home to hundreds of companies and offshore trusts and was little more than a place to display a nameplate. The directors of Chewbeck were a couple of local professionals, no doubt officers of countless companies managed as part of their business. They didn't own the asset; in reality, the shareholder owned the company. Unfortunately, the published data showed a meaningless nominee shareholder, which concealed the real owner of the block of flats.

Ratso had got Tosh to put a watch on the block and to photo everybody coming or going. Yesterday evening, Tosh produced a photo that pulled Ratso up short. No question—the man was part of the couple he had seen approaching Bardici's Range Rover. Now there he was entering the block, after which a light had come on in a second-floor flat. Nobody had seen him leave.

Ratso glanced round the shabby concrete walls of the entrance. The faded green stair rail looked filthy and the walls were covered in spray-painted slogans written in what Ratso guessed was Albanian. A used condom lay discarded by the wall leading to the ground-floor flats. Ratso reminded himself to wash his hands when he returned to fresher air. Fastidious he was not but there were limits.

"Gotta be pretty desperate to have a knee-trembler here," muttered Tosh. "No sweet music or soft lights. Just cat's shit and a smell of urine." Red and blue graffiti stained the communal letter box. Its door had been forced open and hung off one of its hinges, the results of typical mindless vandalism.

Ratso pointed to the meaningless Albanian words on one wall. "I think it says *Sharon was shagged here.*"

Tosh nodded agreement. "Yeah and isn't that last word *twice?*" They chuckled all the way to the second-floor landing.

The bottle-green door to number five had been severely kicked at some time in its history and though now repaired, the door had also been forced with a screwdriver or chisel. The splintered wood was a dead giveaway. The bell had been pulled from the wall and the bare wires hung loose. Tosh gave Ratso a despairing look and then banged loudly. After a few moments of silence, the sound of movement came from inside. A light came on. "Po?" Ratso knew from his trip to Tirana that the word meant *yes*.

"Police. Open up."

There was a longer pause and Ratso imagined the man's brain struggling into top gear to work out what was wanted of him and what to say. Slowly the chain was unhitched and the door opened.

"Mr Skela? Mr Klodian Skela?"

The man nodded, albeit reluctantly. Klodian Skela was wearing a vest under a dressing gown with a pair of slippers that looked so worn and stained it was hard to believe they had ever been new. Ratso flashed his ID. "I'm DI Holtom. This is Sergeant Watson." As he spoke, Ratso was already pushing inside, taking in the smell of stale air and last night's garlic-flavoured meal. "We have some questions for you."

The man retreated a pace or two but blocked the way into the next room. He looked unshaven and his thinning hair hadn't been combed today. His eyes looked bleary, as if he had not slept a great deal.

"We'll need some time. We'll need to sit down with you." Ratso nodded in the direction of the open door to the main room. Skela burst into a torrent of Albanian spoken at a furious pace.

Watson tapped his toes impatiently as they heard him out. Then he thrust his face forward. "Cut out the Albanian crap, mate. You speak excellent English."

The man shrugged.

"Stop pissing us about, Mr Skela. We listened to the recording of the call you made reporting a stolen vehicle. You spoke well and understood what was being said to you. Now. Take us in there." He glanced at the almost closed door from which came a sliver of light.

Reluctantly Skela led them into what proved to be a bed-sitter with a table for four near the window and a double bed against the far wall. The curtains were drawn but the bedside light was on and sitting in the bed, sheets pulled to her chin on seeing the three men enter, was a young woman certainly under twenty, with tousled long black hair and heavy pink lipstick. Ratso enjoyed taking a second look. She had high Slavic cheekbones, giving her a haughty look beyond her years. Ratso had expected to see the woman who had been on the jaunt to torch the Range Rover but this woman was too young by nearly twenty years.

He wondered how much Skela had paid this bint for the night and whether his assumption that Skela was married was correct. Ratso pointed to the young woman and motioned her to go next door to the bathroom. She looked uncertain, though Ratso was sure she understood English. Skela rattled off a few words and she swung her long limbs out of bed, dragging the sheet with her but not before Ratso had spotted an eyeful of tit and a flash of trimmed, jet-black pubic hair. He watched her wiggle into the bathroom and close the door. He drew up a chair at the table with Tosh beside him. After some hesitation, Skela took a third chair opposite them.

"Where's your wife?" enquired Tosh.

"Manchester. No here till four day."

Tosh cocked his head toward the bathroom and winked. "A secret, eh?"

Ratso watched for the Albanian's reaction; he didn't look too proud of his conquest, so she must have been paid for the night. That or he was worried about something. Maybe his wife had a good way with rolling pins.

Tosh leaned forward and looked at his notes. "You reported Mr Bardici's vehicle stolen at 5:25 p.m. When did you first know it had been stolen?"

"Maybe morning, maybe a bit later. I not so for sure know. I went collect car. Not there."

"You went to Mr Bardici's home to collect the car? 22 Westbrook Drive. Right?"

Skela nodded.

"Alone? Nobody with you?"

"Me. Nobody else."

Ratso marked the first blatant lies but let Tosh continue. "So why not report it, then?" Ratso noticed the man fidget, his fingers opening and closing on the tablecloth.

Skela shrugged. "I not know for sure. Maybe I make mistake. Wrong day. Maybe Mr. Bardici, he out in car."

"So what made you sure at 5:25 p.m.? Had you spoken to Mr Bardici?"

"No. Not talk. Erlis Bardici away."

"Oh, where?"

"Away. He not say. Back tomorrow."

"Abroad, is he? Tirana, perhaps?"

Skela shrugged again but still looked composed.

"You work for him?"

"Like…bit this, bit that."

"Such as?"

"Take car to garage. Work in garden. Paint wall. Buy things. B & Q. HomeBase. Maybe drive him."

Ratso nodded. He always enjoyed questioning a witness when he had every ace in the deck. But he liked to build it up, let whichever sergeant was with him do the spadework, set the tempo before going for the jugular. "So when did Mr Bardici ask you to take his car to the garage?"

Skela seemed unperturbed, replying without hesitation that it had been the day before the theft. "The garage in Twickenham. Meltbys."

"And how do you know Mr Bardici?"

"He my cousin."

"Mr. Bardici? Who is he? What is his job?"

"Ask him."

"I'm asking you. Now tell me." The final three words were snapped out, causing Skela to flinch.

"Maybe he own one, no, maybe two stores. Like corner shops."

"And her?" Ratso pointed to the bathroom, where a shower was running. He saw Tosh change positions uncomfortably on his chair and he would have bet a pony that Tosh's bladder was giving him hell with the sound of running water. Then his attention returned to the witness, who either shared Tosh's problem or was uneasy. "This young woman. Her name?"

"Lindita." The name was accompanied by a small bead of perspiration trickling down the man's forehead to the black stubble on his cheek. A study of Skela's heavy features showed that, given a good wash and brush-up, he would be quite attractive to some women; he had a strong jawline, a steady gaze and designer stubble that he had yet to trim this morning. His eyes were deep-set, suggesting a depth to his character but judging by the squalor in which he lived, perhaps he was less intelligent than his features suggested. His mouth looked smiley though at present he had little about which to smile.

Ratso was puzzled by the man's unease. "How old is Lindita? Fifteen?"

Very quickly, too quickly, Skela retorted that she was eighteen but now his forehead was gleaming with a line of sweat from side to side. It started between the thinning strands on top of his head and was almost a stream now, so much so that the Albanian searched in his dressing-gown pocket and mopped his brow with a grubby blue-spotted hankie.

The draught from the ill-fitting window whistled across the table, matched only by another from the hallway. The small gas fire was not lit. "Not hot in here, is it, Mr Skela?" Ratso was curious. In fact the place was bloody freezing and the best way Ratso could think of to keep warm in a dump like this was to be shagging Lindita twenty-four-seven. Short of that, thermals all year.

Ratso stood up, stretched and yawned loudly as if he were at home. He wanted time now—time to gather his thoughts as he pottered his way round the bedsit picking up ornaments, looking at the pictures on the walls. *Who's this woman Skela is bedding?*

He paused at the end of the bed. Lindita had taken the top sheet but the bottom sheet was still there, rumpled and creased. Halfway down, there were a series of wet patches where Skela's orgasm had dripped from the girl's thighs or been shot into the bed. Elsewhere were other stains that he did not care to study too closely. On the far side of the bed, he saw the jumble of male and female clothes lying in a heap on the floor.

For a fleeting second the discarded underwear took his imagination to Wolsey Drive. His animal instincts toward Charlene had been heightened by a second overnight stop. Last night, they had even walked down to the pub by the Thames for bar food and a glass of wine. It had been one of those awkward events, sort of dating but not--their first public appearance. Yet he could almost feel her urging him to hold her hand in the dark side streets on the return journey. Though his sap was rising, he had somehow refrained. *F'Gawd's sake, Ratso, you can't go walking through the streets hand in hand before the funeral.* But at least there was no sign now of Caldwell's lot, who had interviewed Charlene and left with nothing of value.

Ratso continued his tour of the bed-sitter, leaving Skela to worry about whatever was worrying him so much. Tosh knew better than to fire any questions now while Ratso was letting the witness stew. There was no kitchen as such, just a small area where you could stand on the lino by the sink or cooker rather than on the stained fawn carpet. The remains of takeaway for two and an empty bottle of Bulgarian red stood beside unwashed dishes. Ratso reached the sideboard, the place that had been his ultimate goal without making it obvious. There were almost a dozen family photos, including one of Klodian Skela's wedding to the woman he had seen walking toward Bardici's house in Westbrook Drive. The adjacent photo of husband and wife was quite recent and appeared to have been taken with Southend Pier in the background. Ratso picked it up. "Your wife?"

Skela nodded. "Rosafa."

Ratso's eyes moved along the line of snaps and portraits of the loving family—several were of a young boy at different ages. In the most recent, he was about nineteen and posing outside Old Trafford wearing United's red top. But it was the photo of the other young child that made him look and then look again. *No. Surely not? But yes.* He said nothing as he turned away and pulled back the faded curtain to peer down at the wet pavements below. He felt slightly sick and wished he had tucked into a bacon buttie in the greasy on the High Street like Tosh. Empty stomachs were not good at times like this. He returned to stand, towering over the witness. "So where were you during the day? I mean, between when you saw the car was missing and when you phoned the police."

There was a pause. "Ah! With Rosafa."

"Where?"

"Goldhawk Road. Shopping. Then here. Then I go to Erlis house. No car still. I phone police."

"Did you phone Mr. Bardici to tell him his car was gone?"

"Yes, yes. I phone. No answer. Many time."

Ratso was unconvinced. He decided it was time to sit down and he did so, drawing his chair closer to Skela's fit-looking frame. The sweating above the hairline had stopped but the smell of stale underarms was now very evident. "Okay, Skela. I've listened to enough bullshit. From now on I want the truth."

"What you mean? I swear all true. Car stolen."

"I am going straight to Manchester and I am going to speak to Rosafa. Where is she staying? Your son's address?"

Skela looked everywhere but at the officers. He licked his lips nervously, proving to Ratso that the guy was small-time as he had always suspected. Certainly his crap bedsit showed no sign of drug wealth.

"Your son's address." This time Ratso barked out the words so that Skela flinched. "Now!"

"I no remember. Fallowfield."

Ratso had driven through the Manchester suburb on a few occasions. It was full of students and kebab houses. "Oh, you'll remember by the time this interview is over. You'll remember a great deal. There'll be no more bullshit." He paused for effect before pushing his head even closer to the man's face. "Listen and listen hard." He waited, watching Skela's now sullen eyes stare at the worn carpet. "You, you dirty snivelling bastard, are screwing Lindita…your own daughter. When Rosafa's away, you are screwing her here in the family bed."

Ratso sensed the shock as Tosh heard the words. He saw Skela's eyes move furtively, seeking an escape. He could almost hear the Albanian's brain whirring as he measured the depth of the pit in which he now was.

"Where does Lindita live?"

Skela was slow to answer. "With friends. Ealing."

"So when Rosafa's in Manchester, you screw her like you have done since she was a kid."

"No."

"You'd go down for fourteen years. Maybe much longer. Sex offenders can expect no mercy from other prisoners." Ratso was unsure whether he was bluffing or not. What he had learned about the law on incest had been long forgotten.

"Mind you," intervened Tosh, "I guess Rosafa will use her kitchen scissors on you when she gets the chance."

"No. Not tell Rosafa. No, please."

Ratso never relented when he had someone pinned to the ropes. "Unless I get every answer I need from you, I am arresting you for incest with a minor *and* I am going to Manchester to get statements from your son and your wife on what they knew."

"Then I answer. What you want know? Okay? You no tell Rosafa."

"No deals. No promises. You speak. I listen."

Sweat was again pouring down the Albanian's face. "I pay you money. No tell."

"Piss off, Skela. Answers. That's all." There was a long silence as the fish wriggled on the hook.

Tosh looked across at Ratso. "Let's interview the girl." He nodded to the bathroom. "Let's find out how old she was when this started." Ratso signalled agreement. Tosh eased himself up and headed to the closed door but before he reached it, Skela broke down completely, shaking uncontrollably, sobbing with his head bowed.

"Hold it, Tosh." Ratso turned to the snivelling wreck. "I think our friend here wants to sign a statement. Look at me, Skela and listen. I want every last detail. Believe me, I'll know if you are lying. One single porky, one lie and you will be charged with incest but not before I've told Rosafa the truth. Worse still for you, I'll let her return home to speak to you before I take you down the nick."

"I answer."

Ratso signalled Tosh to sit down. "You were not taking the Range Rover to be serviced, were you? You torched it. What was going on?"

"Erlis, he kill me if he know I speak. You no tell him."

Ratso shrugged and his lips narrowed. "Look, Skela. You have no choice but to speak. I don't give a toss whether you are more scared of Rosafa or Mr. Bardici. Just talk."

Skela started to sob again. Sweaty fear oozed from the man's skin. Tosh and Ratso exchanged glances. They had seen this situation before and there was only one way to go. Foot down, hard on the throttle. No let up. No deals. Or, as Ratso had said a couple of months back, keep one foot on the throat till the gurgling has nearly stopped.

"Erlis. He phone. He say take car. Go to place in country. Meet man. Burn car. Then say stolen."

"Did you go alone?"

"Rosafa did come."

"Who did you meet?"

"Man. No know name."

"You see him before?"

"No. Never."

"After you torched the car, what happened?"

"Man drove us to Acton. Never see again."

"Why did Erlis want the car torched?"

"He no say."

"He paid you well?"

"He promise one fifty pound."

"One hundred and fifty pounds, eh? Easy money, Mr Skela. Where is he?"

"I not know." Ratso could tell Skela was lying. There was just that flickering moment when the man's small brain had decided that he just might get away with a denial. The rapid eyelid movement was a dead giveaway. A curt nod to Tosh.

"You're lying, you stinking lump of shit. Get the girl in, Tosh."

Watson headed for the bathroom and opened the unlocked door. Lindita was sitting on the edge of the bath, still shrouded by a sheet but now with a towel wrapped around her head. He motioned her to join them and she came through, her eyes lowered, the haughtiness apparent only in her face, not in her movements. Tosh remained in the bathroom and Ratso sat silently, waiting while Tosh splashed his boots. There was silence as the three awaited his return, though Ratso observed Lindita staring hard at her father as if seeking a lead from him.

"That's better." Tosh reappeared, grinning contentedly.

Ratso flicked back his cuff to reveal his watch that did nothing more than tell the time. If he wanted a watch that could control a Space Shuttle, be waterproof at 10,000 metres and play "Jingle Bells," he would save up. Till then, this H. Samuels fifteen quid on special offer would do. "I'm bored with this. I've no time to waste on perverted scumbags like you." He leaned forward and barked full into Skela's face so that he flinched, drawing back in shock. "Tell me and tell me *now*." The final word might have been heard in the next apartment. "Where did Bardici go and when?"

He stood up, seeing no sign of progress.

"Okay. I am now asking Sgt Watson to take Lindita to the police station. I am going to Manchester. We'll locate your son and your wife quickly enough."

Tosh looked at the girl. "Get your clothes. Get dressed." Lindita looked sullen and sought guidance with an enquiring look at her father but he looked away, still torn between his fear of Bardici and the destruction of his family life.

Ratso glared at the witness but then softened. "Do you really want to put Lindita through all this? Are you *that* scared of Erlis Bardici? A guy who runs corner shops selling crisps and Mars bars."

Even as he said the words, Ratso knew the answer. Skela was indeed shit-scared. With good reason: if Bardici suspected he had been dumped on by Skela, his death would not be pretty. He motioned the woman to the bathroom. "Get dressed. You have two minutes."

A long silence followed in which Tosh and Ratso stared silently at Skela, who sat with his head in his hands, looking down with his eyes closed. It was only when Lindita reappeared that he looked up, his hands and lips trembling. "Okay. I will say you."

He motioned his daughter back to the bathroom. Not even she was permitted to hear where Bardici had gone to ground.

18

Fort Lauderdale, Florida

Detective Kirsty-Ann Webber of the Fort Lauderdale Police Department cruised along East Sunrise, prepared to turn south toward the Hilton resort. Though assigned to the Strategic Investigations Unit, she had been temporarily pulled from her present role on a team targeting some new suspected mob activity.

As usual, she was driving an unmarked vehicle, everything low profile. *Play it cool, keep it casual* had been her instructions from Bucky Buchanan. According to the chief, the word from Washington was that this assignment was *more important than it seemed. What the heck did that mean?* A guy from DC had checked in at the hotel the Friday before and hadn't returned to DC. *A missing person! So what? Happens all the time. Debt problems. Woman trouble. Just wanting a new start. Got lucky with a new date and can't get his pants on over his erection. Could be all kinds of reasons. Didn't mean the guy had been dumped in the Everglades to feed the alligators.*

She chewed on a granola bar and felt better for it. It was the start of a long day, *another* long day after another disturbed night. Little Leon was now eight months old, with lungs that could crack concrete. She sighed. Balancing being a single mom and keeping her reputation as a smart cookie in the FLPD was harder than she'd expected. Thank God her own mom was available round the clock to provide support.

She knew the missing guy worked for the government, kinda high in the State Department. So was he a spook, living a secret life beneath the cover of his day job? Or was he working for an enemy state? Russia? China? Iran? It was hard to remember who was a friend and who was an enemy anymore. But if he *was* a spook, surely the CIA or Feds would have been down here. Or perhaps their presence would have been top-heavy. Not casual.

The familiar tower of the Hilton came into view, dominating the skyline. She viewed her task with mixed feelings—not because of the task itself but because it was the first time she had been inside the Hilton in three years. She and her husband had luxuriated there for their honeymoon. Andy had been the one love of her life, not like the charmer last year who got her pregnant with Leon and then returned one-way to Chicago. Her husband, a federal agent, was murdered near Peachtree Plaza just days after the honeymoon, shot dead on duty.

Afterwards, she had applied for a transfer to Florida and with rave testimonials about her tenacity, she had landed a position with FLPD. She wanted, or *thought* she wanted, the feeling of being close to where she and Andy had been happiest during their ten months living together. Now, as she parked and then entered the huge open space of the marbled lobby, she had to fight the temptation both to cry and to cry out at the unfairness of a young thug with a gun stealing the future they had planned. Slowly, her mind locked in a time warp, she walked to the front desk and asked for the duty manager.

While she waited, she took a seat on a white bench, *where they had sat* and gazed up at the chandelier and tasteful designs, *just as they had done*. This time she saw everything through watery eyes, which she fought to conceal as the duty manager appeared, hand cheerfully extended. After she flashed her ID, he took her into a private office behind the front desk and offered her coffee, juice, soda. She declined.

"Lance Ruthven, you said?" He was tapping at the computer as he spoke.

"Checked in last Friday. Should have checked out on Sunday."

The tall, rather elegant Puerto Rican, whose nametag read Santiago Buffete, looked across. "Yes. He checked in. But so far, he has not checked out."

"Can we take a look at his room?"

"Sure." He rose to a full six foot two and was about to escort her to the lobby when he paused. "This is Tuesday morning. Plenty of our guests stay long or leave early. It's part of the business. Why are you guys involved?"

"It's outta character." As an afterthought, she added, "He a regular with you?"

Buffete sat down again and after a few quick keystrokes he nodded. "He's been down here five times in six months. Always arrives Friday and…hey! Always checks out on Sunday. So this trip *is* different."

"Maybe he got lucky," laughed Kirsty-Ann, showing her well-kept teeth that glowed against her Florida tan. Had her hair been black instead of blonde, she might have been mistaken for an American Indian, with her oval face and unblemished skin.

"Let's find out."

A few moments later they were outside Ruthven's suite. Buffete rapped on the door a couple of times and announced himself. There was no response and no sound from the room. The detective glanced at her watch; just 8 a.m., a strange time for a guest to be out. Buffete slipped the card into the lock and opened the door.

Ruthven had chosen a king-sized suite with ocean view and the small step Kirsty-Ann took into the room was like taking a step back in time. It was identical to the room *they* had shared, chasing each other round the suite with pillows before tumbling into bed. For a moment she imagined Andy, a beer in his hand, lying on the king-size in his beach shorts and T-shirt, watching something on ESPN.

"The bed wasn't slept in last night. The maid wouldn't have gotten to this room yet...so he's paying for a room he doesn't need."

"Playing away somewhere, maybe." She noticed Buffete wasn't listening. He was calling the head of housekeeping and asking her to drop by with the maid.

"Mind if I look around?" the detective enquired mostly out of courtesy, already about to open the closet door. Buffete nodded as he turned to gaze out to the wintry-looking Atlantic, the greyness of the surface blending into the distant horizon. She moved the formal suit and white shirt along the rail—nothing else in the closet. On the floor were used boxers, a pair of grey socks and a very Washington, DC, pair of black shoes, big, heavy, sensible ones for walking in winter weather. There was a locked room safe, a brown Gladstone bag lying on the luggage stand; the bathroom contained his wash-kit - shaving cream, a disposable razor, expensive shampoo, a toothbrush and toothpaste. The toothpaste looked fresh out of the box and the brush looked unused too.

The disposable razor was a puzzle. Great for emergencies but would a guy on a serious salary travel with a disposable?

Andy used to describe them as the invention of the devil. He always ended up with at least two cuts when he shaved with them.

"Hello?" She heard Buffete calling her and returned to the main room. The head of housekeeping and a Spanish-speaking maid had arrived. Kirsty-Ann's Spanish had improved to no end since joining the FLPD and she followed the question-and-answer routine with little difficulty. She saw surprise on Buffete's face and heard him repeat a question. The doe-eyed maid who was seriously obese held her ground.

Buffete turned away from the maid. "So Ruthven may have stayed Friday night. The maid remade the bed on Saturday but not since then. Right?"

"Correct. But she's unsure if the room really was used Friday night. The shower had not been used; neither had anything but a hand towel. The toilet wasn't used at all. The paper on the roll is still tucked under."

"Unless Ruthven made his own little pointed end after using some."

Buffete laughed along with Kirsty-Ann as he dismissed the staff. Once they were alone again, she asked Buffete to get the safe open.

It was Buffete's turn to joke. "Impossible. We don't know the code that the guests put in." Kirsty-Ann chuckled. Moments later, the safe door swung open, activated by the electronic back door. The detective removed a credit-card holder, a return ticket to National Airport, Washington and a driving licence. There was an Amex card in the name of Lance Ruthven and the photo on the driving licence matched the picture sent down from Washington.

"I'll take these," she said. "I'll sign for them. You can store his clothes and bag."

"Okay. This sure does look unusual. Have a coffee downstairs while I sort out the receipt and check something else. I've had a thought."

"Sounds good. I started early." Kirsty-Ann flashed a smile and followed him from the room. While concentrating on her task, thoughts of Andy had disappeared but as she stepped into the corridor, she was rocked by a memory of walking hand in hand to the elevator. Andy was dead. But what of Lance Ruthven?

Play it cool. Those were her instructions. But it didn't look good.

19

Chiswick, West London

While Tosh was having yet another pee, Ratso had ordered Cumberland sausage and mash for himself and a double cheeseburger with extra fries for his sergeant, who claimed to be *feeling peckish*. Seated by a frosted-glass window, Ratso took a deep slurp of Shiraz. He needed it. On arrival at the Drum & Candlestick gastro-pub, the first thing he had done was wash his face and hands. Even then, he still felt unclean, reminding himself of Lady Macbeth trying to get rid of the blood. In his case, there had been no blood—just the filthy surroundings and the even more disgusting memories of Klodian Skela.

To Ratso, sex was a carnal, lusty thing. But this was different, big time. Father and daughter, for God's sake! What Skela had admitted to made sex seem sordid, worse than animal. Anxious to forget the stale smells, the grime and squalor of Skela's flat, Ratso flicked through the messages on his Blackberry and fired off several replies while Tosh chatted up the Hungarian barmaid. Then he surfed through to Cricinfo and read the latest speculation on team changes for the next test in Perth. Reading of the team's heroics, life seemed clean, decent. All was right with the world with the lads two-nil up in the Ashes series already. He was just about clear of images of Skela when Tosh re-joined him, followed by the immediate arrival of his huge plate of gastroposh sausage and chips.

"Fancy him admitting to sodomising his own daughter because his wife wouldn't let him have any," Tosh muttered as he sat down.

"Change the subject. We've got enough evidence to prosecute. She was only fourteen when it started. We have Klodian Skela right here." He cupped his hands as if the Albanian's testicles were nestling in them. "Now we know Bardici's been to the Caribbean. We don't know why. On that, I believe Skela's ignorance. Bardici would not have confided the details." He hacked off a large chunk of sausage. "But I'll bet you a tenner we hear from Skela before Rosafa returns."

"Boss, I don't much care if I ever see or hear of Skela again."

Ratso shrugged. "He could be the key we need—a key to a new door."

"I don't get it. The kid was up for it. Drops by for an overnighter when her Mum's *oop north*." Tosh chewed angrily at his burger. "I mean, she's a pretty kid. I could sort her out."

"In your dreams." Ratso fell silent, indicating the subject was closed while he ate his lunch.

"Fourteen years old. The bastard," Tosh persisted.

"Tosh. No more!" Ratso's tone was unusually snappy. The sergeant got the message and chomped away noisily as they both turned to watch the TV. The Sky TV News weather girl was predicting snow when Ratso finished the last of his wedged chips. Tosh, with twice as much food, had wiped his plate clean long before.

Coffees appeared and Tosh saw that Ratso was ready to chat again. "Reckon she was eighteen like he said?"

"Nah! See the way the sweat poured from him. She was still a minor. Seventeen at most. More importantly Skela gave us a pointer. Our job is to find out where he's pointing us. And quick too."

Tosh looked concerned. "You under pressure or something, boss?"

"Caldwell's complaint is still ticking. Thank God Arthur Tennant is not my defending counsel. I'd be dead."

"No worries, boss! Not if the AC's behind you."

"Yeah but he doesn't want his name in this."

"Then someone else needs to fix this Caldwell creep."

"Right?" Ratso's voice was interested and his face creased in thought. He was also rather impressed. Tosh was not much given to original thoughts. "That's a plan. But who? Ideas?"

"A word from on high. *A quiet word*. From the very top. Not straight from the AC to Caldwell but *a quiet word* to Caldwell's guvnor."

Ratso was even more impressed. "I like it. I like it a lot." Ratso's face did not break into a smile but his eyes showed appreciation. "All your own work this idea, was it?"

Tosh grinned. "I spoke to Jock when I was having a piss. We both want to help."

Ratso laughed. "Pity! I was going to nominate you for a Nobel."

"I told Jock about the incest. He reckons there's nothing wrong with incest so long as you keep it in the family." Tosh burst out laughing and after a moment's uncertainty Ratso's craggy features broke into a smile and then a hearty chuckle. "Jock added that in life, *everybody* should try everything once—everything, that is, except incest and Morris Dancing."

They both high-fived amid belly laughs. "I never fancied poncing about with white hankies and bells on my legs." Ratso returned to his notes. "Now, listen. Bardici went from Heathrow. Skela couldn't remember the destination—probably the Bahamas but he couldn't confirm Nassau, Paradise Island, or New Providence Island."

Tosh accepted a slice of Ratso's Juicy Fruit. "You sure he wasn't giving you a load of pony?"

"Yeah, because being a cousin, Skela's not just Bardici's gofer." Tosh looked unconvinced. Ratso flicked open his Blackberry and pulled up a map of the islands. "Could be any of these little blobs. They've all seen their share of Colombian cocaine passing through. But if not Nassau, the most likely destination is Grand Bahama Island."

"Maybe he's just topping up his tan?"

Ratso knew Tosh was joking. "The Bahamas government used to be the epicentre of drug running from Colombia to the USA."

"But Bardici's no deal-maker. He's a hammer. And more than that, Zandro's mob get their gear from Afghanistan, not Colombia."

Ratso was pulled up short but only just for a moment. "You're right, Tosh. But the word I got was that this next deal was going to be mega. So maybe cocaine as well."

"Which means Bardici's gone because there's trouble—big trouble with a capital B."

"I'm seeing the AC at four. Get someone working on where Bardici has been. If Skela's right, Bardici could be back as soon as tomorrow."

"Suggestions?"

"Check flights to Florida linking to the Bahamas—airports like Miami, Orlando, Fort Lauderdale—on the day Neil's body was found. Check for Bardici's name on flights and cross-check for a return landing tomorrow."

"But..."

Ratso anticipated the hesitation. "No, you're right. Unless he really did pack his bucket and spade, he'll have used a false ID."

"So check all passengers by camera?"

Ratso's lips almost smiled at the mindless optimism. "Pointless." He saw Tosh's puzzled look. "First identify guys with routings London to the Bahamas on these precise days, *then* we check the closed circuit and put US Homeland Security and our Immigration boys to work. We'll know his name *and* where he has been." Tosh did not look enthused about data mining. Hard graft and meticulous homework was for the others. "Go to it, Tosh!"

With a final nod of goodbye, Ratso headed out into the wintry blast of Chiswick High Road and the uncertainty of what lay ahead with Wensley Hughes.

20

Fort Lauderdale, Florida

At the end of her third day making casual investigations, all low-key with no media on her back yet, Kirsty-Ann Webber edited her report. Everything seemed to point in one direction as she scrolled down the screen to check her Summary and Conclusions:

1. Ruthven had stayed in the Hilton on five occasions but never once had he charged anything to the room from the poolside or restaurants. He had never eaten there on a card, or even paid cash as far as anybody could recall. He was not a familiar figure around the hotel.
2. The computer confirmed he always left on Sunday at a similar checkout time of just before noon.
3. His personal toiletries were slightly unusual (all never ever used).
4. Without a false driving licence, he could not have hired a car because his driving licence was in the safe.
5. The bellmen and car jockeys have no recollection of him leaving the hotel this trip. He always arrived by taxi. The bell captain thought he remembers him arriving.

6. Enquiries of local restaurants and bars within walking distance were negative.
7. His Gladstone bag was interesting. First examination revealed nothing but on closer inspection, it had a false leather base that could have concealed a few items. It was empty but might have been used. The bag has been seized as evidence.
8. Forensics confirmed a couple of long brown hairs found in the suitcase's hidden section were from a wig; see their report in Appendix A.
9. The return ticket to Washington had not been used.

Conclusions

10. Ruthven left the hotel on Friday (almost certainly) and definitely by Saturday.
11. He must have taken cash because his Amex card was in the room.
12. He was never seen in a rented car and was not recognised at rental agencies at the airport.
13. Assuming this trip was like the others, he never used his credit card while in Florida (see printouts from Amex for the periods covered by every trip, nil usage). No other company has any record of him owning a credit or debit card.
14. Taxi drivers have *not* been approached. Their testimony would be a long shot but may be essential. **Speaking to them would lead to immediate media awareness.** So far, I have kept this under wraps.
15. Assuming Ruthven did not plan to disappear on this trip and was following a familiar routine, he would have returned to DC on Sunday. Therefore, either this trip was the one he was building up to for **a planned**

disappearance in a brown wig OR something unusual has happened to him while wearing a brown wig and operating under an identity other than that of Lance Ruthven.
16. The false bottom was just large enough to conceal false identity cards, passport(s), the wig and other odds and ends.
17. Ruthven could enter the Bahamas with only a photo ID but would need a passport to return to the US. I suggest a search be made in DC for his genuine passport. If not found, he must be carrying his real one as well, UNLESS he has hidden/stored it somewhere in the FL area.
18. Enquiries at nightclubs, saunas and gay bars have been negative.
19. As this was his sixth identical trip, he either (a) visits a friend(s) here under an assumed ID or (b) uses the airport to fly to a destination easily reachable from here but not from DC. That could include many cities on the mainland but more probably islands like the Bahamas or Grand Cayman. Alternatively, (c) he may use a cruise or other ship.
20. There are about forty **international** flight destinations from Fort Lauderdale Airport. I discount twenty-seven as being either too far (e.g. Germany) or inappropriate to reach from Fort Lauderdale (e.g. Quebec, Canada) rather than using a better/more direct routing. I have **not** checked US city destinations, of which there are sixty-three excluding Washington DC.
21. In effect, Ruthven has barely fifty hours unaccounted for on each previous trip, so I infer he does not travel far. We should check airlines to the Bahamas, Grand

Cayman and short-cruise companies. I will work to identify a passenger using another name, sailing from here or flying to the islands on dates consistent with all of his visits. Failing that, checking other destinations for the six visits could be done.

Satisfied with her conclusions, she took the report to Bucky Buchanan's office two floors up. She wanted to take it further. She had no idea where this was leading but finding out could be just the boost she'd been looking for.

21

Heathrow, West London
Ratso and Tosh had been delighted that the Miami flight was due at Terminal Five at 0935, so they hadn't needed to start out early. Ratso had even given himself extra time for his shower and breakfast, catching up with the cricket from Down Under. The previous night he had not spent at Kingston, a decision over which he had agonised. However, as he sat in the swaying clatter of the speeding train, his thoughts were neither of Charlene nor cricket. Amy Winehouse belted out a bluesy number, filling his ears but not his mind. Instead, he was reliving yesterday's meeting with Wensley Hughes as the train swayed and rocked westwards.

He always got a buzz passing the familiar revolving sign outside New Scotland Yard, headquartered in its otherwise featureless tower in the heart of Westminster. In here, decisions to make or break police careers or operations were being made every day. During the meeting with the AC, Ratso had felt pleased; he even got in a couple of digs against Tennant. Hughes had said nothing in response and his taciturn face gave away nothing but

Ratso was confident that a black mark, maybe two, would go into the book against his superior. He liked the thought. And as for Jock's idea that *the word* reach Caldwell but not from Hughes directly, the AC had been impressed. Fixing Caldwell with no fingerprints left behind suited him well enough to offer Ratso a chocolate digestive.

After leaving the meeting, Ratso had grabbed the District Line westbound from St. James's Park and was looking forward to getting home in time to watch the West Indies match from Antigua. After breezing cheerfully out of Hammersmith station, he had crossed the Broadway and chatted supportively to Charlene, saying all the right things. But in truth, he was quite glad for a night away from her. He needed some space before going to Wolsey Drive drifted into something permanent.

Am I just a straw for a drowning woman to cling to? Or am I indispensable? Once the funeral's over, will she still need me? Would she want to settle down—two kids and a nine-to-five routine? She had pressed Neil. Is that for me? Nine-to-five—that's a non-starter. Kids? Love 'em to bits but giving them the time they deserve...now that would be a problem. And I'd be living a big secret, a huge guilty secret that it was me who sent Neil to Westbrook Drive. And if that ever came out, what then? Shitsville, baby! He killed the line of thought as the train slowed for Northfields.

Something else had been nagging away at him, like a sore tooth or a stone in his shoe. The previous evening, as he'd been scrambling eggs, he'd had a flash of inspiration. St Paul *en route* to Damascus had nothing on this—but writing the idea down had been impossible. As quickly as it had come, it was gone, that momentary flash of inspiration. He wished now he had let the eggs stick to the pan while he scribbled it down. Try as he did for the rest of the journey, he never retrieved the lost thought. He knew it had to involve Skela and as he made his way up to

T5 Arrivals, he ran through everything from the past thirty-six hours, searching for a trigger. But the thought died when Tosh Watson appeared from a food outlet.

"Baggage in hall," volunteered Tosh, devouring the remains of a McMuffin dripping with brown sauce. He gulped down a mouthful of coffee as both men confirmed they were wired up with covert body sets and tiny wireless earpieces.

"Tosh, you stay at the end of the walking-out area. I'll watch as they come out of Customs. Is Varley in position? Wired up?"

"Up there. And Madden too. I checked. They're both ready." Tosh pointed to a middle-aged man in a dark grey coat, who held a miniscule camera trained to film every person coming through.

"Where's Madden?"

"By the bookshop."

"They know Bardici's codename is Alfonso?"

"Correct. You ID Bardici and Madden and Varley will be ready."

They moved into position about thirty metres apart. After ten, Ratso saw new labels on the luggage coming through, showing that travellers from BA's Miami flight had arrived. But first would come the ones with EC passports. Non-EU citizens like Bardici were held up by the longer queue waiting for Immigration clearance.

From last night's great report by young Nancy Petrie, Ratso was confident they had identified Bardici by elimination. Nobody had travelled using the name Bardici—no surprise there. Eight passengers had changed flights to Nassau from Miami but their return dates were not even close. Only three persons from the Miami flight had flown to Grand Bahamas. The honeymoon couple had been quickly eliminated. That left a

Mr Mujo Zevi. The UK Border Agency had been most helpful, producing a photo taken of someone calling himself Mujo Zevi from Montenegro, who had passed through Immigration on his outward journey. The man had the same frame as Bardici.

It had been easy to persuade the AC that Bardici must be allowed to continue to use the false ID if he wished. Knowing his false ID could be a godsend on some future date. In turn, Wensley Hughes had persuaded top brass at the Border Agency that on arrival, Zevi should be waved through, nothing done to make him feel threatened or suspicious.

Ratso was on edge for the next toe-tapping twenty minutes. Every new face had to be checked and discarded but just as he was starting to wonder if he'd crapped out again, he saw his target. Zevi stood out because of his bulk and familiar swaying walk, like a gorilla looking for food. His large right hand gripped an overnight bag, just as he had gripped Neil before savaging him to death. For a moment Ratso was consumed with hatred and wanted to leap out at him—but now was not the time for an arrest.

Mujo Zevi looked somewhat different from his outgoing Immigration photo. Today, he wore a Miami Dolphins cap pulled low across his forehead and it looked as if he had not taken a razor on the trip. But that walk, swaying from side to side, was a dead giveaway. Ratso had watched hours of film of Bardici and he had no doubt Zevi was their man.

As the Albanian ambled past him, Ratso spoke softly. "Standby, standby. Contact. Alfonso entering walkway from Arrivals Hall. Subject wearing Miami Dolphins cap, unshaven, no beard, gorilla-like walk. Brown bag in right hand." He gave his call sign and said *over*. Within a few seconds, he got confirmation of *eyeball* from Tosh, Madden and Varley. Satisfied, he imagined Varley filming the unsuspecting target's every movement.

He saw geek-like Madden half visible behind a revolving bookstand. The target showed no reaction to anybody or anything, as far as Ratso could judge from his disappearing back.

Just to be sure, Ratso wanted to be there when Zevi reached Westbrook Drive. DC Nancy Petrie was already by the corner shop in the white O.P. van—the abbreviation for an Observations Post vehicle. Normally it would be plain vanilla, no name on it but Ratso had used it before for watching Bardici, so today magnetic signs had been fixed for Wickers, Plumbers & Heating Engineers.

He and Tosh hastened to the car park, a relative term where Tosh was concerned as he panted to keep up. They grabbed the VW Golf that Tosh had brought out and headed for Hounslow. While Tosh drove as fast as he dared, Ratso warned Petrie that Zevi could appear by taxi or private car within twenty minutes.

Tosh dropped Ratso close to Ali's corner shop. In seconds he was inside the Wickers van. "He should arrive from this end of the street, so drive past number 22, turn round and park beyond it so we can move toward him as he enters the house. Camera ready to roll?" Ratso heard the grunted *yes, of course*, though he had suffered five-star snafus when nothing had been recorded at all. Slowly they advanced to the apex of the bend, where he had lost sight of Klodian Skela and his missus last week. Now they had a perfect sightline to number 22 without being so close as to be obvious.

Within four minutes, a black cab appeared and slowed outside number 22. Ratso felt his pulse race. From ninety metres away, he watched Mujo Zevi emerge and pay the driver. As the cabbie moved slowly away, the Wickers van was cruising by number 22 and captured a great full-face view of Bardici as he picked up his bag and rolled his way to the front door.

"You got all that?" Ratso saw a satisfied nod. "Okay! Drop me off round the corner. I'll go back with Tosh. And you, Nancy? Coming with us?"

"I'll go back in the O.P. van. Leave you men to talk cricket or whatever."

"That's our loss, then." Ratso almost smiled goodbye as he climbed out and joined Tosh in the Golf.

They had barely travelled for ten minutes when Ratso sensed his companion needed a leak. But Tosh didn't like admitting to it. "Mattrafact, boss, I was just thinking I could murder a steak and kidney pud. I missed out on that yesterday. There's the Waggoners in about a mile. You up for it?"

Ratso was not up for it. He'd been fighting to retrieve that flash of inspiration, running through every step taken since they had arrived at Skela's squalid flat. "What! At this time? No, we're not stopping to eat. Get me back. I'm onto something even bigger than your steak and kidney pud—if I can only remember what the hell it is."

"Take my advice, boss. You can never, will never, forget a good steak and kidney pud and that's a fact."

"I'll take your word for it." Ratso laughed. "Stop for a piss if you must. But I want to get straight back."

After watching his sergeant scurry across the tarmac and through the side door of the dreary-looking pub, Ratso returned to his mental filing cabinet, opening and closing each drawer and each file in turn. But still that nanosecond of inspiration eluded him.

22

Fort Lauderdale, Florida
Kirsty-Ann Webber kissed beaming Leon goodbye and gave her mom a loving hug, promising to be back as soon as she could this evening. She had suffered a sleepless night, not because of Leon but because of the events of the previous day. After a last lingering look at Leon's chubby face and laughing eyes, she was gone, leaving behind the cosiness of her private life for the harsh reality of being a detective in the FLPD.

Every day was different. The day before, she had gotten involved in what the radio shock-jocks and local media were calling *a chase*, when in fact it had been nothing of the kind. She had followed a Buick sedan through the toughest part of town after stumbling on a gang confrontation. The Buick left the road and crashed into a wall, leaving the driver dead. Webber said she had played it by the book. She reminded herself for the umpteenth time that from her unmarked car, she had seen the guy, known locally as Muscles Mitch, shoot dead a father and son, both known drug dealers. By chance, she had witnessed every moment of the slaying—cold, brutal, clinical murders. Muscles had been well-known to FLPD and had a short life expectancy anyway, being an unemployed drug user and dealer. After killing two guys from a rival gang, it would have been even shorter.

She doubted Muscles even knew he was being followed, let alone chased. High off the buzz of the murders and cocaine, he had driven as if he were invincible and had paid the price. But after any incident like this, there was always a full investigation—looking for *lessons to be learned* and verifying the officer hadn't behaved inappropriately. Left-wing activists had packed the airwaves, calling for her head on the block. Right-wingers applauded her courage, when she knew she had done nothing brave at all.

Short of letting the guy disappear without getting his car registration number, Kirsty-Ann was sure she had played it proper. She'd radioed for support but for a vital seventy-five seconds she was alone—just her, the killer, his Buick and a concrete wall at a sharp bend. *Good riddance* had been her reaction on seeing his very dead body slumped across the front seat. He looked similar to the young thug who had shot her beloved Andy. But being a professional, she'd still checked the body to see if she could do anything.

It was a twenty-minute drive to HQ through the morning traffic. She was nearly there when the radio squawked and the chief's voice came on the line. "Morning, K-A. How ya doing?"

Kirsty-Ann tried to sound positive. "Hi, Chief! As you would expect."

"Rough night, I'll bet. But relax. Yesterday we got rid of three guys who were going to give us grief for the rest of their lives."

"Thank you. Listening to the radio phone-ins…"

"Ignore them. The investigation will be brief and conclusive. Got it? Anyway, I'm not calling about that. I've heard from DC." He cleared his throat noisily. "Your report was well received.

You can continue enquiries with the cruise ships, the casino trips to nowhere and the airlines."

"Still playing it cool?"

"If you can but the story has broken in Washington. The media know nothing except that Ruthven flew down here and stayed at the Hilton. I've already called the hotel and they're going to release a brief statement that he was there but did not check out. Period."

"Understood. But Ruthven—who is he? It's been odd, investigating the disappearance of someone I know nothing about."

"Well, I was never told either. But if you believe the *Washington Post*, he worked in Iraq and more recently Afghanistan."

"So he could be a political target?"

"In theory. But based on your report, I'm not convinced. You want to capture, kill, interrogate a guy like Ruthven, hell, it's not that hard. The guy's got no twenty-four-seven protection. He's a government servant. Could be picked off any time in Washington."

"Reckon he worked for the CIA?"

"We'll never be told if he had another role working undercover." Bucky Buchanan laughed. "A spokesman for the State Department put out a statement expressing mild concern but emphasising that there were no security implications."

"Which means there were?"

The chief laughed. "Keep an open mind. Ain't nobody has a better ear to the ground here than you. What they know in DC and ain't telling us, hell, we can't work on that." He paused. "You coming in?"

"Sure, I'm nearly there. I'll grab the file and eliminate the possibilities one by one."

"Good! It'll keep your mind off yesterday."

23

Clapham, South London

Ratso opened the pack of M&S sandwiches. Today he had prawn salad on brown with a mango smoothie. He enjoyed a quiet lunch at his desk. It gave him time to think, or, if Test Match Special was on, to get lost in that for half an hour—as lost as you could get with a constant flow of texts, calls and emails coming through. Anything was better lunchtimes than swilling down a pint or two in the Nags Head while watching Tosh and the rest devour soggy chips and burger baps as if they might never eat again.

In front of him was everything on Klodian Skela—his signed statement and notes about the interview, things Ratso had not wanted to include in the statement. Ratso had always believed in mental thumbscrews. *See a soft spot, go for it.* On his second visit to Skela, he demanded regular updates on *everything Bardici* on the condition that Ratso would not say a word to Rosafa and he *might* not be charged. *No promises*, he had emphasised.

Though his tiny office was well heated, Ratso shivered. He wondered if he was sickening for a cold, or worse still, for flu.

The Underground in December was a damned sneeze zone, with germs flying everywhere. He sniffed as he dumped the sandwich packet in the bin and returned to his notes. Then, impulsively, he got up, deciding to visit the team.

The Cauldron was quiet. Jock Strang was still in Glasgow. Most of the detectives were out on assignments or over at the Nags Head scoffing cholesterol. After cursory exchanges with DC Venables about Chelsea's bad away form, he went over the scribbles and pictures on the whiteboard. It was all too familiar. No roads led to Boris Zandro. His name and a photo of Wisteria Lodge were at the bottom right corner of the board but nothing pointed his way at all.

He was about to turn away when a single scribble, just two words—*Land Registry*—triggered a flash of light. And then he knew. Not that it was on the board—it wasn't even mentioned. To the astonishment of Venables and Nancy Petrie, he thumped his fist into his left hand and then furiously scribbled *solicitors* on the board beneath *Land Registry*. "Yes! Got it! I've got it!"

Petrie muttered *what's that, charm or looks* but Ratso ignored her, already heading back to his office and the remains of his sandwich. Compared to his thoughtful journey down the stairs, his return was supercharged, energy at full bore. Suddenly a whole new line of enquiry lay ahead.

One small step for man but one giant leap for truth and justice.

He munched on a prawn, anxious to get his desk clear. *Arkwright, Fenwick, & Stubbs, solicitors.* He had never heard of them till he discovered the firm had acted for the Gibraltar company that bought the block where Skela lived—a block full of Albanian tenants.

London had thousands of lawyers, most of them law-abiding but beneath the surface were others Ratso had learned to despise. Besides those who simply stole client money by *teeming and ladling*, dishonest lawyers fell into two camps. One type used every dirty trick in the book to get acquittals for villains who were guilty as hell. The other camp comprised low-profile firms who quietly got on with business, uncaring about the laws against money laundering. Only the previous week, an investigatory report had confirmed that more money was laundered through London daily than passed through the offshore islands in months, perhaps years. If the transactions were big enough, the report concluded, the City's banks balanced risk against reward, turning a blind eye to massive dodgy transfers that would never be permitted through the tight regulatory corset in well-run financial centres like the Isle of Man or Jersey.

Was Arkwright, Fenwick, & Stubbs in that camp? He would check out the partners, check out their business. Everything. For a moment Ratso gazed out of the window at the endless grey of a wintry afternoon. He watched a bus splashing through the December rain and a woman wrestling with a broken umbrella. His hands were sweaty and his heart was racing—good signs that he was onto something. That, or he had man-flu coming on.

Boris Zandro, I'm coming to get you.

It was a rare moment of euphoria to be savoured, like winning the lottery and momentarily living the dream. . But just like that daydream, harsh reality was swift to return as Ratso studied his notes and pored over the research done during the Wensley Hughes investigation. Nobody had checked out these solicitors or the purchase of Wisteria Lodge. Just a few keystrokes revealed Terry Fenwick was the senior partner and that Boris Zandro's London home was owned by an Isle of Man company called Menora Holdings Limited with a registered office in Athol Street, Douglas. Zandro must be a tenant.

Damn it! He had hoped for another Gibraltar link. *But was Menora just a front for Zandro?*

Ratso kept on digging, trawling through the data from the Manx Companies Registry, hoping that Terry Fenwick's name would leap off the screen as a director of Menora. It did not. *Another bloody wall.* The directors were Manx chartered accountants from a reputable firm. The real owner was hidden by nominee shareholders. Ratso's thoughts flashed back to a visit to the island on a sunny day, when Douglas Bay was a Mediterranean blue. Over a plate of delicious local Queenies on the promenade, an advocate from the attorney general's department had explained that a nominee shareholder typically held the shares under a trust deed for the true owner. That owner's name was not publicly recorded.

Boris Zandro, I'm coming to get you. But it's bloody difficult!

He surfed the web for anything more about the firm, about Terry Fenwick. These days, most law firms used websites and press releases to cram Google with enough puff and stuff to raise profile. But not this lot. All roads led to nowhere. The solicitor had no profile; he never appeared in Law Reports, never wrote articles; his website did not boast of deals done or victories achieved. The Internet revealed only a simple web page offering the firm's services for corporate and commercial law. One of his partners had the same name and was probably Terry's brother or son; another was a woman. None of them had a photo beside their profile. None of them had a profile at all.

Boris Zandro ran his affairs through companies. Was Terry Fenwick his lawyer? Was Fenwick the man who used Zandro's wealth to invest in blocks of flats, in Wisteria Lodge and God knew what else? It was possible. It was certainly worth flogging the idea.

Was Terry Fenwick a heads-down-get-on-and-service-the-clients type of solicitor, as the website implied? Ratso wondered how the hell a three-lawyer firm, tiny by City standards, could survive with the heavy overheads of Lime Street EC3. Surrounded by giant Square Mile companies with thousands of staff spread across the globe, Arkwright, Fenwick, & Stubbs apparently survived with a size and structure more suitable to London's outer suburbia.

Don't get ahead of yourself. The partners only need a handful of clients with large property transactions to make a good profit. Ratso doodled heavily with a thick black marker pen as he argued with himself. *No. Something smells here.*

While no cause for celebration, his instincts encouraged him to risk a machine coffee and a few moments later he was returning with the flimsy paper cup, its heat nearly scalding his hand. He looked again at the printout for Chewbeck Holdings Limited—Klodian Skela's landlord. The nominee shareholder was called Beckchew Limited—obviously from the same stable and also registered in Gibraltar. His fingers flying over the keys, Ratso muttered, "Surprise me," but the search on Beckchew Limited only produced yet another nominee shareholder. *You could dig till you reached Australia but you would never find the name of the true owner, the mastermind, the real moneybags.*

For a moment, Ratso's head drooped as he let out a sigh, his eyes shut tight. He drummed the desk in frustration. The identity of the true owner, the moneybags, would be recorded on that Rock—or should be. The KYC rules meant the Gibraltar agents *should* have checked true ownership *and* that the source of money was kosher.

No easy way of knowing who or where the purchase money for the apartment block came from.

No! Wrong!

Terry Fenwick, as a London solicitor, had to know his client, had to be satisfied about the source of funds when acting for the Gibraltar company. So go and ask him. Twenty minutes and you'll be in his Lime Street office.

Oh, sure, Ratso! Go jump in with both big feet? Risk alerting Boris Zandro that you're sniffing around his lawyer? You don't even know Boris Zandro's solicitor is Terry Fenwick.

He logged onto the Law Society's website. It offered advice to solicitors if money laundering was suspected. For thirty minutes, he read through endless pages of hair-splitting jargon. One thing was clear: if he had acted for Zandro on these property deals, Fenwick would protest he had no reason to suspect any fraud or money laundering and therefore had no duty to make a Suspicious Activity Report.

Okay, so I go and interview him. What would Fenwick say—assuming he's bent, that is. He'd ask who's under suspicion. So I'd say Boris Zandro. And he might say, never heard of him. Or he might adjust his pinstripe and say, yeah, I've acted for him or his companies but I'm under no duty to disclose anything.

So I'd say well whatever you do, not a word to Mr Zandro that Det. Inspector Todd Holtom has been making enquiries. If you do, it's the criminal offence of tipping off. Understood? And Fenwick would nod solemnly and shake my hand, promising to keep stumm. Door slams. End of meeting. And as soon as I've gone, Fenwick tips off Zandro.

No, Todd. No size-tens on Fenwick's plush carpet. Gotta link Fenwick to Boris Zandro.

Terry Fenwick = Possible Key

He drained the coffee, grimaced and decided to clear his head by popping round to Café Nero for a real cup. Sometimes he'd found a change of scene from his broom cupboard triggered an idea. But not today. By the time he finished his latte with an extra shot, his notepad was full of circled doodles but at their heart were just four words. *Fenwick: Connect the Dots*. In other words, Sweet FA. Or perhaps within those four words lay an opening. But how?

24

Central London EC3

"Jock's back tomorrow," volunteered Tosh. "He's got his boy Gordy thinking positive."

"Not the same as kicking the winning goal in the World Cup, though, is it? The coach told Jock he had that in him, given a few seasons. Now he's finished."

Ratso really felt for the lad. As a youngster, he had dreamed of playing cricket for England. Being left-handed, he had modelled his batting on David Gower and his bowling action on Wasim Akram, the great Pakistani left-arm quickie. As an eleven-year-old, he had imagined himself walking through the Long Room at Lord's as a genuine all-rounder. The realisation he would never be good enough to play for England had come in his late teens. The coach's arm round his shoulder had been kind but the words, though sugar-coated, had been brutal. Years of dreaming gone in a moment of harsh reality. His dad had been pretty choked too; from his wheelchair, he had lived his dreams through his son.

The two detectives were heading for Arkwright, Fenwick, & Stubbs' offices on Lime Street. They fell silent as they walked along Eastcheap and into Philpot Lane. Ratso had insisted they get off the Northern Line at London Bridge and walk across the river to get more miles into his daily routine. Tosh had not been appreciative.

"Jock would have enjoyed what you're going to do," Ratso said.

"Yeah, he's a great bullshitter," Tosh agreed.

"And you?" Ratso turned to look at his sergeant, who grinned back but Ratso remained uneasy. Jock was a safe pair of hands. Besides that, Ratso was still struggling to understand why they were approaching Fenwick at all – reversing his decision that it would be a crap move. *Desperation* – that was it. Chuck a rock in and watch the ripples. But still the nagging doubts had him on edge. Tosh Watson was younger, less experienced and less adept at thinking on his feet. "Get the feel of the place, any brochures, magazines, artwork on the walls, antiques, threadbare carpets, whatever." He popped a Polo into his mouth as Tosh unwrapped another Mars bar from his endless supply. "Get an impression: is it busy, lots of clients in reception, sounds of typing everywhere, phones ringing? And most important—there should be a board listing the companies that have registered offices at this address. Photograph it if you can. Don't get caught! Above all, ID Terry Fenwick. Does he look like the photo we got from DVLC?" They stopped at the end of the street to wait for a bus to trundle by. "You got the patter?"

Tosh's grin nearly split his face as he nodded enthusiastically. "I'm well up for it boss. When I phoned for the appointment, I told the girl what it was about. Just a ten-minute meeting with Mr Terry Fenwick, I said. No more." As they dodged a cruising cab while crossing Fenchurch Street, Tosh grinned again. "I'll get a photo of him and the other partners if I can."

"Risky. Not needed."

They headed north along Lime Street, the narrow road that had long been synonymous with Lloyd's of London insurance. Further up the street lay the Willis Tower and the Richard Rodgers Lloyd's building, the latter very avant-garde when it had opened in 1986. Now it looked rather tired. But the offices of Arkwright, Fenwick, & Stubbs bore no resemblance to the neighbouring towering buildings. Its entrance was a narrow doorway close to the Ship public house. The gloomy entrance led to a flight of unstained wooden stairs, no carpet or lino. Both men studied the four-storey building dating back maybe hundreds of years. "Where will you be, boss?"

"Doing a spot of thinking, Tosh."

"I'll see you in the Ship, then."

Ratso laughed but then turned deadly serious. "Remember. No risks. Got it?"

Ratso went on to the pub still regretting that his impatience had meant Tosh making the visit. Jock would have been more nimble on his feet if anything went wrong. But Tosh had been so enthusiastic that Ratso's own impatience prevailed. He glanced back at the slit-like entrance. It was too late now; Tosh had gone up the stairs. He checked the time. *Too early for a scotch. More like tea and cake.*

He entered the pub, which was still busy with noisy city types who would never make it back to the office from lunch. The place smelled of roast beef, green veggies and beer. A weepie Dolly Parton number mixed with the sound of braying laughter. He thought of Tosh and his size-tens and abandoned the idea of coffee. "A Famous Grouse. Make it a large one."

He poured a splash of water into the whisky and settled down to read the *Standard*. The whisky was almost gone when a beaming Tosh reappeared. Ratso tossed back the last drops and rose to follow his sergeant at a discreet distance till they reached Mark Lane, well away from Lime Street. By then, Ratso was sure nobody was following.

Ratso could sense his sergeant's excitement as Tosh ambled along, slowly swinging his teddy-bear arms, his toes pointing slightly outward.

Just nine minutes later, as Tosh and Ratso rounded the corner by Tower Hill Station, Terry Fenwick was studying a picture of Sergeant Tosh Watson photographing the list of company names. He put the photo in his briefcase, checked the time and announced to the receptionist that he would be leaving early after all.

25

Fort Lauderdale, Florida

At first Kirsty-Ann Webber had intended to take in the airport but by the time the tall radio mast at Police HQ on West Broward Boulevard came into view, she had decided to work the phones. Relegating a check on casino cruises to her third priority had been a no-brainer. Like everyone in Florida, she knew all about these cruises to nowhere. Daily cruises sailed a few miles into the Atlantic to get round gambling regulations, while the hopefuls aboard slaved over slots and blackjack till the ship docked hours later.

Kirsty-Ann had tried it just once and vowed never again. She had quickly grown disgusted watching people who could barely afford to lose a dime endlessly feeding the slots, which almost always channelled their money to the casino owners. The throng cheerfully formed long lines at the buffet, chowing down mountains of fast food and sinking Atlantic quantities of booze before returning to feed the slots till their last nickel was gone.

But Lance Ruthven? Would he go even once on a casino cruise—let alone six times? *Hell no!* That left the longer two-night cruises to

Grand Bahama, where gamblers stayed in hotels for a couple of nights. *Young guys having a blast might party that way once, maybe twice in a year.* But would Lance Ruthven do this five or six times? It made no sense. Frankly, the whole thing made no sense— him visiting Florida so often—unless he had friends here, or some sinister business. *A hobby? Snorkelling? Fishing? Well…maybe.* It was a thought. So where else might he go? The Bahamas, the Caymans?

Walking slowly, equally preoccupied with the media storm hanging over her and how to unravel the Ruthven mystery, she entered the white three-storey building with its familiar blue stripe getup. Some colleagues she passed encouraged her to give the proverbial finger to the media critics, while others praised Bucky Buchanan for refusing to crawl to the shit-stirring lefties who wanted her suspended…or worse. On reaching her desk, she unlocked her computer for updates on overnight events before hitting the phone. As the chief had said, there was plenty of coverage in the Washington media about Ruthven, including a serious-faced image of him, identical to his passport. But the local journalists hadn't majored in on the story yet.

She glanced at the photo on her desk, her Mom with Leon in a floppy sun hat. She hated being apart from them. Being a single mom had not been the plan—quite the reverse. If she had tried to encapsulate her vision, it was a family unit—Mom, Dad and two kids, cocooned by peace, happiness, respect and understanding. But that smooth-talking trader from Chicago had charmed his way into her life during his long weekend visit and abortion had not been acceptable to her, despite her malevolent feelings toward the bastard. The only good thing was the trust fund he had provided without even wincing. He had no interest in ever seeing her or Leon again.

Despite Leon's gurgles and smiles, she still felt an emptiness, especially when times were tough, like now. Leon needed a father. She needed someone to tune into her wavelength and hold her through the media attacks. She wanted someone like Andy to teach Leon to play catch, how to kick a goal and how to shoot baskets. She turned away from the picture, just a hint of tears in her eyes as she refocused on airlines flying to the Bahamas. From Fort Lauderdale, there were four obvious possibilities—Vision, Bahamasair, Gulfstream International and SkyBahamas—but she jotted down a reminder not to overlook private charters and to check that Ruthven was not a qualified pilot. But that would come later, if the airlines didn't pan out.

She decided to start with Bahamasair.

"Hi! How ya doin'? Detective Kirsty-Ann Webber calling from the Fort Lauderdale Police Department." She explained what she wanted, held for a few minutes and was passed to a woman with a deep, husky voice who seemed about to chuckle at any moment. She introduced herself as Darshelle King. Kirsty-Ann could almost picture the woman from her voice alone. She judged Darshelle to be African-American, mid-to-late thirties, overweight with a rounded, warm smiling face and large brown eyes. Big earrings hanging low. A red sweatshirt straining somewhat against the fullness of her bust. Kirsty-Ann smiled at her mental picture as she explained the information she needed.

"I'll get right back to you. Give me an hour, honey."

"Thanks, Darshelle. Appreciate it."

She dialled SkyBahamas and repeated her inquiry to a woman with a remarkably similar voice. Maybe all airline employees sounded like this.

No sooner had she ended the call than the phone rang. It was Darshelle. "That was pretty darned easy," Darshelle laughed.

"You mean negative?"

"Nope!" Another chuckle from deep in the throat. "I mean there was jus' one person who booked every one of those flights."

Kirsty-Ann's face lit up. "Including this most recent one?"

"Depends what you mean. The guy flew to Freeport but he was a no-show for his return flight."

The detective paused. "And his name?"

"Kurtner. Hank Kurtner."

"Hey, Darshelle, that's terrific! I'll drop by to get a statement. You available in an hour?"

"You're in Nassau right now?" Darshelle's surprise was evident.

Kirsty-Ann fell silent. *How could she have been so dumb!* The airline's HQ was on New Providence Island, not Fort Lauderdale. She laughed. "Well, maybe not an hour. The Concorde's stopped flying!" Both of them laughed. "I'll check flights. Budgets here are so damn tight I'll need to speak to my chief. I might be swimming!"

"Wouldn't recommend it. The water's not so warm now."

26

Central London EC3

Ratso stood with Tosh on the platform at Tower Hill Station, waiting for a westbound train. "So we have our first twenty-four-hour surveillance data on Terry Fenwick." Ratso checked the message just received. "He's predictable. Leaves home early. Train in. Walks to the office. Goes home just after six."

Tosh was still on fire from the success of his visit but this info was a downer. "Get a life, mate!" He showed Ratso the picture of Terry Fenwick he had taken. "Pretty damned good, eh?"

"You're sure he didn't…?"

Tosh shook his head as the District Line train rumbled into the station. "Cinch! The girl at reception knocked on his door, told him I was there and he called her in. He was pointing her to a corner to get him something. He was watching her, so I got a clear shot of him."

"And the list of company names?"

"Displayed right beside me in reception. By the time she returned, I was…" The rest of Tosh's answer was drowned out as the carriages stopped noisily beside them. The train was standing room only and they fell silent, swaying and bumping into strangers as they passed through Mansion House, Cannon Street and Blackfriars. They were almost into Temple when the train stopped in the tunnel. A moment or two's delay was not unusual but when it became rather more, Ratso looked at Tosh in the near-silent carriage. Passengers were either staring mindlessly at the adverts, reading books, the evening paper, or fiddling with iPods or MP3s, nobody speaking.

"Reminds me of the 7/7 bombings," Ratso volunteered. "I was stuck in the tunnel near Westminster for a bloody age. All types of explanations were given but blowing up Tube trains was never mentioned."

"Cheerful sod, aren't you," intervened a laughing Aussie with ridiculous sideburns.

Ratso grinned. "Well, it's not our train, so why worry, mate?" He was about to make a dig about the last test match result when the driver came on. "Sorry about the delay. All trains are stopped. There's someone on the line near Stamford Brook. I'm waiting for instructions on whether the power will be kept off and you can walk into the next station. It's about two-fifty metres."

"Selfish bastard," said Tosh, so half the carriage could hear. "Why didn't the sod just jump off a roof. Inconvenience nobody." Ratso nodded as he watched murmurs run through the strangers. No doubt there were as many shades of opinion about another suicide as there were skin colours in the carriage. "This is your fault, boss," continued Tosh, unsure whether he was joking or not. "Your keep-fit routines. Walking to Tower Hill. If we'd gone to Bank, we'd be back drinking cups of tea with our feet up."

Ratso enjoyed the chance of a wind-up. "Good exercise, though, standing here. Keep moving your legs. Stand on tiptoes and back again." Their immediate neighbours grinned and the Aussie was obviously debating whether to make a dig about Tosh's waistline when the driver came back on.

"Sorry, ladies and gentlemen. The District Line controller says we're to stay on the train. Maybe twenty minutes."

"Pity. I fancied walking. There's rats down there the size of cats." In the near silence, those close by looked toward Ratso, a head higher than everyone around him. The women and even some men looked uncomfortable at the thought.

"You'd eat them an' all," added Tosh, enjoying the attention.

Ratso grinned from ear to ear. "Nothing like a bit of rat, eaten raw. Maybe a dash of Worcester sauce."

The Aussie laughed and several others joined in, enjoying the banter that kept their minds off the mounting sense of claustrophobia in the packed carriage. Had it been a blazing hot August day, the panic factor would have been ten times higher. "You think he's joking," Tosh said.

"Only about the Worcester sauce. Rat tartare. Goes down a treat."

"Will you shut up?" The sharp interruption came from a woman in her early thirties, with disapproving eyes set behind severe glasses and an accent from one of the finest finishing schools. Her glare showed her contempt but Ratso gave her what he thought was a sexy wink, forcing her to look away and then return to her *Guardian*. Tosh caught Ratso's eye and said nothing. Fortunately, the driver came on soon after.

"Better news. We'll be on the move in two minutes." And they were. The relieved passengers settled down into silence again.

At Embankment, Ratso and Tosh changed to the Northern Line. Between the two platforms, Tosh regaled Ratso with more details of his meeting. "Not the shyster type you see down the Old Bailey or Southwark Crown Court. Fenwick's more like an accountant. About fifty. Quiet voice, shrewd face. Mean with words. Almost like a Gestapo officer in a movie. Calculating."

"If he's so clever, you sure he didn't rumble you?" Ratso was worried, not just about Tosh's cheerful optimism but because even a company lawyer like Fenwick might know that crime prevention for a Lime Street address was the role of the City of London police.

Tosh was adamant. "No. He fell for the cover story. I gave him some spiel about a gang targeting professionals to launder money on the pretext they were buying a chain of motels. He said he'd never been approached but would alert us if he was. I also lobbed in some crap about a spate of break-ins—a gang nicking computers. Fenwick said he was pretty safe, showed me his security system. Plus he's one floor up, so a ladder in Lime Street is the only other way in. He said they kept little cash on the premises but I warned him that laptops, iPads, computer chips and techie things were the hot targets."

"What took you so long?"

"Ah!" Tosh tapped the side of his nose. "I saw a brass plate for some accountants above Fenwick. I visited them too, just in case Fenwick was suspicious."

Ratso was surprised. "Good thinking. Anything else at Fenwick's place?"

They descended the escalator, Ratso noticing he had a missed call. Tosh looked uncomfortable. For a moment, Ratso was concerned but it was just Tosh's bladder sending urgent messages. "The offices were pretty dull. Low-key. Cheap carpeting, no magazines. Not even a *Financial Times*. Just four rooms off the reception. One PA for the three fee-earners and the girl on reception." He paused to think. "As we knew, there's Terry, his brother Adrian and a young woman partner called Lynda Dorwood. Adrian was out but I glimpsed Lynda—she's about thirty. No artworks. Just the bog-standard legal prints on the walls. Practical furniture, rather old and faded but the computers in reception and Fenwick's office were the real deal."

"Nothing else?"

"No other clients. Just the list of companies with a registered office. Shall we go through them tonight?"

Ratso checked his watch and shook his head. "It'll keep overnight. I've cricket nets at Shepherd's Bush. I'll just shift some crap from my desk and then be off. Anyway, Jock's back tomorrow. My office—nine thirty before meeting in the Cauldron."

27

Clapham, South London

Ratso had spoken to Charlene the previous evening after nets. She sounded miffed that he had not been to see her. But her bombardment of text messages made him uneasy. He had no wish to become her permanent crutch. He had calmed her with a promise never to leave her side during the funeral and wake but had added that he would not be staying overnight. "With your sister back, you've no need for me. Stay strong." He had ended the call to the sound of her blown kiss.

Afterward, his thoughts were only of the cryptic message that had hit his Blackberry yesterday afternoon, at 3:20 p.m. to be precise, when he and Tosh were on the Underground heading toward Lime Street. It had been from Klodian Skela and had been just a few words: *Erlis go there about boat. No more.* Ratso had scribbled the words on his pad. After the meeting with Tosh and Jock, he would pay Skela another visit.

A boat? A rich man's toy, like you see at Monaco or Puerto Banus— seventy metres long at a million dollars a metre? A floating gin palace like Roman Abramovich might own? Or did Skela mean a ship?

He had to press Skela for more details. Bardici would hardly fly to the Bahamas to talk about a fishing boat. So it had to be flashy or commercial. Bardici would not want a gin palace for himself, nor could he afford one. Zandro already had the *Tirana Queen* moored at Gibraltar or somewhere on the French Riviera. Would he want another eighty-million-pound gleaming white hulk that shouted I am so stinking rich I can afford two? Maybe. But if Zandro wanted to buy one, he would go himself.

Ratso had breakfasted early on Cheerios and fruit but as the milk had turned, the cereal he ate dry and the coffee he drank black. The machine coffee now in front of him seemed unusually welcome as he flicked through his latest messages. Nothing new from Skela. He checked the time on his screen and saw it was coming up to seven. He hit the web page for London area news to see what had been happening around the city overnight.

Below the national news items he saw that the trial of a rapist was about to start at the Old Bailey, there had been a double stabbing in Walthamstow and a shooting in Camberwell. He sometimes wondered why he bothered reading this stuff; the stories would be the same tomorrow and the next day. Same crimes, different locations.

He was about to turn to the cricket pages when he caught the headline *Tube Incident: Victim Named*. Immediately, his mind flashed back to the previous afternoon. He opened the page. He didn't take in the details, not at first anyway. All he saw was the name Klodian Skela. His eyes went in and out of focus and for several long seconds he stared at the screen, not taking anything in at all. Klodian Skela, aged thirty-eight, of Chiswick. Pronounced dead at the scene. The female driver being treated for shock.

At 9:30 Tosh and Jock arrived together and overfilled his office. After politely but impatiently listening to Jock's news from

Glasgow, Ratso told them of Skela's death. But Jock wasn't ready to work just yet. "Heh, get this. I meant to tell ye. Last month after Poppy Day, I went into Arthur Tennant's office. Ye'll never guess what the mean bastard was doing!"

"Using a teabag for the fourth time?" suggested Tosh.

"Go on, then," said Ratso, always happy to hear the latest shit about his boss.

"He wis only putting his poppy in a wee box to keep for next year." The listeners laughed. Tennant's mean streak was the stuff of legend. When he had been based in Eltham, his nickname was Crime—because Crime never paid.

"Probably been using it for years," Tosh summed it up neatly.

Ratso got them back on message with a decisive chop of the hand. "Right, then. Skela. I checked with Transport for London. Time of incident, 4:47 p.m."

"So that was *after* I met Terry Fenwick," suggested Tosh, already anxious to avoid any blame.

Ratso nodded reassurance. "*If* Fenwick is connected to Zandro. *If* Fenwick *had* smelled a rat." He almost smiled as he used the word. "*If* he had acted at once, there was still no time for him to warn Zandro to get his lieutenants to tell Bardici to scare the crap out of Skela."

"Even if Fenwick was suspicious," Tosh added, over-hastily, "which he was not."

"So you said." Ratso watched Tosh pull a Mars bar from his cardigan pocket. The chocolate was cracked and the bar squashed but Tosh's enthusiasm for it was not dampened as he took a huge bite. "Either Skela's wife Rosafa was after him, or Bardici, or both. Whatever, he just couldn't cope."

Jock looked pensive. "Ye hadna spoken to his wife?"

Ratso shook his head firmly. "No. I preferred to keep the threat hanging."

Jock looked thoughtful, his steely eyes staring at nothing in particular. "I'm no saying this is what happened. I'm just playing devil's advocate. If Fenwick was suspicious when Tosh fixed the appointment, then Bardici might have been tipped off in time to intimidate Skela." After being back in Glasgow, Jock's accent was more pronounced than ever.

Ratso was not convinced. "Why should Tosh phoning about crime prevention trigger an alarm?" He saw that Tosh looked especially relieved at hearing this. "For now, we assume it was general pressure that drove Skela to jump."

"He wasna pushed?" suggested Jock, showing teeth somewhat misshapen from his days of pipe smoking, a habit he had kicked seven years before.

"I checked. The poor woman driving the train was pretty cut up. She collapsed in the cab. But she was sure: Skela was alone near the end of the platform. Simply dived across the rails."

"Whit aboot Lindita, his daughter? Would she be blackmailing him?" Jock's Glaswegian hung for a moment as the listeners thought it through. Before Ratso could comment, Tosh responded.

"Get real, guys! His daughter was no prisoner. Not like the kid kept in a cellar for twenty-four years by that Austrian pervert." Tosh lobbed the Mars wrapper into the dark green bin. "Lindita was gagging for it. Know what I mean?"

Ratso nodded. "You're right. She didn't live with her folks; just came round for dinner and nookie when her mum was away. Would she have put the screws on him?"

"Maybe it's sort of the done thing in Albania." He saw Ratso's dismissive look and Jock's smirk. "Shagging your kids—it can be legal in Belgium. Just the thing after moules and chips down Ostende. Lots of other countries too, like Turkey. It's legal. Different sort of stuffing there, that's all!" He was rewarded with a wry look from Ratso and a barking laugh from Jock. "So maybe that's what they do in Albania when they're not out shooting each other and dealing drugs."

"You're a sad, sick bastard, Tosh. Don't let's go there." Ratso turned a page in his notepad. "Tosh, you interview Lindita. I reckon Skela was shit-scared of his wife; see if Lindita knows what drove him to it. See her on her own, mind. We never told her why we were interviewing her father. 'Course, we've no clue what he said to her later."

"And Mrs Skela?"

"Question her too but tread carefully." Ratso clasped his hands behind his head and stared at the cobweb in the corner of the ceiling as if seeking inspiration, like Robert the Bruce in his cave. Suddenly, he leaned forward and flattened his fingers on the table. "No. Scrub everything. We keep out of it for now. That block is too full of Albanians."

"Aye," Jock agreed. "Bardici, Zandro, whoever—they've got to believe Skela's death is being treated as routine."

"Tosh, check with the coroner's officers. See what they've discovered."

Tosh looked disappointed at his change of assignment. "You ask me, the kid won't have mentioned our visit to her mum or the coroner's officer."

Ratso nodded, anxious to move on. He tapped his notes impatiently. "Item two. Take a listen. Skela's last message—he left it about ninety minutes before he jumped." He played back the dead man's words. *Erlis go there about boat. No more.* The broken English hung over them till Ratso continued, "I was going to ask Skela today what he understood by the word *boat*."

"Those words, *no more*," Jock repeated them. "I'd say it either means Bardici was only there about a boat and *nothing more...*"

Ratso finished the alternative. "...Or *no more* help. Because he was pissed off with me...or with life." Both sergeants nodded in agreement.

Jock leaned forward, hands clasped under his chin. "Boss, let me check out the Grand Bahama scene."

"If you think you're flying out tonight with your water wings and sun oil, think again."

"Wi' my rugged charm, I dinna need a tan to pull the birds." This was a dig at Ratso, who enjoyed a touch of bronzing. They all laughed. "Anyway, boss, hot sun and me are a no-no. Give me Copland Road, a Rangers home win and a fish supper any day." His eyes showed he was momentarily living the thought. "No, I was actually thinking of using the Web."

"Agreed." Ratso was moving on. "Got your pics, Tosh?"

The sergeant pulled two photos from his folder and laid them on the desk. The first was the list of company names, each on a small plastic plate slotted into a board. "I had the photo of Fenwick enhanced for the surveillance boys." The second photo showed Terry Fenwick seated at his desk, his right arm pointing across the room.

Ratso produced the picture from the DVLA in Swansea. "Here's the one on his driving licence. Taken three years ago but looks very similar. Anonymous-looking bugger, isn't he?" added Ratso, taking in the regular but thin features, the half-frame glasses low on the man's nose, the traditional short back and sides and the smooth, well-shaven cheeks. "Height? Build?"

Tosh laughed. "Medium height. Medium build. As you say, anonymous. Say five ten. Not thin. Not fat. Not burly. Just average. Aged fifty-seven, according to Swansea. That surprised me."

"The quick blast of surveillance gave us a taster. Now let's go in depth. Get Google images of his home in Bickley. Get its value, the outstanding mortgage. Family circumstances. The usual." The listeners knew there was more coming. "But I'm more interested in what he does during office hours. Surveillance morning and evening was pretty damned dull."

Tosh leaned forward as he spoke. "You ask me, he sits at his desk and makes money."

"Maybe. Let's see how many clients come and go. Photo them too."

"Use the O.P.?"

"Not a good street for that. I don't want to overuse it, anyway. Try and fix an office opposite."

Jock looked pensive. "Expecting Boris Zandro to drop in for a wee chat and coffee with Fenwick? Get real. Wensley Hughes would have got that years ago, when Zandro was under constant observation."

Ratso snapped his fingers. "You're right! Never once was Zandro near Lime Street." He looked down at the list of company names. A quick glance showed maybe fifty names. But as Ratso knew already, there were more—probably many, many more where Arkwright, Fenwick and Stubbs were involved but with a registered office in the BVI, Isle of Man, Jersey, or Gibraltar. "You studied the names yet, Tosh?"

"Meant nothing to me."

Ratso and Jock leaned over the photo and looked at each name in turn. Nothing jumped off the paper. No Albanian names. Nothing that linked in with Zandro or his address. They looked random, almost computer-generated. Anonymous like the thin-faced solicitor with the forgettable features. The typical city gent on the 8-17 from Bickley.

Tosh rose. "Sorry, boss. I need a leak. But the names, they're meaningless. Right?" He got no reaction from Ratso, who was deep in thought, his brow furrowed. Tosh scurried out as Jock stretched out a hefty fist and picked up the list. He too admitted defeat after a second read-through. It was only when he handed the photo back to Ratso that something finally sparked.

Ratso's eyes widened as he looked down the list. Suddenly he jumped up, punching the air. "I got it! I got it!"

"Explain, boss."

"I was looking for anagrams. But it's easier than that. Three are a dead giveaway."

"All yer hours on the Daily Mail crosswords. Time well spent." Ratso was unsure whether Jock was taking the piss or not.

Ratso grabbed his pen and pointed to three names, then read them out. "Etro, Oulsden and Egent."

Jock looked puzzled. "Say it quickly and it could be a law firm."

Ratso's eyes disagreed. "Oh! I missed another one. Onduit Investments Limited."

"Come on, boss. Give."

28

Clapham, South London

After Tosh returned, Ratso suggested they all pop round to Café Nero to top up Tosh's bladder and keep his urinary tract in regular order. While Jock and Tosh grabbed the only spare table, Ratso stood in a long line for the coffees. "You'd never think there was a recession," grumbled Ratso to a total stranger. "Always the same. Every time you blink, there's another coffee shop open and they're always full."

"Yeah, in my next life, I'm coming back as the guy who started all this in Seattle. You need a second mortgage just for an espresso and a muffin."

"These places breed quicker than rabbits," Ratso agreed as he handed over his money to the young Polish girl behind the counter. "I'm told you can still visit the daddy of them all—the first ever Starbucks in Pike Place Market, Seattle. I expect our American cousins would say, *It's kinda neat*." Ratso collected his tray with three coffees and muffins for the sergeants.

At the table, Jock had been joshing Tosh about the company names. Tosh's frown said it all. Ratso sat as the sergeants wolfed down their muffins, though that didn't stop Jock from almost choking with laughter. "I asked Tosh if he'd worked it out," he spluttered to Ratso. "Okay, I said, I'll give you a clue. These four names: Etro, Oulsden, Egent and Onduit. They're code for four London clubs. So he only says, Spurs, Arsenal, West Ham and Fulham." Ratso joined in the laughter while Tosh scowled, asking what was so bleeding funny.

"Tell him, Jock."

But before Jock could answer, Tosh volunteered again. "Tit-and-bum clubs, then? Like those joints in Soho? Sunset Strip and that."

"Come on, boss. Put the poor sod out of his misery."

"Etro, Oulsden, Egent and Onduit. Add one letter to each you get Metro, Poulsden, Regent and Conduit."

Jock put on a passable imitation of a Hoorah Henry's London accent. "Each one is a posh, blue-chip London club—hangouts for toffs like the Lord Doodahs and Sir Willerby Muppets of this world. Oh yaah! Spiffing, what?"

"Plus loads of media types, city slickers, minor celebrities," added Ratso. "The royals—some of the male ones, that is—belong to the Poulsden in Hill Street, Mayfair."

Tosh was miffed at his ignorance being so exposed. "So what's your point?" he asked huffily.

"I'll explain, Tosh. I'll use big writing to make it easier. Or would you prefer a cartoon?"

"Bollocks!" Tosh replied, grinning as he shifted uneasily.

"Okay, imagine you're Terry Fenwick."

"With his money, too?"

Ratso ignored him. "You form dozens of companies. Most names have been used already, so you can't register them. You need to invent new ones. So you're having lunch in the…"

"Metro Club in Charlotte Street," suggested Jock.

"And you're talking to a client who needs a new company," continued Ratso. "So you think, what shall we call it? Ah! Metro Holdings Limited but of course you know that a good name like Metro will have gone." Tosh looked up, his expression showing that he was now on message. "So today I want a list of members from those four clubs. I'm off tomorrow; it's the funeral."

"And no' just off for an hour, eh, boss?" Jock's remark was well loaded and Ratso saw Tosh smirk.

Ratso's poker face gave nothing away. "Afterwards? I'll go to the wake. Meet the family."

"Ye'll be back the next day, will ye?" Now Jock's voice was deadpan but Ratso had no doubt what the gossip had been behind his back.

"Why not?" Ratso ducked the bouncer as well as any England batsman. "After I've been through the membership lists, I'll decide about surveillance but if Fenwick's a member of these clubs, then we might get to fast-track what's going on."

He turned to Tosh.

"Tomorrow, for Neil Shalford's funeral, I want you in an O.P. van. I want everyone who attends the service to be photographed. Plus, of course, anybody who might be hanging round watching."

"Expecting Bardici?"

Ratso's look was foxy. "If he heard both Hogans would be there as mourners, he might stop by." He twirled his coffee cup. "They won't be, of course. No way they want to be linked to Neil Shalford. Especially not to his corpse." Yet the listeners knew Ratso had a subplot in mind. They had spotted the dancing look in his eyes.

"But?"

"But if my snout gets the word out..."

Jock thumped the table. "That both brothers will be there? Aye, that'll attract Bardici like a fly to dung."

"And in Bardici's mind, link the bugging to Dan and Jerry Hogan." Tosh was getting there in bite-sized chunks.

"He might try something. Or he'll want to know who attends. So you will be there to watch any watchers, Bardici or someone we don't yet know. Maybe we'll add another photo to the whiteboard. Perhaps even ID him if you follow him onto a bus or tube. Or better still, into a car with a number you can scratch down. Got it?"

Tosh grinned. "Piece of cake, boss."

Ratso was less confident. Jock had said nothing, his mind somewhere else. "Jock. Anything to add besides the shenanigans at Rangers?"

Jock stirred from his thoughts; Ratso had guessed his mind kept drifting back to Glasgow. The Scot shook his head and sighed. "It's a right mess up there. Double-dealing. The fans deserve better." He reached for the last crumbs on his plate. "Any special instructions for me, boss? While ye're, er, comforting the widow?" But Ratso had already left the table and if he heard, he was not rising to the bait.

"He'll be well in there," volunteered Tosh with Ratso out of earshot. "Charlene's a right little raver." The two sergeants grinned at each other as they held back, watching Ratso hold open the door for a frail-looking pensioner.

"Aye, right enough!" added Jock. "Remember that night at yon pole-dancing place in Streatham? That piss-up after banging up those Yardies?"

Tosh looked sheepish. "I prefer to forget that night."

Jock rewarded him with a belly laugh. "My money? The boss won't be in next morning. Not early, anyroads."

The two men laughed and were still laughing when they caught up with Ratso near the traffic lights. He looked at them suspiciously, pretty damned sure he was the butt of their joke. Ignoring their mocking grins, he crouched to chat with a scruff who was seated cross-legged on a coconut mat, an even scruffier mongrel beside him. The two sergeants looked on as Ratso exchanged some banter before slipping a fiver into the man's grimy hand.

"God bless you, mate," the man said with a strong Yorkshire accent. Ratso knew the beggar had started life in Rotherham.

"Don't piss it all against the wall, will you," Ratso responded as he smiled his goodbye and the three officers moved on.

"You're a soft touch, boss. A fiver! Five quid to a lazy bastard who's too idle to get off his fat arse." Tosh's face matched his indignant tone.

"Ending up like that is never so far from any of us. That fiver means more to him than to me."

Tosh was unrepentant. "One day you'll see the real him, all togged up in his best whistle and flute coming out of the Ritz after a slap-up dinner. Conmen, the lot of them."

"You are so wrong. This guy likes a chat, a kind word." Ratso's voice had grown irritated. "And I know a damned sight more about him than you ever will, with that pig-ignorant attitude. Talk to him—find out for yourself."

Ratso wasn't going to give Tosh the pleasure of knowing the horrific story of the guy's rail crash in Africa that stole his wife and his baby daughter. He had used a crutch since the age of twenty-nine. His frontal lobe brain injury had made him unemployable.

There was an embarrassed hush as they walked on before Jock broke the surly silence. "Reckon Zandro might be a club member, boss?"

Ratso shrugged but his face revealed a glimmer of hope. "I don't know much about these pukka joints. You need a shedload of members to support your application to join. One blackball and you're out. It happened to that Jeremy Paxman once at the Garrick. But maybe Zandro *would* get elected—all that patronage of the arts stuff and his swanky dinner parties."

"I'll check for his name anyway," Tosh said as they turned into the car park and their drab, cheerless block.

Ratso stopped in his tracks and turned to face the sergeants. "I've an idea. Tosh, take five random pictures along. Any old sods—City types, landed gentry. Get them from the Web. Nobody well-known but include Zandro among them and then ask the porter at the entrance whether he knows any of them."

"And if they recognise Zandro?"

"Act disappointed. Make out you were after one of the others."

"And me?" Jock sidestepped a puddle and glanced up at the drizzle that was now settling on Ratso's hair.

"When you've cracked Klodian Skela's boat, help Tosh on the clubs."

29

Kingston, Surrey, England

Ratso sat in the rear of the Daimler limo. Next to him was Charlene, dressed in black and clutching a white hankie in her black gloves. Outside, the sky was endless pale blue against which every branch of every tree was sharply edged. The early morning frost had just about thawed under the winter sun. In the middle row of the stretch limo were Charlene's sister and Frankie, her insipid-looking husband, who had a thick ginger moustache to match his ginger comb-over. Over milky Nescafé and biscuits, he had bored Ratso rigid, full of crap about his job in credit control at a sanitary ware company in Folkestone.

Neil's only known relation, his brother Patrick, was working on a mining project in West Australia. He had emailed that he could not travel. The brothers had not seen each other in seventeen years and Patrick's indifferent tone was loud and clear. Charlene's brother was on an oil rig in the Falklands and was not attending. Neil had a handful of drinking buddies, so Ratso expected maybe a dozen or so mourners to be at the church.

Ratso had felt very close to Charlene, enjoyed her squeezing his hand as they left Wolsey Drive. She was staring straight ahead, her thoughts goodness knew where. Yet his thoughts kept drifting back to the new evidence that Tosh and Jock had gathered. In the silence, the details swirled around his restless mind. As the Daimler turned into Fernhill Gardens, he wondered how Tosh was getting on in the O.P. vehicle—presumably okay, as Ratso's phone was silent in his pocket.

Occasionally Ratso glanced at Charlene and gave her what he hoped was a reassuring smile. She seemed well in control, not tearful, just quiet and tense. He guessed the tears would come during the service. Suddenly, Ratso's phone rang, grotesquely intrusive to the chilly silence as the limo glided slowly toward the cemetery behind the hearse. Frankie, the credit controller, turned round and glared at Ratso. "Turn that bloody thing off. Got no respect?"

Ratso glared at the irritating sod. "Look, chum. Neil was murdered and don't you forget it. I can't. I'm on duty twenty-four-seven. Got it?" He watched the absurd moustache disappear as the boring little man turned away. Ratso answered the call. It was Tosh.

"Right bog-up, boss. Our van's just been sideswiped by a delivery vehicle. About two minutes from the cemetery. Not our driver's fault. But by the time the traffic boys arrive…"

"Yeah, yeah." Ratso had a big decision to make.

"We'll never make it. Plan B? You want me in the church?"

"What you wearing?" Tosh got as far as explaining he was wearing a lilac T-shirt and jeans before Ratso stopped him. "I've got the North Face job."

Ratso's mind was racing. It was at moments like this that you earned your crust or screwed up. "Grab a camera with a decent zoom and skulk somewhere close by. *Skulk* means discreet, okay?"

"You got it, boss. Where are you?"

Ratso wiped the window that had started to mist over. "Driving along Richmond Road. We'll be ten to fifteen depending on traffic on the gyratory."

He ended the call. Immediately, Charlene turned to him. "I'm glad." Her face was sincere. Ratso looked back, puzzled. "Glad you're on Neil's case. I thought…"

"You're right. DCI Caldwell's running the show but…I mean, Neil was a mate. I'm doing what I can." The gratitude in Charlene's eyes made him feel uncomfortable deceiving her about this…and perhaps too about his conflicting emotions. She gripped his hand tighter and he felt her thigh press close against him. Ratso swallowed hard and looked away.

He peered out as the procession turned into the winding road leading to the church and cemetery. Ahead, he saw blue flashing lights of a patrol car and a motorbike. Someone Ratso did not recognise, presumably the delivery driver, was on the street corner looking like a whipped pup as he was questioned by two uniforms. Of Tosh there was no sign as they inched past the two vehicles, Ratso scanning the wing of the O.P. van. It had been crumpled deep into the deflated nearside tyre. He saw young Reynolds, the police driver in his overalls, talking on his phone.

Ratso looked away and gave Charlene another reassuring smile, hoping she would not ask questions. She squeezed his hand and then stuffed the still-dry hankie into her black shoulder bag. He offered her a Polo but she declined. "I'm told it helps," he prompted but again she shook her head. Finally the vehicle stopped. Moments later, they stood restlessly outside the church watching the pallbearers lift the casket from the rear of the leading Daimler. "Here we go, then." He grasped her elbow and they walked to the coffin, which Charlene touched briefly, staring blankly at the abundant lilies and white carnations.

Ratso never saw Tosh but Tosh saw them. He was pretending to read a headstone. In Dallas, Texas, his position would have been called *the grassy knoll*, about sixty metres from the entrance to the chapel. His loud lilac T-shirt was muted by his North Face. He felt glad of it on the chilly morning. So long as he leaned round the gravestone beside him, the camera's powerful zoom gave him a great chance to photo the very few mourners. It all looked very predictable, nobody out of place.

He had photographed the nine mourners who had awaited the arrival of the hearse. They looked like a group of pub mates, chatting spasmodically, all of them seeming to know each other. No Hogan brothers. One solitary woman of about twenty-six with a wide-brimmed black hat stood alone smoking a cigarette, gazing around her, obviously nervous. *An ex-lover, perhaps? Or a current one? Or Bardici's spy?*

Far down to his right, Tosh saw the empty grave, the earth piled up, everything ready for the burial. Nearer were low shrubs and a clump of trees, perhaps six of them, their leafy branches drooping toward the ground. *Holm oaks, probably*, he thought, grappling back to lessons at school. His casual glance changed to a stare. *Was that movement behind one of them? Surely not a mourner.* He could hear a doleful melody, perhaps an organ or canned music cutting through the crisp air. Then came the strains of "Abide with Me" being sung feebly by the few mourners.

There it was again. *Movement. The air's still. Can't be a branch swaying. A sniper? A snooper?* He crouched low and backed off, moving away from the trees, the singing fading with each step as he dodged and ducked from one headstone to another. He headed up the slope away from the church, planning to turn back once he was positioned above, behind and beyond the trees. If it worked, he would end up concealed close to but behind the unknown watcher. One thing was obvious: whoever it was had a sniper's view of the grave.

In short bursts, still crouching low and panting with nervous tension, he travelled a good forty metres beyond the trees before circling. Was it one of DCI Caldwell's team? *Possible. But poofter shoes had been told by his superiors to back off. A toady like Caldwell wouldn't risk his career by defying orders. So if not Caldwell, who? Bardici?*

Okay. Assume it is Bardici. He's not out to shoot Ratso. Doesn't know him. But Charlene and the other mourners? The mysterious bit in the big hat? Surely not. But... A nasty uncomfortable thought struck him, went right through him. The bacon buttie with brown sauce he'd devoured in the van crashed through his intestines like lead falling from a roof.

If Bardici sees me, he'll not know I'm a copper. He might think that but even worse he might assume I'm a Hogan gofer—one who doesn't want to be seen at the funeral. So where does that leave me? Not in an effing good place at all. Tosh's mind and stomach were both in turmoil as he covered the last few metres, moving slowly down the slope, pausing behind the occasional headstone to catch his breath.

Now his damned bladder was sending him unwelcome messages too, adding to the pressures from the buttie and the toast, cereal and last night's chicken korma. He checked the time: perhaps four minutes till the mourners emerged. Then, depending on what the mystery man was doing, he could race to the chapel and find the lav. *Christ!* Holding on while crouching was bleeding agony.

He reached an oak that stood a good eighty feet tall with a massive trunk. He edged in behind it and took the pressure off his knees, easing himself into a standing position for the first time in ten minutes. His innards felt better for not being squeezed and he started to relax as he worked out where the figure had been. It had to be close now and just down the slope.

Nothing. Nobody. Zilch. He was sure he was in the right place, maybe thirty metres from the tree with the broken branch that he had used as a benchmark. Had he been mistaken? Had it just been a seasonal robin fluttering its wings? He peered round the other side of the trunk and was rewarded with a clear view. There he was: crouching down behind the next tree, a camera next to him on the mossy earth. No sniper's rifle. He let out a long, low sigh of relief. This was no hired killer. This was someone interested in who'd attended the service. *A copper, then.*

At that moment, the vicar and coffin appeared, its silver corners glinting in the noontime sun. Ratso shuffled out with Charlene's head almost resting on his left shoulder, their pace slow behind the pallbearers. Tosh saw the watcher in front of him fiddle with the camera and then focus it on the empty grave.

Decision time. Tosh knew Ratso would give him hell if his only photo was a rear view of a dark green hooded anorak and black jeans. Tongue lashings from Ratso were rare but memorable. He would have to move again. *Risky but a calculated risk.* The watcher was photographing the procession. *Go for it!*

Slowly, Tosh stepped away from his cover. If the man turned round, there was no hiding place till he reached a solitary bush twelve metres away. But why should he turn round? He was intent only on the people in front of him. The ground beneath Tosh's feet was soft and his progress silent and swift. His destination was a scrubby bush that stood only about five feet high.

Its evergreen nature would be perfect cover while he captured at least a side-on view and hopefully even better.

"I am the Resurrection and the Life." The priest's words carried up the slope on the still morning while the watcher snapped countless pictures. *Five metres to the bush,* thought Tosh, his quarry now just fifteen metres away. *Five metres to safety.* He slowed slightly, doubling his care to avoid anything that would make a noise. Four metres. Three. Two. At that moment, a pigeon flew from the bush, its wings cracking like a rifle shot in the stillness.

The photographer jumped and looked round, totally shocked.

But not as shocked as Tosh when he realized who he had been watching.

His sphincter strained under the renewed pressure and he struggled to contain himself. For a second, their eyes met but then the watcher turned and ran across the hillock toward the cemetery gates.

Had he been recognised?
Had he, hell!
Christ! He needed to tell Ratso. And quick.

30

Clapham, South London

Ratso went through the motions at Wolsey Drive—handing round ham and tomato sandwiches and offering cans of lager or slugs of scotch. But his heart was never in it, not since he had taken Tosh's call. It was a sinister and unexpected development—even worse if Tosh had been recognised, as seemed inevitable.

Despite mounting frustration with the mindless chitchat, out of politeness Ratso lingered at the wake till just after three. For a time, he amused himself by irritating Frankie, the brother-in-law from Folkestone, while seemingly playing the good host with Charlene. But as the clumsy-looking brown clock, a relic of the 1950s, struck three, he could take no more. While listening with half an ear to stories about Neil's antics in a pub in Mitcham, inwardly he was cursing the delivery driver who had smashed the O.P. van—and even more vehemently regretting his own decision to let Tosh attend. *We'd have struck gold if only Tosh hadn't been spotted.*

Ratso whispered to Charlene as she carryied a tray of macaroons that there had been some vital developments and he had to leave. She led him into the hallway, pulling the sitting-room door closed behind them. "Will you get back tonight?" She rested her head on his shoulder and Ratso felt the enticing warmth of her body clinging to him. "My sister's not staying. Everybody will be gone soon. Todd, I'll be *so* lonely."

She squeezed him tightly and tiptoed to plant a lingering kiss on his mouth. Ratso was acutely aware of her firm breasts, prominent beneath the simple black dress and her single silver brooch. All morning, he had been admiring her shapely figure and until Tosh's call, he had regretted that her sister was overnighting. *Lust over logic.* But Tosh's worried voice had taken the lead from his pencil. Only the inviting rustle of Charlene's black stockings was now coming close to tilting the scales.

Ratso nodded to the closed sitting-room door, where the noise was rising with the alcohol. "Charlene, if I can, I'll be back. But in my job, the only certainty is uncertainty. There's been a nasty turn of events today. One of my team caught someone watching the funeral."

Charlene gasped. "The murderer?"

Ratso was giving nothing away. He shrugged.

Charlene's eyes filled with tears and she tightened her grip. "Are you in danger? Was someone there watching you?" Ratso did not answer. "Todd. No, I couldn't bear that. Not after Neil. You're my rock. Remember?"

Ratso drew away, held her at arm's length and looked deep into her green tearful eyes. *Strange how she has tears for me and had none for Neil.* "I'll call you." He pulled her close once more, stroking the back of her neck until the stirrings started down below and he pulled away.

Back in Clapham, he went straight to his office, black coffee in hand. The room smelled stale despite the cleaner's lemon-scented spray. He summoned Tosh and Jock and they squeezed in, both clutching their own paper cups of coffee. As they sat down, he removed the black tie and hung his suit jacket behind the door.

"Jock. You're one step removed from this deep shit. What's your take?"

"Boss, this last ten minutes it's a whole lot bloody deeper. I've just had the coroner's officer on the blower. Yesterday he hadna interviewed Mrs Rosafa Skela. *Too distraught*, the widow said. But they took her statement last night." Ratso saw he was holding a document. Jock handed over Rosafa's statement and as he started to read, Ratso glanced up at Tosh and took in his ashen look.

The statement was four pages long and Ratso's eyes scanned through it, knowing whatever had spooked his sergeants would jump off the page. "Bloody hell!" Ratso threw down the statement. "We're in bigger shit than the local sewage farm. Christ! Where does this leave us?" He picked up the paper cup, drained it and screwed it up angrily, hurling it into the bin so that it bounced from side to side.

The two sergeants knew better than to interrupt Ratso's train of thought. Ratso picked up the statement and read again the paragraph on the third page—a few words that changed everything. At last he spoke.

"So Klodian Skela duped us." Ratso's stare was uncompromising. He leaned toward them, eyes hard, his fists now clenched on the desk. "This changes everything." He frowned, shaking his head in bewilderment. "She says their daughter died aged thirteen." He spoke quietly, almost as if thinking aloud. "So why did Klodian Skela confess to shagging Lindita, his own daughter?" With barely a pause, Ratso answered his own question. "Because he had to conceal her identity."

Jock looked concerned. "Did ye no read to the end?"

Ratso looked sheepish. "It gets worse? I thought I'd found the bad point." He flicked over the final page. "Jee-sus! It was Erlis Bardici's daughter!" He put down the statement and looked at each sergeant in turn. "Rosafa says when she got back from Manchester, her husband confessed he'd been screwing Bardici's daughter. Then he left the house and twenty minutes later, he jumped." He looked at Jock and saw the concern on the Scot's face. Tosh was pulling at his already long earlobe, his face a mask.

Jock's summary said it all. "Better admitting incest than to screwing Bardici's little princess. He was right."

"Tosh, ever since your call, I'd been struggling with why Lindita was watching the funeral. It made no bloody sense. I kept thinking, why would Skela send her? But that made no sense." He paused. "Now we know. Bardici sent her and she saw you." He debated whether to add more. "That makes it ten times bloody worse." Ratso saw that Tosh needed no warning.

Jock stretched out an arm and put it over Tosh's shoulder. "Ye're positive she recognised you. So…ye're compromised. Big time." Ratso and Jock exchanged a glance before Jock continued, his voice low. "Suppose Terry Fenwick *was* suspicious and had checked up on ye. Did he see your ID?"

"Yeah, briefly. I flashed it at him but he'd have learned nothing in that nanosecond."

"The receptionist had yer name from when ye made the appointment. So he sends Lindita. Point two: we must *assume* Bardici knows you interviewed Skela about the Range Rover."

Tosh clutched at a straw. "He wouldn't know Skela was interviewed. Lindita would never have told her dad she and Skela were shagging."

Ratso's glare was as sharp as his tone. "Three: he knows you were watching the funeral. Four: we don't know if he is aware of your visit to Fenwick's office. But I fear the worst." He spread out his hands despairingly. "What a goddamned mess! He now knows or at least fears he is under suspicion for Neil Shalford's death *and* the burning of the Range Rover." Ratso's eyes closed as he struggled to get 360-degree vision on the new situation. "And what Bardici knows, we have to assume Zandro knows. That means Zandro could be aware we're after him despite the official line that he's off radar." He stood up in a sudden movement to bang the desk from a greater height. The remains of Jock's coffee spilled as the flimsy cup toppled over but nobody moved. "Gentlemen, Operation Clam is…well and truly fucked."

Tosh stared out of the window as Ratso stood with hand on chin for a moment before sitting down. The anger had gone. Months of careful planning had been blown. He spoke slowly, wearily. "Bardici's no fool. He'll suspect now that Neil was working for us, not the Hogans." He turned another page in his notebook. "When they burying Skela?"

"Tomorrow afternoon."

"Right. We watch Skela's funeral." His lips narrowed as he added sardonically, "From an O.P. van, unless there's a good viewing point from an adjacent building. Tosh, I'll keep you on the team but never again where you may be seen by Bardici or his daughter."

"But, boss, Bardici doesn't…"

Ratso cut him off with another hard-eyed stare. "I'm not taking any chances." He then turned to the Scot, who was mopping up his coffee with a tissue. "Right. Jock. Before we discuss the club lists, tell me about this boat Skela was on about. What do we know?"

"Boris Zandro owns a yacht. A rich man's toy. More like a cruise ship. Helipad. Twelve staterooms. Jet bikes. Disco. Home cinema. Ye ken the stuff. It's called *Tirana Queen*. That was in the old file. Today it's heading for somewhere in the eastern Med."

"So Bardici wasn't going to the Bahamas for anything connected to her."

"Aye, right enough but on Grand Bahama there are plenty of wee fishing boats. Some for inshore and others for big-game fishing for tourists, as well as commercial operations."

"Bardici wouldn't be interested in them, surely."

Jock disagreed, explaining he might use a fishing boat for offloading his Class A from a bigger ship.

"Or, I suppose, he might have wanted one for *exporting* cocaine from the Bahamas to a bigger ship that could cross the Atlantic." Ratso was thinking aloud and didn't sound or look too convinced by his own point.

Jock checked his notes, written in red pen with lots of underlining. "Then there are the pleasure craft. All sizes. Hundreds, maybe thousands of small sailing boats, cabin cruisers, speedboats, plus the top-end toys. Many of the smaller ones are for sale. The recession."

"But would Zandro send a thug like Bardici to check out a purchase? Bardici's front is running a corner shop. His value to Zandro is as an enforcer. Thirteen stiffs and counting."

Ratso stood up, yawned noisily and stretched. Outside, it was now dark and the wind was edging up to gale force, rattling the windows. For a moment, he thought of Charlene, probably alone now with the wind howling round the house. Waiting for him. Hoping for him. He should be there. But…he checked his watch.

"Okay, Jock, Tosh. What do you think?"

Tosh, who had been very quiet, nodded distractedly. He had been reliving the visit to Terry Fenwick's office and the confrontation in the graveyard. "I'm with ye, boss," concluded Jock. "Ye send Bardici to the Bahamas to sort out a *prob-lem*. Scaring the crap out of folk. That's why he was there. But somehow it's connected to a boat." Jock paused. "There's one other thing. There are two shipyards, boatyards, call them what ye like."

"Small craft?"

"Och, no. Cruise ships—the big ones. Cargo ships, big and small. No huge supertankers but plenty of freighters big enough to carry a shiteload of dope."

"You checked them out? What's going on in the yards?" For the first time Ratso sounded interested.

"Remember the detective constable who came over from the Bahamas? Darren Roberts. We took him up West."

Ratso turned from the window and smiled. "Yeah. Good guy."

"He's just been promoted again—up from detective sergeant. He's a DI now. So I had a wee word. He's taking a shufti at the two yards, checking out what's going on."

"Long shot but that's good." Ratso turned to Tosh, whose face was pallid. "You look knackered."

"I'll get over it."

Ratso nodded. He knew that if Bardici got hold of Tosh, the end would not be quick. The memory of Neil's todger was still vivid. "From now on, till I say otherwise, your profile is lower than a snake's arsehole. Take no chances. Different routes home." He saw the fear on Tosh's face and toned down his vehemence. "Look, Tosh: Bardici's a killing machine, like a giant schnauzer bred to attack. He needs no reason to kill and you've given him one. If Fenwick was suspicious and his daughter mentions you, the jigsaw's complete. I can't take that chance. Fenwick may even know you work from here, in which case, so may Bardici."

"No fear from Fenwick," protested Tosh, who looked like a dead man walking.

"Y'know what Bardici did to Neil." He saw Tosh flinch and his bulk shift uneasily on the chair as he wiped one hand nervously down his face. "We know zilch about Fenwick or Zandro's lieutenants but Bardici won't believe that." He saw Tosh nibbling his finger nervously. "So maybe don't even go home; stay somewhere different. Just for a while."

"Ye can stay with me," Jock offered. "I've a spare room."

"The missus would divorce me. It wouldn't take much."

The comment proved everything Ratso had always felt about coppers being married and he sighed in sympathy. Tosh's wife's tongue was the stuff of legend. "We'd done so well, so bloody well this past day or two. Months and months of investigations and Bardici never twigged we were onto him. All buggered by a pig-ignorant slob admiring his tattoos while driving his delivery van."

"And that bleeding pigeon," Tosh added with a thin smile.

Ratso snorted angrily. "Okay. Let's move on—think positive. The club lists." Ratso had read the report what seemed like a lifetime away, on the train going to the funeral. "I've seen the members' names. A pretty good cross-section of blue bloods, captains of industry, judges, actors, media types and professionals." Tosh said nothing, barely even looking at his colleagues. Ratso doubted he'd even heard the invitation to contribute. "So, Jock? What happened when you dropped by the clubs with the photos this morning?"

"First, Terry Fenwick lives well but not flash. House in Bickley, worth just under a million. Wife. Two sons being educated at Tonbridge School. Drives a Chelsea Tractor. Wife has a Mazda. Member of the local tennis club. Pretty typical for a solicitor of his age."

"Check out both his partners."

Jock scribbled a note before continuing. "Fenwick's a member of all four clubs—has lunch or dinner in one or other every week."

"Go on."

"Sometimes, he stays overnight at the Poulsden in Hill Street."

"A shag-a-thon?"

Jock shook his head. "Impossible. No women."

"Who did you speak to? Discreet, is he?"

"The club secretary. Roger Herbison. Good guy. Ex-military. One of the chaps. At each place, I spoke about Fenwick only to the club secretary, not the main entrance staff. I'll come to them in a moment."

"Reliable, then?"

"The club secretaries? I'd say! Shit-scared about any scandal. That was the reaction I got from every one. *Not on our doorstep.*"

"And Boris Zandro? His name appeared nowhere. Tell me he's a member."

Jock laughed. "I will if it's what ye want to hear…but it's no true. He's no a member of any of them."

"But?" Ratso looked expectant.

"Zandro *is* known at each of them as an occasional guest. Comes in for lunch or dinner. Never with Fenwick. The porters never mentioned that name once. At the Regent, Zandro's usually a guest of Lord Brockstone or Sir Ian Templemore. The door staff recognised him but none of the others in the photos." Jock pushed across the photos he had used—all suited individuals, well turned out, the types you would expect to find in London clubs with pedigrees dating back two or three hundred years. Ratso looked at the photo of Boris Zandro and his knuckles whitened at the aura of respectability and charm.

"He gets signed in?"

"No, not exactly. Typically, the front entrance just need to know from their members who to expect as a guest."

Ratso was disappointed; he had hoped for a paper trail. "Anything else?"

"At the Metro, Zandro's sometimes a guest of Lord Tramoyne from the Arts Council. The Conduit, he's been there just once as the guest of some songwriter I'd never heard of. At the Poulsden, he's usually the guest of Sir Antony Pulvenhof, the city financier, or Lord Brewham, the former prime minister."

Ratso's voice rose in excited enthusiasm as he stood up— his stand-up, sit-down routine, familiar to his watchers when the adrenalin was flowing. "Jock! Tosh! There's the link. Bent solicitor and Zandro with regular chances to meet, to exchange messages, whatever but never seen together or linked at all." He fell silent as he turned to watch a bus go by beneath the huge swaying trees running toward the Common.

"Fenwick's partners are no members at any of the clubs."

"I still want them checked out."

"Fenwick doesn't use the Poulsden that often. Never goes to their steam room or sauna. Rarely goes into the library. Doesna' spend hours in the bar. Just the occasional lunch or dinner." Jock looked at his listeners in turn. "But as I said, sometimes he kips there."

Tosh had been silent, locked in his own private hell. "Being a member of the Poulsden is the dog's bollocks. Isn't that what you said, Jock? Royalty and all that. Perhaps it's a status thing for Fenwick."

Ratso was dismissive, his fists still clenched. "Nothing about Fenwick suggests he's interested in profile. No, he's a member there for a reason. Let's prove what it is."

He doodled for moment, drawing interlocking squares, fired up. Then he looked at them both, his eyes once again alight after looking so drained just moments before.

"We're coming to get you, Boris Zandro." Ratso said the words slowly and with relish. Suddenly, they did not ring so hollow. "Check out Terry Fenwick's travels. We presume he yo-yos back and forward between Bickley and his office. But let's see if occasionally he goes to the Bahamas, Gibraltar—any offshore places. I reckon he could be a key part of the money laundering, setting up companies and trusts to receive the drug profits once laundered, then buying properties, shares, art, whatever. Let's prove it."

"But it's still dirty money, even if he uses Persil on every note." Jock made the word *Persil* sound like a long wash at the Laundromat. "We need to see if any of these companies like Egent, Oulsden, Etro show up in Gibraltar. Could be he uses variations of the same name over there."

"Sure. But he needs a sloppy or corrupt banker and maybe some relaxed, complacent professionals in Gibraltar."

"The City's full of greedy banks, even the big clearers. So why not in Gibraltar?"

"Why not indeed!" Ratso stood again and clapped Tosh on the shoulder, though the sergeant had contributed nothing. "Cheer up, Tosh. You've got life insurance."

"Fat lot of good that'll do *me*. I'm not dying just to make the missus rich." Tosh was beyond banter. "I'm going down the Nags Head. Gonna sink a skinful. Anyone up for it?"

Ratso shook his head. "Not tonight, Tosh. But not the Nags Head. Go somewhere different. The Flute & Flag. Remember my warning, right?"

"I'll join ye," Jock said. "And maybe a fish supper after?"

The two sergeants were almost out of the door when Ratso stopped them. "Jock, check out if there's any pattern to the club visits. Particular days. Know what I mean?"

"Aye, right enough. But I dinna think we'll get lucky."

"Try anyway."

"We going to follow Zandro?"

Ratso shook his head. "He never does *nothing* that isn't kosher." He broke into a huge smile, cheeks creased in places rarely used. "Waste of time watching…just yet." He opened his arms expansively. "But now we have the golden key. Terry Fenwick. Let's use it." After the sergeants had closed the door, he said it again. "We're coming to get you, Boris Zandro."

He felt good. Good enough to trek back to Kingston Station. Good enough to buy a couple of bottles of red and help Charlene get over her loneliness.

31

Fort Lauderdale, Florida
Detective Kirsty-Ann Webber yawned, though it was barely 10 a.m. Leon's teething pains had given her a tough night. She stretched across her cluttered desk to answer her ringing phone. It was Bucky Buchanan. "Mind droppin' by?"

"Now?"

"Sure. Convenient?"

"On my way, Chief." She immediately felt more alert. She'd done two hours of paperwork and needed a break. She stretched to her full height of six feet, arms high above her head, the bottom of her fawn-tailored slacks rising to show a hint of ankle and black shoes with a generous bow on top. She tossed her hair into place and touched up her pale pink lipstick. Satisfied, she set off down the long corridor. She spurned the elevator and climbed to the top floor, nodding distractedly to colleagues who muttered support.

What could the chief want? Probably that damned car chase again! But just maybe it was about the disappearance of Lance Ruthven. She hesitated before knocking and then entered the anteroom to the chief's office, which straddled the end corner of the building and boasted large plate-glass windows with great views of nothing worth looking at. "Go right on in," said the bespectacled secretary.

"Ah! K-A, take a seat." Buchanan was in a short-sleeved shirt, his arms bronzed and covered in light brown hair. He stretched to pour her a black coffee. "Family okay?" It was his regular opening remark unless there was trouble ahead. She relaxed at once.

"Just great. But Leon's teething. That guy has the loudest yell this side of the Rockies but hell, I wouldn't change a thing."

The chief grinned in agreement. He had five kids from eighteen down. "You gotta know when you're blessed." He flicked open a slim folder. "This is not about the media feeding frenzy. Toughing it out's done good; it's goin' quiet. And this is not about Lance Ruthven either." Kirsty-Ann raised a pencil-thin eyebrow. "Not yet, anyway." The chief's grin was infectious. "We had a request from London. A guy they regard as an enforcer for a drug baron entered Florida with a false passport and went on to Grand Bahama. They know that was his destination but..." He sipped a 7-Up. "They don't know why he was there."

"Not our problem, is it, Chief?"

His smile was wolfish. "Come on, K-A. I wouldn't be wasting your time and mine for no reason. You work it out."

"Brit killer goes to Grand Bahama. Lance Ruthven goes missing, probably in Grand Bahama." She tapped her head with a well-manicured finger. "US State Department honcho parties with London drug enforcer? Not sure any jury will buy that." Her dry humour was well received. "What's the connection?"

"None yet that they've made in London."

Kirsty-Ann smiled as a thought struck her. "But we know Ruthven visited Afghanistan."

Buchanan whistled through his teeth. "Hey, K-A. We need guys like you out there." He pushed the file toward her. "Right on."

She first looked at the two photos—one of Erlis Bardici and the other from his false ID for Mujo Zevi. She flicked over the few pages of notes. "Thirteen suspected executions in three years, the most recent just two weeks ago. Don't those Brit cops ever catch their murderers?"

"He kills scumbags. Does Scotland Yard a favour. But they're cutting the guy some slack to get evidence to arrest their untouchable, a drug baron called Boris Zandro."

"Okay but why would Bardici want to kill a State Department high-up? Even one who worked as a diplomat in the world's heroin capital?"

"No reason. Yet."

Kirsty-Ann laughed. "C'mon, Chief! Give. Whaddaya holding back?"

"Both on Grand Bahama the same weekend. Both using a false ID."

"And Ruthven never returns. That's game, set and match! Slam dunk! High-fives all round." They both laughed.

"There'll be fingerprint ID for Bardici—once when arriving from London and once on returning from Grand Bahama."

Kirsty-Ann scanned the details. "These papers were sent over by a Detective Sergeant Jock Strang care of his boss, Detective-Inspector Todd Holtom. Know them?"

Buchanan offered her a cookie. "Never met them but Todd—he's called Ratso by his pals--he's helped us a few times with tips. Y'know, drug stuff. We owe him."

"Okay, Chief. What next?"

The chief shrugged. "Maybe you get a trip to Freeport. Get a break from the baby. That's if your mother can cope?" He saw her cautious smile, almost wistful, as if a night or two without comforting Leon would be more than welcome. "Washington liked your work and would rather have you check it out than get the island's cops involved. Discretion, I am told, is still king."

"You reckon Ruthven's a spy working at State? And maybe close to exposing Zandro's drug empire?"

If the chief knew, he was not saying. He looked out of the window, staring at an ugly red-brick. "Guy's bound to know confidential stuff. He worked the Middle East for ten years."

"This Ratso, he over on the island now?"

The Chief shook his head and patted down the thinning hair on his tanned scalp. "He's still trying to figure out why Bardici went there with a false ID. But as you'll read, he...er...lost an informant. His trail is cold."

"So I guess he wants fingerprints from Homeland Security and anything suspicious at the airports. Like him meeting someone." Kirsty-Ann saw the chief glance at his wall clock. She rose at once. "Anything more on Ruthven?"

"Nix. Just stay alert. I know *you* don't need to be told that, K-A."

With a smile, the detective turned and left.

32

Kingston, Surrey, England

With a bunch of flowers and two bottles of Argentinean Malbec, Ratso felt a bit like a kid on his first date as Charlene let him in. She gave him a kiss in the doorway. Not caring if Caldwell was snooping again, he deftly kicked the door shut. He'd picked up the last rather tired flowers at the shop near Kingston Station, a place that did a roaring trade selling peace offerings to city gents returning home late.

"They're beautiful," Charlene breathed in his ear. "Thank you." She stepped back to stare at him. "This evening, tonight—we start a new chapter. The past is gone. We can hold hands in public. Be an item. Go shopping, the cinema, *be seen together.*" Her green eyes were heavy with intent.

Ratso felt queasy as he listened, trying to look more enthusiastic than he felt. No, he wasn't like a kid on his first date. He felt more like a co-respondent slipping in for a quickie while hubby was working nights. But she didn't want that. She was talking commitment. *And with Neil dead less than two weeks. Buried just ten hours ago. I mean, Charlene's just great—smart, cute, sexy, fun. But I need a no-strings deal.* "Sorry I'm so late. But I brought these too." He pulled the two bottles of red from a carrier.

"Perfect! I've got lasagne on standby. It'll take twenty minutes."

"Just time for a shower, then. Okay?" He hesitated. "But I've no change of clothing. I came straight here."

Charlene laughed. "Can't have you sitting around in the nuddies, can we? You'll find Neil's dressing gown hanging on the bathroom door." She eyed him up and down. "But it won't cover, er, everything."

"I'll chance it. But no peeking on the stairs." He was rewarded with a dirty chuckle. *What in hell am I doing? Silly question, Ratso. Your dick's in charge. Not for the first or last time either.*

The purple hem of Neil's dressing gown barely reached his thighs and the material strained across his back. As he'd looked at himself in a full-length mirror, he felt even queasier. *Dead man's shoes. Wasn't that the expression?*

"Get you!" Charlene giggled as she saw him, not in the least abashed by him wearing Neil's clothes.

"Besides you, something else smells good. I'm famished. I'll open the wine." He joined her in the kitchen and busied himself with finding glasses and unscrewing the bottle tops. Meanwhile, Charlene lit a cinnamon-scented candle and adjusted the cutlery on the small square table with its bistro-style red check cloth. She disappeared into the next room and soon the soft, sultry sound of Sade singing "No Ordinary Love" seemed to come from all corners of the room.

"You sit down and pour. I'll dish up," she told him as she sashayed over to retrieve the lasagne from the oven. He admired the wiggle and then the deep red as the Malbec tumbled into the glasses. Moments later she joined him, sitting opposite but very much within reach. "Here's to the future." She raised her glass and chinked with his.

"But never forgetting the past." He looked into the endless depths of her eyes and saw them harden for a moment, as if memories of life with Neil were far from her mind. "Hard to believe what we've been through today. And I'm not just talking of the funeral."

"Meaning?"

He quickly explained about the Observation Van being in an accident and the funeral being watched by a woman. "Unexpected! Can't say no more than that."

"You knew her, then?"

"Yes." He spoke the word slowly, realising he might be painting himself into a very unwanted corner.

"And Caldwell. How's he doing? He's pretty smart."

"Smart as in Carnaby Street or smart as in street smart?"

Charlene paused, head cocked appealingly to one side. "He dresses well, I'll give him that. But he's a clever bastard. Know what I mean?"

Ratso nodded. "Oh, yes." He played with the beef and tomato sauce. "Delicious. But Caldwell? I've not heard of any progress."

"What about you? You getting anywhere?"

"It's Caldwell's case, not mine. But if I hear anything, I'll give him a bell. His sort makes me puke." He wrinkled his nose in disgust. "Loafers...tasselled and all."

"His sergeant told me he was a high-flier."

"Yeah. Right up his own arse. Let's change the subject, shall we?"

Charlene fell silent for a moment and then brightened. "You got a load of Frankie today!."

"A right tosser! I know more about bad debts from selling sanitary ware than I ever wanted to know." He smiled. "I suggested he went round collecting with a pair of Dobermans. He thought I was being serious!"

She laughed in an exaggerated fashion, as if everything in her life tonight was in full, glorious Technicolor. "You're right! Can't see what my sis sees in him. He's not just boring—he's boring *and* unattractive." She clinked glasses again. "Unlike you." Her other hand stretched out and stroked his. "Todd, y'know I've dreamed about an evening like this ever since we first met, that night up West." Ratso looked at her quizzically. "I wanted so much, y'know, you and me spending time together. Quiet dinners. The cinema. Dancing in clubs. Picnics in Kew Gardens."

"You're a dark horse. I had no idea. That must have been... God... years ago. That joint in Bruton Street." He pushed aside his empty plate and wiped his lips.

"Don't get me wrong. I never strayed." Ratso's face was blank and he said nothing but Neil had told him differently. He reckoned she had done her thing with more than one work colleague while he had been away. What had she said the other day – *we had an understanding*. Charlene gazed dreamily across the table. "Sometimes, I just thought, *well, sod it, two can play that game*. But I never did. Why? Because it was you I fantasised about. You were the one I always wanted to, y'know..." She squeezed his hand tighter. He still did not believe her—certainly not the faithful bit.

Ratso cleared his throat. "Since it's confession time," he spoke slowly, "I can only say I always reckoned Neil was a lucky sod. But I never thought of, well...making a play for you. Never thought you were interested."

"Good things come to them that wait. Isn't that an expression? And I'm not just talking about you. I'm talking about me." She blew a kiss over the candle, which flickered in the slight breeze. "I'm not looking for wham, bam, thank you ma'am. I need a relationship. I need you. And from today, I'm free."

Ratso gathered the crumbs from his bread roll and marshalled them together. Then he looked across the check tablecloth and absorbed her loose-fitting cream cutaway blouse, an open invitation to feast. "Charlene—I mean, you don't feel... well, getting serious like this is just a bit hasty. We were only burying your *numero uno* and my good mate this morning."

The remark did not go down well and Ratso saw the irritation on her face before she rose sharply and rounded the table. Standing beside him, she leaned forward, kissing him hard, forcefully, on the lips. Ratso felt himself pushed against the chair back. He responded by clasping his arms round her buttocks and pulling her closer. Perfumes did little for him but nevertheless he was acutely aware of her scent. She eased back, seated herself on his lap and stroked his bare thigh. "Neil's not sitting up there on God's right hand watching us and saying *tut-tut*. He's not saying *me old mate Todd's dicking my missus too soon*. He's not saying *no sooner am I dead than the missus is getting serious for a best mate*. I don't believe any of that crap. Neil is gone. History. Six foot under. He couldn't give a damn." She kissed him again. "And neither do I."

Ratso found that his hands were caressing her buttocks rather more intensely now, sensing the outline of her briefs under the burgundy skirt. Her delicate fingers were sending a powerful message and he knew he was losing control, even if he had the will to fight. Another gentle touch and any thought of challenging her visions for the future were gone. Suddenly, he didn't give a fig either. *Forget your good intentions. Go for it, Ratso. Sod the future! For now, relax, relent and feast.*

But just as her cool, slender fingers slid between his muscled thighs, they were both startled by the intrusion of his phone, its metallic ring creating an unwanted barrier between them.

"Sorry. That could be important." He pushed her off as gently as he could and stood up. His dressing gown parted, revealing his erect manhood, which immediately seemed like an intruder in the new situation, already starting to wither as he looked round for his phone. Charlene sighed, her face tense as she followed him to retrieve it from the mantelpiece.

Ratso stood, elbow against the wall as he answered.

"Boss, it's me. Jock. Sorry but…"

Charlene flung her arms round his neck from behind him, piggy-back style, hot breath on his neck.

"It had better be important." Ratso listened, his mind somewhere between Charlene's gentle massage and the urgency in Jock's voice. He listened for maybe thirty seconds, all the while acutely aware of Charlene's excited breathing. "St George's, you said? Okay. See you there. Maybe forty minutes."

He killed the call and tousled Charlene's hair.

"I've got to go. Can you call me a minicab to go to Tooting?" She rose, her eyes that had been wild with excitement now narrowed and hard. He stroked her cheek "Sweetie, I'm sorry, really I am. Everything's changed."

"Do you really have to go?" She pouted. "This was going to be such…"

He quietened her, pressing a finger to her lips. "I know. For me too. I think you could see that I was…er, up for it."

"Is it really so important? There's enough bloody coppers in London. What's the problem?"

Ratso eased her away, more gently than he felt. If this was how she was going to be, she never would understand what it meant to be in a relationship with him. "One of my sergeants was attacked a short while ago. He's being taken to hospital, condition unknown."

33

Tooting, South London

Ratso stepped out of the minicab, still unsure whether the Pakistani drove faster than he spoke or spoke faster than he drove. He had managed the journey in twenty-six minutes flat. Ratso felt relieved to be alive and standing in the night air of Blackshaw Road. The Toyota saloon had been grimy, with no working rear seatbelts and seemingly no front suspension or brakes. The upholstery was ripped and the stuffing was such that Ratso felt something was trying to invade his back passage every time they hit a bump.

Ratso paid off the turbaned driver, making a mental note to wash his hands at the first opportunity. He glanced around to get his bearings and then strode off beside the huge red-brick building to A&E Admissions. The Christmas decorations in the brightly lit reception area did nothing to disguise the fact that this was a soulless place where endless life-or-death dramas were played out. At least fifteen worried-looking visitors awaited news from the emergency rooms down the corridor.

He spotted Jock standing close to the Christmas tree. The Scot's face was sombre but brightened when he saw Ratso. "How's Tosh?" enquired Ratso at once.

"He'll be okay. He was lucky. He's badly shaken—suspected fractured ribs, bruises and a possible fractured left ankle. The nurse says we can see him in a few minutes."

"Can we get a cup of tea here?"

Jock nodded at a machine. "I'll get you one." He started to move off but then turned. "Ye reek of curry. Chicken tikka, was it?"

Ratso cursed the minicab. "My taxi doubled as a delivery vehicle for a Pakistani restaurant in Morden. That bad, is it?"

"Bad enough to put Tosh into cardiac arrest."

"I'll wash my hands."

"That's never enough. Ye need to give yer clothes to Oxfam and then have an all-over scrub-down, a blanket bath. I'll ask yon nurse." They both laughed as Ratso headed for the Gents'. When he returned, Jock had put two steaming paper cups on a table.

"So what do we know?"

"There's a team at the scene but I'm no hopeful. The best chance is…"

Jock was interrupted by the nurse waving them over. She took them along the clinical emptiness of the corridor into a small room where Tosh was sitting up, his face turning purple down one side. Somehow, he managed a lopsided smile. The room reeked of disinfectant and floor cleaner. "Ten minutes," warned the Filipino nurse.

"Mr. Watson can take more than that. Nothing really wrong with him. He just wanted free B & B," said Ratso. The nurse appeared not to understand but she left with a smile. "So, Tosh, what happened, me old son?"

"Bruised ankle where the car hit me. Not the worst, the doc said. Two suspected cracked ribs, left side where I hit the corner of a wall." He gingerly touched his temple. "And this hurts like hell where I hit a gate."

"Okay. Take it from the top." Ratso sat down on the tubular steel chair and pulled it close.

"Good curry?" asked Tosh.

"Don't go there, or you might have a sudden relapse," Ratso growled with a wink.

"Well, after I left Jock going to the chippie, I headed home. The missus had phoned telling me to bleeding well get back home pronto. Till then I was planning on the scenic route but after her bloody rant, I went home direct, my usual route. I turned into our street, Welbeck Avenue. It was quiet as usual. It's one-way, traffic from behind me. No on-street parking allowed. Our place, number 73, is a couple hundred metres down there."

Already Ratso was scowling but Tosh continued. "So I was gone maybe ninety or a hundred metres when I heard a car swing round the corner from Trinity Road. The engine was revving a bit, so I looked back. It was accelerating, full headlights blinding me. It could have been nothing but…"

"I had warned you," interrupted Ratso, sounding more sympathetic than he felt.

"Something told me."

"Probably my warning, don't you think?" Ratso observed, rather less gently.

Tosh looked sheepish as he paused to gather his thoughts. "Then I saw the car's lights were aiming at me and I realised he was going to mount the pavement. I watched a split second longer to be sure. Next moment…bang. It was on me. Don't laugh, boss but I dived to my left. Saved my life, no question but just too late. The car hit my ankle with its front near corner. I landed half inside someone's front yard. I yelled like buggery."

"Ye were lucky," Jock commented.

"Luckier than you know. The car stopped up the road and two men ran toward me. I never saw them, mind, just heard the running footsteps. But five blokes came out of the house beside me, where they'd been playing poker. When the two from the car saw them, they hoofed it and drove off."

Ratso shared a look with Jock. Tosh saw the mounting anger on the boss's face, saw the lids of the hooded eyes close and the cheeks narrow, always sure signs of trouble. But instead of the fury he expected, Ratso's anger was cold, clipped but just as deadly. "No way can I cover your arse over this. You were warned. What in hell were…? Oh yes, the missus."

Tosh looked across at Ratso and wished he had not as he put in his mitigation. "The missus. Sounds like a shit excuse but… right, Jock?"

"Aye, ye wanted to go to the chippie but with yer marching orders from Patsy, ye left at once."

Ratso had met Patsy on a couple of occasions and Tosh had his total sympathy on that score. "No excuse, Tosh. None at all. Arthur Tennant, the AC – they'll need a full written explanation." He stood up. "The thugs were going to cart you off. Interrogate you. Or kill you straight off, if you were lucky."

Jock's face showed he had not thought that through but after the shock passed, he broke the long silence. "Ye were lucky, son." He looked down at his good mate, whose face looked even more swollen now than a few minutes before. "Ye got the vehicle make and number, of course," he joked. They all laughed, though Tosh's laughter stopped with a gasp as the searing pain spread from his ribs.

"Yeah, right. The number was PI55 OFF."

Jock looked at the two colleagues in turn. "Best hope is damage to the car."

Ratso shook his head. "They'll torch it tonight."

Jock laughed. "Two cars! Bardici will be getting a knighthood for services to the car industry." Ratso's face flickered toward a smile but no more. "I've got the boys checking every CCTV in the area. But at just gone eleven, Trinity Road is pretty busy. Unless we get lucky and catch a car actually swinging into Welbeck Avenue, it's a long shot."

Ratso stood up. "Tosh, you'd better get a bit of kip. I need you back in the morning. Seven sharp." Tosh looked at his boss, unsure how to take the remark but then managed a smile.

"Yeah, right!"

"While you're lying there putting on even more weight, you'll have time to think. I ordered you to vary your route. So what did you do? Only ponce down Glebeside Lane, business as usual." Ratso's voice lowered to a growl. "You'll get both barrels from the top brass, deservedly. Nothing I can do to protect you. Got it?"

"Sorry, boss. I never expected anything so soon."

"Bardici's a king cobra. He strikes hard and fast." Ratso saw Jock nod, fully supportive. "For now, think back to when you left Jock. That's along Glebeside Lane, into Trinity Road and up to Welbeck Avenue. My guess, no, *my hope* is these bastards were parked near the nick, on the off chance. You probably saw the vehicle."

"Or they were following me all evening."

"Bardici's crapping himself wondering what we know. Maybe Zandro is too." Ratso looked at Jock. "Here's the problem. If these thugs were not there by chance, we're turning the clock back."

"Ye mean…the bad old days?" Jock's eyes were like slits.

"Someone leaking, yes. Someone on Bardici's payroll who provided Tosh's address."

Jock scratched his head. "Someone higher up."

The uncomfortable comment hung heavily in the harsh light of the sparse room. Ratso was about to disagree when they heard a shrewish voice in the corridor and the Filipino nurse entered with Patsy Watson. She was a bit younger than Tosh, about thirty. Ever since his second meeting with her on a quiz night, Ratso had avoided her. She had a face that was perpetually disagreeable, mouth downturned, lips thin and eyes as hard as Charlene's were melting. Her nose was sharp, her jaw narrow with a receding chin. She wore no makeup and her hairstyle was a severe bun, adding to her disagreeable image. But no doubt with Tosh's job, she had plenty enough to put up with.

Whether she had always looked and behaved like a shrew or whether being married to a copper had scarred her, Ratso had no idea. He forced himself to mutter hello but Patsy ignored both him and Jock as she stared menacingly at her husband. Ratso had no wish to stick around.

"Come on, Jock, we've a lot to be getting on with." He pushed the Scot to the door, leaving Tosh to fend for himself. "Cheers, Tosh," he said with a wink that Mrs Watson could not see. Then he was out of the door.

As he and Jock hovered in the corridor, the rasping tirade started. "What you been doing, then? Drunk again? Falling over, was you? Drinking down the pub when the kids was expecting you bleeding hours ago? You always was a selfish bastard. I got better things to be doing than visiting A & E after you get pissed." There was a slight pause for breath. "You been eating bleedin' curry again! This room stinks. I warned you—no more curry, stinking the place out, farting everywhere. Selfish sod."

Jock started to snigger. "A right mess ye've got him into, boss, you and that minicab." Ratso grinned and urged them away with his head. When they were out of earshot, Jock continued, "So what now?"

"Stay here till someone from uniform can keep guard twenty-four-seven. We can't take any chances."

Jock thought for a moment. "Maybe Tosh visiting Terry Fenwick was the trigger, not the funeral?"

Ratso did not like being reminded of that. He sucked in his cheeks. "Maybe Tosh wasn't as smart as he thought in the lawyer's office." He reached the main entrance and pulled up the collar on his windcheater, grimacing as he saw the sleet now falling on the path outside. "I might just make the last Tube from Tooting Broadway. Anything but Anwar's Luxury Minicabs."

"Hammersmith, is it, boss?" There was a touch of insolence in Jock's eyes.

Ratso played it dead-bat, a real Geoff Boycott–style forward defensive. "At this time of night? Where else?" But as the sleet slapped against his cheeks, the image of Charlene alone and the miserable way the evening had ended left him uncomfortable. Still, no way was he heading back to see her. The moment had passed. A slice off a cut loaf was one thing but he didn't want to own a bakery. More importantly, his life, his lifestyle, was not for sale. *For once, Ratso, let your brain rule your dick.* He decided to phone her in the morning.

When he got to Tooting Broadway, the station was locked for the night. He looked up and down the High Street. If he was lucky, a black cab would be heading into Central London after dropping off in the suburbs. Trouble was, he didn't feel lucky.

And he wasn't.

It was nearly two when he stumbled into his apartment, the air chill and the atmosphere desolate. The central heating had been off for hours and no way was he going to put it on now. But he wasn't ready for bed. *Tired? Yes. Exhausted? Definitely.* But he was beyond sleep. There were too many loose ends troubling him. Tosh, the boat in Grand Bahama, the role of Bardici's daughter, a possible leak...Charlene alone in bed with her baby-doll nightie.

He drew the curtains, switched on the main lights and then used the dimmer. From his collection he selected Guns N' Roses and set it to a volume that was almost intrusive on those above, below and next to his open-plan living room. He felt hungry but there wasn't much in the fridge except cheddar cheese. The bread was several days too old but he toasted a couple of slices with cheese and sprayed it liberally with sauce. He was about to open a can of lager when he changed plans and made a mug of instant, into which he poured a slug of Cointreau—*to keep the cold out*, as he told himself, tipping in a second slug for luck.

Munching and listening, he flicked through the accumulation of text messages that had come in during the previous ninety minutes—endless admin with just the occasional nugget from the scene of Tosh's attack. Then he remembered there would be cricket from Perth. He turned off the hard rock, flicked on the widescreen digital TV and was quickly transported into the warmth of Western Australia, where once again the Aussie bowlers were under the cosh from England's top order.

When he awoke, his mouth parched, his legs stiff, England had crashed to 198 all out. While he had slept in blissful ignorance, the Aussie bowlers had suddenly found the right length and destroyed the cream of English batting in twelve overs. Beside him, the now-empty mug lay sideways, coffee and liqueur spilled across the already stained carpet. He felt a wreck, every limb aching from sleeping in the chair. His mouth was furred, his eyes bleary, his toes numb. His hands were frozen and he was stiff in all the wrong places.

He checked the time. Ten minutes to five. The heating would not kick in for another forty minutes. Slowly, he stood up, stared blankly at the spilled mug and then began a long, slow stretch, really forcing his arms up toward the ceiling. Then he touched his toes, did some hip swivels of which Elvis would have been proud and headed for the kettle. He wondered about Charlene. *Too early to ring her.* He'd wait till he was in Clapham.

On second thoughts, he grabbed the Blackberry and sent a text asking how she was and saying it had been a right bummer how the evening got screwed up. But she had to understand. He was a twenty-four-seven kind of copper and that would never change. He ended the message with three X's but then deleted two of them before transmitting.

34

Clapham, South London
The pavements on Glebeside Lane were icy, so Ratso's usual brisk walk was much slower and more cautious than usual. The overnight sleet had frozen and the sight of a young woman falling heavily outside Hammersmith Station had been a good reminder to take care. On his headphones, Queen pounded away. His new iPhone started vibrating and he paused to check it under a street light. It was from Charlene, timed at 6:20. *Sorry. My fault. But I had the hots for U. Maybe C U tonight? XXX.*

Ratso crossed the gritted road and swung his arms faster to get his circulation going. He went straight to a greasy, its windows almost opaque from the condensation. Alf's Caff was not his scene—he had no intention of joining the Met's unimpressive obesity statistics with three bangers and six rashers of streaky—but the disturbed night and the freezing temperatures had made the prospect of a bacon and egg bap washed down with piping hot coffee irresistible.

He carried the hot paper bag to his desk. There he munched through the bap, HP sauce oozing onto the paper napkin as the laptop booted up. He checked the London headlines but there was no mention of Tosh; neither was there any report of a burned-out vehicle found. *Give it time*, he murmured.

He phoned St George's and asked to be put through to Tosh but the nurse said he was sedated and to call back later. *At least Patsy didn't murder him.* He had scarcely put the phone down before Jock was on the line. "We still meeting at nine, boss?"

"Except for Tosh."

"Ye free now?"

"If it's good news, yes."

"I'll be right in."

While he waited, Ratso looked at the replica of the whiteboard from the Cauldron. Each day, he took a photo and loaded it onto his laptop. Too rarely, it gave him inspiration. Today, it looked just the same: a glass half empty. Euphoria at linking Terry Fenwick to Boris Zandro seemed less thrilling in the cold light of dawn after a short night that had left his brain in slow motion. But as he sat wondering what news Jock might bring, his experience convinced him Tosh had been uncovered while visiting the solicitor's offices.

He wiped his mouth as Jock entered, his cheeks rosy, everything about him alert, almost radiant. He had a couple of folders in one hand and a flask of tea in the other. "You look better than I feel," Ratso observed. "I had a lousy night. The cricketers got a first innings stuffing and I fell asleep in a chair."

"I was home just after three. I waited for young Armstrong to arrive. There's a couple of uniforms taking turns outside Tosh's room. Ye heard from the hospital?"

"He's asleep. I guess he'll be released today."

"The lads downstairs are more worried about the damage to the wall. Ye ken—from him diving into it."

"Yeah. There'd have been less damage if the car hit it. Anyway, you've news?"

Jock poured strong builder's tea from the flask and sipped appreciatively. "Ye want the good or the very good?"

"Work upward."

"Here's the Florida report. It's from a Detective Kirsty-Ann Webber in Fort Lauderdale."

"Like the name."

"Bardici travelled to Grand Bahama under his false name and passport. But of course, with their beefed-up Homeland Security, they took pics twice *and* got his dabs." He handed over a Perspex folder.

"His dabs? Impressive! Mind, I've done the chief there a good turn or two. What's the even better news?"

"I'll get there. But there's more from Detective Webber. Just a throwaway one-liner. She didn't know what she was telling us—just mentioned it in case it fitted. She says it is top, top confidential. Seems an important government servant from Washington named Lance Ruthven disappeared on Grand Bahama the same weekend Bardici was there. And this geezer from the State Department was using a false name too."

"Coincidence."

"Well, maybe. But guess where he did the diplomat bit when not in Washington? Kabul."

"Afghanistan!" Ratso almost breathed the word with reverence, his eyebrow raised.

Jock grinned. "Bang on, boss."

Ratso looked stunned by the magnitude of the information. "We need the entire lowdown on the circles Ruthven moved in. If he's a high-up, then…"

"He might have come across Adnan Shirafi."

Ratso was so excited that he stood and punched the air like Freddie Mercury. "And there's better news? Surely not better than that?"

"Boss, before we move on...I'm no saying ye're wrong but we're at the hypothetical stage only."

Ratso was in no mood for negativity. "Give me the best news."

Jock pushed across a series of photos taken around the two boatyards. There were three vessels in for repairs or checks. One was a small yacht of probably about twelve metres. The next was a mixed cargo vessel. Ratso looked up. "According to Detective Inspector Darren Roberts, it is undergoing extensive repairs after hurricane damage." Jock nodded but his face was almost puce with excitement.

Ratso picked up the two photos of the third ship. According to the printout, it was a former Coast Guard vessel undergoing a refit in the boatyard that had lasted some months. The Coast Guard had used it for oceanographic research but apparently it was outdated and too rusted for a government agency to use. It was apparently being updated by new owners for the same purpose, having been picked up for a song.

Jock looked at his boss. "My money's on the third one. No reason except the size."

Ratso stared hard at the two larger vessels before reaching into his drawer. After pushing aside old cricket fixture lists, an invite to the Spinal Injuries Association AGM, a bus timetable, chewing gum packs, dried-up biros and an unused WH Smith diary, he produced a powerful magnifying glass. He pored over the photos of each vessel in turn. Suddenly, to Jock's astonishment, he jumped up again as if a swarm of bees had invaded his anus. "Nomora! Nomora! Nomora!"

Twenty minutes before, his eyes were those of a fish on a slab. Now they danced with excitement. Ratso's pulse was racing, his nerves jangling, all his senses in overdrive.

Jock tried to share the excitement but could only manage bemused interest. He sat waiting for Ratso to scrape himself off the ceiling. "Ye'll need to explain, boss. Something I'm missing?"

"Klodian Skela speaks from the grave." He rummaged in a different drawer and produced the recording of the Albanian's last words. The broken English accent echoed eerily round the room. "Erlis go there about boat. No more."

At first, Jock sat impassively but when he heard the words, he leaned across the table and high-fived Ratso. "No more. *Nomora*. That's what he was saying!" They both stood up, almost ready to do a quick twirl of the Dashing White Sergeant but the room was too small. Ratso gave Jock the type of hug he normally reserved for the opposite sex.

"The *Nomora*. That's why Bardici went there." Ratso was almost breathless as the words tumbled out.

"It wisna being adapted for cargo, though. Just a cover story?"

"Maybe," Ratso agreed, "until we storm aboard and find no men in white coats."

Jock laughed. "Aye! Or maybe a couple of Bunsen burners and a phial of copper sulphate for show."

"But Bardici wouldn't go there just about a boat. He's a *hammer*. Maybe he went because of this Ruthven guy."

"Maybe Ruthven was the link to Kabul and something had gone wrong, so Ruthven was…er…eliminated."

"Or Ruthven knew too much. Jock. You take the meeting. I want to see the AC."

"Not our friend Tennant? He *is* our boss."

"You've missed the good news?" Ratso's grin was rare but spectacular. "He's off from today till after Christmas. Gone to his place in Majorca. But anyway, I need authority from Wensley Hughes." He looked round furtively as if expecting a spy to jump out from behind the potted plant on the windowsill.. "Remember, we may have someone in our team leaking. Don't tell anyone about the *Nomora* or the missing American."

"Tosh?"

Ratso shook his head, eyes closed in thought. "No need yet. The stuff from Kirsty-Ann is marked *Top Confidential*. This must be a hot potato in DC. We didn't know how Zandro was going to shift this mega consignment. Now only me and you know the vessel that's to be used. How vital is that?"

"Aye! If Zandro thought we knew, he'd abort." Jock stood and edged the couple of feet to the door. "You don't trust one of our team?"

"Until I'm sure how Bardici's thugs knew where to find Tosh last night, I don't trust anyone."

"I don't buy that, boss."

"I don't want to sell it either. I'd have said every man jack downstairs was straight up and Wensley Hughes too. But bastards like Bardici, they sniff out a weak link like Tosh looking for burgers." He saw from Jock's troubled face that his caution was sinking in. "Someone downstairs might be short of money—woman trouble, gambling debts. Any pressure point and Bardici's type can twist the knife."

"Put like that…"

"Answer me this. Who knew Tosh would be walking down Trinity Road and into Welbeck Avenue last night?"

"Me. Nobody else…unless Tosh told somebody. But it's his normal route."

"That's our best hope. Oh and get someone to cover Skela's funeral."

"Waste of time, ye ask me."

"I expect you're right but we do it anyway."

"This ship *Nomora*. Yon mega shipment. When's it happening?"

"Still vague." Ratso paused for a moment. "Mind you, my snout is well down the chain. But he was warned to stand by for something very big in November and then it was this month. Now he's unsure."

"Reliable, is he?" Jock had been let down by informants before.

Ratso's face showed his mixed feelings. He tilted his hand both ways. "But if the *Nomora's* not ready, that would explain it."

Jock paused, hand on the doorknob. "Tosh's route, boss? The leak? It wisna me," he said, his face suddenly as forlorn as his voice. In his concern he'd dropped into his strongest Glaswegian accent, like Kenny Dalglish at a press conference when he disliked the question. "No gambling, no women and no drinks I canna handle standing on my head."

Ratso gave the big man a reassuring nod and started making notes for what he wanted to say to the AC. At that moment, his phone rang. He listened to the brief call, ending it with, "I'll be there."

Wanting to see the AC was one thing. The AC *summoning* him was rather less welcome.

35

Westminster SW1

Ratso was ushered into the well-ordered office of the AC. Wensley Hughes had a reputation as a ferocious worker but you would never know it. Besides a Nokia, a landline phone and a laptop, his long, narrow desk was empty except for a copy of the *Billboard* magazine, a publication designed for all coppers high or low.

"Morning, Todd. Grab a seat." Wensley Hughes had not stood as Ratso entered. The AC was wearing a white long-sleeved shirt with a starched collar and very formal tie. He asked for two coffees to be brought in but then got straight to the nub. "I heard about Sergeant Watson. But not from you." The accusation was obvious.

"I was typing up a report for you this morning when my other sergeant, Jock Strang, brought what he thought was good news."

"But it wasn't?"

"On the contrary. It was *fantastic* news but Jock Strang hadn't joined the dots. Sir, on top of linking a City solicitor to Boris Zandro, we've had a major break today."

"Tell me about the hit-and-run." Wensley Hughes' narrow nose seemed even more prominent than usual this morning, probably because of the rimless half glasses that were perched way down it to check his monitor. Ratso glanced at his scanty notes. He knew Hughes hated waffle and so his report was a series of pithy headlines starting with the cock-up at the cemetery.

"Close judgement call, that," Hughes commented. "You needed to have the funeral covered. I see that. But you were there as a mourner anyway."

"True, sir but look at it this way—I'd never have spotted Bardici's daughter. Tosh did. He just got unlucky with that damned pigeon."

"Was he warned yesterday? Afterward, I mean. About Bardici?"

"We discussed it, yes, sir." It was a gentle way of saying that of course Tosh had received a clear order that he had ignored.

"But he took no special precautions. It was his usual route home?"

"Correct. He didn't expect anything to happen so soon."

Wensley Hughes showed no sign of irritation at Watson's lapse. That was the man, Ratso felt. Always an even keel. No highs, no lows. And all the more effective compared to Arthur Tennant's histrionics. But Ratso knew the AC would not ignore the sergeant's stupidity. Hughes spread his hands flat on the desk and then held them together as if in prayer. "Luckily for you, your sergeant wasn't killed or held for torture. Your team dodged that bullet. But things were tricky enough even before that. Caldwell's still griping about Neil Shalford's murder. He's persistent, I'll give him that."

"Can you hold him off for another month?"

"Look, it was bad enough letting Bardici run when we believe he murdered your mate Shalford. Now we suspect he took a swipe at one of my officers." He stood up to his full six foot four, leaning against the window. "Things look different when you sit in my chair." He wiped some dust off a plaque on the wall and sighed. "Todd, you're running an operation that has the potential to bring down Boris Zandro's empire. I've been there. I remember what it was like—the obsessive need to win. But that overwhelming drive can make you ignore the risks and get on with the game as if nothing but the end result counts."

Ratso nodded, still bursting to explain the breakthrough but assessing that this was not the moment. Wensley Hughes returned to his swivel chair with its navy moquette padding.

"Bardici may or may not take another pop at Watson. I'm inclined to your view that, having failed, he'll move on but precautions must continue." He sat down and peered at Ratso over his glasses. "Here's the worry: Bardici kills again. We—and that means I—cannot keep ignoring evidence pointing to Bardici while he slaughters at will." He raised his right finger in warning. "If Watson had been murdered last night, that would have been the end. I would have had to bring Bardici in and gear all resources to finding the driver."

"I understand, sir."

"These days, the slightest deviation from the fundamentals and I can get summoned before some Parliamentary Committee to be asked ludicrous, long-winded but occasionally penetrating questions by a bunch of flatulent-mouthed MPs seeking to boost their own profiles." He selected a biscuit with all the care of a surgeon doing a brain implant. Then he pushed over the plate. "At present," he continued, "I can still hold the line that I do not *know* Bardici was involved in both incidents. But now Bardici realises he's being watched." The AC looked at his screen and Ratso wondered whether it displayed his bullet points--his ducks in a row. "But *you* know and *I* know that if the shit starts flying from the pinko politicians and they rabbit on about us not doing enough, or *anything*, to prove Bardici's guilt, heads will roll. All because you believe you can land Zandro."

"Can I cheer you up, sir?"

"You can try." The tone was dry, ascetic. *Come to think of it*, Ratso decided, *the AC does have a monk-like quality about him. Always calm, measured, contemplative. Persuading him now's my best hope.*

"Arresting Bardici now would blow everything. First, why would Bardici tell the lieutenants or *anybody* that he has been rumbled? My guess is that's why he moved fast last night—making a point. Second, let me tell you where we're at."

When Ratso had finished explaining about the *Nomora*, Lance Ruthven, Adnan Shirafi and the London clubs, Wensley Hughes asked for the Fort Lauderdale report. In character, he had taken the good news with quiet satisfaction, concluding with *you've done well* at the end of Ratso's summary. He scanned Kirsty-Ann Webber's report in seconds, only pausing to reread the final comments about Lance Ruthven. "As if we didn't have enough trouble with Bardici's capers, now you're going to bring the MoD, the Foreign Office and maybe the PM himself down on our heads. Mine particularly."

"Sir?"

"Look—for years, British policy in Afghanistan has been to cosy up to Adnan Shirafi. He controls the heroin scene in Helmand Province. If we took out the poppies and his endless flow of smack, world supplies would be stifled. To us fighting the drug barons, Adnan Shirafi is the man to take out. But to the

MoD, he's been an asset helping to control the Taliban rebels in Helmand Province." He shook his head in despair.

"Crazy position, sir. Right hand–left hand nightmare."

The AC prodded a report on his desk. "When he was prime minister in 2001, Tony Blair pledged to kill the poppy fields—a pillar of his rationale for the Afghan war. Good call until you upset bastards like Adnan Shirafi. But Blair was not alone. In 2006, American counterintelligence experts also wanted to destroy the entire Afghan poppy industry." Hughes laughed in despair. "They were too late. The goalposts and our poppy field policy were, well…just poppycock! The Americans uncovered that the British Army in Helmand had distanced themselves from the war on the heroin trade. They had even put out a leaflet to local criminals to reassure them. Why? Because it was interfering with our military operations."

Ratso was unimpressed. "My nephew Freddie died in a Kilburn bus shelter because of Afghan heroin."

The AC shrugged, obviously frustrated. "Tell me about it. Him and hundreds, thousands of others globally. I attended a meeting in Washington where their narcotics guys almost cried on my shoulder."

"And you cried on theirs?"

"More or less. Law enforcement wanted poppy crops destroyed from the air, killing off 90% of the world supply. The local population would have been compensated in some way. But the Pentagon was hostile, just like MoD."

"You mentioned 2006. What about today?"

"*Realpolitik* has won. The war is ending but *three times*, I repeat, *three times* as many poppies are grown today as in 2001. Nobody wanted body bags returning to the USA or UK. Lives of our troops depended on what the military chiefs out there recommend. Their voices held sway." A resigned shrug said the rest.

"So Shirafi rules!" Ratso's sucked-in cheeks and steady eyes made him look unusually rat-like. "Corruption wins while we fight a drugs war that could have been killed stone dead in Helmand."

"There's a report saying British troops themselves were active in opium trading. I don't buy that but it might be true."

Ratso's anger was mounting. "There's more spin than from Shane Warne's leg-breaks."

"That's politics. It might be spin. But look at the stats." He swivelled the monitor.

Ratso absorbed the summary in a few seconds. "So 7,000 tons of opium sold by growers at about £100 a kilo becomes about 1,000 tons of heroin worth around £4,000 a kilo on the European market."

"And the traffickers pocket around a billion." Hughes turned back the monitor as if to close the conversation.

"Here's to Zandro's next jet!"

Wensley Hughes' gave a resigned nod as he drained his coffee and topped them both up again. "Ironic, isn't it? You want me to turn a blind eye to Bardici's murders because of the bigger picture—bringing down the entire Zandro empire, including Shirafi. Yet you don't sympathise with our military bosses, who turned a blind eye on Shirafi for their bigger picture of defeating the Taliban."

"Are you saying we *are defeating* the Taliban, sir?" Ratso was rewarded with a glance that said *touché*. "Rock and a hard place, then."

"You may be right. But where does this leave us? The Lance Ruthven link is pure speculation but must be investigated.

Whatever you prove, when it comes to it, our political masters may want a cover-up, dancing to the US president's tune."

"Ah, yes. The *special relationship* between our two nations that means we are special if we follow the Yanks blindly but meaningless if we need their support." Ratso saw Wensley Hughes was bored with his rant but he continued anyway. "But heroin, the drug trade, kills more people, ruins more lives than al Qaeda or the Taliban ever did. For that, Shirafi's accountable. I want to bring him down."

"Accountable?" Wensley Hughes brushed away some crumbs as easily as he swept aside Ratso's irritation. "Wrong word. He may be to *blame* but he's not *accountable*." His eyes turned hard. "And no way will you try to bring down Shirafi. Stick with Zandro."

"I get Zandro and days later Shirafi starts supplying the next chancer."

"Don't shoot me, Todd. I'm only the messenger."

"Sorry, sir. My team spends its shrinking budget battling the drug barons while the politicians spent billions on a war in Afghanistan *supporting* the guy who…"

Hughes stopped Ratso with a decisive wave of his arm. "Don't piss into the wind. You know and I know that from *our* standpoint it's crazy, insane. But our political masters won't countenance any attempt to strangle the source. Shirafi is untouchable, at least for now."

Ratso's fingers clenched, unclenched and clenched again. "So?"

"I want Cyprus watched. Send your Scotsman. Sergeant Strang, isn't it? You've convinced me *Tirana Queen* is headed there. It's still being tracked?"

"Yes, sir. But unfortunately we couldn't wire it for sound. An oppo of ours on the Gib force got aboard delivering veggies. Reported it was too risky to get up to the bridge."

"I gave up ideas of bugging Zandro in 2008. He has his home, his jet and *Tirana Queen* swept for bugs, though I gather the latest tracking devices can beat the sweep." He checked his screen again. "Your friendly - Giles, isn't it?. Is he reliable?"

Ratso nodded. "Giles Mountford? Good guy. So far, sir, straight as a gun barrel."

"Good, good. Then we can be sure Zandro's Gulfstream flies to Cyprus tomorrow. I'd guess he must be meeting up with his boat. I want Strang and one of the women on your team in Cyprus tonight. There are two airports, Larnaca and Paphos. Could be either. They must cover whichever airport Zandro will use and track down the *Tirana Queen*."

Ratso thought for a moment. "As I recall, those airports are about fifty miles apart. I'll get Giles to tell me which it is once Zandro files his flight plan."

"You say heading to Cyprus is outside Zandro's normal routine?"

"Normally, he has the vessel sent to Barbados for Christmas. He's been there every year since 2003."

"Oh, yes. That's right. I was always green with envy. So this trip is not pleasure."

"Important enough to screw up his usual Christmas routine. That's a pointer that he's up to something." As he thought back, Ratso realised why he was disappointed. "But you don't want me in Cyprus then, sir?"

"No." The AC's face broke into a warm smile. "I want you to sniff around Grand Bahama." He checked the time on a clunky Sekonda watch. It had been a twenty-fifth wedding anniversary gift and it gave him a load of data he never needed. "I think there's a BA flight to Miami after lunch. Be on it today. Susie will book it and a hotel. Stop off in Fort Lauderdale to meet that police chief."

"Bucky Buchanan."

"You know him?"

"No, sir but he owes me a favour or two."

"Good. See that detective, too. Keep her in the loop. On the downside, I've got to inform the Feds in DC about the possible link between Bardici and Ruthven's disappearance." Ratso's face screwed up, showing his concern. The AC was quick to spot it. "I can see what you're thinking, Todd. But if you're correct, the link is very bad news for the State Department." For the first time during the meeting, Ratso got the finger treatment. Everybody who had a one-to-one with the AC was liable to get it at some point. The AC's wagging finger pointed straight at Ratso's chest, delivering the message that this was deadly serious. "So when you're out there, do nothing to upset Washington's low-key approach. Understood?"

Ratso's look said he would obey orders but through gritted teeth. "Of course, sir."

"I want you to find out everything about the *Nomora*. Owners, when the work will be finished, what's happening next. Itinerary. Where the crew will come from. Maybe there's even a master signed up."

"I was thinking about how the *Nomora* was paid for, sir."

"I like that. Link it to that solicitor in the City. One of those companies he formed." The AC typed a note onto his computer.

"Someone will have to get aboard the *Nomora* to plant a tracker. Not a job for us."

"Report back to me on how to get aboard. I'll get the boys to do it." Hughes looked thoughtful, rubbing his chin slowly. "No. Second thought, no tracker on board. I'll get the boys at Vauxhall Cross on it. They can do it remotely."

"It's in a secure shipyard."

Wensley Hughes stroked his smooth-shaved cheek as a sly smile played out around his lips. "Don't underestimate your own ingenuity to get aboard if it's essential. Lawfully, I mean—use a pretext, got it? As for the boys if we have to use them, a locked gate and a couple of guards won't stop them. I say boys but there's some damned brave women in that team working under the radar."

"Anything else, sir?"

"Before you jet off for those piña coladas, get Sergeant Watson to send me a report on why he ignored your warning last night." He paused. "And to provide a full debrief on his walk home. Because if he was not followed along Glebeside Lane and Trinity Road, then someone in your team is. . ." He let the unspoken words hang. "And I don't want to think that."

Ratso rose and shook the AC's hand. "Me neither, sir."

"When Watson is able to return, keep him close to base. And make him a damned sight more careful."

"He's learned, sir."

"Lost any weight, has he?" For a moment, Ratso was puzzled at the question, so the AC continued. "You saw that report saying Met Police are very overweight. Those jokes about Scotland Lard or Blobby Bobbies. If the rumours are right, we're unfit for purpose. Watson, as I recall, has the body mass of a humpback whale."

"Unfair on the whale, sir."

"He ought to lose weight. He might have dodged that vehicle if he'd been more nimble."

"But how would McDonalds survive, sir?"

36

Fort Lauderdale, Florida

Ratso had never found the drive north from Miami on I-95 to be a pleasant experience. Even by day you needed the skills and courage of an F1 driver to survive. The multi-lane highway linking Miami to the rest of the USA was always busy. Now, after a disturbed night, a tiring day and a long flight, it was distinctly unnerving. In the dark, after a squally shower, his headlights showed a constant sheen of water and sometimes blinding spray, thrown up by the thundering wheels of the huge trucks and semi-trailers. His rental car felt tiny and feeble with such awesome power speeding by.

Each driver behaved as if they'd discovered the secret of how to stop suddenly in the wet, when in truth they had no more chance than a puck on an ice rink. With constant lane-changing for the stream of exits up the eastern coast, the slightest error and carnage was just a second away—more fodder for the contingency fee attorneys who advertised on billboards, TV and the radio, all promising massive accident compensation.

Ninety minutes later, Ratso was relieved to be turning the little Nissan off I-95 rather than being carted off in an ambulance or to the morgue. He headed eastward, letting the nasal-voiced sat nav guide him to the Blue Ocean Motel. It had been a long day that had started twenty-three hours before when he had awoken in his chair at home.

But the flight had been smooth and after the economy-class meal, a vodka tonic and some red wine, he had slept soundly. When he awoke, the 747 had been only eight hundred miles from touchdown. Surprisingly refreshed, he had pulled out a scribbling pad from his black carry-on, intending to create an action plan but thoughts of his conversation with Charlene kept intruding.

After throwing a few clothes into his grip, he had called her. Looking back on it, the call had been good or bad depending on how he wanted matters left. Hell, he liked her enormously, sympathised with her hugely, fancied her something rotten. If he could be sure her only demands would be in bed, then, as his mother would have said, everything would have been *just tickety-boo*. But his copper's instinct had flashed too many warnings.

Being a twenty-four-seven detective put the mockers on rose-tinted views of parenthood. *Look at your mates, Ratso! Half of them are divorced or separated.* But for his kids, Tosh would have been. Rare were the wives who could say, *Don't worry I know your job comes first*—and really mean it. He had ended the call promising Charlene she'd be the first to know when he was back, whenever that might be. *Before Christmas for sure. Christmas lunch together? If I'm not working that day.*

He swigged his bottled water before putting the perplexities aside to return to his to-do list. His top priority, besides meeting Detective Kirsty-Ann Webber and her boss Bucky Buchanan, would be assessing whatever data arrived from the IMB about the *Nomora*. While in the departures lounge at Heathrow, he had spoken to Bob Whewell, the director of the International Maritime Bureau in London's Docklands. Formed over thirty years ago to fight crime at sea, the Bureau had become a treasure trove of information. On several occasions, Ratso had received valuable support when drug trafficking by ship was involved.

As the aircraft's wheels came juddering down, he felt heartened. So many new leads had opened up. Soon, after Christmas, he could start piecing together the final strategy. *Nomora* was the key. Surely it had to carry Colombia's finest from the Caribbean and collect a huge stash of heroin from Cyprus or Turkey. His dream of Boris Zandro being frogmarched from his mansion in handcuffs was interrupted by the bump, bump of touchdown and then the screaming engines, reverse thrust at full bore. *Welcome to Miami and the horrors of the US Immigration system.* Not that the cabin staff announced it in quite those terms.

As he finally turned into the parking lot of the Blue Ocean Motel, it was gone 11 p.m. local, 4 a.m. in London. He killed the Nissan Versa's engine and abandoned it among a line of similar nondescript small saloons. He stood for a moment, shivering in the chill evening air, then flung his black leather jacket over his plain white T-shirt. He stretched, rubbed his tired eyes and walked stiffly to the car's boot to retrieve his grip. But the prospect of some beers, a hot dog and a shower—in any order—brought a spring to his step as he crossed the asphalt toward the brightness of the sparse but efficient-looking lobby. Inside, he took in the desk clerk, lines of drink machines and a cash dispenser. Nobody else was checking in. Perhaps everybody was in the bar watching ESPN.

An hour later, he was seated in the bar himself. It was busy with sales reps, *road warriors*, mainly under thirty-five and mainly staring at the TV screens dotted around the soulless room. In front of him was a giant hot dog with lashings of mustard. It was ludicrously large for any normal person but no doubt the Americans around him would take such a monster in stride. *As would Tosh*, he told himself, briefly wondering how to tell his sergeant that the AC wanted him on a diet.

Ratso had grabbed a vacant barstool. Though basketball filled most screens, there were also a few on Fox News, talking heads without sound. *Best way to listen to them*, Ratso thought as he turned away. Neither programme was of the slightest interest. With these tall black guys, basketball seemed far too easy. After the third beer, he vowed to email the NBA telling them to raise the baskets.

An oaf sat down next to him, wanting to pour out his heart after a skinful. With a curt nod, Ratso picked up his beer and moved to a corner table. En route, something alerted him to a new idea—something he should have concluded a great deal sooner. Perhaps, he decided, it was simply distance giving him objectivity. As he plumped himself down on the tired red leather banquette, it was all so blindingly obvious.

No way could Tosh Watson have been targeted just from a fleeting sighting in the cemetery. Bardici's daughter may have told her father that a copper who had interviewed Skela was skulking between the graves—assuming she dared tell him that she was being humped by his cousin. He drained the beer and signalled to the bartender for another. Tosh could never have been traced by anything Lindita had seen. Tosh hadn't left any details with Skela after the interview. The chain of events *must* have started at Terry Fenwick's office. Tosh *had* flashed an ID card but the print of name, rank and warrant number was so small that a casual glance would reveal nothing. Where Tosh was based was not on his ID anyway.

Had Fenwick, suspicious, gotten his PA to try a dial-back after Tosh phoned for the appointment? No. That would have revealed nothing. Then a thought struck him. He grabbed his iPad and started typing furiously as the bartender arrived with another bottle, the condensation running down it onto the absorbent mat. When the message to London had gone, he felt satisfied, confident now about what had happened. It was the only way. Now he just had to prove it. There should be a reply in the morning.

In just six hours, he would meet Bucky Buchanan, to say nothing of Kirsty-Ann Webber. He was still thinking about her as he drained the bottle and headed for his room. He peeped round the closed curtains but found himself staring at the darkened window in the next building barely twelve metres away. Despite the name, the Blue Ocean was several blocks back from the Atlantic. He might just as well have been at home in Hammersmith. At least there he got the screech of gulls from time to time.

And the cricket would have been on TV.

37

Fort Lauderdale, Florida
The meeting with Bucky Buchanan was cordial—an informal chat over stacks of pancakes at a fast-food joint just across from police HQ on Broward. But any secret hopes Ratso harboured of getting to meet Kirsty-Ann Webber were dashed when Bucky explained she had flown to Freeport on Grand Bahama.

Though Bucky's pancakes disappeared at an alarming rate, along with crispy bacon, orange juice and decaf, the chief was still able to get his message across loud and clear: nobody was stopping Det. Inspector Todd Holtom from joining the dots linking Bardici to Lance Ruthven but on no account must anything like that become public. "Seen this?" Bucky handed over a Washington, DC, newspaper cutting.

Ratso got the drift from the headline alone. "I see," he responded, taking in the spin that Ruthven had "most likely" drowned.

"The message from DC is that Ruthven must become a non-story." The chief's grey eyes bored uncomfortably into Ratso's head. "You ain't heard that from London yet?" He saw Ratso's face break into a frown. "Then you sure will, son." Recalling his meeting with the AC, Ratso turned away to take in the room, which seemed to contain half of Fort Lauderdale's finest scoffing pancakes and maple syrup. "You do what you have to do. But if Ruthven's real or false name becomes involved, you are to report to London at once. Assistant-Commissioner Hughes, isn't it?"

"I knew Wensley Hughes was speaking to the Feds yesterday. I haven't heard what happened."

"You will. They were very appreciative of the contact but I'd say they were crapping themselves at what you might uncover."

Ratso tried to play dumb. "Politics involved?"

Bucky showed a full set of whitened teeth. "Right on! If this story blows back onto the State Department, Commissioner Hughes will be carpeted." He waved his fork for emphasis. "Probably by someone in your Foreign Office or in Defence. If I'm wrong, then my name ain't Bucky Buchanan."

"So what is Detective Webber doing? I mean, she's poking a hornet's nest, surely?"

Bucky grinned. "If she found pointers, anything consistent with drowning, now would that surprise you?" He pushed aside his empty plate and ran his fingers over his *en brosse* grey hair.

Ratso thought he had the drift. "Look for the convenient facts only." He saw a slight flicker in Buchanan's eyes. "Did Ruthven enjoy snorkelling?"

"I'd bet you ten bucks to a dime that Kirsty-Ann will find someone who rented out the gear to a man fitting his description. She's a smart kid."

Ratso grinned. "Does that answer my question about snorkelling? Or your problem that nobody called Ruthven ever went to Grand Bahama?"

Bucky's eyes narrowed at the reminder before he nodded respect. He left twenty dollars on the table and started to shepherd Ratso toward the exit.

"Sounds as if there's no point in my meeting Detective Webber," Ratso continued as they stood in the morning sun. "If I'm right, my enquiries will point the other way."

"Heck no. You two gotta meet. She's staying at the Double Palm at Lucaya. Kirsty-Ann knows the time of day, okay. I ain't worried for her. No, son, it's *you* I'm worried about. One snafu and your career is done. Our guys in DC will see to that."

Ratso's pleasure at the thought of meeting Kirsty-Ann was immediately overshadowed by an image of another summons to the AC's office. "I get the message."

"Sure you do, son." Bucky clapped him on the shoulder. "Sure you do."

38

Freeport, Grand Bahama Island
It was 12:40 p.m. when Ratso dumped his bags in his room at the Pelican Pointe Motel on Grand Bahama Island. As he had waited at Fort Lauderdale International, he'd spoken to Wensley Hughes on the phone. The call had been short and to the point. The UK's Foreign Office and the US State Department had shared a mutual love-in and the brief call emphasised Bucky's warning. "So pull me from the job," Ratso had challenged.

That suggestion met with a sharp rebuff. "Even the Foreign Office toffs accept you must discover the truth. It's just what we do with our knowledge that's making them twitchy. So go ahead—prove the Shirafi to Boris Zandro connection. Prove the link between *Nomora* and Bardici's visit and somehow link Bardici to Terry Fenwick."

"And Ruthven's murder to Bardici?"

"We can nail Bardici on something without digging up a possible crime against a US citizen on a Caribbean island. Unimportant to us but..." The transatlantic connection went quiet while Hughes picked his words carefully. "If you prove a link between Bardici and Ruthven, fine. But if you proved that Bardici slit the American's throat, that would be too much information."

"I understand. A snorkelling accident would be, er, suitable to you, sir?"

"I knew you would understand. Tread carefully."

"I have some ideas." Ratso hoped his confidence was justified.

Just over an hour later, while waiting at the Freeport carousel for his bag, Ratso had called Detective Inspector Darren Roberts.

"Hi, Darren. Yeah. Good journey. Can we meet as planned? Excellent. Jerk chicken or curried goat? That's what you recommend? Sounds good. The food's shit at my hotel? Now you tell me! Okay. You pick a place and I'll be there." He scribbled down the name and directions. Almost at once he was alerted to an incoming text. He checked it and a satisfied smile played round his lips.

A burden had been lifted. But the smile faded as the wider implications became clear. Someone had indeed phoned the switchboard at Scotland Yard the afternoon of Tosh's visit to Fenwick's offices, asking where to contact him. So the good news was, there was no leak. But the bad news, the much worse news, was the certainty that Fenwick knew he was a suspect.

Just like Erlis Bardici and Lance Ruthven had done about twelve days before, Ratso parked in the sprawl of the mud earth car park of the Pink Flamingo Calypso Bar. Here and there were puddles from a heavy overnight shower. There were over forty other dusty and dented saloons and SUVs filling half the parking area. Lunch trade was obviously good. He had no briefcase, nothing to make him look like a London copper or someone on a mission. He had debated wearing Bermuda shorts but had settled for a tropical blue and white T-shirt with sand-coloured slacks.

He locked the car, his head swirling with thoughts of what he could or could not say to Darren Roberts. The guy had done a great job photographing the shipyard and though Ratso had warm, comfortable memories ever since their wild night in London, Ratso's concern was about secrecy and small islands. Maybe he was a tad paranoid but everybody on small islands seemed to know everybody else. That had been his experience in Guernsey and the Isle of Man and he doubted this Caribbean island was any different.

Last night's evening chill in Florida had given way to a steamy heat that sapped his energy. The lush trees that surrounded the car park increased the sultry atmosphere as the sun beat down beneath scudding dark clouds. Overwhelmed by the oppressive steaminess as he strolled slowly away from the dusty orange Datsun, Ratso's copper's instincts never warned him that he was within a few paces of whatever remained of Ruthven's body, buried in the unappealing tangle of mangroves and pines.

Having completed the walk down the footpath, he stood motionless, awestruck by the beauty of the scene that opened in front of him. To his right was the wooden cabin-come-shack from whence came noisy chatter and the smell of spicy cooking. A reggae number Ratso did not recognise was also blasting away. But in every other direction there was serenity, unspoiled views of white sand, swaying palm trees and turquoise water, with a ripple of salty white where the water lapped the shore.

Through the maze of both black and white faces surrounding the shack, Ratso struggled to find DI Roberts among the diners seated either on the balcony or under bright red sun shades on the terraced area beside the beach. He had not seen Roberts close on two years but Darren Roberts spotted him at once. The inspector rose to his feet and hollered with a deep, booming voice and a wave of his arm. No name—just a single "Hey, mon!"

Unlike many of the locals, who were big, burly with gleaming muscled arms, Inspector Roberts was below average, standing only five foot nine with slim arms, toned but not bulky. He was wearing a short-sleeved purple shirt and navy flannel trousers with no sign that he was a detective, though Ratso's paranoia warned him everybody here probably knew anyway. Ratso joined him at a table that seemed to be in a prime spot, shaded from direct sun yet with endless views of the curving bay.

"Not a pole-dancer in sight, Darren! What kind of place do you call this?"

The ice was immediately broken and within moments they were chatting, laughing and reminiscing about Kinky Katrina, the Nigerian dancer with thighs like a bison who had taken a shine to Darren.

"You owe me for rescuing you from her," prompted Ratso.

The toothy grin appeared at once. "Ratso," he said in his strong local accent, "I can tame her kind, two at a time. I do have them mewing like kittens."

Ratso punched his arm playfully. "Dream on, pal! Kinky Katrina, mewing like a kitten? You'd have been having bloody kittens, more like! One flick of her hips and your arse would have hit the ceiling."

The banter continued until beer and spicy chicken appeared, served by a young woman who obviously knew Darren as a regular.

"I've got the IMB working on the background to *Nomora*. Oh and remember Tosh Watson?"

"Big appetite, small bladder, right?"

Ratso laughed. "He's working to prove Zandro's mob bought the *Nomora* and how it was paid for."

"How is Tosh?"

Ratso briefly updated Roberts on the attempted murder but moved on to what Bardici was doing in Freeport.

"You did say Bardici...he was a hammer?"

Ratso was not going to get into delicate areas. "Right but we think his visit was linked to *Nomora*. That's what we need to prove. Any recent deaths linked to the shipyard? Any bodies found strangled—a favoured method? If Boris Zandro was ripped off during the refit, he might have sent Bardici."

Darren Roberts shook his head. "There were a coupla deaths last week but that was a domestic—husband he did shoot his wife and her lover while they goin' at it like crazy. He done shot the man's wedding gear first." He cackled in a *tee-hee-hee* kind of way.

"Or what he could see of it," prompted Ratso and they both laughed, Darren rocking in his chair. "So the shipyards? What's known?"

The Bahamian shook his head. "They do repair the ships. They been done that since I was a kid. But business at this one is bad, kinda slack."

The comment was not lost on Ratso. "You round the quay, the docks often?"

"Sure thing but my wife, she do work at the yard too. You got docks, you got crime. Muggings of drunken crew, smuggling, drugs, theft from ships, pilfering. Mon, we always is round them parts."

"So the *Nomora*? How long has she been there?"

He scratched his receding curly hair and weighed his answer. "Maybe July."

"Seems a long time. What's going on?"

"You said low-key, correct?"

"If I'm right, *Nomora* is going to be carrying Class A drugs. The last thing we need is for anybody to know we have the vessel under scrutiny."

Roberts grinned. "My wife Ida, she done work as PA to the boss, Lamon Wilson. I did ask her, not like I care. Just casual like."

"And?"

"The owners they did buy the vessel cheap. They modernise it for studying seabeds and the like. But Ida, she don't know nutting what happen on board."

"When is the job complete?"

"I never done ask her. But I tell you, the work cost big bucks." He whistled softly.

"In sterling?"

"In your money, over one million pounds."

"What!" Ratso was startled. "Either *Nomora* was rusted to hell and back or there's something *really big* going on."

Darren grasped Ratso's arm. "I got more, mon! My cousin's son, Chuckie, he does work doin' welding at the yard, so he and me, we done had a beer."

As he listened, Ratso's paranoia about small islands intensified. "Discreet, is he?"

"Relax, mon. We was just chilling out—me, him and his old man. And the boy, he did say that the ship, she rusted, filthy. Then, sudden-like, he did stop talking. Real sudden. Like he remember to keep the trap shut."

"Did you press him?" Ratso had mixed feelings when he saw the Bahamian shake his head. "Like you said, I kept it cool."

"You did well." Ratso looked around and waved for two more beers. "Access to the yard?"

"There's a guard at the gate. For to stop the kids—they get chance, they do nick the paint, the tools."

"But I couldn't get in? Or get aboard?"

"Without permission? No way. But me? I get in easy, go sniff around. Plenty reasons." He saw Ratso's doubtful look. "I done go there often. The boss there, he no way suspicious."

Ratso felt his iPhone vibrating and checked his messages. There were four. The first was from Kirsty-Ann suggesting meeting at the Crow's Nest bar at 5 p.m. The second was from DC Mason reporting the discovery of a burned-out 2004 Vauxhall Astra without plates on waste ground near Dartford on the Kent-London border. The front nearside wing was badly damaged. The last message was Tosh asking him to call urgently, *very urgently*. The fourth was from Jock hoping he had remembered to pack sun-oil and water-wings. He grinned momentarily before turning to Darren. "Excuse me. I must respond at once." He accepted Kirsty-Ann's offer and sent a text to Tosh promising to call within the hour. He wondered what had happened that was so urgent. Klodian Skela's funeral, perhaps? Something with Terry Fenwick and Gibraltar?

Darren waited till Ratso had pocketed his phone before continuing. "I guess you wanna know when the ship's gonna be ready." He tapped the side of his rather bulbous nose in a familiar gesture. "I find out, let you know." Two more cans of Kalik Gold were delivered to the table.

Ratso flipped his ring pull. "One more thing, Darren. I'll send through a couple of photos. Either or both persons may have visited the yard. Show the gatekeeper and your wife, see if either recognise them."

"Not ask the boss at the yard?"

Ratso shook his head. Something deep inside warned him that the yard might be involved, though he had no idea how.

"Got names of these two guys?"

"Not for sure, no." Ratso put his fingers to his lips. "But keep it close, Darren."

"Who are they?"

Ratso shook his head. "Persons of interest." Ratso caught the resentful look on Darren's face and so hurried on. "Nothing personal, mind. Just that we don't yet know what's going on."

The inspector's face brightened. "No sweat." He drained the last of his can, left some cash beside it and stood up. "Send me the pics soonest, mon, huh?"

Ratso followed him down the three rickety steps from the balcony to the beach and they strolled side by side toward the cars. For a few seconds, Ratso wondered if he was letting Darren get too interested in the mission. It seemed absurd not to trust this dynamo of energy and enthusiasm. But it was a small island. The thought nagged away at his satisfaction that things were moving better.

After promising to meet the following day, Ratso drove into town, following Darren's directions to the Crow's Nest bar and Kirsty-Ann Webber.

39

Freeport, Grand Bahama Island
Ratso had phoned as soon as he was parked close to the Crow's Nest. "Hi, Tosh. How're you doing?"

"I'm at my desk but I can't laugh and I'm stiff as hell. How's it going?"

"How's the wall?"

Tosh's laugh started and as quickly died. "No jokes, please, boss!"

"So what's so urgent at your end?"

"One of my snouts got wind of something. Those Hogan brothers is going to do over a house in Brighton. Bankside Gardens."

"And why am I interested?"

"Because there's 30 kilos of cocaine stored there. At sixty grand per kilo, that's a street value of, say, £1.8 million. Seems the Hogans are a bit short on gear, so they're gonna nick this."

"Stealing from a rival gang? Risky." Ratso had come across this several times before—turf wars, hijacking gear from another gang. "Could start an all-out war, lot of tit-for-tat murders. How's it relevant?"

"My guy only knew the address, not the owner's name, so I checked it out. It's a four-bedroom detached place. Upmarket. Sort of place you'd see a Mercedes outside and maybe a Toyota Land Cruiser." Tosh paused to build the excitement. "The house is rented by an *Albanian*. Someone called Rudi Tare." Ratso's brow furrowed and he closed his eyes, deep in thought as he checked his internal database of names. "You still there, boss?"

Ratso feigned irritation. "So you thought the Albanian connection seemed significant? Worth bothering me with? You've nothing more?"

Tosh could tell his boss was now several moves ahead. This was a wind-up. "Not enough, boss? You want the size of his dick or what?"

"Check out that dead end we reached early on. Remember? That story about a distributor for Zandro's network. We thought he was in Sussex, around Crawley."

"Oh, yeah. About seven months back?"

"Maybe six. We met *omerta* but my gut reaction was that the chain went from Zandro to a lieutenant and from him to this distributor in Sussex."

"Terry Fenwick is from Kent."

Ratso was dismissive. "Fenwick somehow gets instructions from Boris Zandro…we assume. But my take is he's the brains on companies, not part of distribution. Besides Fenwick, there has to be a big distributor. The Crawley lead was wrong but Brighton's just thirty minutes farther south, so an Albanian down at the coast seems tasty."

"Rudi Tare's place looks suitable to stash away a load of drugs. Discreet—set back behind a line of trees, with a courtyard big enough for cars to come and go without drawing attention."

"Posh area, then?"

"Yeah—not Bishop's Avenue posh but not Harlesden neither. Not a street where you live in your neighbour's pocket. But you're sounding more excited by this than me, boss. What gives?"

"Here's why." Ratso imagined the whiteboard in the Cauldron as he spoke. "Way back, I asked Jock to watch that meeting in Tesco's car park between Bardici and someone unknown. Bardici was in a Mazda 4x4. The other hooded guy arrived in a Ford Focus. They chatted in Bardici's motor. When the meeting broke up, the unknown man threw away what Jock thought was a ciggie. After they'd gone, Jock found it was a piece of screwed-up paper. On it were the initials *JF*, with an arrow pointing to the word *Tearaway*." Ratso paused to let it sink in.

It was a few seconds before Tosh admitted defeat.

"Tare equals Tearaway." Ratso almost heard the clunk as the penny dropped. "Back then, we had nothing to go on: the number plate on the Focus was false and trying to suss out the letters JF was a dead-end. We never could ID the mystery man. Now we may have Tearaway identified." Ratso watched a group of white youngsters shouting cheerfully as they bounded their way into the Crow's Nest bar. "Could JF be Terry Fenwick's brother? I can't remember his first name. Anyway, when's Hogan's mob going to attack?"

"Christmas Eve. About 11 p.m." Tosh waited for the explosion and was not disappointed as Ratso broke into a torrent of abuse about inconsiderate bastards screwing up everybody's Christmas plans. Tosh heard him out before continuing. "You're wrong, boss. They had no intention of screwing up *your* plans. They don't want or expect you around. They reckoned us lot, we'd all be wearing Santa hats and guzzling whisky and mince pies."

Ratso saw his point. "I'll be back in time. Just. Tell Arthur Tennant." Ratso stopped in mid-flow. "Oh, he's away, isn't he? I'll brief the AC, then. Ask your friendly if the Hogans are going tooled up. I assume so. Danny Hogan sometimes carries a sawn-off. We'll need the works; this could be like the St Valentine's Day massacre."

"Boss, nobody else knows about this. Just you and me. So we could do nothing—just watch and move in afterward. Let these scumbags sort out their personal war. Leaves you free to sing falsetto at the midnight carol service."

Ratso chuckled. "You've heard my balls are on the line, have you?" Then he fell quiet, chewing his lower lip, weighing up the position. The idea of these thugs beating the shit out of each other had its attraction. "No, Tosh. We must intervene. That damned Osman court case—the judges ruled we cannot stand back if we can prevent a crime."

"Oh yeah, that crap decision about the Wood Green job. Bloody daft if you ask me. Let the ignorant shits fight it out, that's what I say."

"You're not yet the Lord Chief Justice or Prime Minister. When you are, you can change the law. Till then, we abide by it. But if Rudi Tare *is* Tearaway and we intervene, we'll find laptops, money-laundering chains—names, dates, dozens of pay-as-you-go phones. We may get pretty damned close to the beating heart of Zandro's empire." He paused, savouring the prospect. "*And* we put the Hogans' hit squad away for a seven-to-ten stretch for armed robbery."

"And we pull in 30 kilos of Class A—maybe other gear, too."

Ratso was barely listening now as he watched a tall, upright and slim woman with shortish blonde hair park a Toyota Corolla at precisely 5 p.m. From a distance, he placed her age as thirty, certainly no more. His spirits rose. He felt sure that the woman walking with the swivel in her hips was Kirsty-Ann Webber. He certainly hoped so. "Tosh. I got a meeting. You've done good. We'll talk about Gibraltar and the London clubs tomorrow. Just one last thing."

"Yeah, yeah! I know, boss. I'm sure, at least I *think* I'm sure: a parked car did start its engine in Glebeside Lane shortly after I walked past it. But I don't recall it passing me as I walked."

"You reported that to the AC?"

"My statement went through an hour ago."

"That makes me feel better. Talk tomorrow."

Ratso got out, stretched and then walked the few metres to the beachside bar. It was less authentic than the Pink Flamingo, better painted and altogether too twee for Ratso's taste. The Crow's Nest was designed for tourists and as Darren Roberts had warned, so were the prices. But once again, the location was to die for and Ratso stopped to take in the sweep of the bay and the small craft that cruised or sped across the gentle swell.

He removed his shades as he entered. Inside, he saw the blonde buying a Coke that was more ice than Coke. Up close, she seemed even taller, slimmer and more naturally blonde than his first impression. But what struck him most was the tanned complexion, not brown but lightly coloured, adding warmth to her oval face. He approached the bar, introduced himself and asked for a lemon and lime. "Outside or in?" he asked her.

"Inside." Her tone was decisive and Ratso looked at her with the slightest question on his face. "It's gonna rain in ten minutes, mebbe even five." They headed to a table away from everyone else in the bar. "You met Bucky this morning?"

"Seems like years ago but yes. Over pancakes."

"That's his daily fix. Never varies but that guy just never puts on weight." She laughed, flicking her hair so that it danced around the back of her neck before settling.

Ratso was about to comment when the sound of torrential rain started beating down on the corrugated roof. "You're in the wrong job. How about TV weather presenter?"

She smiled, a gentle one, perhaps even affectionate. "You mean I'm a lousy cop?" She spoke in a slow drawl with an impish look on her face. Ratso guessed she had been brought up somewhere else in the Deep South, maybe America's Bible Belt.

Ratso laughed, liking the way she had turned his comment around. "Sending you here on a job this sensitive—that says it all."

"Well, thank you, kind sir," she replied, raising her glass to chink it with his. "You Brits sure know how to say all the right things. I gotta tell you, I'm a ways outta my comfort zone doing this." She let her deep blue eyes linger on him for a moment or so too long.

Ratso looked away. This Kirsty-Ann was cool, über-cool. He leaned forward so she could hear him above the rat-a-tat-tat of the rain on the roof. He smelled no perfume but vaguely recognised lavender soap. It was fresh and not overpowering. "Your chief explained you got one hand tied behind your back."

"Is that what Bucky said?" She shook her head. "He's wrong. It's both hands."

"Looking with one eye shut," Ratso replied confidently, adopting an expression on the hoof that seemed to fit what she was doing.

"Nuts to that, Todd! There's a hidden agenda up in DC. I call it *perverting* the truth. Concealing reality, if you will." She grabbed a handful of pistachios and munched angrily for a moment, her serene face now revealing her inner confusion. "Not my scene. My job is to catch criminals, investigate crimes, not to play CYA games for politicians in the State Department. When I started checking on Ruthven, I made a good breakthrough. I was excited, just hoping to see it through." She shook her head, eyes lowered. "And now I'm...you know...Washington's gofer.." She tossed her head dismissively.

Ratso sympathised, knowing he would have felt the same. "You mean both eyes shut?"

"Maybe that's what DC wants but Bucky, no way he would agree to that. Sure, Todd, I can look – maybe even find. But anything I uncover goes to Bucky, no media, no local cops. Bucky tells the guys in DC and ..."

"Nothing more happens unless it suits the suits." Ratso finished her explanation with a chuckle. "You've got to think big picture. *If* I'm right, this Lance Ruthven guy was helping a power broker called Adnan Shirafi in Afghanistan. Did you know that? Come to that, I don't know what you know!"

Kirsty-Ann laughed. "Assume I know nothing."

Ratso leaned forward. "For starters, Shirafi is king of the drug trade from Afghanistan but he's off-limits, a no-go zone; he's just too big in DC and London. Besides recent opportunities for contact in Kabul, Ruthven and Shirafi were at Harvard together."

The American looked impressed. "I did not know that." Each word was articulated to emphasise how important the information was.

"But I bet someone knows that up in DC. They just keep it close. Anyway, Shirafi *deserves* life sentences, keys thrown away." He drained his drink. "You want some Coke with your ice this time round?"

She rocked back her head. "Your British humour slays me."

He ordered more for them both. "The lives that bastard has ruined. But he's not even on my radar. Shirafi sits at God's right side and together with a guy called Boris Zandro, they dominate the European drug industry. But I can't prove it. Yet!"

"And if you did?"

"Zandro will get life. Shirafi will remain untouchable."

"So you and me both then. Same boat." They laughingly chinked glasses.

Ratso paused to wipe the steam from the window, watching the rain bounce off the stacked chairs on the patio. "If you can prove Ruthven probably drowned, no I guess *might have* is closer, what happens next is for them in Washington. I guess they might like that. My position is worse." He deliberately displayed one of his best smiles, demonstrating that the burden was light on his shoulders. "I'm here to *find* out why Bardici was here but if he killed Lance Ruthven, then either I bury the truth … or bury my career." He chopped his right hand sharply downwards.

"So give—tell me what's going on." Her eyes extended an invitation that was hard to refuse. Though her hands never moved, Ratso felt as if she were caressing his arm to encourage him.

"It'll take time."

"Time I got." It was her turn to grin but it was sardonic. "Tomorrow I'm to follow up *information received*—that someone was seen snorkelling the weekend Ruthven disappeared. Infer a shark attack. My guess, there were hundreds snorkelling." She grabbed the menu. "Want a bite?"

"Is that what one shark said to the other?" Ratso's comment stopped her short and she laughed so infectiously that he joined in. Though he had barely digested the fries from lunch, he wanted to be with her. "Yeah, I could murder some fresh conch, squeeze of lime. How about you?"

"A green salad. I'll order. This is on FLPD, by the way. No expense spared—not till you put in the expenses claim, that is." She made her way to the counter, her long legs and backside shown off to perfection by the pale pink hip-hugging slacks that didn't seem to be slack anywhere at all. Ratso watched her chatting freely to the bartender, her face quite angular in profile, her nose slightly beaky and commanding. There was certainly a *don't mess* vibe in her demeanour until she laughed or smiled, when her aura changed to *I don't bite really*. Ratso found the mixed message to be a real turn-on but he guessed with looks like hers, she was bound to be propositioned constantly. Her deep pink cutaway vest top, decorated front and back with a couple of palm trees, showed off her breasts—slightly larger than average. Ratso bet no surgical enhancement; if he was right, Kirsty-Ann was a no-nonsense type who would never have contemplated silicone.

When she returned, Ratso gave her a potted version of the painstaking efforts to nail Zandro. She was a good listener, only asking occasional but very pertinent questions. When he finished, she turned to the matter in hand. "So you have our Homeland Security pictures of both men, right?"

"Yes. And my pal in the Bahamas police here is using them right now. On a pretext." He spotted her concern. "Relax. Low-key. He understands where I'm coming from."

"Anything I can do for you?"

There was no hint of flirtatiousness in her remark and Ratso played a straight dead bat. "Did you find out where Ruthven was staying? Did he have a hired car? Was it parked near a beach or returned to the airport?"

"No idea. Not yet. But I have no plans to go to every beach looking for a neat pile of Ruthven's clothes."

"Some of what I might discover may be, well, inconvenient in Washington." Ratso looked thoughtful and rather sombre but then he brightened. "But with luck, I may not need to check out car rentals, hotels, bars, clubs. It all depends what I get from the shipyard."

"Meaning?"

"Meaning if both Bardici and Lance Ruthven went there, I've got the connection."

"And the ship?"

"We're working on who paid for it—the name of the owners, who is to be the master and so on."

"You may look confident," she paused, "and don't take this wrong but to me you sound, oh, kinda worried. Cautious maybe."

"Do I?" He had hoped it hadn't shown. "Bitter experience, I suppose. It's like Snakes and Ladders. Up the ladder only to slide down a snake!" Ratso grinned ruefully and shrugged. "Let's change the subject, shall we?"

Kirsty-Ann leaned forward. "Sometime…oh, hell, right now—let me tell you about the stuff I'm dodging back in Fort Lauderdale." She took a deep breath and then began. "I'm being investigated regarding a fatality." She clasped her hands so tightly that the joints cracked. In a few clipped sentences, she gave Ratso the details. "So, it gets me down—the media, the assholes who phone in to the local radio stations, the tweets, the hate messages. Being over here is an escape from it." She looked up and Ratso saw the bitterness in her eyes.

For a fleeting second, Ratso brushed his hand across hers in a gesture of solidarity. "It'll blow over. I'd trust your chief.

Bucky will back you. Anyway, something else will catch the public imagination. Your story will die."

"You're some listener, Todd. Thank you. Now let's talk about something else. This was kinda funny. After I checked in last night, the concierge at my hotel must have thought I needed some male company. He told me about the Red Poppy Bar just along from my hotel."

"I saw it."

"He said if I wanted hot dates or to chill out some, that was the place."

"Right! I saw the sign outside saying *THE Singles Joint*."

"I didn't need any hot dates. Or cold ones, come to that." Her eyes danced as she spoke. "But anyways, I checked it out. Sure is a great pick-up joint. But not for a homebody like me. My priority back home is Leon, my baby son, not listening to testosterone-charged men in bars hoping for a one-nighter."

Ratso nearly asked what her priority was when she was *not* in Fort Lauderdale but there was an iciness in her eyes that warned *don't go there*. His mental image of Kirsty-Ann was falling apart. "Your husband? He in the police?"

"I'm a single mom now. My husband was murdered in the line of duty. He was FBI. Now it's just me, my mom and baby Leon."

"I'm sorry." Ratso waited for further details but none came. "But the Red Poppy. Why were you telling me? You see a glint in my eye? You reckon I'm testosterone-charged?"

"No way," she laughed. "Hey, that sounds kinda insulting whatever I answer! I was thinking about where you would find loose tongues. A place the crew of your ship or the shipyard workers might go to get laid."

Ratso wiped the remains of lemon juice from his mouth. "I like it. This Red Poppy could be useful." He watched her push aside her empty plate. "When do you leave the island?"

"After I've found a store owner who thinks he rented snorkelling gear or a wetsuit to a guy looking like Kurtner. Or any pointer." She paused thoughtfully. "Or I'm getting nowhere. So maybe a coupla days."

"But as I said to Bucky, Ruthven never came here. Sounds like someone is interested in why he came here but dare not admit it."

"And no Feds involved. Fool's errand isn't it! But perhaps we can meet up, exchange news? Tomorrow evening."

"Sure. I'd like that. And some escape from work."

"Do we ever escape? Still, it sounds good to me." Ratso looked out of the window, which was still wet with the rain. "It's nearly stopped. Shall we?" He started to rise and she followed but neither moved away from the window. They stood, side by side, watching the rain dripping down from the trees and the roof above them.

"You'll be back in England for Christmas?"

"I'm working there on Christmas Eve. We're piggy in the middle—one gang stealing another's gear. Could turn nasty."

"Some thief in red with a beard going down the chimney?"

"Not a *ho-ho-ho* will be heard, I can tell you." He paused to adjust his shirt, which was clinging unpleasantly to his back. "My Christmas present to myself will be banging up a few thugs and hopefully nabbing a key distributor."

"You'll be in charge?"

"Not at the scene. I'm leading the planning but the County of Sussex will provide what we call the Tactical Firearms Unit.

They'll handle the heavy stuff, even though I'm trained and allowed to carry a weapon."

"Take care, then. You don't want to be caught in a shootout."

"Yeah. I'm working on a plan."

She nodded abstractedly, obviously deep in thought and then glanced at her watch. "Now, if you'll excuse me, I'm gonna ring Mom and say hi to Leon. If I wait till I'm at my hotel, he'll be asleep." Moments later, they had parted, an awkward moment when neither party wanted to be so formal as to shake hands or to be so relaxed as to throw in a hug. They parted very simply with a warm smile. Ratso hurried toward his car, the rain still dripping from the palms that lined the beach. As he walked away, Kirsty-Ann's eyes followed his every step till he reached his car, admiring the athletic figure with the languid gait. Only then did she turn her attention to her phone.

Before Ratso had even started the engine, his phone rang. It was Darren Roberts. "I've some news."

"Good or bad?"

"Urgent."

"Let's meet at the Red Poppy Bar."

"You wanna go *there*?"

40

Freeport, Grand Bahama Island

After a swift shower and a change of clothes, Ratso approached the Red Poppy Bar. The evening air was fresh after the rain. The dust and windblown sand had all settled beneath a cloudless dusk and the drying foliage exuded scents to mask drifting diesel fumes and the salty sea tang. The unmade track to the beach had turned to reddish mud and his canvas shoes soon had a dirty rim around each sole. He enjoyed the image of DCI Caldwell ruining his poncy loafers as he squelched along here. *Yes, I like that a lot!* As he dodged the puddles, every step revealed his sense of purpose, what with action in Cyprus, Gibraltar, London clubs, Brighton and now right here. Dead-end streets now seemed to be opening up.

I'm coming to get you, Boris Zandro.

But who was JF? He still needed background about Terry Fenwick's partners. The F pointed to Fenwick but Tosh had texted that his brother's name was Adrian. Tosh was now checking on Google for Albanian surnames beginning with F in West London. "Like looking for a Mr Chin or Mr Li in Beijing," Tosh had muttered on being instructed.

At the large mat outside the entrance, he paused to scrape off the worst of the mud, noting with irritation that some had splashed onto his sandy slacks. Above the double doors was the garish red strip lighting depicting a poppy. The bar was barely a mile from the shipyards, as the crow flew—conveniently close for ships' crews to drop by. And it looked the type of place where loose tongues might wag after a few beers or stronger. Beyond the low-rise housing, he saw the distant, powerful overhead lights and the towering height of a giant cruise ship. From somewhere in that direction came the rumble of cranes. Though he could not see the *Nomora*, just knowing it was there quickened his pulse.

He pushed through the swing doors and was surprised how quiet the bar was. Not in terms of sound, because the thump of heavy metal shuddered round the dimly lit room. It was spacious but the dark colours and the alcoves and booths for canoodling made it seem smaller. Apparently, the island's fast set had yet to appear. Ratso glanced toward each corner, wondering if the inspector was tucked away at a table behind a flickering candle. He took in the rock-star artefacts, the fishing nets, the conch shells, the stuffed flying fish and a blue marlin that all somehow blended to create the ambience.

Satisfied that Darren Roberts had not arrived, he swaggered toward the bar. Sitting at a table with a clear view of the door was a group of young women. Ratso reckoned by their raised voices and raucous laughter that they had been hitting the rum for several hours, maybe young Americans on a bachelorette party. Judging by the hungry way they eyed Ratso as he crossed the room, they were already flying. Quite reluctantly but with a cheery smile and wave, he refused an invitation to join them and headed for the line of barstools.

He shuffled up beside a couple of local girls who looked drugged out and who he assumed were anybody's for a hundred bucks, perhaps even less. Their full lips were caked with red lipstick and their once unblemished skin was coated with blusher to highlight their cheekbones. The prettier one, relatively speaking, had dyed her hair a deep red to match her lips; the other had her hair close-cropped. She must have thought this improved her looks but Ratso reckoned it added ten years to her clapped-out eighteen.

The redhead gave him a tired smile but Ratso simply nodded hello and turned to the bull of a barman, who asked him his pleasure. Ratso ordered a Hurricane, picking it at random from the list of cocktails he had been handed. He stood, one elbow on the bar, watching in disbelief as the barman filled an hourglass-shaped goblet with dark rum, coffee liqueur, Irish cream and Grand Marnier. A green parasol, pieces of pineapple and a cherry added to the Del Boy appearance. He sipped cautiously, liked the flavour and so sucked a hefty draft through the twin straws as he skirted the empty dance floor and settled in a booth close to the pool table.

He had almost drained the glass when Darren appeared, beaming hugely as he crossed the room. "What you drinking, mon?"

"A Hurricane."

Darren's eyes rolled in amusement. "You looking to get laid tonight?"

"No plans but..." He grinned "Right now I'm flying high."

"That's just fine, Todd, 'cos I got good and bad news."

"Better get me another Hurricane, then. More rum, less Irish cream." As he waited for Darren's return, he gazed at a faded photo of Freddie Mercury, arm defiantly raised. As if from nowhere the red-headed hooker appeared close to him, her large backside bulging around her white denim hot pants. She stopped beside the pool table and gave him what she assumed was a sly and sexy come-on. She picked up a cue, turned it upside down and suggestively stroked the thick end, rolling her eyes in apparent ecstasy. As her performance ended, she gave Ratso a huge wink of her false eyelash. "How 'bout it, big boy?" she suggested.

Ratso was wrong-footed. His immediate thoughts were to tell this overweight tart to piss off and stop imagining that a bloke like him had to pay. "Hi, sweetie! Tempting." He looked round defensively. "But my wife." He winked. "She's arriving soon." The woman shrugged and gave him a sad smile as she turned away, revealing an unsightly purple bruise on her left buttock.

Darren returned with a beer for himself and a reddish-brown Hurricane tinkling with ice. "Got an offer you could easily refuse from Cassie?"

"You know her? Both of them?"

"Sure, it's our job to know the working girls."

Ratso nodded to the four American women who were whooping over something. "With so many freebies around, I'm surprised they have any takers."

Darren grinned hugely. "You'd be surprised. Plenty of guys, they do like the power when they buy a woman. But you right. These American women, they be plenty cutters, mon."

"Cutters?"

"Freebies. After a coupla Hurricanes they is anybody's."

"Okay. Business. Give me the good news."

Darren produced the photos of Ruthven and Bardici in disguise. "Ida, she done recognise both men. So did Hubert, the security guard at the gate." He pointed to Kurtner. "He done been at the yard four, maybe five times."

"Why?"

"He do check the progress."

"Or not, as the case may be," added Ratso, thinking how the drugs' arrival in the UK had been postponed twice. "And Mujo Zevi?"

"Just one visit. He too do chasing Lamon Wilson. But..." The Bahamian put down the photos and fixed Ratso full in the eye. "Ida, she been check her boss diary. These two, they done both been booked to visit together."

"And?"

"That guy never showed." He pointed to Kurtner.

"Did your wife know anything about Kurtner's visit to the yard?"

"She served him and the boss coffee. She do say it was a short meeting, maybe twenty minutes but mon, there was a shouting, plenty shouting. She do hear the visitor plenty much. Then they done gone inspect the ship."

"Did she speak to her boss about the visit?"

"When the guy, he left, her boss he scared. Mon! Lamon, he was shakin', just staring at a wall. She done fix him a large Johnny Walker." Darren cackled at the thought. "Then later he did kick ass in all directions."

"Why?"

"Because he say this Kurtner guy, he mad, wild-eyed mad."

Ratso nodded thoughtfully and then sucked long and hard on the straws. "That fits."

"So...you want the bad news?" Darren waited for Ratso's shrug. "The ship surveyors, they a-gonna inspect *Nomora*. The crew, they all been done hired. That Panama Ship Registry they soon gonna approve the paperwork—certificates, crew an' all. Then the *Nomora* she do sail."

"Where to?"

"Ida not know."

Ratso needed time. "Like when?"

"Ida say mebbe 10 days latest. Before the New Year."

"What! *That* quick."

"This guy," he pointed to Mujo Zevi, "he do take no shit. He did dictate the date. *Nomora* she done gone, finished before New Year, he say. Or else big shit happen!"

"So Mujo Zevi scared the crap out of your wife's boss."

"Ida reckons the bosses, they is a barrel-load of monkeys. They always cackalin' and sniggerin' after Kurtner had gone. But Ida she damn sure she take care. Her bosses, they done bought the yard maybe a year back. They is hard men. But this guy from London, he did give their asses a right whipping." He *tee-heed* loudly at the image.

Ratso heard what Darren was saying but his mind had moved on. With the crew arriving shortly, time was tight if the boys from Vauxhall Cross were needed to plant a bug on *Nomora*. He sensed Darren was looking at him, wondering about the long silence.

Ratso shoved over the pictures. "The barman know you're a police officer?" He saw Darren's toothy grin that said *stupid question*. "Check out if he saw either of them. Low-key. Pilfering enquiries or something. I've got to get a couple of texts away."

As soon as Darren had moved off, Ratso sent an urgent text to the AC and another to Bob Whewell at the IMB. The messages gone, he checked the time. It was nearly 8:30 p.m., 1:30 a.m. in London. Nothing would happen till the morning.

He glanced across the room and saw that the tables and booths had now filled up considerably, with a wide cross-section of singles out on the pull. Many were locals but some were crew from the luxury yachts, sporting that perma-tan look from a day job cruising the Caribbean every day of the year. Others, their faces pallid, had probably flown in from wintry US cities for a whoopee weekend. The decibel level was rising with Van Halen reverberating from all corners. Ratso stifled a yawn until he noticed Darren sitting at a table for two in animated conversation with the red-haired hooker. As he drained the last of the Hurricane with a satisfying slurp, he idly wondered whether either of the two men had been desperate enough to dip their wick inside Cassie's much-abused body. He did not have to speculate long before Darren bought the girl a drink and returned, beaming.

"My shout." Ratso stood up.

"Thanks but I promise Ida, I not be late."

Ratso sat down again and looked enquiringly at Darren, who explained, "The American, Hank Kurtner, he was a regular. The barman, Joel, he did recognise him for sure and pointed me to Cassie. She done been spent the whole night with him several times. She did know him as Hank. Just Hank. He sell auto spares and comes from Detroit, Michigan. He did always stay at different hotels."

"When she last see him?"

"At the Marlin. The weekend he disappeared. He did spend Friday night with her. She did say he was a regular guy. Like plenty doggie-doggie." Darren grinned at the thought. "Not like some weirdoes. Mon, she do say they kinky bastards."

"She know why Kurtner came to the island?"

He shrugged. "The usual - to chill out, catch the rays. Maybe go snorkelling."

Ratso nearly reacted at the word snorkelling but managed to remain poker-faced. "That it? That's all she knows after four or five all-nighters?" Ratso shook his head. "Still, I guess he wasn't paying for polite conversation."

"Nobody know the other guy." Darren stood up, keen to get away.

Ratso rose, dwarfing the Bahamian and clapped an arm round his shoulder. "You've done a great job. I'll be in touch." As he said the words, he was already troubled; if the IMB didn't deliver, tomorrow was going to be tough. "I'm not staying."

"Hey! After those coupla Hurricanes, you'd be flying soon. I thought you liked to party, mon!"

"Sad sod now, aren't I? Too many things doing my head in. Besides Van Halen." They walked to the exit. "I need some night air and then later a quiet place serving beer, chicken, peas and rice."

After parting from Darren, he decided to take a look at the shipyard. It was no distance but the route proved to be a zigzag maze of darkened back streets, a mix of residential, auto repair and small industrial units, a rough part of town. Every step made him more wary. Stray mongrels roamed at will, trash fluttered in the light breeze. But there was nothing specific to make him feel uneasy.

Except experience.

He touched his belt for reassurance. He had bought it in a personal security store in Dallas, Texas. Though it just looked like a chunky buckle, it doubled as a knuckleduster that could be freed from the leather in a trice. On flights, he had to put it in his checked baggage for fear it would be confiscated. No question, it was a fearsome and effective means of self-defence. A snarling dog bounding up to a fence beside him convinced him to be prepared; he unclipped the buckle and gripped it tightly in his right hand, leaving the leather belt flapping freely around his waist.

Moving farther from the bright lights, he entered a broken-down area of strange smells, rusting bicycles, scooters and unloved cars, a part of Freeport that was full of unfamiliar sounds and voices drifting from the shabby single-storey homes. He had never been close to these timbered shacks with their corrugated iron roofs but he had often seen ones like them on TV, wrecked after a Caribbean hurricane.

He passed a few locals, embryo basketball players judging by their height, all of them towering over him. They seemed uninterested in him but Ratso knew that walking in deprived areas where you look the odd man out or the richest guy around was a ticking time bomb. He'd learned that working round the backside of Kilburn in northwest London. But he soldiered on, hoping he looked more confident than he felt, all the while heading for the brightly lit port area and the massive cruise ship with its yellow funnel.

The first shipyard of four that he reached, next to the Grand Bahama Shipyard, was well protected with a close-boarded fence topped with razor wire, at least nine feet high and heavily locked at the main gate. In the dry dock he saw the cruise ship standing aloof between lines of lights and four huge cranes. He walked on for another five hundred metres before he saw his goal. There, in a dry dock, was the *Nomora*. Its green hull and low-level white bridge stood out under the glare of overhead spotlights. He could see no sign of activity. One thing was obvious: as Darren had warned, casual access was impossible with a fence made from mesh and razor wire. But peering through it, he could see that the ship looked freshly painted. Whether the rust was still underneath or had been properly treated would be for others to find out when the vessel was caught in a Storm Force Ten.

His eyes studied the vessel from end to end. Like he always did, he used a cricket pitch for comparison. Probably she was up to fifty metres in length. What had been done in the refit costing a million quid? He had no clue as to what to expect but one thing was for sure—within those fifty metres, there was plenty of room to stash away drugs with a London street value into the billions.

Ratso moved on down the side of the yard, passing a solitary security guard who was seated in a sentry box smoking a cigarette, the smell of tobacco drifting from him. A quick glance at the heavy-duty gates was sufficient to convince him that Darren had been right—for the average Joe, getting inside the yard was a no-no. Everything now turned on his message to Bob Whewell at the IMB. As the AC had said, he'd have to use ingenuity to get aboard.

He was just bracing himself for another unpleasant walk back to the tourist area when he got lucky. A taxi pulled up to drop off someone who, though in mufti, looked like a crew member—officer material, too. While the man paid off the driver, Ratso noticed that his build was familiar, as was the bald head with tufts flying sideways by each ear. As he stepped forward to claim the taxi, Ratso was sure. *My God! It's him!* He wanted to yell out with satisfaction. Immediately he half turned his own face away but he need not have worried. The drunkard seemed uninterested in anything other than keeping his balance and persuading one leg to step in front of the other without collapsing. The man belched loudly and the smell of rum lingered as Ratso took in the side view of the familiar pugnacious face, clearly profiled by the security lights along the perimeter fence. There could be no doubt.

Another duck had joined the row.

41

Freeport, Grand Bahama Island
Once inside the cab, Ratso turned round for a final look as the man fumbled and dropped his ID card at the security guard's feet. For a moment, Ratso ignored the driver's request about where he wanted to go. His heart was pounding, his pulse racing and his brain racing back to when that face had haunted him. Though the memories were unpleasant, he felt on fire, his nerve ends tingling with excitement. The driver repeated the question, this time more aggressively., Ratso had to force himself to answer, asking to be taken somewhere quiet where he could chill out with the *very best* local cooking, no singles crowd and no loud music.

Ten minutes later, the taxi dropped him at a small bar not far from his hotel. He needed some downtime. He was desperate to catch up on the injuries involving two of the English fast bowlers as they prepared for the Melbourne Test but now this face from the past danced before him like a kid's Halloween lantern. *Oh God! And then there's Charlene, too late to phone now—long gone 2 a.m. over there. What to say, anyway? Will I make Christmas Day?* He'd text her. That would work.

The exterior was scarcely inviting—drab colours, peeling paint and a cracked window—but inside, a cheerful woman, who Ratso took to be the wife of the owner, showed him to a table for four, which she cleared for his solitary use. The restaurant area was small, seating ten at a push but it was under half full. Ratso reckoned he could see the husband standing in front of a cooker laden with steaming pots. He ordered a beer and jerk chicken and was about to text Charlene when his phone vibrated. He saw it was Jock Strang.

"Hi, boss." The unmistaken rasp cut through the several thousand miles between them. "How's it going?"

"Bloody fantastic. You'll never guess who I just saw." He paused for effect. "Only our old friend Micky Quigley."

Ratso heard Jock suck through his teeth. "That Irish bastard? He'll be the ship's master, then?"

"I guess. We missed the sod on that freighter bust in Lyme Bay. Now we have another chance. I wonder where he's been hiding up."

"Play this right, boss and we'll know where he'll spend the next twenty years." Jock's laughter carried the miles easily. "But, boss, I'm no going to cheer ye up."

"Go on, then!" He nodded to the woman as she delivered his beer, admiring the red ribbon bow in her generous ponytail. "You're still in Cyprus?"

"Aye, right enough! I wish I wisna. It's been a right scunner— or in English, a dog's dinner." Ratso poured his beer as the Scot started to explain. "I'm here with Nancy Petrie, ye ken. We stayed overnight at a crap flea pit near Larnaca Airport, run by an ex-RAF electrician who used to be based at Akrotiri. The lamps were screwed onto the bedside tables. At breakfast there was a big sign: *Our cutlery is not medicine. Do not take it after meals!*"

Ratso snorted a laugh. "Yeah. I get the drift but get on with it."

"Zandro's pilot phoned but not from the UK. Said he had no chance after Zandro gave him instructions. If you believe that."

Ratso made a mental note to worry about that later. "So he landed while you were still kipping or noshing, eh?"

"Now, now, boss! Ach no. It wisna like that at all. He phoned from...Istan-bul."

"Istanbul?"

"When Zandro arrived at Biggin Hill Airport, he wanted to go to Cyprus right enough—but not the southern side that we all know and love. He wanted to go to the Turkish side. It's called the TRNC—the Turkish Republic of North Cyprus. That's the part the Turks kept after they invaded back in the 1970s."

"Go on."

"But the point is, no flights from Europe can land on the Turkish side. It's regarded as an illegal state with the Turks as illegal occupiers." Jock paused to let the message sink in. "So flights go via Istanbul or Ankara. Of course, when your guy phoned from Istanbul, he was about to take off again. So there we are, stuck on the Greek side while Zandro's jet lands at Ercan Airport across the border in the TRNC."

"So you jumped into your rented car to drive across?"

"Aye, right enough. I was advised I could cross with a car at a godforsaken place called Metehan."

"Easy, then."

Jock snorted. "I was queuing to get across when I got chatting to a Welsh fella in the next car. He told me it was illegal to take a rented car across to what he called *bandit country*. He said it was deep shit to take rented cars out; the hatred on the Turkish side is too intense. In the war nearly forty years ago, there was ethnic cleansing, with thousands murdered by both sides. Each blamed the other. From what this Welshman said, *both* sides were barbaric. Muslims were butchered or cleared out of the Greek side and vice versa."

"Get on with it! I'm in no mood for history lessons. You got across?"

"Aye! *Eventually*. At first, we decided to walk across and rent on the other side. But this Welsh guy offered us a lift, so we crossed with him."

"So?"

"He was heading to a port called Kyrenia, which the Turks have renamed Girne. He said we could easily rent a car there. Looks like a great spot for a holiday, boss. No a bandit in sight! Great hotels, casinos, bars, clubs, beaches and a port. Anyway, we rented no hassle but the sick bit? We could have driven across. It's only cars rented in the TRNC that can't cross into the south. The Welsh guy was wrong! So I rented and drove like the locals—that means like ye've no fear of death and with less skill than a learner driver with impaired vision. It was about thirty kilometres to Ercan Airport but we were too late. Zandro's jet had landed over ninety minutes before."

"You spoke to the pilot?"

"Aye! *Eventually*, yes. Giles had gone off for a bite tae eat and, if you believe him, said he'd left his phone on the plane. *Eventually*, when he did answer, he said Zandro had gone to… wait for it…only Kyrenia. To join his boat."

Ratso bit his tongue rather than arse-kicking Jock for not checking that out in the port before dashing to the airport. "Any clue who Zandro was meeting?"

"The pilot didn't ken, if you believe him. Says Zandro never volunteers."

"How long till Zandro flies back?"

"The pilot's on standby for tomorrow—sorry, that's today now. It's 4:50 a.m. here and bloody freezing, too."

"So you found *Tirana Queen*, did you?"

"Aye! *Eventually!*"

Ratso mimicked Jock's accent. "*Aye eventually* seems to be the story of this trip, Jock."

"Right enough! *Eventually's* a great word for this lousy snafu. I raced back to Kyrenia harbour and found out that even if a yacht eighty-nine metres long could get in, the berths are all full in winter anyway."

Ratso sighed. "So, next? *Eventually?*"

"Someone suggested I try the Delta Marina about a mile away, so we dashed there, busting the backside of the Kia. No joy. *Tirana Queen* wisna' there. I spoke to a couple of crew on a wee sailing boat who'd seen a floating gin palace moored just outside the marina but it had sailed, *weighed anchor* as they said, about forty minutes earlier."

"So where are you now?"

"We're sitting in the Kia, heater going full blast, using our night glasses. We never ate yesterday evening except Nancy shared her Crunchie bar with me. My stomach's rumbling like Krakatoa." He sounded more pissed off than Ratso had ever heard him.

"You'll feel better after a good breakfast. You should be able to get stuck in after daybreak without Zandro arriving and leaving unseen."

Jock sounded hesitant. "Our luck, as soon as I've started to murder bangers, egg and bacon, his damned boat will moor and he'll be gone."

"So where's your observation point?"

"We're in a lay-by on a narrow road about two hundred metres above sea level. When it's daylight, we should spot the vessel for ten miles in any direction."

"Nautical or Statute miles?"

"Sorry, boss but I'm no in the mood for banter."

"Ah! Thanks." Ratso acknowledged his meal being served. "Sorry, Jock. I was just thanking the serving wench for my dinner of jerk chicken, peas and rice."

"Boss, stop, stop! If this goes on much longer, I'll have to eat Nancy."

"Okay, now listen. I want photos of every person leaving the boat *and* those who stay aboard. Let's hope for Shirafi. Close-ups on anything they're carrying. You've got the zoom lens?"

"Aye. When they drop anchor—heh, how'd ye like that nautical jargon—we'll mosey on down to the marina. I guess they come ashore in a wee speedboat."

"Tenders, they're called, since you're so into the *hello sailor* scene. And bring me back some Turkish Delight. The pink one."

He ended the call and turned to the steaming plate in front of him but his mind was troubled. He pushed the food around as if marshalling his thoughts. The highs of just a short while ago were gone. Was the pilot to be trusted? Or was he playing games? It hadn't sounded good. *Not good, not good at all.*

42

Freeport, Grand Bahama Island
While waiting for his coffee, Ratso sent a friendly text to Charlene promising to talk when he could. The message gone, he looked around the dining room, which was almost devoid of any features except for an incongruous solitary picture of Neil Armstrong on the surface of the Moon. Back home, the small caff would have been called *a greasy spoon*, especially given the curiously bent fork he had been given. But the homemade rum and raison ice cream made up for the naked-light-bulb atmosphere.

At least his to-do list was now finished. Using Cricinfo, he updated himself about the build-up to the Melbourne Test. One day he would be there watching the English batsmen walk out, trying to look confident with 80,000 Aussies baying for their blood. *One day*, he told himself again. *Like when I've nailed every drug baron in London and won the Euromillions.*

Seeing flaming sambuca on the drinks list, he ordered one. When it arrived, correctly served with three coffee beans, the hostess lit the liqueur and after a few seconds he blew out the flames. "Here's to common sense," he muttered, thinking of the dickheads back home who had banned setting the drink alight. *Health and safety regulations. Eurocrap from Brussels! No doubt you could set your nasal hair on fire, or even the hairs on your arse if you were daft enough. Consumer activists gone mad!* Ratso sipped the warm, sticky glass with relish, remembering La Casalinga restaurant near Lord's where he'd sunk several on days when rain had stopped play.

His thoughts turned to Kirsty-Ann and tomorrow night. She was an enigma—warm, friendly but with an invisible shield that warned him not to push his luck. But someone must have done, or there would have been no Leon. But what were *his* intentions? Once upon a time, hell he'd have been after her like a rat up a drainpipe. But now with the big four-zero approaching, life was different. No more hitting a Saturday night party with a cheapo Spanish red and ending with a shag on the shagpile.

He sighed at the flood of memories of the wild days and wilder nights but as the second sambuca kicked in, nostalgia gave way to uncertainty. These days, arresting Zandro, getting the lads in their wheelchairs up to Lord's or bowling some late out-swingers seemed more important than chasing bits of skirt in noisy clubs. And if Kirsty-Ann fancied him, a big if, well Charlene didn't own him, for God's sake. But thoughts of her alone in her semi-detached in Kingston cast a long shadow over the final sambuca and lingered even after he had paid his bill. He drained the coffee and promised himself a local beer at the hotel bar before turning in.

Back in his room, he flicked on the TV and caught the end of a CNN news programme as he undressed. Then, just as he was about to climb between the tired-looking sheets, his phone vibrated. It was Bob Whewell from the International Maritime Bureau. "Christ, Bob! You're at your desk early."

Ratso was rewarded with a laugh. "Sorry to spoil the workaholic image but I'm in Singapore. We're thirteen hours ahead. I already did a presentation on piracy this morning."

Ratso laughed. "Sorry that I butted in, then. You must be busy."

"No problem. I haven't got all the answers yet but I expect to reply tomorrow. It's not straightforward. But you wanted cover to get aboard the *Nomora* urgently. That's fixed. I've spoken to the surveyor who does the classification and survey work for the State of Panama where the vessel is registered. I persuaded him to advance the ship's survey to today and for you to join their surveyor. You will meet Tito Comores at 8 a.m. at the Pelican Bay Hotel. He will have notified the yard and is fixing your credentials."

"Thanks, Bob. You're a star. I owe you one."

He lay in bed, restless from the time difference and unable to sleep. For sure, Tito would know the owners of the vessel but he'd bet it would be a faceless company and nominee shareholders. *Useless.* He needed real names - a trail to tight-lipped lawyers in Gibraltar would be another cul-de-sac. *But what about source of funds?* The thought shot through him. He sat up and turned on the light. *The source of funds. Hell. I've nearly missed that open goal.* He checked the time: it was far too late to phone Darren, so he sent him a text, his fingers fairly flying over the keys. *For God's sake! How could I have overlooked such a basic?*

The room was small, the air stale and there was no minibar or tea or coffeemaker. He paced around, stared at the blackness outside the window and reluctantly poured himself a glass of sparkling water. Then he sat on the solitary chair sipping it, his angular face locked in a deepening frown. He had nearly emptied the glass when his iPhone alerted him to a message. Wensley Hughes wanted him to call when he awoke.

Brownie point time, he decided as he dialled at once. *Good to be seen to be alert at this time of night.* But what the hell did the AC want? It had to be trouble.

43

Freeport, Grand Bahama Island
Surrounded by the smell of fresh paint, Ratso walked along the deck beside Tito Comores, an amiable South African approaching retirement with enthusiasm. The deck was cluttered with hawsers, torn matting, old bedding, new bedding, a broken chair and fast-food wrappers. But even the new paint could not disguise the lingering smell of decay, saltwater, seaweed and old rope. No real attempt had been made to smarten up *Nomora* for her inspection but Tito seemed content, not in the least surprised by the signs of rust still visible or the broken-down feeling that pervaded a vessel on which one million pounds was being spent. Besides several cans of paint to cover the rust, Ratso found it hard to understand what the money had bought. True, the hull was freshly dark green and the crew's quarters spanking white but under that façade of beauty, *Nomora* was a shithole. Or so Tito had decided after completing the tour of inspection.

Hoping not to encounter Micky Quigley, Ratso ran his eye down the short list of work to be inspected. Some rusting parts of the A-frame at the stern had been replaced. The dry and wet labs had been cleaned and looked ready for new scientific equipment to be installed. The old stuff had been ripped out and dumped. *Apparently*. But the vessel had been in dry dock for days, weeks, months. Ratso stopped at the bow, gazing down the entire length of the vessel with Tito beside him. They were alone but Ratso still spoke quietly.

"Tito, everything seem in order to you?"

Tito looked at his checklist, each one ticked. "Todd, this was what is known as an *additional survey*. That means it was needed only because of a refit or renewal. Being an oceanographic research vessel means it also has to comply with RVSS—Research Vessel Safety Standards. *Nomora* passed its annual survey just before she sailed here." He checked the records. "That was just six months ago, so this is not a full survey. I only have to check some minor repairs, the work on the A-frame, check the suitability of the winches, the knuckleboom crane over there and the modest refit." He pointed to the midships area. "There's been only limited adaptation that must comply with safety regulations and I only have to certify that the standard of workmanship is satisfactory."

"The previous owners were Coast Guards but it never carried weaponry?"

"Not officially. Not obviously, either. Most of the space below decks was used by the boffins testing water for the fish urine content or whatever it is they do." He chuckled, something that had come easily to him all morning. "Straightforward job, a no-brainer really." He tapped his list with a pen bearing a hotel logo. "Finally, I have to certify that the vessel complies with various maritime rules and because nothing unusual has been done to the vessel, I am satisfied." He ticked the final box.

Ratso's puzzlement was growing with every word. "Can you see work worth a million pounds or even dollars?

"Pounds," Tito confirmed from his spreadsheet. "You can see why the Coast Guard dumped her. She *was* a rust bucket. She *remains* a rust bucket...but smartly painted - all fur coat and no knickers. So to answer the question--no, this job was overpriced. What I've seen was worth maybe a third to a half of that. The owners got their bollocks tweaked." Tito laughed, a gold tooth glinting in the sunlight. "It happens."

Ratso liked the answer. It ticked a box on *his* personal checklist and reinforced his opinion that he had to be wary of Lamon Wilson and all he stood for. Darren's wife's opinion had stuck with him. No legitimate owner paid a million quid for work worth just a third of that. No legitimate company hired Micky Quigley, either. Nobody would send Lance Ruthven on six trips just to see a few locals slapping paint onto a rusting hull.

Ratso tapped his foot, which resonated on the deck. There had to be more. Something not obvious had been done to *Nomora*. Something not on the job specification. Something not apparent from the sheaf of scale plans that Tito had been given. Something that the yard had charged heavily for—or something *Nomora*'s owners were happy to pay an extortionate price for. *Like silence.* He turned to his companion. "Thanks, Tito. I'll have to dash. I've another meeting in twenty minutes."

"If you want me, I'll be checking stuff in the offices. Your chap Quigley may be there with the CEO."

Ratso shook his head. "Thanks. I've one more meeting before racing to the airport." *Thanks, Wensley, for screwing up tonight's date with Kirsty-Ann,* he muttered under his breath as he clambered down the gangplank. He had sensed disappointment in her voice when he had broken the news but the call had been briskly efficient too. And now he'd also miss meeting Darren's contact—a young fitter called Chuckie who was flying back from Disney in

Orlando. He had worked aboard *Nomora* and Darren reckoned he was a relative who could be trusted. Not the ending he had hoped for and it showed in his taut facial muscles as he strode out of the yard, barely saying goodbye to the guard at the gate.

Twenty-one minutes later, Ratso was seated at the dining table in Darren's modest single-storey home. *Hurricane-proof*, Darren had proudly explained when Ratso arrived, pointing at the concrete blocks that made up the walls. Sitting beside Ratso was Ida, a petite, almost bird-like figure with gentle features, aged perhaps twenty-nine. Her hair was long, hanging in rivulets either side of her face. She wore little makeup and her skin was not as black as her husband's. Her eyebrows were perfectly groomed, boomerang-shaped, arching high above her eyes to enhance her open, enquiring look. Darren meanwhile was heating shrimp gumbo on the cooker across the room. The air was filled with the enticing smell of shrimp, onions, garlic, stewing tomatoes andouille sausage and mixed herbs.

"I really appreciate this," Ratso said, addressing them both. He was looking at printed pages from the company's invoice ledger kept on QuickBooks. There it was: addressed to Onduit (Enterprises) Limited of Gibraltar, an invoice for 1.62 million Bahamian dollars, equalling one million pounds sterling give or take. The services to be provided were *as per specification discussed and agreed with your representative.*

Darren dumped bowls of steaming gumbo in front of the two diners and then joined them. "You know that company?"

"I know the name. The team in London are working on the way money moved around using offshore jurisdictions. This is pretty damning material." He noticed Ida was simply playing with her spoon. "Ida, you look worried." She gave him a weak smile and shook her head but Ratso was unconvinced.

"Ida, she be happy to help." Darren was quick to intervene but Ratso could see she was in torment. "Did you get to copy the bank transfers, honey?"

As if pulling herself out of a deep swamp, Ida slowly removed a thin bundle of printouts from her orange sack-come-handbag. She never said a word and Ratso was unsure whether her attitude was just sullen or fearful. She turned away as Ratso flipped the pages. There had been four stage payments totalling the full amount. Each one had come from Onduit's account in Gibraltar using the seemingly reputable Royal United & Universal Bank of Canada.

"Perfect." Ratso's eyes said it all as he folded the papers and slipped them into his briefcase. Ida looked troubled, her stare locked on the floor but Darren seemed unaware or uncaring as he spooned the steaming gumbo into his mouth. Ida still hadn't touched hers. Ratso's eyes at last met Darren's and he motioned him to say something.

"Ida, you don't never need to worry." Darren shook his head vehemently. "No way. 'Cos Todd here will never use these documents in court. I telling you, sneaking out this stuff, nobody will ever know nothing. No shit."

"Darren's right, Ida. This is vital information but it's not evidence. If we need to prove this, we would get the shipyard to disclose these documents officially, as if I had never seen them. So you can relax." Ratso watched for Ida's reaction and was concerned that she still stared down, her lips pursed, her whole body taut. Ratso had seen similar body language often enough in interview rooms to be convinced something was bugging her. But what was it? Was she so scared of her boss? Did she know more about what work had been done on board? He gulped more of the hot, spicy soup during an embarrassing silence. Darren too had now caught the vibes.

"Ida, my honey-love, you is not in any trouble."

She suddenly pushed back her chair from the table and stood up. "Fuck you, Darren for using me—you using *your own wife*. You putting me, my job on the line. But you don't give a shit, do you? You mussa be think only your own career." She turned round sharply and grabbed her bag, tears pouring from her eyes. "You just using me. Make me feel like shit to my boss." The words tumbled out as Darren dashed toward her. He tried to put his arms round her shoulders but she shrugged him off and headed for the door.

Ratso was desperate to do something. "Ida, you can't go back to work crying, looking all shaken up. People will want to know why. Come and sit down. I'm not asking you anything else." He saw her waver and pressed on. "Look, I'm really sorry. It's my fault, not Darren's. I've been leaning on him to make this vital connection." He paused for a moment's debate with himself. "And I'd like to tell you why."

Ida turned to look at him, her almond-shaped eyes streaming. Ratso opened his wallet and from one pocket produced a photo of a healthy-looking Freddie receiving his bronze medal for completing the Ten Tors event on Dartmoor. "This is my nephew, Freddie. Young, fit, popular. Three years later, Freddie died alone in a London street, killed by drugs imported by the gang that own this boat." He saw he had her attention. "This is why I must win. And it's not just Freddie. There are thousands of others—kids, mums, dads...they've all had their lives and families destroyed. Does this drug baron care?" He paused. "We need all the help we can get and these papers are vital to bring these bastards down." He moved toward her, smiling. "I am so, so grateful."

Slowly, Ida's determined stare softened. She took the photo from him and studied the strong features of Freddie in his prime.

She wiped away a tear and then handed back the picture. Darren grasped her shoulder and gently eased her back to the table. She slumped down with a final sudden movement, blew her nose and then sat, looking down and away as if ashamed of her outburst.

"You scared, my sweet? Worried about something else? Something you is not telling me?" Darren was standing behind her, one hand on one shoulder, the other softly caressing the back of her neck. "Is that your problem?" There was a long silence broken only by the bubbling sounds of second helpings boiling on the cooker.

At last she spoke, turning toward her husband. "Darren, believe me. I got no part in all this. No way." She shook her head vehemently. "I know nothing, no shit. But *Nomora*, she was like special." Then she burst into more tears, her shoulders heaving uncontrollably.

For now, Ratso had heard enough. The rest would have to wait. He wanted to give her both barrels, peppering her with questions till the full story emerged but no way could he do that to Darren and Ida. He picked up his grip. "Enough, enough! I've got to get my flight." He saw Darren silently mouthing that they would speak later. "Ida, just remember the thousands of Freddies and when you're ready, tell Darren anything else you know. Please."

44

Freeport, Grand Bahama Island
An hour later, Ratso had checked in for a direct flight to Miami so he could make the evening connection to London. Still cursing Wensley Hughes for the order to rush back to plan the Christmas Eve raid, he crossed the check-in area at Grand Bahamas International. He had barely gone a few paces when he heard his name being called. Turning sharply to look over his shoulder, he spotted Kirsty-Ann, who had just entered the terminal.

He started to walk toward her, his body language oozing pleasure. Her face made no secret of her pleasure at catching him. "I'm glad I got here in time."

"Heh! What a great surprise," he replied. There was an awkward moment again when neither was sure how to greet the other in the middle of a crowded terminal. "Let's stop by the bar. I needn't go through just yet." Moments later they were perched on high stools, he with a beer, she clutching a Virgin Mary, easy on the ice.

"That was a real bummer about tonight." She spoke softly so that he had to lean in to hear her against the backdrop of chat from all sides. "After you called, I felt kinda lost. I'd no idea how much I was looking forward to dinner till you cancelled."

"Me too. You would not believe my language after the AC ordered me back!" He briefly touched her hand as they clinked glasses.

"Your enquiries finished? Go well?"

Ratso's mind raced through what he had achieved. "Seven, maybe eight out of ten. But given more time, it might have been a perfect ten." He appreciated her sympathetic look, her head cocked and her eyes lowered. "And you?"

"I guess." But Ratso could sense her unease. "I'll have a wrap tomorrow. My questions about hiring snorkelling equipment haven't spooked anybody. Those beach-bum kids are pretty laid back." She imitated their lazy drawl. "*Oh, really? Oh, yeah, could be. Sounds like someone. Sunday? Like two weeks ago? Sure. Mebbe! Yeah, there sure was a guy, yeah!*" Ratso laughed as Kirsty-Ann pressed on. "If the folk in Washington want to conclude Ruthven came here and got ate up by a shark, my report won't make them choke on their croissants."

But Ratso was concerned and she was quick to sense it from his raised eyebrow. She too now looked uneasy, her leg swinging to and fro.

"If DC leak or spin a suspected shark attack, the local media won't want those headlines. Not good for tourism. Tell me more but I'm concerned for you. Slightly better than headlines about a murdered tourist," added Ratso. He was thinking of the shocking Bahamas murder statistics that Darren had mentioned.

"You? Concerned? For me?" Kirsty-Ann saw his nod and her cheeks coloured as if she was touched quite deeply. "That's all, really. I wasn't briefed to dig deep about Hank Kurtner. Just to find out enough to let DC know that Kurtner may have died here. Bucky's sure they don't want any murder investigation in Freeport."

"There isn't one, I can tell you that," Ratso snorted. "Stinks, doesn't it?" He leaned toward her and found that he was lightly clasping her bare arm just above the wrist. It just seemed so right and she never flinched. "Look, if the Feds and Washington want a cover-up, the Atlantic out there," he nodded toward the sea, "is surely where you draw a big, fat line." She looked puzzled so he continued at once. "Forget Grand Bahama. Someone called Hank Kurtner flew here and never flew back. But nobody will miss Hank Kurtner. Why? Because he never existed except here."

"Go on."

"Lance Ruthven is different. He checked into the Fort Lauderdale Hilton but never checked out. His belongings were in the room." Ratso debated before continuing but then decided he should. "You ask me, which you haven't," he grinned, "I'd go for drowning in Florida and no sharks. Enthuse Bucky about investigating a possible sighting near Fort Lauderdale - somewhere others have drowned in difficult currents." He saw she was interested. "If DC play up a shark attack here or in Florida... and I don't think that's their game, wow—the world's media will invade. It'll be like Amity Island in *Jaws*. And that means intense scrutiny...of you and your investigation."

"Which, right now with the car wreck fatality, I want as much as a root canal." She seemed to be pushing deep into his mind. "Todd, you're a regular guy. But there's more, something else you haven't told me. Don't go holding out on me. And anyways...what is their game?"

"Okay. Hank Kurtner checked out of the Marlin Hotel."

"What! You found this out?"

"A hooker from the Red Poppy told me where he stayed, so I dropped by the Marlin as a friend expecting a birthday gift left for me the front desk. The girl said he'd long gone, nothing left in the room, nothing at the front desk. He'd paid his bill. But he never took the flight under the name of Kurtner and he abandoned his car."

"So he may be alive?"

Ratso shrugged. "He... maybe returned to Florida. Different ID. As you Americans say, don't bet the ranch. Kurtner's hire car was retrieved by the rental guys from the Marlin Hotel."

"Suits the shark story, then?"

Ratso did not look convinced. "Kurtner never showed at the boatyard." He pulled out a photo of Bardici and they both stared at the swarthiness of the man's face, his heavily built frame and large, thickset hands. "Bardici's smart, animal smart. My guess, he stripped Kurtner's room and checked out for him before going to raise hell with the boss at the yard about delays to the refit."

"You think Ruthven was ...?"

"Silenced, I'd say. He could link Shirafi to the *Nomora*. But Bardici murders for the hell of it; disposing of Ruthven for incompetence would be no big deal."

Suddenly, she looked sad and tired, her head shaking at the mess she was in. "I hate all this double-speak from Washington. Based on these facts, if he drowned here, he checked out and then walked fully clothed into the sea carrying all his belongings." She shook her head angrily. "This could unravel like crazy if the journalists get a sniff of scandal. So you're right, it can't be here. It has to be back home. But again, Todd, tell me what is Washington's game?"

"They want this story to disappear. They don't want Ruthven or Kurtner reappearing. Their problem is they know from you he reached here and they don't much like that. Untidy."

"So?"

"Well, he might be alive but I doubt it." He tried to sound reassuring though in his guts he was unconvinced. "Kirsty-Ann, if I were you...you make a full report to Bucky Buchanan. Tell him what you uncovered over here, being something and nothing. Run the *missing in Florida* approach by him. Tell him I proved Kurtner had seemingly checked out over here. My guess - that's what DC wants. Nice and vague. Nothing sinister, No skeletons in Ruthven's closet."

"You think?" Kirsty-Ann sounded hesitant, surprisingly so.

"Those guys in DC, they *know* the truth. Not what I've just told you but the rest of it. Wensley Hughes has spoken to them. They'll have tracked every opportunity for contact between Ruthven and Shirafi in Kabul. So it's KYA time! Don't get cornered where you can get hung out to dry. Make them decide which of their lies works best. To me, Florida is the place. That's where his belongings were found. Look— there's no corpse here. If the story breaks that Ruthven came here leading a double life with another name, hell, every professional and amateur sleuth will be crawling all over this."

"Yeah, I can just see Greta van Susteren from Fox News going real big on this. Once the media start asking questions…" She let the sentence die. "And so?" She clasped her hands across her knees. "If you make arrests, will Ruthven's name come out? That Bardici may have murdered him? If so, everything that Washington wants buried will…"

"Float inconveniently to the surface?" Ratso saw her torment, sensing she knew that one wrong move and her career was in a lose-lose spiral. "Ruthven's *existence* is irrelevant to us in London unless we are nailing Shirafi and the AC says that won't, can't, must not happen." Kirsty-Ann was surprised at the bitterness in his tone.

This time, it was Kirsty-Ann's hand that rested across Ratso's fingers. Despite the coolness of her touch, the warmth came across in the message she was sending. "You're right. I'm gonna tell it like it is…and then some. Let someone else decide."

"That was my last call. Time to go. You ever get to London?"

"Not so far." She smiled almost teasingly. "I've never had a reason."

"You should. I'd enjoy that. And Ruthven and those guys in DC would be off-limits."

She smiled very differently, her face lighting up for the first time since their heavy conversation started. "That's a cool idea. My mom can care for Leon for a few days. What's the weather like in February? I'm due some vacation."

"Don't pack a bikini or sun lotion." He rose to leave. "But the welcome will be warm, that's for sure."

"Deal," she said. They strolled slowly toward Immigration and Security as if reluctant to reach the moment of parting. He stopped just short of the line and they stood facing each other for a silent moment before Ratso put his bag on the floor and grasped her gently around the waist. She responded at once, pushing herself forward as he gave her a gentle, affectionate kiss on the lips.

As he drew back, Ratso was feeling almost lightheaded, debating whether to miss the flight. The Christmas Eve raid seemed an intrusion on something far better. For a second, nothing seemed to matter but being here with this woman that he barely knew and yet so much wanted to. But damned duty and common sense prevailed. The raid in Brighton was too important to screw up.

"I'm going to miss you. We hardly know each other but it's like, oh, I don't know—maybe like there's magic dust all round." He paused, feeling a bit silly.

She pulled herself close. "I kinda feel that, too. Magic dust, huh? Yeah. I'll buy that."

"So, see you in London. Promise?"

"Can we see those soldiers with the funny hats?"

"The bearskins? Busbies, they're called. Yes. At Buckingham Palace. But I can't promise you'll see the Queen."

"Seeing you'll be just fine." She pulled at his free hand to turn him toward her. "Maybe I'll get to see *your* bearskin." She winked with an impish smile. Then she gave him a warm hug, turned sharply away and was gone. Ratso watched her till she had waved at the corner and turned out of sight.

On the hop over to Miami, Ratso dozed fitfully, disturbed by every change in the noise from the turboprops but once cruising on the London-bound 747-400, he tucked into the evening meal of salad, beef stew and a rich chocolate dessert. He accepted the flight attendant's offer of coffee and brandy and dismissed thoughts of Charlene and Christmas Day. Her obsessive texts were an irritation but somewhere lay a kind and gentle solution. More urgent was the Christmas Eve plan and updating the whiteboard.

Micky Quigley was a big plus. Probably somebody loved the Irishman—perhaps his mother but Ratso doubted even that. There was plenty enough of the bruiser but little that was likeable. He was a drunk and had done time for a violent attack on a woman. He was scruffier and stank worse than a scrapyard mongrel. But none of that bothered Ratso. He had no wish to get nearer to the Irishman than to slip on the handcuffs. In a dawn raid on a previous vessel, the Dubliner had escaped, slipping over the ship's side. He had vanished, never once appearing in his usual haunts. Ratso had even wondered whether he might have drowned and had hoped for weeks that a body would wash up along the South Coast. Until last night.

Why have I been thinking about Quigley's escape? He sniffed the brandy and swirled the glass in his hand, savouring the fiery fumes. It was a few moments before he had the reason. Quigley had escaped because the local cops had been in charge and been stubbornly pig-ignorant. And now the raid on Rudi Tare would be handled by the Sussex Tactical Firearms Unit. He could see no way around the problem; he would have to delegate the delicate operation to the Sussex TFU. But that didn't stop him creating a plan, a good one, so good that the Sussex top brass would have to buy it.

The Sussex Constabulary's Tactical Firearms Unit had an excellent reputation. *Sure, I respect their professionalism but this is my baby. I don't want another Micky Quigley snafu.* On his iPad he studied the data he had downloaded at Miami Airport. To strangers, Bankside Gardens was part of Brighton but actually it lay in Hove, though the join between the two was seamless. Ratso knew the area from years back but much had changed since then. The old music hall image as a resort for dirty weekends for Londoners or for a paddle had been lost to a new flashier, faster-moving image. And with the changes had come crime and drugs. Increasingly, the seaside town, under fifty miles from London, with its pier, antique shops, fish-and-chippers, amusement arcades and miles of beach, had become a neo-capital for the gay community. Additionally, it was a mecca for young adults, with clubs, pubs and bars - all easy pickings for the pushers.

Before take-off, he had mined his way through Google Maps and done a virtual drive along Bankside Gardens. But now he was offline, so he browsed the map and photos that Tosh had sent through. Tosh had also tracked down some agent's particulars from when Rudi Tare had rented Flinders. It was described as a "highly desirable gentleman's residence." Being in Brighton, Ratso wondered whether the agents meant that it was the gentleman or the house that was *highly desirable*.

The property had four beds, three reception, a conservatory and a double garage with two up-and-over doors. Others in the street were valued on Zoopla at over £1.1 million. It was a substantial two-storey building, painted white and mock Georgian in style with a portico over an impressive front door painted navy blue with brass fixtures. At the rear was a rather neglected garden and an impressively large gravelled courtyard wrapped around the front. Ratso could see why Rudi Tare had selected it. There was plenty of room for cars or small vans to be loaded while concealed from the neighbours by a mix of tall hedges, towering evergreens and thick clumps of shrubs.

Tosh had also sent a dozen aerial photos of the street and the entire neighbourhood. This was an upmarket area but by no means Brighton's finest; most houses looked as if they provided white-collar families with comfortable homes, garaging for more than one car and space for the kids to play football or cricket in the garden.

As he studied the view from the road, he tossed back the dregs of the brandy angrily as the implications of the Osman ruling struck him. Whoever sat above Rudi Tare on Zandro's muck heap was likely to take fright at coppers ripping Rudi's place apart. Thanks to the pinko idiots in the legal system, the cat was not just out of the bag but was bolting straight to the one person Ratso did not want tipped off.

The Hogans would come tooled up, no question, so the top priority was preventing injury to decent coppers protecting a shitbag like Rudi Tare. By the time he met them, the Sussex team would have their own plan and would not welcome any input from a smartarse in SCD7. On the plus side, they would have started the groundwork, checking with neighbours about using their drives or even their homes as observation posts. Surveillance would be underway too and planning where and how to position roadblocks. But something else was needed, something special to create a win-win from this lose-lose situation.

Ratso sighed and then buzzed the attendant for another coffee while his neighbour snored, mouth open. The Osman ruling could hardly mean turning up at Tare's home and saying, *Please, Mr Tare, we are coming in to protect you from the nasty Hogan boys and once we've done that we're going to arrest you for offences that will bang you up for twenty years. Come on Ratso, there has to be a solution.* He yawned, checked the time and realised it was 4:30 a.m. in London. He turned off his iPad, reclined his seat and switched off the light. Within moments he was gone.

He slept through breakfast and only awoke when asked to put his seat into the upright position. He was offered a coffee and welcomed it and as he sat looking at the darkness outside, he realised that he had a plan. *Why did sleep so often provide an answer?* As the plane parked at the gate, his brain was still in overdrive, puzzling now how to discover the identity of JF. He was missing something.

45

Brighton & Hove, Sussex, England
Later that day, on the drive down to the South Coast, Ratso felt none of the Christmas spirit. There was no chance of tossing back whisky with Crabbie's green ginger or getting into party mode, not with a dangerous mission ahead. He had called Charlene, who now knew she would not be seeing him on Christmas Eve and that Christmas Day was iffy. During the chat, her disappointment had turned to surliness and understandably so but he had ended the call with no regrets. It was bad enough having to work on Christmas Eve without being nagged by someone who said she understood. *Like hell she did!* Ratso had told her gently that dating him was always going to be full of ruined plans and disappointments and she could never expect that to change.

Tosh had confirmed that the sharp end of the operation would be handled by a Chief Inspector Graeme Uden, a uniform in the Sussex force. Tosh had dismissed him as an awkward sod. "Trouble is, he was never breastfed as a baby," he concluded with all the confidence of a Harley Street psychiatrist. Uden was the Tactical Firearms commander reporting to the Strategic Firearms commander, who on this occasion had proved to be an assistant chief constable called Rick Longman.

Tosh described the curt phone call with Uden as being as pleasing as having a witch doctor with sharp nails treat an overgrown boil on your prick. Longman, in his view, had been only slightly better. But Ratso knew Tosh's breezy cockiness would not travel well to the Sussex coast. Even so, Ratso assumed that his plan would be rejected by Longman on the basis of *not invented here*. After standing all the way into Hammersmith on the Piccadilly Line, Ratso had then gone straight on to Wensley Hughes to get him onside. Selling his startling plan had been as easy as plucking teeth but by the second cup of Darjeeling, he had won Hughes over. Yet even Hughes, with his urbane charm, had struggled to get the assistant chief constable in Sussex to unravel the plan he'd been developing for twenty-four hours. The most he had achieved was an agreement that the ACC and Ratso would meet to talk it through.

"Despite what your sergeant said, Longman sounds a decent enough bloke," said Hughes after he ended the call. "It's not easy to have some jumped-up detective inspector in the Met pissing on your parade. Treat him gently. You may persuade him. After all, yours *is* a bloody good idea." It was the first time Ratso had ever heard Hughes swear. *He must be impressed*.

On entering Brighton just after 4 p.m., Ratso felt the first twinges of festive spirit as he took in the coloured lights crisscrossing the streets and Christmas trees of all sizes perfectly placed to catch the eye. As he approached the seafront, a Salvation Army band was belting out *O Little Town of Bethlehem*. Everywhere pedestrians were laden with carrier bags stuffed with food, drink and gift-wrapped goodies.

After leaving Scotland Yard, he reached Clapham just before 2 p.m. There he had been updated on missing facts, absorbed the information from the IMB and had listened to Jock's Cyprus report. Ratso had then dropped by the Cauldron, studiously avoiding the sprig of mistletoe hanging near the whiteboard. He explained he would not need any of them in Brighton; Chief Inspector Uden's armed unit would be providing the support. "And getting the overtime," grumbled Tosh. "I was looking forward to that."

Despite his exhaustion from the short night, Ratso smiled. "Tosh, you're still grounded. No overtime for me either. DI's work their bollocks off for the love of it! But with luck, I should be tucked up with cocoa before dawn on Christmas Day."

"Who's Cocoa? Bahamian, is she?" enquired Jock. "Some dusky maiden ye brought back from Freeport?" There were several dirty chuckles, which Ratso acknowledged with a grin before hurrying on with details of the London end of the operation.

"Ye'll be there at the hoose yersel', though?" asked Jock.

"Leaving now. Longman's the SFC but Uden's team will be at Flinders. I fully intend to be there."

"Uden won't like that, boss."

Ratso knew he was right.

After parking in the hotel's car park, Ratso hurried through the biting easterly wind into the Old Ship Hotel. It was on the seafront but the sea might as well have been a thousand miles away for all the Channel view Ratso had from his single room. As arranged, he phoned the assistant chief constable at once.

"I'll head over with Chief Inspector Uden. Save you trailing out to HQ. Ten, maybe fifteen minutes." The ACC sounded cheerful and friendly. But would it last?

As Ratso slurped tea and relished the squashed-fly biscuits in the lounge, he received confirmation that Wensley Hughes had made arrangements for *some of the boys* to visit Freeport to see if *Nomora*'s bridge and the captain's cabin could be bugged. The plan was to enter the boatyard covertly over Christmas, though Ratso warned that some of the crew might now be joining Micky Quigley on board. He had just poured a second cup when Longman appeared, Uden trailing respectfully behind him.

The ACC was late forties, nudging six feet and looked as if he had led the lifestyle of an athlete. His face was almost cherubic, certainly boyish with fair hair flopping over his forehead. He was dressed in full uniform with shiny, heavy-duty black shoes. Ratso gave him a second look, trying to place where he had seen the man before. Had it been in the newspapers, police magazines, or had he come across him elsewhere? Whatever, the assistant chief constable showed no sign of recognizing him.

Uden looked very different, his face aggressive, the set of his square jaw defiant, screaming *don't piss with me*. His *en brosse* silvery hair was revealed after he removed his cap as he sat down. He looked mid-forties and his grey, rather drawn features were designed for late-night poker, the steely eyes revealing nothing. The handshake was cold but firm. There was no smile.

"Tea or something stronger?" enquired Ratso of Longman, studiously ignoring Uden.

"It's Todd, isn't it? Todd, I could murder a builder's tea with a teacake. Too early for a seasonal scotch, even for Graeme Uden here."

"Only just," Ratso replied but the senior officer let the joking tone pass. As Longman turned his head to the young waitress, Ratso took in his profile and knew at once where he had seen him before. "We've met. Sussex Martlets Cricket Club. You were the opening bat and you took a hundred off us at Arundel...oh, six, maybe seven years ago."

Longman's face lit up. "You were there? The best innings of my life. Seven seasons ago. So you were playing for the Revellers."

"Nothing to revel about that day. You stuffed us. I opened the bowling and my figures were none for sixty-seven off twelve."

"We won by eight wickets, I remember that too. But the Revellers are and were a good touring team. You a County player ever?"

Ratso shook his head. "The Met came first, second and third. The odd game for Surrey Twos if they were short. These days I'm playing for Shepherd's Bush." As he spoke, Ratso could sense Uden fuming that the two men had found a shared love to kick-start the meeting.

"I've pretty much hung up my boots now." Longman paused while his chief inspector ordered a ham sandwich with plenty of mustard. "Now I'm happy just to be selected for the occasional golden-oldies match."

As Longman and Ratso shared banter about grounds they had visited, players they had met and above all crowing about the Aussies being stuffed Down Under, Uden stared around, his thoughts locked behind impassive features. But once the tea was poured and Uden was taking great lumps out of his sandwiches, it was down to business.

Ratso's fears about a hard sell gradually disappeared as he explained the two prongs of his plan. As he spoke, he kept scouring his memory for where he had come across the name Uden before. Did it have bad vibes? He was unsure. He just could not place it. At least with Longman, Ratso's enthusiasm for the plans and his own coolness under Longman's astute questioning seemed to have the ACC playing defensively off the back foot. But Uden said nothing, even after he had devoured the last crumbs from his plate. He sat, eyes lowered, head tilted forward, all the while watching and listening, revealing nothing. Ratso had met his type before - until Uden had decided which way the wind was blowing, he would say nothing. Then he'd back Longman, eager not to step a centimetre out of line.

Ratso was right. Forty minutes later, the ACC grinned across the empty plates and cups. Then he nodded to Uden. "Graeme, that's a better plan than ours. The two prongs. Clever idea. Tricky, though." He steepled his slender fingers as he peered across at his chief inspector. "We can make it work, can't we?" Uden gave his monosyllabic approval without a smile.

Ratso knew just what to say. "I can see you're a real detail man, Graeme," he lied cheerfully. "You'll need to be. Maybe we can regroup later? Give you a chance to sort out the small print, local knowledge and all. I need all the help I can get." Ratso knew that the final words would hold sway and was not disappointed. A flicker of smug satisfaction crossed the chief inspector's face.

Longman intervened almost instantly. "Todd's right." He turned to Ratso. "You're CROPS trained?" Ratso nodded. "Then I want you there. You're an AFO, too?" Again Ratso quickly confirmed he was an Authorised Firearms Officer. Only then did Longman's slender finger point at Uden. "My take is this: you deal with the bigger picture round Bankside Gardens but have Todd concealed on the premises. Work for you?"

With barely a second's hesitation, the taciturn Uden responded, "Good plan, sir. I'll get started right away."

The ACC studied his slim black watch with care before continuing. "Let's meet in two hours at HQ. That'll give you time to put the meat on the bones, eh?" He saw Uden almost smile. "Meanwhile, I'll give Todd a tour of Hove, let him get a feeling for the area. I won't stop at the property, not dressed like this. The less activity near Flinders, the better."

Ratso watched Graeme Uden replace his cap with all the careful precision of a surgeon. Then he was gone, walking across the room with clockwork soldier strides. They watched him go.

"Man of few words, Uden but he's a fine officer. Brave and good on the ground. He'll be Silver, of course but with your knowledge of the Hogan mob, having you close to where they'll start their raid makes sense. With a push, he'd be happy to play second fiddle to you during the raid." *Yes,* Ratso mused. *He'd be scared to fart without a written chit from the chief constable.* "But," Longman continued, "it's best for his team that he's in charge, even though the details will largely depend on you."

So be it. Ratso smiled, pleased simply to have won over the ACC. Sensitivities between the Met and other forces could be as taut as banjo strings and just one false step could have led to another Quigley balls-up. As they braved the icy blast of the easterly to cross the car park, Ratso thought again how lucky it was that they shared a love of cricket. But it had been more than that—he had remembered Longman's face, from seven years back. *Now that wasn't luck. Not at all.* The thought pleased him as they headed inland, leaving behind the restless grey of the sea.

46

Brighton & Hove, Sussex, England

Over twenty-seven hours later, with Christmas Eve nearly Christmas Day, Ratso crouched among the shrubs in the pitch black of Rudi Tare's front garden. The Hogan gang were on their way. He was in full camouflage, night binos round his neck and a Glock to hand if needed. For what seemed like the hundredth time, he went over the plan, rehearsing what lay ahead, trying to assess the weaknesses and all the while hoping things would continue to gel.

Ratso quietly unwrapped a Yorkie bar amidst the rustle of the foliage. He peered through the dark at his watch. Another ninety minutes till Christmas Day. From a house a few doors down came the strains of "Silent Night." *All is calm, all is quiet.* The irony of the lyrics was not lost on him. *Fat chance of that once Hogan arrives.*

It was a cloudy night, the freezing wind having died away during the day. Even so, he was thankful for the black gloves and the warmth of the balaclava that shrouded his head. The cold night air penetrated every limb and he yearned to stamp his feet to stir up some body heat. His two-way earpiece linked him to Uden, who was outside the property in the garden of the house opposite. Uden was hooked into the wider circle of personnel dotted round Hove, watching for Hogan's Transit to enter town, or concealed in side roads ready to man the roadblocks on his command.

Outside the property and well concealed were Uden's shots, all armed and ready for whatever lay ahead. Ratso's plan had called for at least seven of the armed team to be concealed around the grounds to arrest the Hogan mob. Longman read it differently. "Too risky," he concluded. "We don't know how long Danny Hogan's men might be at Flinders." Ratso had conceded the point. He knew from a right bog-up on a job near Woking that maintaining total silence for too long was a mounting risk. Someone like Tosh would be desperate for a piss. Give it long enough and somebody would cough, sneeze, belch, or fart and all hell could break loose. So Ratso alone was inside Rudi Tare's front garden, concealed in the thick and unkempt shrubs and tall evergreens that lined the entire perimeter.

He finished his chocolate bar and stuffed the wrapper into his pocket. If everything Tosh's snout had told him was solid, Dan Hogan would be leading a team of six while his brother Jerry remained in London. A navy blue Transit van would enter Brighton on the A23 at around 10:45 p.m. It should then take the A27 west before ducking down Dyke Road Avenue into the hinterland of Hove's residential area. There, just over a mile back from the seafront, was Bankside Gardens. Once the van was at the property, officers from the Sussex Constabulary would be on standby to set up roadblocks and to lay stingers but for now, they were hidden well away from the junctions. *Nothing* must spook Dan Hogan.

Hidden in a driveway just one hundred metres away were two unmarked Mercedes people carriers. They were big, heavy and suitably close to being built like tanks, each filled with six armed officers ready to surround Flinders' front gates. Once again, Ratso relived the small details agreed upon with Uden and Longman: when the gang was ready to leave, if it got that far, the first Mercedes would move in to block the driveway. The shots from the two Mercs would already be running to cover the gates. Dan Hogan and his thugs would be caught *like rats in a trap*—an expression Ratso had deliberately used to amuse Jock when bouncing the plan off him the day before.

It was 10:40 p.m. The van should be getting close. It had left London almost precisely at the time the snout had predicted. He looked across at the large, detached house from his hiding place. There were a couple of lights on, one upstairs, one down but the wide open space of the impressive gravelled courtyard lay in darkness.

A crackle in his ear provided confirmation from Uden. "From Silver. *Santa One.* Contact."

Ratso took a sharp breath; the Transit had turned into Dyke Road Avenue. Uden would be the first to see it arrive. More vitally, he had to alert the Mercs when the Transit was ready to leave. Ratso felt very alone in the bushes, yet he was not bothered. This was where he wanted to be, at the pivotal point of the action. He now knew Hogan's lot were coming armed with guns, chains and crowbars—at the very least. He eased his position slightly for the last time, desperate to avoid triggering the sensors that would floodlight the yard. Once activated, Ratso knew they would remain on for two minutes but with so much movement expected from the Hogan mob, he had to accept that the lights might remain on for longer, leaving him vulnerable… unless Hogan knew how to cut off the power.

A minute passed and then two, before Ratso heard the throb of a diesel cruising slowly along the tree-lined street. In his planning, Ratso had assumed it would drive in and park. It didn't - stopping unseen somewhere short of the open double gates He trained the night glasses on the entrance. The engine went silent. In the stillness, he heard a door open and seconds later came the sound of someone entering the drive. The crunching on the gravel suggested there was just one person and he was running. No sooner had the figure entered the property than the floodlights were triggered. Ratso could see him now—a stocky figure with full balaclava concealing his face. Was it Danny Hogan? It was impossible to be sure but the chunky build and lack of height made it likely. In his hand the intruder carried what looked like a pair of long-handled cutters.

The man seemed unconcerned about being caught in the full glare of the overhead lights. As soon as the large empty space in front of the house was illuminated, he began running, passing close to Ratso and then down the side of the garage to the back. Unless anyone had been on lookout at a window, they would have seen nothing before the figure had disappeared. *Damned well informed*, Ratso thought as he guessed where the man was headed. *Hogan must have expected an empty house.*

According to the drawings Uden had obtained from the landlord's solicitor, the backup batteries for the alarm system and the mains electric switches were in an outhouse behind the garage. Uden had also established that it was secured by two large bolts, each padlocked but surely no match for those long-handled cutters. Almost instantly, he heard muffled scrunching sounds as the padlocks were cut, followed by the creak of a door.

From down the road, the strains of "Away in a Manger" drifted across the blackness, reminding Ratso that tonight was supposed to be a magical night for kids, a time for peace and goodwill to all men. *Not with Danny Hogan around.* Still, Ratso was impressed; Hogan had done his homework. *Perhaps he did have someone working on the inside.*

If the intruder really knew his stuff, he would disable the two batteries before cutting off the power. If he didn't, flicking the mains switch would still leave the house alarm system activated. For almost a minute, nothing happened but then the yard went black, the house lights went out and Ratso could see nothing at all. No alarms sounded. *He's cut off all power.*

Ratso heard the sound of feet on gravel and his binos picked out the man as he returned to the van. Once again, he passed within two metres of Ratso. Then the sound of feet on gravel stopped. Ratso assumed the man was now on the pavement, briefing the gang in the Transit. Moments later he heard the diesel engine fire up; the throb grew noisier as the van advanced, lights on and swung into the blackened yard. It passed him and stopped about twelve metres away, parked up facing the road, ready to leave.

From the neighbouring property Ratso now heard the lyrics of "We Three Kings." The headlights were extinguished and the sound of doors opening filled the night. *You ain't bearing any gifts, though, are you, Danny? More of a takeaway tonight for you.*

"Wot you reckon, Danny?" The voice was gravelly, pure South London.

"No sweat, mate. Place is empty. That Tare bleeder ain't due back till after midnight. Not a sign of him or his mate even after we cut off all his fucking power. His telly must be on the blink, everyfink."

"So?"

"Ned, you stay with me, Alfie round the back. Jack, watch the road. If he comes back early, you know what to do. Right? Shooters ready?" Ratso heard muttered responses. "Right—let's do the bleedin' garage, grab the gear and load the van."

"An' if the buggers come back?" The lookout sounded worried.

Hogan sounded exasperated. "Like I said, Jack. Yell like fuck. Right? Then it's into the bushes and we grab Tare and his gofer when they get out their motor."

It's going to be kinda crowded in the bushes, Ratso thought. Ludicrously, a variation of the lyrics of the "Teddy Bears Picnic" flitted through Ratso's mind—*If you go into the bushes today, you're sure of a big surprise.* But as for Danny's plan, it was piss-poor. No way would Rudi Tare drive in once he saw a Transit parked in his drive. Not that he could dial 999, either.

Ratso thought about the feverish activity now taking place in the neighbourhood. The roadblocks would be in place, stingers across the road. *Danny, you're trapped.* The thought was warming—not as good as a snifter of scotch with Neil Shalford but pleasing enough. He wondered how Hogan would tackle the garage. Both white doors were metallic up-and-overs with a lock built into the twist handle in the middle. Perhaps Danny had somehow got a key. Even in a secluded location like this, to force the door with the Transit would be far too noisy. Every kid for miles around would think Santa's sledge had fallen from a roof, reindeers and all.

He heard footsteps disappearing in all directions and then the clunk of something being moved. There was a solid thump as whatever it was hit the gravel. Ratso could now guess what was going on but still could see nothing, his view blocked by the van. After a few minutes of undefined movements, the yard was illuminated, suddenly and eerily by the business end of an oxy-acetylene cutter. The bright golden yellow flame showed three men as shadowy figures standing by the white garage door. Then the flame was fine-tuned to a razor-sharp pinpoint of light, which cut through half-inch-thick metal in seconds.

Ratso could hear a choir singing "O Come All Ye Faithful" as the cutter completed its circle around the handle. He heard someone wrench the handle clear and then came the rattle and scrape as the door pivoted upward. The black interior of the garage was invisible as the cutter was extinguished. Ratso heard swearing, followed by a clunk as the gas cylinder and blowtorch were loaded back into the rear of the van. Someone laughed as Danny's familiar voice said they needed to leave plenty of room for the gear.

The CD of carols had ended. As Silver, Uden had to decide when to intervene but Ratso's role was to give him a heads up. It wasn't time yet. He saw a torch illuminate the garage before the door was lowered, only the occasional flicker of the men moving around inside visible through the hole. Did they know where the gear was stashed? Unless Danny knew, finding 30 kilos of cocaine in a house that size could take till long after midnight and Danny was expecting Tare back by then.

With someone guarding the gate, he bet Uden would be reluctant to call up the Merc until Jack had left his post to join the others. But getting the Merc to block the exit in time was going to be a close thing...too damned close. Ratso eased his position, stretching now that the sensors were inoperative. He shook some circulation into his aching legs. He had spent too long in his cramped, crouched position. Now every second seemed an age. Two minutes; three, four, five, six minutes all passed with only vague sounds of activity from the garage. He sent out a whispered message on the two-way. "Cyclops to Silver. Santa's boys in the garage."

The sound of the garage door being raised alerted him, followed by irritated voices. "Yer...but finding it wasn't no big deal. We gotta lift the fucker. We know it's full of the stuff. Get it in the van. Get lifting. I got the rest. Bleedin' bonus that is." Danny's gravelly voice carried across the yard. The torch was extinguished but Ratso was satisfied from the grunting and swearing that the men were carrying a safe. No way were they carrying just 30 kilos of Class A in its wrapping.

"Easy, now. Don't fuckin' drop this on my fuckin' foot."

"Over a bit. Your way. To you, Ned. Now push. I said push, you useless fucking dickhead!" More grunting. "Okay. Now one last push so there's room for everyone and we can close the bleedin' doors." The speaker raised his voice just a tad. "Ned— fetch Alfie and Jack. Then 'op in the bleedin' back an' sharpish."

Ratso had heard enough. He whispered a message using his call sign. "Cyclops to Silver. Santa One about to leave."

Uden acknowledged at once.

Ratso waited for Uden's order. He waited one, two and then ten seconds. Still nothing. He was obviously waiting for Jack to return to the van. *Bloody pointless. Don't wait, Uden, or this is snafu time. Jack can get nowhere. We need the Merc now, right now. What are you doing, Uden you tosser? Get that Merc across the entrance. Now!*

Another five seconds passed before Uden's order went out. "From Silver. All units. Attack! Attack! Attack!"

Uden's single command had put the roadblock teams on full alert. Farther afield, police vehicles would be on standby in every neighbouring street. The carpets of nails to deflate the tyres would be rolled out about three hundred metres away in each direction. Wooden barriers would also be blocking the roads as a last resort but the nails laid like a carpet from verge to verge would surely be sufficient. On Uden's command, Ratso knew that a dozen uniforms would be tumbling out of other vans, creating a wider cordon to support the TFU in case anyone tried to hoof it through adjoining properties.

Ratso saw Ned and Jack racing toward the Transit's headlights and then round to the van's rear doors. He heard them scrambling aboard. Then the doors were slammed shut and he glimpsed Danny Hogan's squat figure entering the front passenger seat. At 11:27 p.m., the driver slipped the van into gear to cover the twenty-five metres or so to the gate. The vehicle edged forward, no hurry, no tyre squeal, no panic—more like a funeral hearse than a South London gang making a getaway.

Then came the sound of the Merc's engine roaring as it accelerated to blockade the drive. The Transit had barely travelled fifteen metres when Ratso saw the lights of the Mercedes appear and screech to a stop. He saw armed officers creating a cordon with two of them positioned between the people carrier and the front of the advancing Transit, their shotguns loaded with Hatton rounds, ideal for shooting out tyres. The air was now filled with shouts of "Armed police," mixed with the revving from the vehicle engines and a constant wailing of sirens. As swiftly as he could within the cover of the bushes, Ratso moved closer to the gate, intending to get in behind the Transit to provide cover should any occupant try to leap out.

Ratso could imagine the earthy language and panic in the van at the sudden change of events. *What would Danny do? Surrender? Not his style. Open fire? Maybe.*

Whatever Danny ordered, the driver suddenly responded by pressing his foot down, gravel spraying out around the tyres.

The Transit lurched forward between the brick pillars, slamming the front nearside of the Mercedes, the crunching and tearing of metal adding to the confusion of noise. Ratso hoped the two officers carrying shotguns had managed to jump clear. So far they had not fired.

Ratso edged as close as he dared to the entrance on the driver's side. For a second, from between the foliage, he had seen the profile of the man at the wheel, a look of snarling determination on his face as he had accelerated. Now Ratso brushed aside the greenery, planning to position himself behind the Transit. A glance right showed that the van had failed to shift the front of the Mercedes enough to squeeze between the vehicle and the pillar holding the gate. At that second, a shot rang out, almost certainly of a Hatton round. He heard it smash into the metal of the van rather than thud into the tyre as intended.

Ratso felt exposed, fearful of being caught by a ricochet if another round or two were fired but he was determined to open the rear doors of the van.

He edged forward onto the gravel just as the Transit's reversing lights came on. Too late, Ratso realised that Danny Hogan must have ordered a retreat. The van roared straight back. Standing just four paces behind it, he had no chance of escape, had barely started to run when the rear offside corner struck him, knocking him to the ground just clear of the violently spinning wheels. Stones flew everywhere as the driver raced back a couple more metres before slamming the Transit into forward gear. Ratso rolled off the gravel and lay prone as the blue van thundered past him again.

He heard cursing from inside the van, mixed with shouting from the TFU team as they surrounded the exit. A shot rang out, then another. Ratso knew Hogan sometimes preferred a sawn-off shotgun and that's what it had sounded like. In his earpiece, Ratso immediately heard "Shots fired!" Hogan had made clear there would be no easy surrender.

As he started to raise his head, another shot rang out but from where and in what direction, Ratso could not tell. The van slammed into the Mercedes even harder the second time. This time the driver had struck the Transit into the lighter back end of the Mercedes. *Good thinking, Danny.* The noise of breaking glass and torn metal filled the air. The impact had pushed the people carrier sideways, leaving just enough room for the Transit to squeeze by. With a roar of acceleration, it started to race away when there was another shot, which Ratso reckoned was another Hatton round. This time, there was no metallic clang; he hoped that one of the tyres had been shredded. If it even made it to the roadblock, the stinger would do the rest. The second Mercedes, filled with another six officers, sped away in pursuit.

At first, Ratso had assumed his injuries were nothing serious, the type of blow any sportsman would quickly shrug off. In the heat of the moment, nothing seemed to matter but catching the gang but now with the action moving on, he realised as he tried to stand that he could not. Instead, he slumped down awkwardly by the verge. As he lay there, Graeme Uden appeared and looked down at him. "You okay?"

"Slight knock. I'll be fine. You go on. Catch the bastards."

He heard Uden call for the ambulance that had been on standby. After he had hurried away, Ratso again lifted himself to his knees but rising was impossible as a searing pain ripped through him. *Must be worse than I thought*, he concluded as he lay still, awaiting help. Then from somewhere quite close by came a moan. He could see nothing but it had to be one of the TFU team.

"I'm coming, mate," Ratso called out. Uden had obviously been unaware of the officer down, so the man must be off the drive somewhere. In the pitch blackness and ignoring what he now assumed was a dead leg from the Transit slamming into his thigh, Ratso dragged himself forward, clawing his way slowly over the stones.

Almost before he had crossed the gateway, he heard what he took to be the siren of an approaching ambulance. Teeth gritted, he forced himself to go on into the shrubbery on the other side. Again he heard an agonisingly deep groan out of the dark just ahead of him. It spurred him on. From somewhere came another volley of gunshots and more shouting. Danny Hogan was not going quietly.

Silent night, holy night.

The words haunted Ratso as he peered into the dank shrubbery. He struggled forward, his left leg useless and dragging behind him. At last he was onto the soft moss, damp twigs and wet earth under the shrubs. At that moment, the ambulance pulled up outside, the blue lights flashing across the dark green trees. It was then that he saw a slumped figure lying beneath a giant conifer, staring up at the sky. His gun lay useless near his right hand. He felt the wetness of lost blood close to the man's head. "Hold up, mate. You're going to be fine. The ambulance is here." He could now hear the laboured breathing followed by a chilling moan. He clasped the officer's hand and squeezed. "I'm with you mate. Speak to me, speak to …" Ratso suddenly found he could not finish the sentence as confusion racked his body and his brain blacked out.

47

Brighton & Hove, Sussex, England

It was late afternoon on Christmas Day before Ratso started fully to understand where he was and why. Having been admitted to the A&E Department at the Royal Sussex County Hospital on Eastern Road in Brighton, he gradually became aware that he was in a private room with an officer outside the door. His mouth was dry and his throat felt swollen, as if someone had forcibly shoved a large cucumber down it. He could not see the rest of his body, nor be sure what was still part of him and in what condition.

A nurse came in and wished him merry Christmas with the news that sorry, he had missed out on the turkey and trimmings over five hours before. Somehow he was able to mutter that at least he'd be able to catch a repeat of *Morecambe and Wise* on peak-time TV. Ratso was unsure whether he really cared about the turkey and Christmas pudding anyway.. His head was pounding and his whole body seemed to ache. "Now you're awake," the cheerful-looking nurse continued, "I'll get Dr. Hudson to drop by."

In the next few minutes, Ratso tried to work out what he could remember of the previous evening. The nurse returned with a young doctor, who pulled up a chair to seat himself close to Ratso. "How are you feeling Mr Holtom?"

"I'm not sure which parts hurt the most." Ratso tried to turn his head to look at the doctor but found he could not.

"You've been heavily sedated. Overnight, you've had a naso-gastric tube from your nose to the stomach but that was taken out a short while ago. Your neck is in a collar, just a precaution."

"I'm not paralysed, am I?"

The doctor leaned forward. "You are one lucky man."

"Well thanks for that but it doesn't exactly feel that way. As far as I remember, I was struck on my thigh. Got a dead leg."

"Yes, you certainly had that. When you see your thigh, you'll find it black and blue. But that wasn't the problem. A dead leg, as you call it, soon recovers. When you were brought in, you were pretty much out of it and nobody had seen what happened to you. It's easier if we know what happened."

Ratso tried unsuccessfully to change position. "So?"

"The A&E team checked pretty much everything. That's why you are in a neck collar, just in case of any injury there. But their thoroughness revealed the problem."

"I was struck by a Ford Transit when it suddenly reversed into me."

Dr. Hudson looked thoughtful. "That figures. You received a severe injury to your spleen. There was massive internal bleeding that the A&E doctor fortunately picked up." He stared at Ratso hard. "I was called in to decide what should be done. I'm sorry to say your spleen was damaged beyond repair. I had to carry out a splenectomy—remove it. Sometimes we can repair it but not this time."

"Is that…very bad?"

The doctor shook his head. "Your life will continue pretty well without it. You're more vulnerable to bacterial infections but don't lose sleep over that."

"Can I have some water, please? My throat's giving out." The young nurse tilted a small quantity of water into his mouth. It tasted like nectar, soothing the burning pain that made swallowing agony. "Oh God! I remember now. There was another person I was trying to help. I found him under a tree. Is he okay?"

"That's where the ambulance crew found you, lying flat-out unconscious beside him."

Ratso felt responsible for whatever had gone wrong. "Did he make it?"

"He's fine. Better shape than you. He was struck by a bullet in the chest from point-blank range but his ceramic plating saved him."

"But he was unable to speak, as I recall."

Dr Hudson smiled knowingly. "The impact knocked him backward. He hit his head on the trunk of a tree. That pretty much put him out. The ambulance crew reported he was drifting in and out of consciousness. You though were out cold."

"I'm glad for him. Danny Hogan's a right bastard. He'd have shot to kill given the chance. When do I get released?"

"We'll decide tomorrow. We need to keep you under observation." He paused as the nurse checked Ratso's blood pressure.

"And the gang? Did you hear?"

"All arrested at the roadblock. Two gunmen were slightly injured trying to make a run for it. A load of shots fired but no other police had to be admitted."

Despite the throbbing in his head, Ratso managed to nod just slightly.

"We can get some food sent in anytime if you wish." Ratso declined but instead requested his phone to make a few calls. The doctor looked reluctant but before he could protest there was a tap on the door and Wensley Hughes' head appeared. To Ratso, lying flat out, he looked enormously lean and tall until he sat beside the bed. He introduced himself to Dr Hudson, who excused himself for the moment.

The AC said nothing till both doctor and nurse had left. "Great job. Merry Christmas, too." He handed over what was obviously a bottle in a red bag with cord handles. "That's for another day. Anyway, how are you feeling?"

"Glad you came, sir. Good of you to spoil your Christmas Day for me."

"Truth be told, I'm quite glad to escape the in-laws for a few hours. My wife's sister never stops talking."

"That would do anybody's head in."

"Congratulations. I've spoken to Chief Inspector Uden and to the assistant chief constable. Everybody's well pleased. Shame two of you were injured but with Hogan's mob all armed, it could have been a great deal worse."

"Uden did a good job."

"Maybe but your two-pronged plan worked a dream... and we nabbed Jerry Hogan in Merton before he had a chance to empty his Christmas stocking. Sgt Watson has been busy." Ratso managed a quiet smile at the thought of the overtime Tosh would be receiving. "We also recovered thirty-two kilos of cocaine from the safe and a load more." Hughes leaned forward and rested his hand on Ratso's left shoulder. "Besides that, I read the report. The other prong of your plan worked a charm."

"Has Tare's house been searched yet?" Ratso wanted to relive every moment of it but now was not the moment.

"Before we get to that, Todd, I want to repeat that your plan was first-class."

"Thanks. We were lucky. So much could have gone wrong."

Hughes' tone was dismissive. "No plan is foolproof. But this one worked exceptionally well. It cut through the problems. Razor sharp." He leaned forward again and clasped Ratso's arm. "It may be time for you to put in for promotion. Think about it."

Ratso nodded appreciatively. "And the search?"

"Besides more drugs stashed away, nothing useful found yet. Your two sergeants, Strang and Watson, are coming down to go over the place with a full team. I've no problem with Watson working in the house."

"Sir, I'd like to be there."

"That's for the doctors, not me."

"The important thing is Tare's contacts. Of course we want to nail the riff-raff pushers but we must identify who controls and supplies Tare." He lay silent, exhausted by talking and frustrated at being out of the loop. After a long silence during which Hughes went to the window and then returned to the chair, Ratso spoke again. "Sir, you remember the initials of the mystery man are probably JF. I had an idea I need to check online."

"The bed rest and sedation has done you good, then." Wensley Hughes' chuckle was deep and mellow.

Ratso tried to laugh along but the pain made it short-lived. "It came to me when I was hidden in the bushes."

He saw the AC fumble in his pocket and produce his Blackberry. "What was your idea?"

"Arkwright, Fenwick and Stubbs. The brothers are Terry and Adrian but I want to know Adrian's full name."

Hughes set to work at once scrolling through pages of fodder before he found the simple web page for the firm. "Adrian Fenwick. That's all."

Ratso was disappointed. "Two brothers dividing the role as Zandro's sidekicks makes huge sense. Nothing we've established from watching Terry links him with any other key figure. Observations this past week have shown zilch out of the ordinary. Superficially, Terry Fenwick is a boring man with a predictable lifestyle. But he must communicate with Zandro somehow. We need to look at his business partners, the people he sees daily." The two men sat in silence for a few moments. "I've an idea, sir. Suppose Adrian Fenwick is not his full name. It could be he just chooses to be known as Adrian."

Hughes started tapping away, his thin fingers nimbly flitting over the keys. "I'm checking the Law Society—the Roll of Solicitors." Ratso watched impatiently, frustrated that he could do nothing. "You wanted a letter J, did you say?" Hughes looked up. "What about Adrian Julian Fenwick, then?" The AC suddenly looked even younger than usual, his eyes twinkling in pleasure.

"There's millions of JFs but I'd bet he's our man. It fits so neatly. Yet he doesn't use the name Julian publicly as a solicitor. Can you get someone working on his birth certificate, sir?"

The AC scribbled a note. "Anything else?"

"The shipyard. Any news? Bob Whewell from the IMB warned me yesterday that his information was the *Nomora* is cleared to sail any time."

Hughes smiled. "The ship can't sail without us knowing. We can track every move."

"But the bridge? Micky Quigley's cabin? Did someone get aboard and get the bugs placed?"

"Not possible." Hughes helped himself to an apple before continuing. "If that's what those boys say, you can stake your life there was no chance."

Ratso could only agree but he still looked disappointed. "I was supposed to be phoning someone about seeing her over Christmas. She won't know where I am or what's happened."

"Neil Shalford's woman, eh?" The words were accompanied by a sly grin that grew bigger when Hughes saw the defensive look on Ratso's face. "Planning to comfort her again, were you?" He got no denial. "I'm glad to see that good old-fashioned chivalry isn't dead." He grinned again. "What's her number?"

There was a pause. "No idea, sir. I need my own phone for that." He also wanted to call Kirsty-Ann but he was not volunteering that.

"I'll make sure you get it before I leave." Ratso watched the tall figure stretch, his fingers nearly touching the ceiling. "I must be off. We're playing charades tonight—a Christmas tradition in the wife's family." Hughes pulled a face that spread to Ratso's.

"And my phone, please." Even as he said it, he wondered how it would be when he got through to Charlene and Kirsty-Ann. Very different reactions, he guessed.

48

Brighton & Hove, Sussex, England

Despite Ratso's protests, Dr Hudson would not release him for two days and even then he was reluctant. Around noon on 27 December, Ratso was driven along the seafront in an unmarked Sussex Constabulary vehicle. The Christmas decorations now looked sad and redundant, swinging and swaying in the rain-flecked northeasterly wind.

After two days cooped up, he had asked the driver to take the scenic route along the Prom so he could rekindle some old memories and enjoy the power of the sea. The skies were dark with low clouds scudding not far above the water. The restlessly leaden look of the Channel's swell was brightened only by the froth and foam of the crashing waves as they broke around the pier and onto the shore.

Both the ACC and Chief Inspector Uden had visited with booze and fruit and Longman had given him a potted history of England's glorious day in the field in the Melbourne Test but that was a poor second to actually seeing the Aussies get a pasting in their own backyard. A rerun of an old Bond movie was no recompense.

The pier now behind him, Ratso's thoughts turned to when he had been twenty-two and had spent the weekend in a small hotel on Regency Square with a raven-haired nympho from Dagenham. She had pillioned as they sped down the A23 on his 250cc Honda Rebel. The Aurora Hotel was still standing but to his disappointment, it was currently obscured by scaffolding blighting its frontage, blurring the memories. Then the driver turned into the residential hinterland as Ratso flicked through Cricinfo to check the Close of Play score for the second day. Overnight, England had piled on the runs. He was still smiling when the driver parked up in the spacious yard of Rudi Tare's home.

In contrast to the eerie darkness of Christmas Eve, this morning the yard had five cars in it, all neatly parked. A constable guarded the gate. Men in white outfits could be seen moving around inside the property. Tosh Watson appeared at the door, looking as if he had eaten more than a few Christmas puddings. Ratso got out of the vehicle, his movements slow and stiff.

"You look happy, Tosh! Found a burger under the sofa, did you?"

"Just glad to have you back, boss." For a moment their eyes met and Ratso felt the sincerity in his sergeant's words. As they headed very slowly toward the portico over the front door, Jock emerged, looking about as pleased as his crumpled face would permit.

"Fancy a cuppa, boss," he offered. "The kettle's on." A few minutes later, the three men were seated on tubular steel chairs round the glass-topped kitchen table, mugs of tea to hand.

"How aboot this, boss." Jock gave Ratso a list running into three pages of his spidery writing.

Ratso flicked through it. "Two cars worth over twenty-five grand each. Over ninety thousand in cash." He rubbed his hands.

"We can confiscate all that under the Proceeds of Crime Act. That I like!" He nodded with satisfaction. "Three handguns, a shotgun, a semi-automatic rifle, ammunition, a nine-inch Bowie knife, eighteen kilos of presumed cannabis, four sets of digital scales, sixty-two small bags of coke, cutting and packing equipment, amphetamines, Ecstasy, Poppers, Speed, thirteen pay-as-you-go phones, a laptop, two Blackberries and a radio scanner."

"Tuned in to police bands," volunteered Tosh." But boss we want to hear about arresting Rudi Tare – Wensley Hughes called your plan a *masterstroke*. Give."

Ratso allowed himself a nod of satisfaction as he changed position, switching from one buttock to the other, his stomach, leg and thighs aching. Being back in Rudi Tare's kitchen was kick-starting a flood of memories. "Not being caught in a shoot-out between the gangs was a must."

"But ye had to comply with Osman." Jock added with a nod.

Ratso marshalled his memories starting with the evening he had shared shepherd's pie with Uden. "Get this - I remembered a Reg Uden who had played in goal for Fulham. Amazingly, it had been Uden's old man. Of course, that changed everything! Before then, Uden had been tolerating me just because of Longman but this was a clincher. Sport's a great glue."

"Lucky, muttered Tosh.

Ratso did not retort that his memory of a Fulham player twenty-seven seasons back was more than luck. "With a detective constable from the TFU, we went over to Flinders. There were no security gates. I guess they would have stood out in even in this neighbourhood."

"And the place was only rented," Jock chipped in.

"Interestingly, parked on the drive were a Lexus saloon and a Lexus 4x4 - yet there was a double garage. So anyway, I chucked a handful of gravel into the front-drive. The security lights came on immediately, flooding the courtyard from at least five different locations. We hoofed it behind a privet hedge of the house opposite. This big guy appeared with a Doberman and a hefty metal bar. He called the dog Bonzo. You can imagine – that sod was straining on its leash but they toured the drive only half-heartedly."

"Aye, they'll be plenty of false alarms with stray cats."

"And urban foxes," Ratso agreed. "After he went back inside, the lights soon went out. I wanted to test the trips so I clambered over the low wall surrounding Flinders and skulked around among the thick shrubs and trees that surrounded the place."

"Needed brown trousers for that, eh boss."

Ratso grinned before continuing. "The DC was a trained marksman. But anyway I never triggered the sensors. That was the clincher and so over a couple of jars at my hotel, we completed my plan, much of the time taken up with how to neutralise Bonzo."

"Know what's black and brown and looks good on a lawyer?" Jock waited, taking a slurp of tea while he watched. "A Doberman."

After the chuckles died away, Ratso turned serious again. "We arrived at Flinders long before dawn on Christmas Eve."

"So ye mean aboot sixteen hours before the Hogan mob were due."

Ratso nodded. "Danny Hogan would have still been snoring off the previous night's booze." His injuries were troubling him, so he stood to pace the room. "The TFU guys had shoot to kill orders and Uden had fixed a trained handler with a fire extinguisher, a long pole and lasso. Besides that we had the full works in support. The TFU team hid in the shrubs. I was with Uden near the front door. Nothing happened till 7:15 a.m. when a light appeared in the hall followed by another at the back. I guessed someone was now in the kitchen."

Jock poured more strong brown tea and then clasped his hands behind his head. "Go on. I'm with ye."

"Uden radioed Tom Alleyne, a young West Indian detective constable to enter the drive. Dressed like a yob in a black hoodie, his task was to trigger the sensors and set off the 4x4's alarm."

"Brave lad," murmured Jock.

"All hell broke loose. The yard was immediately flooded with light. As he rocked the 4x4, its alarm started blaring and its lights were flashing."

"You weren't padded up?"

"None of us were except Alleyne. The door opened seconds later. I was bloody terrified when Bonzo appeared, snarling. The guard had his iron bar but only the dog bothered me. As planned, Alleyne then broke cover from behind the Lexus. Just as well he did or that Doberman might have sniffed out me and Uden just a few leaps away. Alleyne ran like hell for the gate, looking just like a car thief in his hoodie. Both dog and handler hurtled across the drive to catch him, Bonzo now unleashed."

"Uden gave the order over the two-way - *all units from Silver. Attack, attack*! Three of Uden's men then cut off the thug from returning to the house as Uden and I raced to the front-door – all behind the thug's back."

"Did Alleyne make it okay?" Tosh finished his Snicker and stuffed the wrapper into his North Face jacket.

"I didn't see much after my sprint to the house. The last I saw was Alleyne a few steps in front of the dog and running like …

"Like he had 40 kilos of snarling dog chasing him," laughed Jock.

"With shouting now from all sides, I saw the minder falter, It was only then that he looked round and saw he was surrounded. As I slipped inside, he was flailing his iron bar at the cordon. So Uden and I were into the hallway. Stinking dump too for a posh place like that. A tousle-headed man, unshaven and aged around forty was coming down the stairs. He was unarmed and wearing a navy singlet over boxers and mauve silk dressing gown that flapped open at the front. Uden warned he was armed and let the guy come down one step at a time. Outside I could hear shouting, barking, screaming and then a single shot. The noise died and I assumed Bonzo had been silenced but who might have screamed or why I didn't know."

"So what had happened?"

"I had no time to be concerned for young Alleyne."

"Sounds a bit harsh," It was Tosh who chipped in,

Ratso shook his head. "We had to be gone by 8:45a.m. latest. Flinders had to look undisturbed. Remember, it was your snout who said the Hogans were monitoring the place each day starting at nine. We had a shit load of stuff to do before then." Ratso saw the nods of understanding and continued. "That's why we planned to get the minder and dog into the yard. We needed to walk into an open house. No siege, No doors smashed down." Ratso sat down again and saw the listeners were impressed.

"So then you had to search."

"I started in the garage while Uden had the guy cuffed. He admitted his name was Rudi Tare of course." Ratso laughed as he changed position. "I was bursting to tell him I'd just done him the biggest favour of his life."

"Aye, the Hogans widna' have been so gentle."

"What about the neighbours - all dialling 999 or calling the local TV crews?"

"All fixed. Total news blackout till Christmas Day. No media allowed in the area, neighbours all being reassured." Ratso led them out to the garage, With each step, he could relive the heart-pounding excitement as he had started his search. Now the place was pretty much stripped. "That morning, like now, it felt bloody cold." He found the light switch and everywhere was lit by powerful overhead lamps. "That morning, there was a long trestle table and two chairs. I spotted a box of five hundred small Ziploc bags, digital scales and a substantial polythene bag filled with powder for cutting with pure cocaine. There were traces of white powder on the table top and a cardboard box with fifty to sixty small filled bags, ready for sale."

Tosh looked round the barren garage. "I heard there was a safe."

"Right! The walls were lined with boxes, trash, holdalls and suitcases all randomly stacked. In that far corner were about ten rolls of carpet, almost reaching the flat roof. Hidden behind them was the safe. Around it was more white powder."

"Big bugger was it?"

"I'll say. If it had landed on your foot, Tosh, you'd have had to give up ballet-dancing for keeps."

"Och no, boss. He could still have been the Sugar Plum-Pudding Fairy, surely."

Tosh joined in the laughter as Ratso continued. "And the safe had a sophisticated lock too. No way could we get into it quickly. But I wanted to leave everything for the Hogans. Seeing as how Danny's boys' brains would fit on a pinhead, we didn't conceal it too well! That's when Uden appeared - chuffed to hell when he saw the evidence to arrest Tare and the guard. That's pretty much it - the Scenes of Crime boys swooped, photo'ing everything and we left Flinders looking undisturbed with nineteen minutes to spare. Sure enough someone did a drive-by at precisely 9 a.m.. All serene."

As he was talking, Ratso had been walking slowly back into the spacious kitchen. He downed a painkiller with the last of his tea. "I went outside to ask about Alleyne. The TFU had gone; so had the ambulance and back-up vehicles. Uden told me Alleyne had made it into the van. But he owed that to one of the lads who had intervened. Bonzo had leaped a couple of metres through the air at him and struck his shield, knocking him flying. Then it had tried to tear him apart while he was on the ground."

"He's okay I heard."

"Uden reckoned he'd be fine till he lowered his bruised arse onto the bog-seat. Bonzo was shot. No choice. The handler couldn't get the lasso round the dog's head and couldn't use the extinguisher while the dog was attacking the youngster. He reckoned it was like the Hound of the Baskervilles, snarling and dribbling."

"So you and Uden became Sherlock and Watson, I suppose?" Jock's raised eyebrow showed he expected no answer.

"With you as Watson," chimed in Tosh - a comment which produced high-fives between the sergeants and a smile from Ratso.

"Better than being compared to a certain Tosh Watson, anyway." This time Ratso and Jock exchanged high-fives to hoots of laughter.

Jock sliced into three and then pushed around slabs of Christmas Cake that he had brought wrapped in tinfoil. It had thick marzipan and a generous coating of white icing. Ratso took a bite with relish until for a second it reminded him of Charlene and the Christmas Day he had never had. And of the problems she presented. "Ye ken we picked up Jerry Hogan. The little sod was about to do a runner. We nicked him with his bags all packed and tickets for Dublin."

"Dublin, eh?" Ratso looked suitably pleased but Tosh seemed concerned, his hands restless.

"A quick thought before I take a leak, boss. If you were JF, wouldn't you be shitting yourself now that we've nabbed Rudi Tare?"

"Dog's dinner, isn't it!" Ratso agreed as he scooped up the last crumbs before pulling out his Juicy Fruit gum. He offered it round, restlessly drumming his fingers on the table. "My take - JF must have read the papers or heard on TV about the raid." He paused to assess the position, playing with the cheap biro he was holding. "You heard that Terry Fenwick's brother is Adrian Julian Fenwick. If *he* is JF I'd bet he's a cool one and won't panic."

"Aye, unless he's worried about clues Tare may have left behind."

"Hard to back off now. Firstly," Ratso lifted each finger in turn, "because *Nomora* has sailed. Secondly, we're not dealing with some lowlife like Jerry Hogan who left school at sixteen and couldn't read. If Adrian Fenwick is our man, this guy has a degree from Oxford. He's a qualified solicitor.

"Aye, these Fenwick brothers must be smart, careful. Had to be to run this operation under our noses for years."

"I agree, Jock. They'll believe Tare was squeaky clean with no convenient address-book. This lot have survived because of minimal contact and all traces and arses covered."

"So his Varsity brain will tell him to follow the old wartime motto: *keep calm and carry on.*"

Jock offered round chocolate in Father Christmas wrappers. Tosh grabbed two before he dashed from the room..

Ratso nodded toward the departing figure. "Santa didn't bring Tosh a new bladder then!" He ran a hand through his hair as he turned serious and then leaned on the table, his hands cupped under his chin. "Way I see it, Jock, nobody could run an operation like this without leaving a paper trail of some kind—credit cards, receipts, tickets, something."

"Pity the Osman law lost us the chance to have Tare followed. But if ye ask me, boss—Zandro's committed. *Tirana Queen sailed to* the Turkish port of Alanya. That's an easy crossing from Kyrenia." He stood up and turned to rinse out his mug. "Afghanistan to Iran to Turkey—that's a major heroin supply route. I'll bet ye a wee dram that Zandro met Shirafi in Alanya and paid for the smack using Hawala. But I'm telling ye, Shirafi was not on board when the yacht returned to Northern Cyprus. We photo'd everyone."

"No surprise." Ratso sighed. "Shirafi rarely shifts his fat arse from his palace in Kabul but he might have reached Turkey for such a big deal. You saw no sign Zandro had picked up any gear?"

"Nothing. Zandro, the crew and some camp-followers came ashore carrying zilch. If he picked it up in Alanya, it must still be on board."

Ratso was thinking aloud. "Unless he transferred it at sea?" He discarded the thought. "Nah! Zandro would never get that close to drugs." He watched Jock bite the head from a chocolate Santa. "I reckon he had no choice but to attend a tough meeting with Shirafi…"

"Because of the delays," Jock finished the thought, nodding in agreement.

Ratso's eyelids lowered as he sat in quiet thought. "If you want to shift hot money, big money or pay for drugs, you're right - Hawala's a great way to do it." He handed over his mug for washing. "And I reckon *Nomora* will head for Turkey. For Zandro to spend a million on a refit, he'll sweat the asset."

"You mean Micky Quigley will first pick up some of Colombia's finest?"

"Yup! Somewhere round the Caribbean. Those ultra-fast speedboats often bring cocaine into the small islands."

"Aye, right enough. Or it gets dropped to *Nomora* by parachute from a small plane."

"Turkey was so out of character for Zandro, it just had to be important." Ratso rose, winced slightly and moved stiffly across the kitchen to grab a tea towel.

"And as for the Fenwicks, however clever they may be, they canna rewrite history—the companies Terry formed, the money trail to Gibraltar."

Ratso chipped in. "And the transfers from the Gibraltar bank to pay for the vessel and the shipyard."

Tosh returned looking less like a man in agony and offered round jam doughnuts. Jock accepted but after the cake, Ratso found it easy to decline. Tosh chewed enthusiastically and a gave a grunt of pleasure as he reached the jammy middle. "Okay, boss, what next?"

Ratso thought for a moment. "We monitor *Nomora*. We watch Adrian Fenwick. We get the reports from the lab boys on Rudi Tare's laptop and phones. But I'm not expecting to strike gold. Trace every phone number used by Tare—follow up all numbers, any names found on scraps of paper around the place."

"Dinna hold yer breath, boss. Rudi Tare seemed to destroy everything. There are shredders everywhere and the word here is that neither Tare not the minder are singing."

Ratso's face showed no surprise. "Tosh, I want the links from Lime Street to Gibraltar proved tighter than a duck's arse. Jock, check out that Turkish port—Alanya, was it? See if it has a history of heroin exporting. That may be the route Zandro's used before. I'm going to concentrate on the London clubs." He rapped the glass table top with his knuckle. "Remember, we have one goal: bringing down Zandro himself. Anything less is failure."

49

Clapham, South London

Ratso was seated in Detective Chief Inspector Tennant's office. There was a strong smell of embrocation. "Done your back in gardening, boss?" Ratso gave no hint that he was being sarcastic. Everyone knew Arthur Tennant had his eye on an apparent workplace injury leading to early retirement with a truckload of compensation.

Tennant groaned theatrically. "Bad fall this morning round the back. The lazy sods hadn't treated the ice in the car park. The pain's getting worse."

"And you just back from your holiday, too! I hope you had some good witnesses." Ratso managed to sound sympathetic. "But you really shouldn't be here. Typical of you, guv! Soldiering on."

Tennant faltered, then answered with glib assurance, his eyes as shifty as a lying defendant in the box. "I've a doctor's appointment—and yes. DC Mason found me on the ground and I made a report at once."

"See you fall, did he?"

"No but I showed him the ice and he helped me up. I couldn't move." He emitted a loud groan, his face screwed up with apparent pain.

I bet you just lay down by the ice and waited for a witness, you lying toad. "Home run, then."

"Coming on top of last year's injury to my spine, not good. Remember I wrestled that yobbo to the ground?" He shook his head in resignation.

Ratso remembered that so-called incident. The yobbo had denied resisting arrest and there had been no witness. "Straw that broke the camel's back, eh, boss?"

Tennant opened the drawer where he kept his annual poppy and removed a couple of Ibuprofen from a container. "I fear the worst, Ratso. This could finish me." He swilled down the pills with a swig of tea.

"Tragic, sir. Not the end to a great career you would have wanted, is it? No more golf either, if you're crippled. You'll just have to spend your retirement counting your compensation. But on the bright side, you'd get to see more of your place in Majorca!"

Tennant shifted uncomfortably in his seat, whether in pain or because the image of him counting damages was a tad too close to the truth, Ratso was unsure. He noticed there was no grimace or groan this time. "Anyway," Tennant continued, "I've read the reports. What a joke! Protecting Rudi Tare!" He snorted. "Any fallout?"

"Hard to tell. Both Fenwicks are under observation. Remember we had the Crawley connection tip but it led to nothing?"

"Go on."

"Adrian Julian Fenwick commutes from Copthorne, just a mile or two outside Crawley."

"Something and nothing. Lifestyle?"

"Like his brother, except he's a bachelor. Seventeenth-century cottage. Two beds. Bit of land. S-Type Jag, under two years old. A small sailing boat kept at Brighton Marina."

"The third partner in the firm? What about her? She must know what's going on."

"Lynda Dorwood? Good thought, sir but she only does conveyancing. She's never filed a single document at Companies House. She's been with the firm only four years and came from Birmingham. Her father was a president of the Law Society."

"How could she not know?"

"Because the brothers do nothing obviously unlawful from the office. If I'm right, Terry meets Zandro *by chance* at a club."

"The brother?"

"Lives barely thirty minutes from Brighton. He could have been meeting Rudi Tare *by chance* in pubs all over Sussex. My good mate Assistant Chief Constable Rick Longman was a tad embarrassed - said Tare had never come up on their radar at all."

"You can prove they meet?" The tone was sharp.

"We will, guv, we will." Ratso spread his fingers wide on the table. "This is my theory. After picking up orders from Zandro, Terry sets up whatever companies will be needed and fixes the money. He briefs his brother. Julian *call-me-Adrian* is the doer, closer to the real action, gets his hands dirty. Julian uses—well, used—Rudi Tare as his main South Coast distributor."

"There's another?"

"We found a couple of phone numbers in the minder's room and an address in Wellington Street, Leeds but no street number. Could be in an apartment block. That's being checked out."

"Where's the gear been coming into the UK? Julian Fenwick's yacht?"

"Convenient but no. Far too small. It's just a dinghy." Ratso checked his pad. "In Tare's bedroom, behind his dressing table, we found a receipt for fitting a new exhaust pipe to a Ford Iveco van in Dover. We're checking that out, tracing the van. Dover's interesting. The date of repair coincided with that rumoured delivery last August. That might point to the van having met a bigger truck coming in from Europe."

"Clutching at straws, aren't we?" Another wince and groan accompanied the comment.

You negative, time-serving shitbag. "Every little helps, boss." Ratso fixed Tennant with a sympathetic stare. "You're not looking too good at all," he lied. "You must be badly shaken, guv. Don't miss that doctor's appointment."

Outside Tennant's room, Ratso let go of his frustration by kicking the skirting-board. He felt better for it. He glared back at Tennant's office and thought of the poor sods in Stoke Mandeville who really did have a back injury. "Shitbag," he muttered as he made a mental note to put in for tickets for Longman and Uden to join him on the next outings. Longman had been keen to help out at the cricket and Graham Uden wanted to treat the patients to burgers at the Eight Bells when they came to watch Fulham.

Making light of his own body-under-repair, Ratso bounded down two flights of stairs, delighted to get away from Tennant as quickly as possible. The Cauldron was almost empty but the stuffy smell of stale sweat and a curry takeaway lingered. After being with Tennant, it was like a breath of fresh air to be with Tosh and the perky Nancy Petrie. They were standing by the whiteboard and writing up the latest position of *Nomora*.

"Definitely heading for Europe," Tosh volunteered. He led Ratso to his cluttered desk and showed the position on his screen. "No way is she going to Nigeria to pick up a load of gear. She's one-eighty miles north of Madeira now."

Ratso leaned forward to study the screen more closely. "Europe, yes—but north or south? If she's going to the UK or Spain, she'd be taking a more northerly route."

"Unless there were sea conditions that kept her south?"

"Check out the reports for the past week. But to me, she's going to enter the Med at Gibraltar."

"Heading for Turkey?"

"I hope so."

Nancy twisted to face Ratso. "But, boss, she's come from the cocaine belt. She must have gear on board. We know it never stopped at Nigeria. It hasn't stopped since leaving Freeport. You reckon she's come all this way empty?"

"I'm with you but if she never stopped, how in hell did the gear get aboard?"

Petrie was dogged as usual. "If she picked up gear from a fishing boat or it was dropped from a small plane, we wouldn't know that."

"No more HMS *Manchester* patrolling down there."

Tosh looked surprised. "Stopped patrols, have they?"

"February 2011. Government cutbacks. Just another sign Britain's going to the dogs. Bust, buggered and bankrupt." Ratso scowled as he warmed to his theme. "We're fighting a war against guys with unlimited cash and Britain can't even afford a naval vessel to stop the drugs from reaching the UK anymore. HMS *Manchester* did a great job. Besides our government licking the hairy arse of the bastard in Kabul."

"The world's mad," volunteered Petrie, flicking her head in an act of defiance.

"Subprime mortgages in the USA. That's what started it," suggested Tosh as he reached for a crumbly Danish pastry.

"Greedy bankers," added Nancy.

"Damn fool politicians," Ratso snapped. "What chance do kids of decent folk have?" He grabbed a chair. "So," he sighed, rant over, "we are where we are. *Nomora* could have picked up a load at sea unmonitored."

"The only other place would be in Grand Bahama."

"The boys had her under visual from the moment she left dry dock till she was about ten miles offshore. Nothing happened." Even as he spoke, a new idea flashed through his mind. That's why he loved these little chats; just sometimes, something new emerged. "The shipyard. She could have taken drugs on board during the works."

Tosh grinned. "You always said there was something hooky about the refit."

Nancy Petrie chipped in. "The cost could have been a huge bung to the yard for a load of gear being taken aboard, disguised as oceanographic equipment."

"Or for work done not on the schedule. Or a bit of both." Ratso gave Nancy a nod of approval. "For now, we assume that vessel is hot with cocaine. My snout only knew this was going to be a mega delivery of drugs—undefined. It was me who assumed it was all coming from Shirafi. Maybe *Nomora* will carry both. If she shows the slightest sign of heading north for Spain and the UK, I want to know instantly. We'll need to alert the Spanish boys."

"You're forgetting something, boss. We've not the slightest evidence there's even one gram of coke on board, let alone enough to get the Spanish navy out."

Ratso grinned. "Tosh, if *Nomora* heads north, she's not entering the Channel to test for plankton—not with Micky Quigley on board. I'm going to phone Darren Roberts in Freeport." He checked the time. "He'll enjoy an early morning wake-up call."

50

Mayfair, Central London W1

Could life be any better than this, Ratso wondered as he walked through the mild evening air. After the recent bitter cold that may have helped Arthur Tennant on his way to a large damages claim, the change in wind direction had made the afternoon and evening unseasonably warm. He had raced home and changed into his best grey single-breasted, a pale blue shirt, chunky cufflinks and a carefully selected sober tie in maroon and navy. Where he was going, mobile phones and other gizmos were banned in the bar and over dinner, so for a while he would be off message. *Bloody marvellous*!

No question—today had been pretty good. Solid progress and no sign of Adrian Fenwick panicking like Corporal Jones in *Dad's Army*. So was he one cool cookie or was he innocent? The call to Darren Roberts had inched matters forward. Now, with those warm feelings already making every step a pleasure, the walk from Green Park Station up Berkeley Street was giving him time to think of his chat with Kirsty-Ann.

Earlier, he and Charlene had met up for lunch in the Rocket by Putney Bridge, the only time he'd seen her since the raid in

Brighton. The trouble was, he had enjoyed her company—had laughed, felt seduced, charmed, whatever. But she had to dash back to work and the magic had gone, leaving him with her invitation for him to move in. *Invitation? It was more of a plea.* He had gently declined. She had made her displeasure clear in bucketfuls.

If only she could be satisfied with the occasional lunch, a night out and then giving each other a right good seeing-to. But fair enough, that wasn't what she wanted anymore. Even though she was as horny as a rabbit on Viagra, she wanted security, two kids—one of each, she had said. "There's nobody else I want or need," she had volunteered sadly as they had parted. "I think I've been in love with you for so long. Too long with your attitude towards me."

"If you need support, count on me. I'll be there for you but semi-detached only," he said as he'd picked up the bill. Plainly, that was not going to swing it. With a huge hug and a wistful smile, they had parted, probably for good.

The doorman outside the Palm Beach Casino wished Ratso a cheery good evening as if he knew him. The intrusion broke the train of thought, leaving him free to anticipate Kirsty-Ann's arrival next month. Their occasional late-night chats, London time and the frequent text messages had filled him with anticipation. Her gift of a bottle of Laurent Perrier champagne in a presentation box had awaited his return to Clapham. Already he was planning her week in London, almost living every moment already.

And tomorrow he would know whether *Nomora* was heading north or into the Med. *God! It had better be Turkey or Northern Cyprus. Otherwise, I'm back to first base.*

Ratso loved walking in London after dark, at least in the better parts of the city. He was now in the heart of club land, just off Berkeley Square in Mayfair. The streets were busy with taxis heading for restaurants or looking out for late shoppers. Round here there were better cars—stretch limos, Bentleys, Aston Martins and smarter-looking totty in designer outfits and coiffured with elegance unseen in his stamping grounds of Hammersmith and Shepherd's Bush.

He had spoken to the secretary of the Poulsden Club the day before and had been invited for the evening, one of the occasional nights when members were allowed to bring a guest. His cover was that he worked in a senior role in the Home Office on matters linked to immigration but that was unlikely to be much of a topic because the secretary had seated him for dinner next to Bruce Sparsfield, the former England cricket captain, on one side and Don Geering, the Olympic rower, on the other. Sparsfield had captained a successful team to the West Indies but had suffered a humiliating tour of Australia, so he had been eased into resignation. Geering had captured gold and since then had delivered the fastest ever time over two kilometres when racing on Lake Bled in Slovenia last summer. If that were not good enough, the secretary, a former brigadier in the Royal Artillery, was going to give him twenty minutes before drinks to discuss Terry Fenwick.

As he entered the club, up a wide sweep of steps and through revolving doors, he felt curiously like a fish out of water. He had never been in an elite members' club where to be admitted was proof of a status to which he could never aspire. Inside the carpeted entrance, beyond the porters' glory hole, was a cavernous, vaulted room filled with deep leather chairs, flowers, statues in marble or bronze and what Ratso assumed were valuable *objets d'art*. Portraits of men famous in their time but now long forgotten hung round the pastel blue of the walls and spotlights picked out the rich colours of the oil paint. At one end, with pleasure,

Ratso saw a portrait he recognised from schooldays as being the Duke of Wellington. *I bet club members would recognise them all. Different upbringing.*

At his local Comprehensive, Ratso had learned how to survive in an urban jungle and not much more. History had been Henry having six wives and Alfred burning some damned cakes. Oh yes and a spider in a cave. His eyes were drawn to a marble staircase that dominated everything. It rose straight ahead and then divided left and right to a balconied area. Everything oozed class, wealth, stability - a throwback to days when the British Empire ruled the world. Now it couldn't afford just one vessel to fight a drug war, let alone protect the Falklands again.

The hall porter took Ratso down a side corridor and ushered him into a wood-panelled room with a desk straddling one corner. The carpet was old, thick and yet in good repair, an Axminster, its colours matching Ratso's tie. Behind the mahogany desk was a crinkly haired figure with a broad smile and what proved to be a fierce handshake. He was aged about fifty-eight and introduced himself as Roger Herbison. He did not return to his desk but instead ushered Ratso to a pair of chairs positioned by a low table on which lay a decanter of sherry and two glasses. "Whisky, if you prefer?"

"Sherry will be excellent." Ratso recalled he had last drunk sherry when still at school, over twenty years back. Also on the table was a printout of what Herbison had been working on. "Shall we get straight down to what I have established?" Herbison's voice was mellow, slow and reassuring.

"One question first, if I may? I know the history of the club—becoming a member is harder than getting a straight answer from a politician. So how did Terry Fenwick get admitted? From what I know, he is an undistinguished solicitor and being a member of a profession is not enough anyway. You require excellence like a rowing gold medal or a knighthood or being one of Her Majesty's judges."

"High Court and above only. Circuit Court judges would not qualify." Herbison ran his fingers through his pepper-and-salt hair and his eyes twinkled. "But Terry Fenwick got in because his father, a property developer from Birmingham, bought out our short-term lease and donated us one for 999 years on the condition that his two sons could join if they applied and would by right be entitled to be on our committee."

"And the father?"

"Tragically, he died a pauper. A property crash revealed he was over too highly geared and he went, shall we say, belly up." He topped up both glasses with pale, dry sherry from the crystal decanter. "Terry did join. The other son never showed any interest." Ratso noted that there was no third son.

"I bet some of the old-time members huffed and puffed about admitting an upstart."

"Very perceptive of you. All hell broke loose. Terry Fenwick would have been blackballed by the majority, if not unanimously. But a pressing rent demand concentrated minds. Of course, the old man had us by the short and curlies. Acquiring a virtual freehold in Mayfair is gold dust. The club would have folded like many others if we had to pay market rents."

"So everyone held their noses and voted yes."

Herbison laughed. "Bang on!" Then he turned serious. "Is the Poulsden going to be mentioned in dispatches, Mr Holtom?"

"Do call me Todd, if you wish." Ratso did not want to scare the horses. "That depends on many things that are at present… unpredictable. But if a member has been a naughty boy, then he will have to come down to the headmaster's study."

"I see." Herbison smiled ruefully and let out a resigned sigh. "I feared you might say that." He sipped thoughtfully. "But there is a bright side. Some of the older members will be able to say *we told you so.*"

"Boris Zandro?"

"Not a member. He has never applied." Ratso reckoned that unsaid was a message that perhaps he too would be blackballed. "He is an occasional guest, sometimes even of a former Labour prime minister. Mr Zandro is a flash money cove, something the chaps don't much care for." He reached forward and handed a lengthy printout to Ratso. "You will not miss the salient point, I am sure."

Ratso glanced at the list of dates going back eleven years. "Is this when records started?"

"No. That is when we got computerised. The older records are available in ledgers if you need them."

Ratso checked the number of occasions when both men had attended the club on the same day—twenty-three times in the last five years and the visits came in clusters. "What does the A stand for?" Ratso asked of the letter beside Fenwick's name. It did not appear every time but was beside all twenty-three times when Zandro had been a guest.

"That means Fenwick had accommodation—stayed the night in one of our club rooms."

"So Zandro only visited the club when Fenwick had a bed here." Even as he spoke, both men's eyes met as if they shared a common thought. "No, I doubt either man is gay. But could Zandro be dining with Lord Bloggs of Tully Blagnett or whatever and then slip off to the bedrooms and meet Fenwick in private?"

"My dear chap, why not? This is a members' club. There's no security. Mattrafact, Fenwick always asks for a ground-floor room, so for Zandro to pop along would be easy."

"Did the two ever dine together?"

"Not to my knowledge. Never saw them speak and I've been here four years now. I had no idea they might even know each other."

"You said they were not here tonight." Ratso's natural suspicion that this was due to a leak had nagged away at him but Herbison was reassuring.

"Quite a few members loathe nights like this when maybe thirty or forty guests, call them strangers, invade their space. They vote with their feet. I've checked; neither man normally attends guest nights."

Ratso drained his glass. "That's good to know. You've been very helpful and I don't have to remind you that this is wholly confidential."

"Mum's the word, old boy. Your secret's safe with me. May I ask what this is all about? Crime boss, is he, this Zandro fellow?"

Ratso put down his glass and rather hoped his next sherry would be another twenty years away. "You may well think that but I couldn't possibly comment. Sorry."

The secretary looked up. "Ah! That wonderful Francis Urquhart line from *House of Cards*. Says it all, really. Well, if there's anything else I can do for you, old chap?"

"I may have a big favour to ask and if the answer's no, I won't be able to accept it. But let's not spoil this evening thinking about that."

"You saw Fenwick's staying overnight next Tuesday?"

"I did and I'll get back to you about that. One more thing. I bet you have pigeonholes here? For members to leave messages or to receive mail from mistresses and so on?"

Herbison stood up, laughing. "You may well think that but I couldn't possibly comment. My lips are sealed on the contents but yes, members communicate via pigeonholes all the time. Mostly it's leaving tickets for Covent Garden or Twickenham but we're not here to question if one of our members is receiving love letters from a popsy in Barnes."

Ratso laughed too but quickly became serious. "I want every letter, note, message left for either Zandro or Fenwick to be photographed or scanned and its arrival time and date to be scheduled, please. By you *personally* but without causing raised eyebrows."

Herbison rubbed his hands nervously. "Not steaming things open, I hope? That would not be cricket."

Ratso quickly disarmed Herbison on that one. "No. Call me at once. Just copy the envelopes, the handwriting. But don't just pick *their* mail. Pick other members at random and keep the nosy hall porters from becoming suspicious. You have a camera?"

"Even better. We have a scanner, believe it or not. We do move with the times here." Herbison chuckled.

"Thanks. I owe you a favour."

"Drugs, is it?" Herbison enjoyed dropping the word into the silence.

"You might think that but I could not possibly comment."

Dinner of Parma ham followed by turbot and saddle of lamb flew by in a blur of repartee and alcohol. Nevertheless, Ratso felt very aware of his lack of education seated among so many with University degrees and a talent with words. But he held his own, living the lie that he worked in the Home Office. It was easy deflecting interest by keeping his celebrated neighbours talking about cricket and the Olympics.

When the evening ended in a glorious haze of fine wines, port and brandies, Ratso was fired up, enervated by the company and the testosterone-charged atmosphere. It had made him feel like a lion on the prowl. During dessert, when the former England captain offered him a lift, saying his driver would be heading for Kingston, whole new vistas emerged of how the evening might end. With the Stilton, the magnificent vintage port had begun circling the table quicker than tassels on a stripper's nipples. After the third glass of Taylor's 1970, Ratso found Bruce Sparsfield's offer irresistible. *To hell with the long-term.* After all, he reasoned, he genuinely liked Charlene, indeed was very fond of her. She knew where he stood, no deception. And right now, being fired up, he fancied her something rotten.

As for spending time in a Mercedes 500 with one of his sporting heroes, that was a bonus that was almost wasted by the rampant urgency that pulsed through him. "Delighted to help you, Todd." Sparsfield's eyes were sincere, eyes that in their prime had seen the angle of the seam on a ball hurtling toward him at over 90 mph. "On a promise, are you?" This time he winked as he put an arm over Ratso's shoulder and they went down the steps into the street.

Arguably the most talented left-handed opener in decades, captaincy had hung heavily on Sparsfield's shoulders. Now, he seemed carefree, though his golden hair had almost gone and what remained was silvery grey. "My driver's taking me to Ham Gate. Your destination is only a couple of miles farther on." As he spoke, a black Mercedes drew up and a chauffeur in a cap leaped out and opened the door. Sparsfield ushered Ratso across the back seat and the chauffeur closed the door behind them.

The journey passed in no time, with Sparsfield answering Ratso's questions about everything from covered wickets to Hawkeye. "What about the Aussie crowd who got at you when you fielded by The Hill at Sydney Cricket Ground?"

"Boy, can they get under your skin," Sparsfield admitted. "I dropped a sitter and from then on, I got hell. I can tell you, there's no hiding place!" From the agony on his face, he was clearly reliving the chanting and jibes he had endured during the Fifth Test—his last as England captain.

"But from what you said over dinner, life's been good to you since then?"

"Cricket opened doors. I'd been to Tonbridge and Oxford, so I'd had a good education. After hanging up my boots, I became a shipbroker and our company got bought out last September. No skill required—just lucky enough to be in the right place to pick up a tasty golden goodbye." He looked at Ratso. "I say. Would you mind if I'm dropped off first? I want to watch the cricket from Australia."

"Sounds a good plan, Bruce. Normally I would do the same but…"

"Say no more. Good hunting, Todd—that's what I say." He turned to the driver. "Drop me off first, would you and then take Mr Holtom into Kingston." He looked at Ratso across the back seat. "Sorry, I've rather hogged the conversation. All this cricket talk. We never did get to talk much about immigration."

"Counting sheep or counting immigrants, always ends in the same thing. It's a conversation killer." The car glided to a stop. As Sparsfield got out, he shook hands warmly and grinned. "Charlene sounds a bit of a cracker. If I were thirty years younger…" Then he was gone, his now rather stooped figure disappearing under an arch into a gravelled courtyard.

The chauffeur turned around. "And now, sir?"

"Wolsey Drive, please." As the Mercedes rolled away from the grand houses lining Richmond Park, the idea of surprising Charlene gave everything an added frisson. He called for the chauffer to stop about a hundred metres from Charlene's house. "Thanks."

"Goodnight, sir."

Ratso watched the car disappear from sight round the kink in the road. He crunched a Polo and then headed for Charlene's semi. The street was silent, lines of small saloons parked neatly. It was only 11:45 p.m. and with the weekend tomorrow, lights were still on in many of the houses. The curtains glowed with the intermittent light of TVs. He reached Charlene's pocket-sized front garden and walked the few steps to the familiar door, where he had been spotted by DCI Caldwell's boys. He turned round and gave a drunken grin for any cameras that may have been watching.

He was about to ring when he heard the sound of laughter from the room to his right. It was Charlene's laugh but the voice he heard next was a man's. Was it the TV she was laughing at? He hesitated, then moved nearer to the window. He could hear voices now, a conversation and then Charlene's flirty giggle.

Suddenly there was movement and the frosted-glass window in the front door filled with light as the couple left the sitting room and entered the tiny hall. Two shadows crossed almost within touching distance, separated only by the door; he heard more laughter and running feet on the stairs. For a moment, he imagined the man, whoever he was, lusting after Charlene's wiggling hips as he followed her toward the bedroom. He found he was shaking. The power of the alcohol had evaporated. All he could feel was shock. *So much for being the love of her life.*

He stood transfixed for a long moment, wondering what to do. The port and brandy encouraged him to bang on the door but the nagging voice of common-sense stopped him. Moments later, the hall light was extinguished.

Slowly, he retraced his steps down the path and turned right along the pavement, pulling up his collar as a misty drizzle started to fall. Thoughts of someone else removing Charlene's skimpy underwear kept his stride aggressive for a good few minutes but once he hit the main road with its sodium lights, new feelings washed over him as if a burden had been lifted. *She doesn't need me anymore. I can play her on my terms now.*

He saw a black cab cruising toward Central London and impulsively he hailed it. *To hell with the cost.* Like a shaken kaleidoscope, the pattern of his life had suddenly changed.

51

Clapham, South London

Ratso dropped an Alka-Seltzer into a tumbler of water and watched it fizz while waiting for Tosh and Jock to enter his office. They did finally, lumbering through the door, reminding Ratso of the joke about how to get two elephants in the back of a Mini. He drained the last dregs. "Heavy night, eh, boss?" Jock grinned as if he was jealous of the king-sized hangover.

"I sank a couple of beers while watching cricket. Stayed up till after 4 a.m. Big mistake."

"Yes," agreed Tosh. "I saw the score."

"I was thinking of brown ale chasing Courvoisier and Taylor's 1970 port," Ratso growled. "But you're right. Our bowlers were tripe. Pie-throwers, the Aussies called them." The two men sat, each with a new mug. Ratso had heard they'd exchanged mugs as Christmas gifts. Tosh's said *Even hairy men can be sexy. Where did you miss out?* Jock had his hand over the slogan on his. "Come on, Jock: give!" Jock relented and Ratso read it out. "Ivor Bigun—the world's biggest liar." Jock grinned sheepishly while Tosh and Ratso did a high-five that Ratso regretted as a pain shot through his forehead.

Unusually, it was Tosh who wanted focus. "How did you get on at the Poulsden?"

"This could be big. We need to move fast. Suppose I'll go up and wake Tennant."

"Tennant?" Both men echoed each other before Tosh continued. "You haven't heard?" He saw Ratso's eager look. "He's got a sickie for at least a month. That fall."

Ratso managed a grin as he flicked on the computer. The lingering effects of the alcohol interfered with his usually adroit fingers. "Here's the early retirement rule: you gotta be *permanently disabled from performing the ordinary duties of a police officer, including operational duties, until compulsory retirement age.*"

Jock rolled his eyes. "On that basis, he's fit. He can continue his *operational duties* just as before—he's been doing bugger-all for years."

"Right on," agreed Tosh amid the laughter.

"I'll speak to Wensley Hughes, then."

"Reasons, boss?"

Ratso rapidly explained why it was highly likely that Terry Fenwick would meet Boris Zandro in a club bedroom next Tuesday night.

Tosh looked pleased. "Bugging and cameras?"

"Yup."

Jock looked uncertain. "I dinna want to watch a pair of shirt-lifters. Or even listen, come to that."

"You won't have to. Not if I'm right."

"'Cos I havna spied on poofters in a lavvy since 1999. I hoped I was done with all that."

Tosh punched Jock's arm playfully. "Memory lane, Jock. You might even get a stiffie."

Ratso laughed, wishing he hadn't as a streak of pain flashed through his brain. "Okay. I've a heap of stuff to clear, starting with my goddamned head. Tell me about Adrian-come-Julian Fenwick and where is *Nomora*?"

"If Julian Fenwick *is* linked to Rudi Tare, he's playing it ice cool. No sign of anything unusual. Maybe JF is not him after all."

Ratso scratched the side of his nose. Even that was an effort. "*Nomora*?"

"You'll like this. She's entered the Straits of Gibraltar."

Ratso somehow managed to look as pleased as he felt. He slammed a clenched fist into his palm. Motivating the Spanish police to raid her on flimsy evidence would have been more than tough. Boarding her in a UK port would be doable. If needed, it was a risk he'd have taken. Now no need. *Yet. But if they found nothing more than white-coated boffins looking for pollutants?* The proverbial would be flying from everywhere – all in his direction. It would be the biggest non-event since England lost by ten wickets in the Stanford Super 20 Final in Antigua. "That gives us time to sort ideas for Turkey, Cyprus. Jock, your take?"

Jock looked up. He'd been fiddling with his Blackberry. "It's 1,816 nautical miles to Alanya from present position. Assuming she doesna stop for bunkering."

"Ooh! Get you, sailor," said Tosh, all effeminate.

"Ach, you landlubbers! That means taking on fuel and water. If it is Alanya, she should arrive Friday."

"Explain."

"She's been making about twelve knots since she left Grand Bahama."

"Let's assume she can average fifteen," said Ratso, looking at the wall calendar.

"That would be around five days."

"Today's Saturday, so assume she berths somewhere in the Eastern Med Thursday earliest."

"Fits in well with the bedroom assignation on Tuesday." Tosh nudged Jock and was rewarded with an exaggerated scowl.

"Tosh, go through these twenty-three dates when the men probably met. See how that fits in with anything we suspected about deliveries. See here." Ratso pointed to the sheet. "Clusters. Look—they haven't met at the club for eight weeks. That's pretty typical. Then suddenly it may be four times in ten days. We may find ourselves in there quite often this next month."

"And they don't meet at the other clubs?"

Ratso thought back to his discussions with the other secretaries. "Open mind still. Their pigeonholes have been used for communications with someone, say Zandro's driver, dropping off messages for Terry Fenwick. The solicitor visited the others less frequently and never overnighted."

Tosh stood up, hopping slightly from foot to foot as if his bladder was sending him urgent messages. "Are we done, boss?"

Ratso gave a half smile. "Monday morning, same time, okay? I'll try to see the AC unless he's off watching Arsenal today."

"I didna' know he was a masochist," Jock threw out as he followed Tosh from the room.

52

Mayfair, Central London W1

Roger Herbison at the Poulsden had proved to be a star act. Though uncomfortable about going behind the committee, a brief chat from Wensley Hughes was the clincher. Fenwick was booked in for Tuesday night but his room had been taken over the previous day by the Technical Surveillance Team. Now, twenty-four hours later, Ratso was in a room three doors along, awaiting action.

In the quiet hours after 3 a.m., the tech boys from Scotland Yard had concealed video cameras in the corridor either side of Fenwick's room to capture comings and goings. In the room, the engineers had installed a couple of audio-visual devices—one in the bedroom and one in the bathroom. Every word would be captured with total clarity by the recorders in the room down the corridor where Ratso was now seated with Jock and the two engineers. Two young Indians were watching their monitors, showing four different views inside Fenwick's room.

Ratso opened a fruit and oat bar while Jock tucked into the remains of a huge club sandwich arranged by Roger Herbison.

The engineers were seated on the bed, finishing a hot curry while Ratso and Jock sat on uncomfortably hard chairs close to a tiny desk-come-dressing-table in the sparsely furnished room.

In Fenwick's equally minimalist room, there was a phone but no TV, Wi-Fi, or radio. The plain curtains hung limply and barely met in the middle. It was all so different from the comfortable opulence of the club's public rooms. As Ratso had commented, the simplicity of the single bed and deal wood bedside locker must have reminded most members of their public school days or life in the army.

Jock wiped his mouth and grabbed a small, dainty cup of tea, which he looked at with mild disgust. "Ye mind the Arab pupil who was murdered? I went to his school in Hampshire. That was *more* comfortable than this." Jock grinned while he chewed. "Ye ask me, only a reclusive order of monks would feel comfortable in these cells." The sergeant drained the cup in a single swig. "Suppose they don't speak, boss? Suppose they just write things down?"

Ratso was dismissive. "They'll speak. Why wouldn't they? Otherwise, they'd use the pigeonhole. But anyway, with the camera above the desk, we'll be able to read every word." He checked his watch. It was 7:45 p.m. "Fenwick has a table booked for 8:15 p.m., so he should dump his overnight bag any time."

"Ye reckon Zandro will slip in at once or later?"

Ratso shrugged. He had no idea. "Whenever, it'll be brief. Five minutes max. But he might drop by twice." He flung the screwed-up wrapper into the waste bin with pinpoint accuracy. "Zandro's dining with Lord Creshaw, so he can't bugger off for too long. Otherwise he'd need the excuse of a bladder like Tosh's." The two men laughed. The engineers, wearing their headphones and intent on their equipment, never heard a word.

From the corridor came the sound of footsteps followed by a key in a lock. Both cameras in the corridors showed the lean figure of Terry Fenwick in a navy blue suit with chalk stripes. He had a dark blue tie with a golden motif running through it and a pale blue shirt. He looked calm and relaxed as he towed a compact roll-along suitcase with a black briefcase perched on top.

After switching on the bedroom light, two other cameras picked up the arrival. His face was placid—the look of a man who was cool under fire and one thousand per cent at ease with himself and his surroundings. He dumped his briefcase beside the desk and plopped the suitcase on the bed. He opened it and extracted a wash kit, which he put in the bathroom. His burgundy pyjamas he hid under the single pillow. He looked round the room and then carried the second chair from one side of the bed to the other so that it was now beside the desk.

He was about to settle in the chair when he let off a hefty fart, looking rather pleased with himself for having done so. Ratso grinned. "Sound system's working okay, then!" He gave the nearer techie a thumbs up. The man responded with a broad smile.

"The jury will enjoy that, boss." Jock grinned as the solicitor open his briefcase and produced nothing more exciting than the evening paper. For the next twelve minutes, nothing happened as he browsed the paper, occasionally running his fingers through his hair.

Ratso looked at Jock. "Wonder what he had for lunch?"

"Vegetarian, I'd guess. Upsetting the ozone layer. Tell ye what, though—at least he hasna put a pot of Vaseline and a condom beside the bed." Moments later, Fenwick tossed the paper aside and left the room. The corridor camera caught him strolling toward the splendour of the front hall and the door leading to the bar and restaurant. "Who's he eating with?"

"Nobody in particular. Down the middle of the dining room is the Club Table, where members on their own must take the empty seat next to any seated member, so it's totally random. Zandro, though, will have a side table for his dinner with Lord Creshaw."

"I know the name. Remind me."

"Ian Creshaw was a Labour MP who became Home Secretary."

"Ye mean?"

Ratso's eyes narrowed and his face hardened. "Creshaw was the bastard who put a stop to money being spent on twenty-four-seven surveillance of Zandro. Killed off the AC's investigation."

"Reckon he's getting a cut?"

Ratso was unsure. "He was reputed to be a greedy bastard." He stood up to stretch his legs. "Last year Creshaw travelled to Switzerland on Zandro's private jet. To Gstaad, I seem to recall. A couple of years back, he cruised the Adriatic on *Tirana Queen*."

"Zandro's so well connected, we did well keeping Operation Clam secret as long as we did."

Ratso walked round the tiny room, stretching. "I betcha Zandro knows—Tosh's visit to Fenwick's office, Tosh in the graveyard and the raid on Rudi Tare. But at least stuff isn't leaking to Zandro the way it once did."

"And the Hogans?"

Ratso paused to peek out of the curtain before responding. He gave Jock a sardonic grin. "Nobody has asked what we're doing now that the Hogans are all banged up!"

"So Zandro must be edgy. Maybe he's leaning on Creshaw to find out what the buzz is."

Ratso sucked in his cheeks. "We should have bugged his table at dinner." Like a caged tiger, Ratso had completed three tours of the room. He sat down on the hard-backed chair and noticed that though the scars were itchy, the pain on movement had all but gone. "Did you read: the Justice Department want more slaps on the wrist for criminals and to empty the prisons."

"Aye! *Give the little darlings another chance*, they said. I'm telling ye, I'm fair scunnered. I get it all the time in the pub. *You lot don't put enough people away*." Jock's face darkened, his brow furrowed. "I always tell them, if I were the Home Secretary, there'd be more prisons and every one would be full."

Ratso gazed at the monitors showing the empty room. "They won't know we've uncovered the Leeds connection. That was good work by young Petrie."

"Aye, she's a bright wee lassie. Pity that Rudi Tare's phones and laptops were clean. But ye're right, that address in Leeds seems to be the centre of operations up north."

"Nothing linking Julian Fenwick." Ratso smiled wolfishly. "But who knows what this evening will bring."

"Are ye no going into his room? Take a wee shufty in his briefcase?"

"From the dining room to the bedroom is thirty-one seconds. Too risky. Anyway, if there's anything worth Zandro looking at, the boys here will capture it. Won't you, Sacha?" The young Indian could not hear until he had removed his headset and then he answered with a smile.

"Can ye no get room service here? I'm fair famished, boss."

"Jock, this is not the Ritz. But I'll call the kitchen. The chef might get something sent in. What do you want?"

"Any burger with chips and vinegar. Irn-Bru, if they have it."

"Ah! The same as Lord Creshaw's having, no doubt."

The next ninety minutes passed slowly. Other than the sound of Jock munching his way through his burger and the two Indian engineers attacking a large bowl of mathari, there was silence. Ratso sent a flirty text to Kirsty-Ann and received a response in a similar vein. He read the details of the one-dayer from Brisbane and was choked to see that the Aussies had won by ninety-eight runs. The stiff-upper-lip England captain said they were taking the positives from the drubbing and that lessons had been learned. *If I had a quid for every time I've heard that drivel about taking the positives and lessons being learned, I'd have retired by now.*

It was shortly after 10 p.m. when the camera showed Terry Fenwick ambling along the corridor, hands in pockets. He entered his room but did not bother to sit down, as if confident that he had a visitor arriving. Sure enough, barely seconds later came the moment that Ratso had dreamed of and Fenwick was waiting for: the aggressively handsome features of Boris Zandro barrelled down the corridor, legs strutting importantly. He knocked sharply and was admitted at once, the door locked behind him.

Zandro pointedly refused a seat. "This RT shit?" His voice, throaty with scarcely a hint of a Mediterranean accent, was unusually clear to the listeners.

"JF says RT is ring-fenced."

"So he must look harder," Zandro snapped. "There's a leak somewhere." He paused barely a second before moving to the next item. "Could the filth have found anything?"

"JF got Benjy as his brief. He reckons his laptop, everything were all lily-white. They would have found nothing."

On hearing this, Ratso and Jock exchanged glances. Ratso made a note to find out who Benjy was—presumably a bent lawyer.

Zandro continued. "RT say anything? Admit anything?"

"Benjy says no. Not a word. And we've felt no heat."

"Good, good." Zandro looked relieved. "But without RT, who'll...?"

"My brother has that sorted." Fenwick looked thoughtful; Ratso could see he was going through an unwritten checklist. "The route?"

Zandro coughed rather nastily and wiped the sputum from his mouth with a pristine handkerchief. "La Coruna."

Fenwick's face showed irritation. "JF won't like that."

"I don't give a shit."

Fenwick sounded resigned. "So the HF hotel? The one near the memorial?"

"Fuck those local details," Zandro snapped. "Not my concern. Get the usual team there."

"Timescale?"

"*Arriving* La Coruna two weeks today latest."

Fenwick nodded thoughtfully. "So you got the money fixed?"

"Done. I paid the fat greedy bastard what he wanted. And a sexy bonus." Zandro was almost at the door now.

Ratso looked quizzically at Jock, who nodded. "Aye! Three young lassies came ashore."

Fenwick was hovering by the door. "Next meet?"

Zandro opened the calendar on his phone. "Two weeks Thursday unless there's a message at the R."

"Agreed." Fenwick opened the door, saw the empty corridor and waved Zandro out.

The team watched Zandro hurry back toward the dining room. Ratso tapped his watch. "That lasted just 85 seconds. Lord Creshaw would scarcely have missed him."

Jock stood up and yawned. "But every second was twenty-four carat."

Ratso's face was flushed with excitement. "Two words. Two magical words—*my brother*. Every other time, it was JF. So Adrian Julian Fenwick is the fixer, the nuts–and-bolts man." He turned to the engineers. "Get that okay? No malfunctions?" He saw their smiles of satisfaction and a thumbs-up. "Okay. Good job. Leave everything running overnight in case anything else happens next door and then slip out around dawn. Jock and I are off now."

"We leave everything in place?"

"Yup! It's all well concealed. We'll need it again. I'll fix it with Herbison."

Ratso phoned Herbison who was at home in Kensington. "No problems, Mr. Herbison. All done. Please reserve the same two rooms for Thursday fortnight. Mr Fenwick will be booking, so please make sure he gets number 8 again and we are in number 11, exactly the same as tonight. Thanks."

"Do let me know if the club's in the doohdah, won't you?" Ratso thought Herbison sounded as if he had sunk a couple of stiff whiskies.

"Count on it. I'll tell you when to put on your tin hat."

"That bad, eh?"

Ratso laughed. "You may well think that but I couldn't possibly comment. Goodnight and thanks again." He made a mental note to send him a good malt when it was all over. Or a dry sherry. He'd be needing it.

"Where on God's earth is La Coruna? I've never heard of it," said Jock cheerfully as they walked down the street, having slipped out the tradesmen's entrance.

"I have. It's northern Spain on the Atlantic Coast but God knows how we get there." He paused. "You catch the hotel name?"

"Maybe initials. HS or HF—and by a memorial."

"We'll need to play that back again."

53

Clapham, South London

As soon as Ratso strode into the meeting room on the first floor, he could sense the mood. Expectation was in the air. There was no applause as he entered to address the dozen or so assembled officers but he saw renewed respect and eagerness in their faces. The Hogan gang's destruction and the arrest of Rudi Tare had been a start but the coup at the Poulsden Club had changed everything. Everyone knew Boris Zandro would be dead meat if the drugs were seized in La Coruna.

Ratso had chosen to meet upstairs in one of the better rooms, airy and bright. Compared to the Cauldron, this room was clinically clean, containing rows of chairs facing a small dais. There was a computer, a fifty-inch screen for photos and movies, a laser pointer, a cork board and a giant whiteboard. Ratso reckoned that the clean, bright emptiness of the room empowered clear thinking compared with the airless clutter and cramped conditions downstairs.

Clutching a plastic cup of tomato soup, Ratso went straight to the empty whiteboard. "Good morning, or maybe good afternoon, as it's just after twelve. Today's meeting is pivotal. We have no time to behave like we're pigs in shit just because we've nearly enough evidence to put Zandro and Terry Fenwick away." He saw heads nodding. "Charging him just on that recording, an expensive brief would get Zandro acquitted. Piece of cake. So near, so far. So, we've plenty to resolve first. I've put the word out round the pubs that since we got the Hogans, we're winding down. Zandro needs to feel his usual cocky self. We don't want the bastard skipping the country. Meantime, we need to make some serious plans—and quickly. We need to cover our backsides from La Coruna through to Dover docks to Leeds."

"Not forgetting the crew of *Nomora*," Tosh chipped in.

"Right. No escape for Micky Quigley this time! And I haven't forgotten Lamon Wilson at the shipyard, either. First, we need to review our priorities." He started to write in capital letters on the board. "Timing is everything." He put a picture of *Nomora* on the screen. "We know she will dock at La Coruna. The Class A could be worth near a billion at street value. So number-one target is to nab every distributor at this meeting. Second, or perhaps first equal, is to seize the drugs and stop them reaching the streets."

"Will we be in Spain, boss?" It was Nancy Petrie.

Ratso said he would be coming to that. He displayed a large map of northern Spain and Southern France and pointed to La Coruna. "I reckon the coke for the UK will be trucked into France. There it will be broken down into bite-sized chunks. Whether it will all be shifted into the UK at the same time we don't know, nor where in France it will be split up." His laser traced a red road from the Spanish port into France. "My guess would be Toulouse on the route north and not far from the Spanish border. It's a big industrial city with plenty of truck movement. In a warehouse, the coke could be transferred into other vehicles, large and small."

"But the smack?" It was Nancy Petrie again.

"Zandro didn't use the damning word smack or heroin. Anyone disagree that's what he meant?" He saw nobody differed. "JF is Adrian Julian Fenwick, solicitor of Lime Street and he's in charge of the split. And it must be *no pay, no takeaway*, as my local Chinese would say." He was rewarded with a few chuckles and rather more groans. "No way can JF handle several dealers and their money on his own."

"He's a damned lawyer—soft hands," Tosh added.

"Ye're bang on, boss. On his own, he'd end up in a paella, ye ask me," volunteered Jock. "But he's done this before. That was clear."

"So we assume Bardici will be protecting his backside," He turned to DC Maynard. "Check all flights Bardici has made to Northern Spain under his own name or his alias."

Nancy Petrie looked disconcerted. She whispered to Vick Maynard, who gave her a nod of encouragement. "Boss, can I put a different view?" Ratso was a touch taken aback but nodded for her to continue. "You're assuming Zandro is selling off the smack to maybe French, Germans, Spaniards, Dutch. Right?" She saw Ratso nod. "Isn't it possible that *every* person meeting the ship is part of a European operation owned by Zandro? They might even all be Albanians. Either way, that would make the meeting low-risk. No money changing hands—all friends together."

Ratso noticed a few puzzled faces but also others were nodding in agreement. He debated what to say as he met Nancy's penetrating stare. *She could go far. Hard as nails and not afraid to voice different and even unconventional viewpoints.* He looked away, apparently checking his notes but actually weighing up the options. He imagined Arthur Tennant being upstaged by a junior constable and being contemptuously dismissive. He decided to react exactly the opposite.

"Thanks, Nancy. Good thinking. It makes sense. You *could* be right." He paused to lob his empty soup mug into a bin. "But even so, we must assume they will be a nest of vipers—hostile, edgy to each other, buying heroin from Fenwick with Bardici as a minder."

"How will we know who's to be there, boss?" Jock was the questioner.

"Only by staking out the place with the Spanish cops. Or other intelligence."

"Because if it's no all pals together, then each dealer will have his heavies. A meeting of even five buyers could mean fifteen arrests."

"My guess? We'll discover the Spanish buyer is one of our old South London friends now living on the Costa del Crime. There's at least a dozen scumbags round Marbella I could name."

"Still in the game, you reckon?"

"Jock…you don't really believe those villains are just drinking San Miguel beer and sunning their tattoos all the time. Some of them have been laundering money via Internet gambling websites, so they must be doing the business. Anyway, anything more from the floor?" Ratso listened to a variety of opinions but most favoured Nancy's standpoint. "Right. Let's move on. We must *assume* it's going to be a hostile, edgy meeting. We've got to be there mob-handed with cuffs for eighteen, maybe more but hopefully it won't be so many."

"Where is *there*, boss?" It was DC Paul Mason this time.

"Ah, Paul. Glad to see you here. I hope *you* didn't injure *your* back picking up Detective Chief Inspector Tennant." He milked the mocking laughter at Tennant's expense.

"Mattrafact, boss, now you mention it…" To more laughter, Mason groaned theatrically on his tubular steel chair.

Ratso shook his head. "*There* is a hotel in La Coruna near a memorial. Name unknown but it should be no sweat – we know it is either HF or HS. Make that your job, Paul: check out every hotel near a memorial with initials like this and give me the possibilities later today."

"If I'm not signed off with a sickie, boss."

Ratso joined in the laughter. "So they meet at a hotel but we can't assume the gear will be divided in the hotel car park. We *can* assume there will be two trucks leaving the docks—one with the coke heading for France and the other with the smack. That means parking up on rough ground, in a seedy hotel car park, in a back street or a warehouse where the gear can be shifted into other vehicles without attracting heat."

"So we follow Adrian Fenwick, boss?"

"My guess is he flies to Asturias Airport, about eighty miles away." He pointed it out on the map and traced the westerly route from there to La Coruna. "Check it out, Jock but I think only Easyjet fly there direct, so we'll know when he books a flight." He flicked over a page of numbered notes. "Nancy, you check with Easyjet for previous flights he's taken. How long he's away, how often he's been—you know what I want. See if it fits with Bardici's movements.

"Tosh, for you, there's good and bad news. The bad: no way will you be anywhere near the sharp end on this. You're damaged goods, too easily recognised now. Sorry." He left the dais to approach his sergeant. "But the good news—before then, I want you to fly to Turkey with Paul Mason to watch the loading at Alanya. Rent a car at Antalya Airport. I want photos of the truck delivering the gear and a movie pinpointing where on *Nomora* the drugs are being stashed, okay?"

"Thanks, boss. And Turkish belly dancers on expenses?"

Ratso grinned. "Permission refused. Watch your own belly in a mirror, pal. How's that 5:2 diet going?" Everyone laughed as Tosh sheepishly looked away and tried to conceal the remains of his KFC and fries. Ratso paused, as if debating whether to add something. "That reminds me, last week I saw a fat bloke, huge belly, sitting on the steps of St Paul's. He was looking pretty damned upset, so I asked him what was the matter. He didn't answer, so I suggested it was because he was so bloody fat. I said to him: 'If I'd seen a belly like that on a woman, I'd have said she was pregnant.' The guy looked up and replied, 'It was…and she is! That's my problem.'"

The room erupted in hoots of laughter. "Be warned, Tosh," shouted a voice from the back. "Sounds like you."

"No way. His missus winna let him near her. Not even with his new aftershave," Jock said.

Ratso joined in the noisy laughter before clapping his hands to get some order. On the board, he wrote *Arrest ALL Attendees*. "We move in as they divide the gear, trousers round their bloody ankles, bang to rights. No wriggle room for smart-arsed briefs to get them off. My guess, whether good mates or not, they just got to be present for the division. Too big to be trusting."

"Are the Spaniards up to it? Do their police carry red capes and shout *olé*?" It was Mason.

Ratso never blinked. "If the guy I'm hoping for is in charge, yes, they're well up to it. I've worked with Antonio Delgado from their National Police before. Top guy."

Jock waved a hand. "Widna we do better to bug their meeting—with help from the Spanish guys, of course? That would fix them. We then get the Spanish navy to intercept the vessel as she is about to enter port. That way, ye get the crew, the Class A with no risk and ye get all the distributors."

"Right but we'd need to know which hotel and which room." He saw Jock's wily old head move slightly in agreement. "And they might have the room swept. Then we'd be in deep shit." He put a photo of the port of La Coruna on screen. "Another thing—if we intercepted the vessel before the meeting, as might happen because we don't know the timing, we'd lose the distribution network. They'd disappear quicker than snow on the Las Vegas Strip."

He wrote *French Arrests* on the board as the next target, followed by *Arrest Crew* and *Arrest Shipyard Management—BUT evidence?*

"So," Ratso continued, "only after these do we reach Zandro, Terry Fenwick, the guy in Leeds and maybe their network of dealers. I'm less arsed about them, the small guys. We want to make this chicken headless. And that's my job: to make sure Zandro does not escape."

"Can we bug the solicitors' offices?" It was DC Nick Millward speaking. "We might get the name of the hotel." He rarely contributed much when it was a full house but one on one Ratso rated him a sharp cookie. This was no time to put him down; the lad needed encouragement.

"Trouble is that their offices are guarded better than the Crown Jewels, right, Tosh?"

"Terry Fenwick showed me himself. This was no DIY alarm system. This is high-tech stuff. CCTV cameras by the main entrance, motion sensors, all linked to a twenty-four-seven security company in Streatham."

"I know even with all that stuff our boys could bug that place while playing a banjo with both hands." Ratso swung himself onto a table top. "If I actually thought we'd tune in to a treasure trove of goodies, I'd call them in. But my guess, these Fenwick brothers won't even chat freely in the office. They both use pay-as-you-go phones. We've had sightings of them walking toward London Bridge Station deep in conversation. They know to take care."

"Aye, that's why it's taken us so long to uncover them," added Jock.

"It's as likely they'll talk over a pub lunch. They were spotted in Dirty Dick's and once in Corney & Barrow. Worth the thought, though." He was about to sum up when he changed his mind. "Nick, I want a complete list of all known Brit drug dealers living around Marbella, Torremolinos, Puerto Banus. Rate them from one to ten as targets based on current lifestyle, unsubstantiated rumours, known online gamblers who may have been laundering drug profits through e-gaming. Oh yes and best of all—known to have visited La Coruna." He saw the puzzled looks. "Okay, that last bit was a joke!"

He turned to Jock.

"I want you to get the French, Dutch, Spanish and German drug squads to watch their top suspects who might make a trip to La Coruna, especially any who are Albanian or have connections there. I want to hear from the French *garçons*, that's 'boys' to you uneducated types, where they believe drugs from Spain might be distributed from. The rest of you, I'll assign other tasks tomorrow."

"And you, boss? Visiting the sick, are you?" Jock's comment brought more laughter.

"Sorry but I've no time to drop grapes into Chief Inspector Tennant's mouth. I'm too busy arranging for the Spanish navy to prevent *Nomora* leaving harbour. I'll be setting up the Spanish police to help on the stakeout. Oh…and Jock and Tosh: a stakeout has nothing to do with barbequing prime Angus. Sorry!" He was rewarded with more laughter as the group broke up.

54

Asturias, Spain

Jock was driving the VW Polo hired at Asturias Airport while Ratso navigated, though the route was not difficult. Neither had ever been in this northwestern corner of Spain before. "So different from the Costa del Sol. That's ruined since I went there on my honeymoon."

"Greed, Jock. Corrupt politicians fixed by unscrupulous developers. This is how Spain ought to look," Ratso observed as he took in wild, sweeping sand dunes and the swell of the Atlantic beyond.

"I've no time for Spain, mysel'," Jock said, adding that he had spent his final holiday with his wife in Sitges. Ratso nodded sympathetically, knowing she had switched her allegiance to an elderly Celtic supporter with a Maserati. For the next fifteen miles, Jock whinged and chuntered on about how he had given Sheena everything she wanted—in bed and out of it—until Ratso had heard enough.

"Jock. Don't kid yourself. You didn't give her *everything* she wanted. You gave her what you thought she wanted. You were wrong. It wasn't you she wanted at all—a decent and hard-working Glaswegian copper fighting crime and doing his best for young Gordy. What she wanted was an elderly Celtic fan with a big dick implant from Los Angeles, an even bigger bank balance, a flashy red Maserati and a grand house overlooking Loch Lomond." Ratso jabbed Jock's knee. "And that is just what she got."

Jock fell silent for over a mile, all the while chewing his tongue. "Ye're right—except for the big dick. She didna' need to stray for that." They both laughed, Jock cheering himself up with a Crunchie, Ratso with an apple. "Your pilot? You still reckon...?"

"He led you a right dance in Cyprus." He examined his fingernails with lingering care. "I want to believe but...he's only as good as his last task." From his slim briefcase, Ratso produced a map of La Coruna and his sheaf of notes. "Head for the port and park there. We can have a late lunch and get our bearings. The Hesperia Finisterre Hotel is no more than ten minutes' walk from the port." He had downloaded Google aerial and some street views of the Spanish town.

"And ye ken Fenwick's staying at this hotel?" Jock was now in the town, crawling at about fifteen mph along a wide boulevard with the port to his right. He saw Ratso nod slightly in agreement. "And *Nomora*'s on schedule?"

"Loaded and left Alanya on time," Ratso acknowledged before his hand shot out and upward. "Just look at that! Jesus! They get bigger every year." Ratso was pointing to a giant white cruise ship moored about four hundred metres away, towering over the entire area. "Like the *Titanic*, it looks so safe, so indestructible."

"They're top-heavy. I reckon you rip it below the waterline, it'll roll over."

"And afterward someone will say *lessons have been learned*." Ratso pointed to a municipal car park on the left. "Park there." As Jock swung over in a sudden swerve, he received a honk from a startled local who nearly collided with their rear. Ratso waited for Jock to finish manoeuvring. "Let's hope we get those ducks in a row. Today's Sunday. Fenwick arrives Monday and so does Bardici under his Mujo Zevi alias. Separate bookings, mind. The meeting is Tuesday and Fenwick's definitely booked into the Hesperia Finisterre for two nights, flying back Wednesday."

"We could have saved him the return ticket."

Ratso laughed as he stretched. "JF has used this hotel before. The hotel name fits with the HF initials and if Mason is right, there's a memorial to a famous British general, Sir John Moore, quite close by."

"Never heard tell of him."

"Shame on you. He was a fellow Scot. Born in Glasgow." Ratso had never heard of him either but had checked him out on Wikipedia. "The guy's a huge hero who died here fighting the French army in 1809. This has to be the best-known war memorial in town."

Jock locked the car and they walked into the narrow streets, which were filled with passengers from the cruise ship looking to buy straw donkeys and leather purses. After a few minutes they found themselves in Maria Pita Plaza, an impressively large square dominated by what looked like a palace with a few bars and cafés open for business on the other sides. The sky was intense blue but it was too chilly to eat outside so they settled for a window table looking across the plaza.

"When do we meet your Spanish pal?"

"Tomorrow at nine. The heavy mob are coming in from Madrid."

"How many?"

"At least forty."

Jock whistled. "Jeez! That is mob-handed!"

"Antonio Delgado is good, damned good. He won't take shortcuts." Ratso pushed the menu aside. "His enquiries suggest Bardici has no room booked under any name. Maybe he gets shacked up with some señorita."

"What about following the trucks from the docks? Reckon we can get trackers on them at the quayside."

Ratso called the waitress over. "Can't bank on that. Let's order and then we'll take it from the top again. See what we're missing and plug the gaps."

Forty minutes later, after a shared carafe of Rioja and some chewy beef, Ratso produced the map of the town. "There's the Hesperia Finisterre Hotel and there, just up the road, is the memorial garden to Sir John Moore—the *Jardin de San Carlos*."

"But the Spanish fought a civil war—Franco's lot and Ernest Hemingway. There'll be other war memorials."

"You're right but not with a hotel initials HS or HF close by."

Jock still looked troubled. "We've just one chance. Is there no anything else we can do to tighten it?"

Ratso fell silent for a few moments while Jock studied the map, looking for war memorials. "Tell you what. JF's room is just a single, so he won't meet in there. Let's check what meetings are booked to take place in the hotel."

"Aye, that may help." Jock still sounded unconvinced. "What other hotels are HS or HF?"

Ratso checked the details gathered by Paul Mason. "We can't be sure about war memorials. Mason double-checked twenty miles around. There are just three hotels HS or HF: the Hispanio Flores, the Hesperia Finisterre and the Hispanio

Sol. But according to Paul, only one has a war memorial nearby."

"Let's take a look at each one. I winna be happy until I'm sure."

Ratso paid the bill and led the way outside. "You're right, Jock. Let's walk the town. Check out the hotels."

"And ye're okay about leaving me here for the arrests?"

"Sure! With Delgado here, I'm not needed. I need to be close to Zandro. Once we've met Antonio and I'm satisfied nothing's been lost in translation, yes, I'll leave you here." He gripped the sleeve of Jock's windcheater. "I *personally* want to arrest Boris Zandro and if I'm here, sure as hell he'll have done a runner by the time I get back." He then pointed. "That's the hotel we're staying in, the Hesperia Coruna. We can check in later."

They turned onto the seafront, passing the long line of traditional apartments, each with large picture windows that looked out across the harbour. The skyline was still dominated by the soaring height of the cruise ship. After winding up the hill, they reached the Hesperia Finisterre and made their way to the desk.

"I'm interested in renting a meeting room," Ratso said. "Tuesday and Wednesday."

"We have rooms for over a thousand. I assume not that big at this late moment?" The svelte receptionist spoke excellent English. Her smile and rounded eyes were a delight. Ratso was so lost in admiring her lips he momentarily forgot to reply.

"Oh, sorry, no. Maybe twenty maximum?"

"I will show you a perfect room. Come!" She led them to a meeting room that would have been ideal had Ratso been minded to book it. They returned to the lobby and she checked on screen. "You could have it on Wednesday but Tuesday…is booked." Jock tried to see her computer screen to get the name but he needn't have bothered. "The Pan-European Timeshare Action Group have it booked for three hours, 11 a.m. till 2 p.m."

She wrote down the price and Ratso gave an unmistakeable wince. "We'll have to look at some other hotels. That looks like a budget-buster."

Outside, the men exchanged knowing glances. The Pan-European Timeshare Action Group sounded a useful cover. They checked the map and continued a short way along the Paseo Maritimo until they reached the large, circular stone-walled garden that served as a memorial for Sir John Moore, a giant plinth taking pride of place in the centre. They walked round the memorial, pausing under the arch to take in the picture-postcard view of the port. They could see the ferry terminal and farther away to the left the cranes used for loading and unloading in the commercial port.

"Look at this, boss." Jock was now thoroughly enthused by this place where a fellow Glaswegian had been buried. "See this poem on this wee plaque. Sir John, he was some boy, eh. We dinna respect our heroes enough these days."

Not a drum was heard, not a funeral note,
As his corse to the rampart we hurried;
Not a soldier discharged his farewell shot
O'er the grave where our hero we buried.

We buried him darkly at dead of night,
The sods with our bayonets turning,
By the struggling moonbeam's misty light
And the lanthorn dimly burning.

Jock paused, strangely moved by the deadly images. "Ye can almost hear the muskets, see the bloodied bayonets, smell the gunpowder. And today it's so peaceful."

"Like Starbucks, you Scots get everywhere. Come on." Ratso led the Glaswegian out between the wrought-iron gates onto the narrow and winding streets of the old town.

"And to think that Zandro's mob use this wee garden as a marker point for a meeting. Fair makes ye want to puke."

"Y'know Jock, I'm coming round to your opinion." They stood by the gate to the memorial as Ratso waved in each direction. "This is no place to divvy up the drugs into several vehicles. Bring a truck round here, into that swanky hotel? No way! Use one of these grand old homes with truck and vans parked up outside? Get real, or as the locals would say, *No way, José.*" He checked the map. "We're looking for a quiet spot or a warehouse nearer the port. Somewhere that vans and trucks don't look out of place."

"A different hotel, then." Jock sounded gloomy. Ratso reckoned it was the thought of more walking that brought it on. He and Tosh were two of a kind.

"If Mason's right, neither hotel has a war memorial nearby but the Hispanio Flores is nearer to the commercial port." Even as he spoke Ratso was striding off downhill. "Come on, Jock. Work up an appetite for dinner."

"If it's like that beef at lunch, I'll go vegetarian."

It took them nearly thirty-five minutes to find the Hispanio Flores, tucked away down a side street in an area where truckers might well doss down for the night. "I can see why JF isn't staying round here."

They both absorbed the broken-down scene. Washing hung from windows in the narrow cobbled street; the pavements were cracked and covered in dog turds. A skinny cat was gnawing at something that might have been a carcass and litter danced in the breeze coming in from the Atlantic. Ratso lashed out at an empty plastic Coke bottle that rolled beside him. From upstairs rooms, more than one baby was wailing its heart out and a broken pram opposite the gloomy entrance to the hotel completed the broken-down image. They toured the area and double-checked the map. Mason had been right; there was no memorial. A quick enquiry revealed the hotel had no meeting rooms and walking round the area proved the nearest parking was four hundred metres in a municipal park. Ratso had already dismissed this hotel. "The area's seedy enough but that's all it has going for it." He shrugged dismissively. "The Hispanio Sol, then. Last chance! Somewhere near the cruise ship terminal."

Ten minutes later, Jock spotted it, looking like what it was—a tourist three-star hotel. The front entrance was through open double doors and the shutters by every window badly needed painting. Ratso imagined that the Atlantic breeze, flecked with salt, must play hell with building maintenance.

"Let's check out their meeting-rooms, if any." Ratso led Jock into a compact reception area where a rather fierce-looking woman in her late fifties waved a dismissive arm and returned to her computer screen. After standing by the desk for what seemed an age, Ratso could take no more. "Hello! Anybody there? We want a meeting room on Tuesday or Wednesday." He spoke slowly, spitting out each word. "Do you have one for twenty people?"

The woman adjusted her swept-back silvery hair, staring at them as if they had crapped on her lino. "*Hablo Español?*" she enquired in a deep voice. Ratso understood enough to know what she was asking and shook his head.

"*Habla Ingles?*" he replied. The woman seemed to understand but shook her head. Ratso looked around for any pictures of the hotel facilities but there were none. "C'mon. We're outta here. Let's go."

The woman watched them leave, adjusting the needles in the bun at the back of her head. As soon as they had gone, she returned to her computer screen with just a fleeting glance at the two Brits deep in conversation outside.

"There's no sign of any war memorial round here anyway," volunteered Ratso as they entered a nearby café, ordered and sat down with their drinks.

"What did ye think of thon Pan-European Timeshare Group?" Jock was warming his hands round tea in a glass cup.

"When we've checked in, I'll trawl the Web."

"Having seen the other hotels, it must be the posh one but it still doesn't seem right." He stretched his legs out and complained about aching feet.

"Let's get checked in. I'm feeling a bit knackered myself."

55

La Coruna, Spain

Next morning Ratso and Jock crossed Maria Pita Plaza in good time for their meeting with Antonio Delgado. At this early hour, the sun was not warm and Ratso was glad of his fleecy lined windcheater. "I met him four years back on a bust at Torremolinos. He's the best I've worked with in Europe. He's a detail freak and none the worse for it but others call him anal retentive."

"Those Pan-Europe Timeshare folk? Ye get anything on them?"

"If they exist, which I now doubt, their online profile is lower than a mole's tunnels."

"Sounds like they're the guys, then, at the Hesperia Finisterre." But Jock still did not sound convinced.

Ratso looked across to the Ferry Terminal. The cruise ship had gone and the red, blue and green fishing boats once again dominated the scene. "It could be an inaugural meeting. I just don't know." They breezed into police headquarters, which was a modern building, more smoked glass than concrete. "Makes our place look what it is."

"A 1960s shithouse," Jock agreed as they were ushered into a small meeting room with chairs for six. The lighting was bright and the view looked onto a vast shopping mall designed to bleed money from cruise-ship passengers. The table and chairs were new, the glass table top matched the windows. They accepted strong, bitter coffee and sat in silence waiting for Delgado. At precisely 9 am, a small, busy-looking man aged about forty-three entered the room alone. Ratso did a double-take. It was not Delgado—not unless he had shrunk six inches and started wearing a toupee to cover the shining bald head Ratso recalled so vividly.

The man sat down at the head of the table, barely shaking hands. He smiled with the warmth of a coal fire that had gone out. From a slim, expensive wallet, he produced two business cards and handed them over. "Good morning. My name is Jesus Botía. As you see, I am a comisario from *Unidad de Drogas Y Crimen Organizado*, Spain's drug squad. I am based in Madrid." His English was impressive but spoken in sufficient accent that both listeners had to strain to be sure what was being said.

Ratso and Jock handed over their cards and showed their IDs, which Jesus seemed to expect. Ratso recalled that a Spanish comisario was the equivalent to a superintendent. He felt rather outranked. Although Delgado was an *inspector jefe*, a chief inspector, he had always treated Ratso as an equal and an old mucker. "Thanks for your support...but I was expecting Antonio?"

"Oh, him? You know him well?" The remark was heavy with contempt.

It was not a good start but Ratso tried not to show his irritation. "We worked together in Torremolinos."

Jesus Botía nodded, uninterested. "He cannot be here." With no explanation and barely a pause, he continued, "So I am in charge. You have any more news for me?"

"I believe you have forty men arriving to support the operation...but where is Antonio? Is he arriving later?"

"Inspector Delgado's father died yesterday afternoon. And no, we do not have forty officers. Just fifteen. He exaggerated the difficulties of a simple affair." Botía saw the horror on his listeners' faces.

"Fifteen? That's crazy—especially if this turns violent." Ratso checked his notes. "Besides the ringleader, Adrian Fenwick, arriving this morning, also flying in is a contract killer called Erlis Bardici. He is the enforcer." Ratso looked at Jock and saw his cheeks were growing redder by the second. "This could be a screw-up of mega proportions. Your officers may face unacceptable dangers."

"You exaggerate too, *Inspector* Holtom." Calmly, Jesus Botía poured himself a coffee and adjusted his heavy black spectacles. "Forgive me but I *have* read the file." The remark could have been polite, perhaps even friendly but the look on Botía's face was closer to contempt. "Your summary has left *me* in no doubt. We need one man at each hotel, watching for a meeting breaking up. But I am sure it will be the Hesperia Finisterre. Wherever Fenwick goes from there for a meeting, by car or on foot, we will follow. If the meeting is there, we can photo all of them and then follow to where the drugs are divided."

Only that part made sense. *A simple affair!* The words almost made Ratso choke. "You'll not follow the lorry to France?"

"No. We will arrest the truck as it leaves town. That will be cheaper. Less risk"

"And lose the chance of more arrests in France."

"The value of the cocaine tells me to take no chance."

"And the truck with the heroin?"

Botía smiled confidently. "The officers following that truck will report to me when the destination is reached. Six of my men in unmarked cars will stake out the area surrounding the truck and will move in when the dealers are dividing it."

"And *Nomora's* crew?" Ratso had been through every detail with Delgado and they had concluded thirty-five men minimum.

"There is no hurry to arrest them. They will have no reason to be suspicious. The ship cannot leave harbour—that has been arranged by you with Delgado. A Spanish naval vessel is patrolling close by at sea."

Ratso could take no more. "This is useless. Nobody arresting the crew? They'll be off, disappear at the slightest whiff of trouble. The skipper's a slippery bastard called Micky Quigley. He'll slip out of Spain quicker than Houdini." Ratso found his voice had been rising with his temper.

Jock's wrinkled face looked ready to explode, his cheeks deep crimson and the vein on his temple throbbing. "With respect, Superintendent Botía," he began, before he was cut off by the little man standing up and slamming shut his notebook.

"You requested our help," the Spaniard snapped. "Now you tell me—a superintendent of the drug squad—how to manage an operation?" He turned sharply and flounced toward the door with all the self-assurance of a matador. "You can observe but will not be involved, not now, not at the scene. Understood, Sergeant, Inspector?" He glared at each listener in turn. "You agree? Yes or no."

Ratso's mind was in ferment. He found himself chewing his lip as he realised the man would have zero interest in synchronising with arrests in the UK. But it was pointless reasoning with someone who thought he could walk on water. In turn, Ratso felt as if his own feet had been nailed but to the floor rather than a wooden cross. He glanced at Jock, who looked as if he'd found ten pence after dropping a pound. "The figure forty was Antonio Delgado's decision, not mine. Let me take you through the breakdown."

"Delgado is like an old woman—everything a big problem."

Ratso caught Jock's eye and shrugged. "You have us by the balls, Superintendent Jesus Botía, so our hearts and minds will follow. Only God can outrank you."

Ratso watched the small man with the big ego flinch at the cheeky comment. He hesitated before returning to his seat. "I take that as a yes, Inspector." His deep-set and cautious eyes still showed his distrust for these interferers from London. "Any update for me, Inspector Holtom?"

Jock wondered whether Ratso would take the piss but realised his boss saw this as too serious for that. "A London drug-dealer who swans about Estepona like villain royalty left there yesterday morning by car. We think he could be coming here."

"His name?"

"He's known as Foxy Boxy but his real name is Arnie Boxter. He's got a sharp face. That's how he got the nickname. He's the only one of our suspects living in Spain who is on the move."

"A car? He won't get much in that. You have a photo of this…Foxy Boxy?"

Ratso tapped away on his iPad and then sent the superintendent several shots of a shrimp of a man, aged late fifties with a thin face, long nose and a slim moustache. "These were taken this week. We think Foxy Boxy could be a distributor for Spain."

Botía nodded. "I think you leave here today, Inspector?" Jock showed no surprise as Ratso explained that no, he was staying on.

"So we meet at seven tomorrow morning."

"I think I should be at the Hesperia Finisterre, where Fenwick is staying."

"No. You look too English."

Ratso had to give that to him. "Fenwick does not know me."

"Seven unless I change it. I am convinced the meeting will be at Fenwick's hotel. The memorial to the English general is the most significant." Jock let the mistaken reference to an *English* general pass without challenge. The past twenty minutes had taught him that silence was the better option.

A short time later, Jock and Ratso were seated at the same small café as the day before. Today, as the clock struck ten, the sun was now striking the red tables so it was comfortable to sit outside. Jock ordered coffee and pancakes with apple, chocolate *and* whipped cream. Ratso, still inwardly fuming from the encounter, admitted to feeling drained and ordered a full English, a rarity for him. While Jock browsed yesterday's *Daily Mail*, Ratso tapped away furiously on his iPhone. "I'm reporting to the AC." The message to Wensley Hughes pulled no punches. "We're facing the biggest snafu in La Coruna since General Sir John Moore died here over two hundred years ago. I want Jesus Botía outranked."

"It's cover-yer-arse time," agreed Jock. "So…ye're staying on?"

Ratso playfully punched Jock's chest. "I'm covering *your* arse by staying on. Mine is up in lights! This could be a five-star balls-up if there's a shootout with the Spanish outnumbered."

"But Boris Zandro? You said…"

"He's under surveillance again and there's no sign of panic. I've told the AC. I've just implemented my Plan B."

"Which is?"

"Turning a high risk of him escaping into a calculated gamble." Ratso winked and Jock knew better than to probe.

The Scot signalled for more coffee. "So we kiss goodbye to arrests in France?"

Ratso nodded. "That's the *only* part of Botía's plan I'm not pissed off about. If we arrest the driver here, he might tell us where he was headed *and* we don't risk losing the coke through a cock-up." He looked at the two runny fried eggs and rashers of limp-looking bacon that had just arrived. "I wish I'd had yours now."

"And Micky Quigley? Do another runner?"

Ratso shook his head and smiled as he dipped his bread into the egg's yellow. "Nah. That was just me being awkward. He'll be off quicker than a whippet if he hears something has gone wrong but otherwise, no way would he abandon *Nomora* here. The Spanish cops would crawl all over it and find drug traces." He chewed thoughtfully on a piece of bacon before pushing the remains to one side. "Remind me—no more full English over here."

"The pancakes are great." Jock grinned. "So what do ye reckon Quigley will do?"

"Refuel and sail. He doesn't know about the Spanish navy blocking him in. He might want to scuttle her in deep water. Off the West African cost is pretty deep. The crew won't get their tootsies wet; they'll be in the lifeboat with some cock-and-bull story. That'll bury the evidence *and* the company can recover some insurance. Either that, or she'll be sold in an obscure port somewhere."

"So what's yer big worry, yer biggest worry?" Jock wiped at smears of chocolate under his lower lip.

"That when the gang transfers and divides the smack, there's a shootout with Botía's young cops. Several die. Some of the distributors escape. Zandro and Terry Fenwick are tipped off and disappear. Quigley hoofs it overland in a stolen car." Ratso's scowl blackened his face. "Bad enough for you?"

"I'll tell ye mine, boss. That meeting willna be at the Hesperia Finisterre Hotel. Botía's wrong."

"Evidence?"

Jock tapped the side of his nose. "No evidence. Just a sixth sense, that's all."

Ratso's intent stare showed his respect as he drained the rest of his black coffee. "Antonio Delgado would agree with you." Ratso stood up and said he would be in the hotel, waiting for the AC to phone. "And you?"

"I'm going over the hotels again. We must have missed something."

For the next several hours, the Scot, having scoured the Web and bought a large-scale map of La Coruna, visited and revisited every war memorial and cemetery in the area. Somehow, he managed to ignore his aching feet and keep going. But nothing else fitted with HF or HS better than the ones they had checked out. While Jock was pavement-pounding, Ratso spent the day working on his plan for the UK arrests, the phone bill to Wensley Hughes costing a fortune. By the end of their third conversation, he had the AC as close to seething about Comisario Botía as Hughes ever went. "Damned cavalier approach. I can't risk that. I'm getting this sorted." Just after 3 p.m., Hughes phoned back. "I've spoken to someone I met at an Interpol convention in Berlin. You can assume Botía's *cojones* are now on the line already."

"Even better in a paella dish."

"Your end? Anything?"

"Jock Strang's been gone all day. He's not happy at all. But the good news is that the satellite data points to *Nomora* entering harbour late this evening."

On a whim, Ratso rang Tosh. "Anything?"

"Tomorrow I'll be up in the Central 3000 room with the AC," Tosh enthused. "Watching the action."

"You like blood, do you?"

Ratso was sure Tosh was holding back. Something was not right. "It's business as usual for Terry Fenwick in Lime Street and there's been no messages using the pigeonholes at any of his London clubs."

"He and Zandro are due to meet on Thursday night at the Poulsden. That won't happen. I'd stake my pension that Terry will know instantly when Botía's men move in down here. So keep up the surveillance on both Zandro and Terry Fenwick."

"We've got our team of eight covering Terry Fenwick like a rash. Wherever he goes, we'll know. Likely time?"

"Dunno. I'll call you. As soon as the raid starts, I want him picked up—and Zandro too."

Ratso heard the slight cough at the other end. "Not so easy, boss. Zandro's given the lads from SCD11 the slip."

"What! My instructions were the sod couldn't fart without us knowing. You telling me he's outwitted the surveillance unit?" There was an uneasy silence. "They'd better bloody find him by tomorrow morning. Where was the loss?"

"His chauffeur dropped him near Fortnum & Masons. He went into Thomas Pink on Jermyn Street. He didn't buy anything. He was then picked up on Lower Regent Street and taken to Plantation Tower in the City."

"Plantation Tower?" Ratso tried to recall the address. "Oh, yes! That huge block near Fenchurch Street Station. Quite close to Lime Street, funnily enough. Why was he there?"

"Unknown. He was followed in at 10:30 a.m. He used a photo ID to get through security and went to the bank of lifts. DC O'Donnell kept watch for him coming out but he never did."

Ratso was exasperated. "It's 4 p.m. now. Is he in a meeting there?"

"The surveillance team circled the huge building and found another exit and watched that too. Then they checked a security camera. He never went up in the lift. He went *down* and two minutes later, exited through the rear entrance on a lower level. Timed at 10:32 on the security camera"

"Lost him! That's all I bloody need. Did he go to Fenwick's office? It's close by."

"No. It's being watched."

"So the bastard realised he was being followed."

Tosh had to agree. "Looks like it. And from the rear exit, he could have gone in God knows how many different directions."

Ratso felt drained. He didn't blame the SCD11 crew; he knew that even with a team of eight using motorbikes, cars and plain-clothes, cunning bastards like Zandro could use local knowledge to give them the slip. "What bothers me is not him losing them. It's that he felt the need to."

Tosh could only agree. "But maybe he uses this dodge occasionally for other reasons. Maybe he didn't know he was being followed."

Ratso scowled as a thought hit him. "Well, I hope to hell there's been no leak."

"I hadn't thought of that, boss." He paused to check his scribbles. "Oh yes - he was carrying a small overnight case."

"Anything else I should know?"

"They say not."

The overnight bag did something to calm Ratso. "Okay. Keep me posted."

"Do you want all ports and airports alerted?"

Ratso was about to say yes when he remembered the note in the thousands of papers he had inherited from Wensley Hughes' original investigation. "No. He had at least one mole in the Home Office, a well-placed one. I can't risk tipping Zandro off. Remember, we haven't been following him at all till now—quite deliberately—letting him think he's off the radar. So our best hope is he's playing away from home. He always used to. Ciao!"

"I didn't know you spoke Spanish, boss."

"I don't. That's Italian, *caro mio*."

Exhausted after a restless night, a worse morning with Botía and now Zandro's disappearance, Ratso slumped back onto the pillows. He needed to unwind, regroup, get his head in gear. *Forget Plan A and Plan B. With Zandro gone, even a Plan Z wouldn't bloody work.* He tossed and turned restlessly, his mind a jumble. Everything seemed a bugger's muddle of futility. Too much had gone wrong at the same time. Only the possibility of Botía getting his balls chewed provided any comfort.

How long he lay there he was unsure. Had he dozed off? Or had every moment been spent treading paths to nowhere? When the phone rang, he was confused, his mind fuzzy. "Yes, Jock. Only give me good news. I can't take any more bad." He listened for a moment before leaping off the bed. "I'll be five minutes." He pulled on his jeans, stuffed his feet into his ageing black shoes and splashed cold water over his face before drying with an abrasive towel. He felt better already.

It was under four minutes later when he saw Jock standing outside the Tourist Office on the plaza. "We've been sniffing at the wrong dog's arse." Jock grinned.

"Explain!" Ratso was already shivering as the light faded and the first of the ornate street lamps came on.

"I went into the Tourist Office. Young laddie in there, a student, he wis an employer's dream—bright, keen and spoke and understood English."

"But you don't speak English."

"Away with yer tedious racist jokes. He understood me just fine and dandy, nae bother." Jock laughed. "Anyroads, he started marking up every war memorial all over town. He seemed disappointed that I wisna impressed. But then I asked him if there were any war memorials near either of the other two hotels." Jock held out the map and it fluttered slightly in the chilly breeze. "The laddie checked his list, mentally ticking off each one and said no. Well, he could see I was fair disappointed. 'But ye're English,' he said, 'so ye might want to visit this monument.' He pointed here." Jock's stubby finger landed on the Mendez Nunez Gardens. I said *no Sir John Moore again* but he said it wisna. It was a bronze statue of John Lennon with his guitar."

"John Lennon? You been on the wacky-baccy? Anyway, why should we be interested in that? We're not here to sing 'Yellow Submarine.'" Ratso didn't mean to sound as harsh as he sounded.

"It's a monument right enough—but it's also an *anti-war memorial*." Jock saw he had Ratso's attention now. "And it's only one hundred metres from the Hispanio Sol Hotel—that dump with the rude receptionist." He pointed to the map. "The Lennon monument isna' even marked. The map's out of date. But it's been there a few years."

Suddenly all the negatives of the past twenty hours vanished. Ratso's blood pumped faster, his eyes flashing with a boyish enthusiasm unthinkable just moments before. "What are we waiting for? Let's go see. It can't be far." Ratso grabbed Jock's arm and gave him a warm look for digging him out of his black hole.

They hurried across the plaza toward the seafront, Jock limping slightly and puffing and panting to keep up. Through the gloom of early evening and across the busy road, they saw a small tree-filled park. They dodged the traffic and found, nestling in the darkness of the trees, the statue of a seated, bespectacled John Lennon strumming his guitar. It was discreet with no pedestal, so low as to be almost anonymous. Ratso peered at it, struggling to read the inscription. *Nothing to Kill or Die For.*

"You're right. Anti-war." He stood a moment in reflection. Why had an obscure small Spanish town raised money to erect this statue? "Back in England, thieves would have nicked this by now for the brass. It used to be lead from church roofs; now they nick whole bloody statues to make a few bob to buy drugs."

He looked across the street and pointed to the Hispanio Sol Hotel. The miserable woman at the front desk could just be seen under the lights of a central chandelier. "It's not even a hundred metres," Ratso commented, more to himself than to Jock, who had moved to get a better view. With dusk, lights had come on in much of the hotel, the first time they had seen it after dark.

"Boss, look at the windows on the first and second floors. Right-hand end. They dinna look like bedrooms to me."

Ratso joined him, staring at the upper floors. "You're right. They're not. They're meeting rooms, so whatever that Spanish bitch never said, she could have offered us a meeting room." Ratso clapped Jock on the shoulder. "One more thing to do."

"My feet are killing me."

"We're not going far. Not if I'm right."

Ratso wanted to avoid walking in front of the hotel and most certainly did not want the woman on the front desk to see them. They crossed farther along the road at the traffic lights and then walked back toward the Hispanio Sol. Just before the entrance, they reached a scruffy one-way street running along the side of the hotel, into which they turned. At the end of the building stood a high wall, blocking any view of what lay behind.

"Come on, Jock," Ratso pointed to the next street, which ran parallel to the rear of the hotel. "Along here and round to the far side. At last, I'm feeling lucky. This is a big area behind a third-rate hotel. I doubt we'll find rose gardens and an Olympic-sized pool behind this wall."

"The laddie at the Tourist Office told me there was off-street parking at the back." Beside him on this busy road, rush-hour traffic was moving steadily in both directions. All around, the pavements were busy with office workers heading home or going to the shops, bars and cafés.

"The car park entrance can't be on this street. It must be up the other side."

Ratso led them another eighty metres or so till they reached the next junction. Here they turned left, the third side of the square, keeping the high wall next to them. Above them the street name was barely visible but a passing car lit the words *Rua de Cervantes*. They had barely taken a few steps when Ratso saw the faded sign saying *Aparcamiento Privado Hispanio Sol*. The two men looked at each other, Jock's face breaking into the huge smile he normally saved for the arrival of his fish supper.

The wall ended and in the gap before it resumed was a perfect view of what looked more like waste ground than a real car park. The surface was dried earth strewn with litter, bits of newspapers, plastic bottles, fast-food cartons and old cans. Pristine it was not but the wide-open space was ideal for a truck looking to divvy up its load into other vehicles.

Ratso was about to pass between the open gates to snoop around the vehicles when he heard a car approaching from behind. "Keep walking, Jock." For a fleeting moment, both men were lit up by the car's powerful headlights before it turned into the car park. After the engine quieted and a couple of doors slammed, Ratso turned back and peered between the open gates. Though the yard was poorly lit by a floodlight fixed to the rear wall of the hotel, Ratso could see a man towing a small suitcase and his companion, a rather younger woman, clinging to his arm. They had their backs to him as they climbed a few stairs leading up into the hotel's rear entrance.

There were perhaps twelve saloon cars in the car park, ranging from a black Mercedes to a small Seat. There were also four vans. That left spaces for dozens more vehicles. There was no security, so they crossed to the nearest car. Jock noted the car's number while Ratso felt the bonnet for warmth. "You won't learn much from Spanish numbers. Delgado told me a few years back that vehicle registrations are national, so you can't tell from which region they come anymore. But check out every one."

The fourth vehicle's bonnet was still hot, as if it had been driven far and fast. It was a burgundy-coloured BMW 7 series and Jock confirmed it had a French number plate. "That couple who just checked in, maybe?" They continued down the line of cars and vans. No other felt as warm. A Mercedes panel van had German plates but the others might all have been rented in Spain. "Some posh cars here for a doss-house like this. I like that. I'm getting good vibes."

"I'd like to see more vans, trucks to shift the gear."

"You're right, Jock. These distributors won't travel with the drugs. They'll supervise the split and then use their delivery guys in case of capture." Ratso led the way back to the street. "Maybe Foxy Boxy might risk driving his share across Spain—no borders to cross. That Toyota Land Cruiser over there could be big enough."

"Are we done? I'm fair famished. I've feet like a pair of dead haddock."

"We'll find the best steaks in town. But first we've got to decide what to tell Jesus Botía."

"He's no going to listen to us," grumbled Jock. "Why not talk to your pal Delgado?"

"Botía outranks him. The AC's progressed it," Ratso muttered as he led them alongside the drab grey rendering of the hotel's boundary wall. As they threaded their way between the pedestrians on the main street, Ratso continued. "Would Jesus buy this? We say, this hotel has a discreet car park. It has meeting rooms. It is near an anti-war memorial. A French registered car has arrived. The receptionist was awkward. That's it."

"Aye, well…put like that." Jock's stride faltered. "Except that Erlis Bardici—call me *Mujo Zevi*—is staying there, fourth-floor room."

Ratso stopped as if struck by lightning. They stood in the shadow between two street lights. Sure enough, standing at an open window overlooking the car park was the unmistakeable figure of the Albanian, his frame almost filling it. He was smoking a cigarette. They watched till he flicked the fag end into the darkness and then shut the window.

"That's a clincher! But if Bardici's there, won't JF be there too?"

"Ye mean no using the other place at all?" Jock was hobbling along and Ratso slowed to accommodate him. "Possible."

Ratso's eyes narrowed as he weighed that up. "Christ, Jock! You're puffing away like a clapped-out steam train." They turned left beside the splendour of the municipal building on the plaza. "Perhaps JF keeps his location a secret."

"Time to tell Jesus where to work his next miracle?"

"We're going to save him from egg on his face."

"Aye, right enough—a three-egg Spanish omelette too, boss."

"But I'm reporting to Wensley Hughes first. CYA rules."

56

La Coruna, Spain

Despite the generous portion of his crab salad and a blood-red fillet steak with tomato and onion salad, Ratso was still unable to sleep. Even the red wine and a couple of cheap fiery brandies were no help as his mind shuffled through how the next day would develop. Erlis Bardici dominated his thinking, especially with Kirsty-Ann's warnings replaying ominously. When the phone rang at 1:30 a.m., it was almost a relief to stop the endless marshalling of facts. "Yes?"

The chocolate voice of Darren Roberts filled his ear. "Hey, mon! What's goin' on?"

Ratso sat up and adjusted the pillow behind his shoulders. "Don't ask! I'd almost given up on you. You got something?"

"Sure but hey, it's been tough shit. I been done try to get something from the boy Chuckie. Remember, my cousin's son who do welding at the yard." Ratso needed no reminding. "He's damned scared and then some."

"I can believe it. You cracked it?"

"The boy, he done tell me. You remember your inspection?"

"Every moment."

"You found nothing strange. Right? No surprise. You done visit the accommodation? The crew's quarters?"

"Yes. But no work had been done there according to the specification. And there was no sign of anything either."

"Under one of them bunks on the lowest deck, they done cut like a manhole. Under there was a big water storage tank. Chuckie, he done work down the manhole—strengthen the bottom."

"How big?"

"Easy take maybe three tons. But I'd say like hell down there—filling it, stacking the coke. Chuckie, he did not see nothing of the coke."

Ratso was now on his feet, pacing the room with giant strides. "Anything else from Chuckie?"

"The boy, he did ask the boss, why is we doing this? He been told to shut the mouth."

"Once the sacks were down there, I guess they could weld over the hole." Ratso was almost talking to himself, thinking through the implications. "Did the boy know of any other hiding place? *Nomora's* now loaded with smack too."

"I did ask him that. He did say maybe the crew's quarters."

"Hold on, Darren. That fits." Ratso leaned over and flicked through pages on his iPhone. "During scientific research, there was sleeping space for sixteen crew, eight officers and up to a dozen boffins—thirty-six total. How many crew sailed with her?"

"Twelve total. I do watch from a crane."

"Tosh Watson saw the heroin going aboard in Turkey. He reckoned it was concealed somewhere around the stern. Perfect." Ratso was already weighing up more changes to the day ahead—big changes. "By the way, I see you got a new murder case on your hands."

"You know that?" There was almost a squeak in Darren Robert's voice.

"I read the papers," Ratso bluffed, not wishing to reveal that Kirsty-Ann was his source. "What's it about?"

"The Pink Flamingo Bar where we done meet? In the mangroves near the car park, a body do appear after a storm. With the high tides and wild seas, the waves they done swept through the pines and mangroves. They done disturb maybe a shallow grave."

"The bar? Is it okay?"

"It sure been damaged but survived."

"What's the story with the body?"

"Male. Around forty. Been dead several weeks. Throttled with a wire noose."

Ratso knew that *modus operandi* well enough to mutter *Bardici under his breath*. "Something to get your teeth into. Local, was he?" He played it straight.

"His clothes, what remained, suggest white male from the USA." There was a pause. Then Darren spoke slowly. "My guess, it's the guy you showed me. Remember the guy with Cassie—liked doggie-doggie?"

Ratso decided to volunteer nothing. "Good luck with that. Anyway, great job on the *Nomora*. I owe you."

"But there's more." Darren sounded hurt and excited at the same time.

"Sorry, Darren! I'm all ears!"

"Ida, she's scared as hell mon, 'bout me telling you all this shit about Lamon Wilson."

"Her name won't come out." Ratso kept his fingers crossed as he spoke.

"On 28 December, she did hear her boss on the phone. He been done fixing something for delivery to *Nomora*."

"Coca-Cola for the crew, of course," joked Ratso.

"Ida, she do say her boss, he did call it *the white stuff*." Ratso whistled. Another piece of the puzzle was in place. "Ida she say them photos of Freddie, they did hurt her real."

Ratso was quite moved. "I'm lost for words. Thank her for me. How're things…with her, I mean? She still sticking pins in my image? Chanting Voodoo curses?"

"She be a coming round. Mebbe soon I'll get back in the big bed." He *tee-heed*.

"I'll drink to that. Thanks for everything. Stay cool."

Kirsty-Ann had told Ratso the victim had been garrotted. "If he's identified, heh, Washington's plans kinda fall apart." She had sounded concerned enough to put the lovey-dovey stuff several steps back.

"Not your problem. Relax." He chose his words carefully. "Bucky won't let the Feds or the CIA hang you out to dry."

He was less convinced than he sounded. He had no illusions about the power of Washington to stage-manage whatever they wanted the public to believe. And Kirsty-Ann still had the road fatality hanging over her—plenty of room for a stitch-up there too.

With too many facts buzzing round his head like demented blowflies, sleep was impossible He poured a glass of sparkling water and phoned Jock, who had also been lying awake watching a recording of a Spanish football match. "Let's have thirty minutes. Come to my room."

"I've still some of my duty-free Famous Grouse. I'll bring that."

As he waited, Ratso slipped on a T-shirt and jeans and opened the action plan scribbled over dinner. The AC had done his stuff. Botía would have to listen. As he savoured the prospect of some malt whisky, he got his red pen ready to make some hefty changes.

Next morning Jock's bottle emptied, Ratso and Jock were seated in the same chairs as the day before in Police HQ. Jesus Botía had left the room to check on the latest news from the port.

"At last he seems to be cutting ye some slack." Jock helped himself to a very plain and very dry biscuit. It was 7:15 a.m. and since their arrival, Ratso had driven home the evidence about the Hispanio Sol. Botía's bronzed face had not blanched but had graduated from disinterest to a *Christ I've screwed up* look of panic. He had left the room hurriedly, prompting Jock to suggest he was changing his trousers.

"Your smart work yesterday, not mine," Ratso acknowledged. "But Botía's attitude has only changed because someone in Madrid has shat on him from a great height."

Wensley Hughes' contact had been a *comisario principal*, a full commissioner and able to *talk nicely* to Botía, as the AC had put it. While not admitting any error, Botía was busily changing his instructions to the assembled team. He had now agreed to position the anonymous support vehicles with their posse of heavily armed officers in a side street much closer to the car park for the Hispanio Sol. He had also just confirmed that the GOES had arrived—the *Grupos Operativos Especiales de Seguridad*, a crack SWAT team ready for a shootout if needed.

Superintendent Botía bustled into the room, his composure restored, with news that a white truck had parked by *Nomora*.

"Just one truck?"

"One only for now." For the first time in twenty-two hours, Botía smiled. "You may be correct, Inspector Holtom. Maybe the cocaine cannot be unloaded until the heroin has gone." The smile turned less friendly. "Or maybe the cocaine does not exist."

Ratso was going to retort but decided to leave it. The conversation between Zandro and Terry Fenwick had been plain. Ida's information was solid too.

Botía took out a packet of cigarettes and played with it, knowing he could not light up. "So I agree with you. As soon as the dealers have been arrested with the heroin, we arrest the crew before they unload the cocaine."

"You have enough support?"

"I have another twenty officers coming." Botía looked away to conceal the climb-down. There was a look of triumph on Jock's face as he winked at Ratso who fought to conceal his satisfaction.

"Coming from Madrid? That might be too late."

"Not from Madrid. From Oviedo. They will be here by nine." Botía was about to continue when his phone rang. Still twirling the cigarette packet with his other hand, he listened intently and then ended the call. "As you suggested, I have two officers already watching the Hispanio Sol Hotel."

"From where?"

Botía smirked quite unpleasantly. "They are using two WCs on the top floor of the shopping mall. By standing on the seats, they can see across the road and into the meeting rooms. In a moment, I will receive a photo of a meeting that has started." He checked his notes and read out the name pedantically. "Adrian Julian Fenwick arrived three minutes ago." Ratso liked it when Botía talked of Julian because he pronounced it more like *hooligan*.

With a swift turn on his heels, Botía disappeared once again, walking briskly with the bearing of a well-trained soldier. When he returned, he showed them an impressively clear 8 x 6 photo zoomed through the meeting-room window. Ratso felt as if his nose were pressed against the windowpane, so detailed was the view. He saw the assembled group all seated with coffee cups in front of them. Ratso could also see what looked like scrambled eggs and bacon piled at one end of the table.

"You recognise them?"

"I can see Foxy Boxy, the weasel-faced guy with the cheroot." He pointed again. "Fenwick is at the head of the table."

"And that is your Erlis Bardici in disguise, guarding the door," concluded Botía. "I recognise him."

"Seven of them, boss," confirmed Jock, "including the one from that French car with his popsy." He pointed a stubby finger and Ratso saw he was correct.

"So the French guy brought no minder," Ratso mused and sounding puzzled. "Must be the *all-friends-together* scenario." He saw a questioning look from Botía so he continued. "We reckon these are all Zandro's own trusted distributors. There's no real risk of them falling out when dividing the heroin. No cash will be changing hands in there."

"But Bar-deechi is there in case of trouble."

Botía spoke in rapid Spanish into his phone before explaining, "I've moved nearly all resources close to the Hispanio Sol."

Ratso smiled and checked his watch. "Jock. Change of plan. I'm leaving. I'll take the morning flight to Gatwick."

"Zandro?"

Ratso tapped his silent iPhone. "No news. He's not been sighted since yesterday." He stood up and shook Botía's hand with an enthusiasm he had never thought possible yesterday. "Good luck, *Superintendent*. I am glad you and I now see things the same way." Botía volunteered no thanks for having been saved from the edge of disaster, so Ratso continued. "And the role of Sergeant Strang?"

Botía walked to the window, tossing his cigarette pack from one hand to the other before replying. "He will join me in the van."

Ratso smiled gratefully. "Tosh is going to be at Central 3000. Contact him the moment the raid starts to get things moving." He saw Botía's puzzled look. "You must have watched Jack Bauer in *24*?" He saw Botía nod. "Central 3000 is a Metropolitan Police facility near the Thames where complex operations can be managed and monitored. We use it for counterterrorist operations or major incidents like coordinated arrests. We've every latest gizmo to hear or observe our targets. Jack Bauer would love it. We will coordinate the London arrests from there." As he spoke, he crossed his fingers that Zandro hadn't carried a disguise in his small bag and disappeared for ever.

Botía looked almost impressed but didn't admit it.

57

London Gatwick Airport
As soon as his flight taxied to a halt, by arrangement with the flight attendant Ratso pulled rank to ensure he was first off, to the irritation of other passengers who had to make way for him. In the terminal, he checked his messages. Nothing from Jock. That was hardly a surprise, as any division of the smack would only take place once the truck reached the car park behind the hotel. As requested before the flight, an unmarked Vauxhall Insignia would be outside the terminal. He phoned Tosh. "No news from Spain?"

"Not yet. No movement."

Ratso adjusted his watch, puzzled that by 1:30 p.m. Spanish time the shit had yet to reach the fan. "Zandro? Terry Fenwick?"

Tosh sounded excited. "Fenwick is at the Regency Club in Upper Brook Street—probably tucking into steak and kidney, if he's lucky." He paused. "His last meal before prison."

"We hope. We hope!" Ratso's anxiety was clear in his tired voice. "And Zandro? Got him back for me yet?"

Tosh laughed. "Good news, boss. He returned home just after eleven this morning. By taxi. Same clothes. Smart, shaved.

Must have a pad up West or along the river where he meets his crumpet. He then went by chauffeur to Church Row, Hampstead. It's some type of Art Society buffet. But seven minutes ago he was collected by his limo and headed home. I saw him on the big screen. He looked calm, unflustered."

"For now," observed Ratso.

"SCD11 have his house under surveillance as we speak. You coming here, boss, or going to Hampstead?"

"I'll let you know. I'm heading for London for sure. *Adios.*"

"Ah! Can't fool me. Italian again boss."

"Spanish, *mon amigo.*" Ratso could laugh with Zandro back under the cosh. He phoned Jock. "So?"

"The meeting broke up an hour back but nobody has come out. I guess they're stuffing their faces. Loading the truck by *Nomora* is nearly finished. You want to speak to the superintendent? He's right next to me. We're in an unmarked van near the hotel."

"Not necessary. Let me know once the action begins." Ratso ended the call and immediately started another. "Brad here," he opened the call using his agreed pseudonym. "What you doing, mate?" He listened for a moment. "In the snack bar? Pizza? Enjoy it. You may have a busy day. Now listen carefully."

The buttie on the flight seemed long ago, so after ending the call Ratso hurried into a fast-food joint, where he grabbed a black coffee and smoked salmon on brown before joining the throng heading for the exit. There he spotted the black Insignia waiting with a driver who looked too young to drive a car, let alone be a police officer. The youngster announced himself as Brian. Ratso climbed in and, through a mouthful of bread, instructed the driver to head up the M23 to London. He settled into the back seat, placed his coffee in the holder and chewed hungrily through the rest of the sandwich. He felt better for it but it did nothing for the stabbing pain behind his sleepless eyes. The car had barely left the sprawl of the airport to turn onto the M23 when Jock phoned.

"The truck's here. Botía's men are moving in now. I'm following."

Ratso immediately ended the call and briefed Tosh. "Move in on Terry Fenwick now. But until I say so, no alert to ports. No Home Office."

Ratso was about to end the call when Tosh continued. "Hang on, boss. There's action. I'm watching live." Ratso gripped the seatbelt across his chest so tightly his knuckles whitened.

Tosh sounded excited. "Fenwick has left the Regent Club. Christ! He's running along Upper Brook Street talking on his phone. We're moving in."

"That quick! Brother Adrian must have hit a panic button." Ratso rang off, anxious to clear the line. He had barely flipped the lid from his coffee when he received the call he wanted. He listened carefully. "Altin Vata, eh? No surprise about that! Thanks, mate."

He phoned Tosh but it was Wensley Hughes who answered.

"Hello, sir. Zandro's just left his house, right?"

The assistant commissioner was stunned. "How the hell did you know that? I was about to phone you."

Ratso laughed. "I'll tell you later, sir. I know where he's going and my suggestion is no intervention. As you agreed yesterday, we don't spook him. Although he doesn't know it, Boris Zandro is coming to meet me." He heard the AC laugh. "I need support. Care to join me, sir?"

"What and where?"

"Hold it, sir." He checked the map on his iPhone and told the driver to head east on the M25 and then take the A22 exit heading south, then onto the A25 toward Westerham. He returned to the AC and explained the backup he needed. Then he sat silently listening to Wensley Hughes issuing instructions in the background. When the AC came back on the line, Ratso immediately noticed concern in his tone as Hughes asked him to hold on. Again Ratso found himself squeezing the life out of his seatbelt and chewing fiercely on his lower lip. After what seemed an age, the AC's voice returned. "We have Terry Fenwick. Sgt Watson saw it live on screen—he was knocked down by a taxi while evading arrest. First reports suggest he'll live. But," he hesitated, "all hell has broken loose in Spain."

"Jock okay?"

"We've lost contact."

58

La Coruna, Spain

After Ratso's sudden departure, Botía had permitted Jock to sit in on the final team briefing at 9:30 a.m., where he was introduced and seemingly quite warmly received. On being informed that Jock was trained in weaponry and permitted to be armed in the UK, Botía offered him a Beretta but Jock was unsure of international legalities and declined.

Sitting in the large windowless meeting room and listened to Botía prattling away in Spanish, Jock could follow the plan easily enough. Every move was being explained using an aerial photo of the area with every position demonstrated by Botía's laser pen. It was so similar to what would have happened back in Clapham that Jock felt increasingly comfortable. All told, thirty men were to be deployed at the hotel. Another ten would then storm the *Nomora* by land whilst a naval team in small craft guarded the seaward side. Micky Quigley was not going to jump overboard and flee this time. Another twelve local officers were on standby to blockade the port gates so that escape was impossible.

The comisario principal got at Botía big-time, Jock thought with satisfaction.

About halfway through his presentation, Botía called Jock to the front and asked him to confirm what they knew of the dealers, which was a decent gesture though he had little to add. He spoke slowly, killing his Glaswegian as far as he could, while Botía translated. "We expected these dealers to have armed protection. However, other than this man," he pointed to three different shots of Bardici's disguised face, "there has been no sign of muscle." He paused. "This man is a professional killer. Others also may be armed. This man is the boss," he pointed to Fenwick. "And this guy, Foxy, always carried a gun."

Jock watched the eager faces. Most were young; all seemed to be under forty. Some looked thoughtful, while others nodded or whispered to a neighbour. Botía received the latest reports. "It is time to get in position. The truck is being loaded," he announced. The assembly broke up with nervous laughter, pats on the back and what Jock took to be mutual messages of good luck.

Across Jock's thighs was a Taser. When everyone had been piling into the van at HQ, Jock had spotted a spare Taser X26, used by the local police. He stretched a point and told Botía he had been trained to use one. After momentary hesitation, Botía agreed to let him carry it. "So okay, with nothing you may feel naked." Botía's words were spoken with a nod of understanding. "Tasers, they are not popular here in Spain. The CNP do not much use them but some local forces do." As Jock fingered the black stubby Taser, it felt reassuring—certainly better than nothing. He doubted it was difficult for a novice to use.

For over three long hours, Jock was seated beside Botía in a red maintenance van parked two hundred metres from the front of the hotel, anonymous among a line of parked vehicles. There had been spasmodic conversation, though most of the time was spent with Botía receiving information and firing off snappy responses. In the rear there was quiet conversation and occasional laughter from the armed group. The atmosphere was tense as the minutes ticked away and the moment of confrontation drew closer. But these officers were the GOES—the elite team, hardened for a confrontation like this.

Copious empty plastic water bottles littered the floor. The air was full of the smell of freshly baked rolls filled with chorizo or some other spicy sausage. Jock tried one and enjoyed the new experience, though hot buttered toast and chunky marmalade was more to his taste. On a couple of occasions, Jock pointed out Erlis Bardici emerging from the front of the hotel. Both times, he looked up and down the busy road but only in a casual way with no sign of being spooked. Each time, he had tossed away his cigarette butt and gone back inside. "He seems pretty relaxed about what's going on," Jock observed. "Otherwise he would have stayed in the room." Botía said nothing.

Of the eight men in the van's rear, two were to remain guarding the lobby after they had stormed the main entrance. Six local police would then arrive to provide a wider cordon around the hotel's front. Botía's plan was that he and the other six, all in body armour and helmets, would race through the lobby, exiting the hotel from the rear into the car park. There, in a pincer manoeuvre with his second team rushing the car park from the side street, Botía planned to trap the dealers as they stood by the truck inspecting its contents.

Jock had been told he could enter the hotel as an observer after the first wave. When he'd met the rude receptionist with Ratso, they had spotted a bar off the lobby that almost certainly overlooked the car park and he decided to head there once the action began.

It was gone 1:30 p.m. before Botía received confirmation that the truck had left the port and was heading toward the Hispanio Sol. By arrangement with Botía, its declared cargo of medical research equipment had been waved through with a cursory inspection by port security and Customs.

Everyone in the van was now like a coiled spring, waiting for the command once the truck entered the car park. Jock had chosen to wear only a bulletproof chest plate while those around him had the full body armour, including a helmet, gloves and chest and leg protectors. As he imagined Bardici's merciless eyes staring at him, Jock wished he were better protected but no way was he going to cower in the van till the action was over. He gripped the Taser tightly, seeking reassurance in its solidity.

Too late now, Jock. If you don't like it, stay in the van. Like a wimp.

Four hundred metres away down a narrow alley, well hidden from the hotel's rear and away from the truck's likely route, was the other group of GOES in an unmarked van. Tucked in behind them were more detectives and support from the local police. The locals were charged with setting up roadblocks with stingers at both ends of the one-way street feeding the car park.

There were even more officers involved now than Ratso and Delgado had thought essential. The boss would have enjoyed the irony. Jock wondered what the *comisario principal* had said to kick Botía into line. Suddenly his thoughts turned to Gordy in Glasgow. He had an urge to hug his son and tell him he loved him. *Oh yes and to encourage him to stay strong—that their beloved Glasgow Rangers would get through the financial turmoil and would be great again.*

Too late for that now, Jock.

Botía checked with the observers perched on the lavatories in the mall. They confirmed nobody had left the hotel but that the meeting room was now empty. A policewoman in disguise with a baby in a pram reported no activity at all on the one-way street. "The truck will arrive in under three minutes," Botía announced. He ordered the team to put on their helmets and to have their long black batons ready.

They waited for what seemed an eternity but sure enough, almost on schedule, the message came through from the pram-pusher. A large truck had just entered the car park. Still Botía did nothing. He was waiting for the next vital data. A few moments later, the woman stopped near the gates and discreetly threw the baby's rattle into the entrance. As she stooped to pick it up, she could see the truck with a group of men standing around it. However, almost instantly, a surly individual approached and slammed shut and bolted the wooden double gates.

The woman moved down the street and quietly reported to Botía, who grunted. He fired off orders and then told Jock what was happening. "Our other van must crash down the gates. That will be difficult."

Botía then spoke to the driver. Their red van cruised forward and parked twenty metres beyond the hotel's front entrance as Botía fired off instructions to all other units, presumably putting them on standby. Once their van had parked, the driver in blue overalls jumped out. He started to inspect the road, marking the surface with yellow chalk as if preparing to dig a hole or trench. He stood scratching his head and kicking at the surface.

Meantime, the other team had entered the side street and jumped out as their driver prepared to ram. When he got confirmation that they were in position, Botía turned to the men in the rear. "*Vamos.*"

As they tumbled out and ran the few steps into the hotel, Botía, now in his balaclava, waited till the last man was inside before barking another order, which must have been to storm the car park. Botía nodded as he jumped down and ran for the entrance. Jock clambered out less nimbly, his knees aching from being seated for so long. As he stood in the road, he heard a mighty crashing sound somewhere out of sight. The gates were under siege. From inside the hotel came a torrent of shouting as Botía's men rampaged through the lobby and down the corridor leading to the rear exit.

The road worker stripped off the boiler suit and grinned as Jock entered the lobby, Taser at the ready. Already two of Botía's men were in position guarding that escape route. No question, the gang were trapped. Now that he was inside, the sound of the vehicle battering the gates was more muted but he could hear the shouts from the GOES as well. Jock could imagine Fenwick and the other distributors confused and panicking.

As he crossed the tiled lobby, Jock glimpsed the brick-faced woman behind the front desk to his far left. He ignored her as he pushed open the door into the bar, saw that it was empty and hurried to the window. He saw the last of Botía's team, followed by Botía himself, jump down the four steps into the car park. First he called Ratso and then Tosh. "The raid has started, Tosh. I'll leave the line open."

Jock could see the laden truck parked about forty metres to his left and by pressing his face close to the glass, he spotted JF, Foxy Boxy and the others in a state of baffled panic, heads twisting this way and that as they looked for somewhere to run. They were nearly surrounded by shouting police, menacing in their riot gear, batons at the ready. The noisy shouts added to their sense of confusion and Jock wished he could have captured the fear on Fenwick's face. His Oxford degree and legal training were useless now. Of Bardici there was no sign. He saw Adrian Fenwick's right hand fumbling in his pocket, producing a phone he must have speed-dialled without even looking at the keys. He never spoke at all, nor indeed did he have time to do so before he returned the phone to his pocket. All the while, the officers were closing on him, shouting and waving batons as the group were herded toward the hotel's rear wall.

Jock's attention was drawn to the car park gates. Even as he looked, he saw them bulge as the unseen van slammed into them again. This time, the hinges were ripped from the wall on either side. The gates fell to the ground with a fearsome, shuddering bang. Immediately, a rush of armed figures raced through, scattering in pre-planned directions to ensure that every corner of the car park was secure. The front of the van then appeared, its bull-bars still intact as it moved to block that exit.

He spotted a movement down to his left in the parking lot. It was Bardici! The Albanian was pulling a gun from under his brown leather jacket. But even before he used it, the sound of semi-automatic fire filled the air. From every direction came the sound of violent action—men shouting, cursing over another round of gunfire. The dealers, including Fenwick, were still in retreat, moving backward one pace at a time to be trapped against the rear corner of the hotel. Botía's men tightened the cordon. But nothing Jock could see explained the gunfire. It was not from the GOES. But no question, the hunters were now the hunted.

To a man, Jock saw the GOES duck down, crouching or crawling to take shelter beside or between parked cars. Given this glimmer of an opportunity, the gang scattered like scalded cats, hoping themselves to duck and weave between the parked vehicles and somehow breach the cordon. But from his lofty position three metres above the car park, Jock could see that there was no escape – the gang were still trapped by an outer ring of GOES at least twenty metres farther out.

As a new staccato burst added to the confused shouting, Jock checked every direction...still no sign of the gunman. In the kaleidoscope of movement, Bardici had disappeared. But who had opened fire? It had not been Bardici. Judging by the reactions of the police, the shooting had come from somewhere beyond the truck that was parked with its rear doors open, its tailgate lowered. As he looked toward the cavernous interior, Jock heard another burst of fire and this time he saw one of the officers just beyond the truck lurch, stumble backward and then fall to the ground

At that moment, two figures armed with semi-automatics appeared from way beyond and behind the wider cordon. No wonder Botía's men had been confused—the gunfire was coming from behind them. Two minders must have been sitting in a vehicle way down the car park. On seeing no chance of escape through the gates, the two now seemed intent on shooting their way to the hotel door. After each move between a line of cars, they fired another burst but their fire was now being met by some of Botía's team, who had spotted them and had turned to face the right direction. Jock recognised the sound of Berettas and Heckler & Koch G36 assault rifles spitting out bullets at 750 rounds per minute.

The air was filled with shouted orders mixed with the whine of bullets and smashing glass as cars and vans were struck. There were shards of glass flying everywhere and Jock saw the vehicles rock as their bodywork was struck by repeated shots. To add to the mayhem, several vehicle alarms had been activated. Too close for comfort, a couple of stray bullets pinged against the outside wall with a nasty thwack. A chunk of concrete fell to the ground. Jock sidestepped from the middle of the large sash window to stand, half protected by the wall. From this position, whatever was happening at the truck's rear was now out of sight but he assumed that Bardici must still be there somewhere protecting Foxy Boxy, JF and the rest.

From his higher vantage point, Jock could just see three armed GOES at the distant end of the car park, all of ninety metres away. They must have circumvented the gunmen so they could close in from behind. Jock watched their slow progress as they crept forward, dodging between Seats, Renaults, BMWs, small vans, light trucks and the occasional upscale Mercedes. Making it into the hotel was the gunmen's only chance but Jock reckoned that once they started climbing the few steps toward the door, they were going to be easy meat for crack-shot marksmen. He had no doubts now—surrender was the gang's best option if they wanted to live.

Jock muttered a few more words down the phone to London as he saw the fear on the younger gunman's face. He looked barely nineteen, maybe part Asian with a boyish, unblemished skin. But however harmless he might have looked, he was toting a lethal weapon and looked ready to use it again. He was only about four metres from the steps and Jock could see that he was weighing up the chances of making a mad dash across the dusty yard. But with the lobby guarded, there would be no escape anyway. Jock was not sure what standing orders the Spanish marksmen had but he assumed they would open fire so long as the gunmen were firing. Suddenly, the young man spun round and let rip a burst of fire, bullets flying in an arc around him.

The gunman shook his head toward someone tucked behind a VW van. The second man raised his head. He was wearing a grey cap with a red logo but beneath it the features were those of a middle-aged man with a whiskery face. He let rip with a burst that flew harmlessly over the yard. Both men ducked down to race for the steps. Jock had a clear view of them crouching low on their knees between two vehicles. They were in an animated discussion, each pointing in a different direction. *Give yerselves up. Do yerselves a favour,* Jock thought, fearful of what would happen otherwise. The older man suddenly stood up, fired another burst to keep the police marksmen down and led his companion away from the hotel. They were both bent double, getting protection from a small Iveco van. Neither realised they were advancing straight into a concealed armed cordon barely ten metres ahead.

Too late to alter strategy, the older man suddenly saw the sinister marksman in his all-black outfit. The older man took aim to fire off a volley. If any excuse were needed to open fire, this was it. Before the amateur gunman could unleash the bullets, the Spaniard shot him full in the chest so that he was lifted off his feet before crashing back across the bonnet of a red Seat. A split second later the younger man was blasted off his feet too, a pained expression on his face. He collapsed at the feet of his dead colleague.

Jock had no sympathy for them. He had earlier wished the end could have been different but any thugs who fired at cops had it coming. He saw the marksmen now closing on the dead men to ensure they posed no threat. Out of sight to his left, Botía's team must have been keeping heads down while the bullets flew, awaiting the chance to advance once again toward Fenwick, Foxy and the rest. Jock could see none of them but he saw a pair of feet sticking out from beneath a Toyota van.

He was about to update Tosh when another familiar figure skulked into view. The man was protected from the police's sight by the line of parked cars, several with their alarms still blaring. The profile left Jock in no doubt. It was Bardici and he was heading toward what he had obviously decided was the only escape route.

Jock did not like that prospect. Not one little bit.

Bardici was heading for the steps, his gun at the ready.

59

Kent, England

He tried Jock's number again but could get no contact. No response. Ratso stared out mindlessly as they approached Junction 6 and the driver eased left to exit the motorway. Suddenly anticipating what lay ahead with Zandro seemed a fool's ego trip. He could have stayed in Spain. He *should* have stayed in Spain. Been there to sit at the top table. Should have let Central 3000 ensure Zandro's arrest. *Vanity, Ratso, sheer vanity.* He dialled again. Nothing. *Pick up the phone, Jock.*

Ten minutes ago, Ratso had felt like he was Jack the Lad, King of the Hill and Master of the Universe able to pull strings and get everyone arrested and charged. But now? God knows what's happening in Spain. He heard horns blasting. *Oh shit!* Not a bloody traffic snarl-up at the exit. Jack the Lad? More like King Henry the 8th's Jester. He phoned Central 3000, who patched him through to Wensley Hughes. "Jock, sir? Any news?"

There was an unpleasant pause. "Sorry, Todd but we're getting nothing."

Ratso wanted to say more on that but raced on. "I'm cutting it close, sir. Where is Zandro?"

"He's advancing on the northern approach to the Blackwall Tunnel. ETA thirty-one to thirty-eight minutes. We have him in sight from a chopper. As agreed, no surveillance from the ground."

Ratso ended the call. It was time to pull rank and use the hard shoulder. He asked the driver to switch on the sirens and reveal the blue strobe lights. But in the instant gridlock that had developed out of nothing, there was no quick escape. Only by forcing vehicles to clear a path to the hard shoulder could they move at all. "Come on, come on." Ratso shook his fist and shouted in vain at a Sunday afternoon driver in a flat cap who seemed to have no idea how to reverse to make some space.

The elderly man in the flat cap, now in a total panic at the noise and shouting, suddenly shunted backward two metres too far, slamming into the front bumper of a Ford saloon. There was no time to waste sorting that out. Ratso's driver swung the wheel sharply and nosed through the over-large space onto the emptiness of the hard shoulder. The Insignia accelerated away as Ratso imagined all the other drivers swearing and cussing at the lucky bastard hurrying home for tea and cakes. He checked with the driver. "With luck, sir, I'll get you there in twenty-six minutes."

Close. Too close.

Damned ego trip.

He dialled Jock again.

Nothing.

For a second Ratso caught his reflection in the rear-view mirror. His eyes looked tired, his cheeks pale and there was black bruising coming up on his lower lip where he had been chewing it. He looked the way he felt—a physical wreck from almost two days and nights without a proper kip.

But Boris Zandro, I'm coming to get you. Better still, you don't know it. If I'm not too late.

60

La Coruna, Spain

Jock saw Bardici pause beside a blue Toyota beneath his window. He did a quick look round to check the position of the armed officers. He must have decided that with luck he could make the steps and get into the hotel. As Bardici looked up, Jock pulled back out of sight, hoping he had not been seen. Though the two had never met, it never felt that way to Jock. What would Bardici have thought of him? Did he look like a hotel guest, terrified at being caught up in the raid? Did he look like a Spanish cop? Or did he look like a knackered detective sergeant from the Met Police?

Bardici made his move. In his brown leather jacket, black roll-neck, black jeans and a pair of sturdy boots, he moved surprisingly fast for a man weighing over fourteen stone. In barely three seconds he had cleared the short open space, mounted the stairs in two leaps and was into the building. He was out of Jock's sight and just had to be in the corridor heading for the front entrance, which he was going to find was blocked by two officers armed with Heckler & Koch rifles.

Though Jock had taken in Bardici's whole appearance, what lingered was the small black gun held tightly in the massive grip of his right hand. What would Bardici do when he found the front entrance blocked? Would he try to shoot his way out? *He'd lose out on that. One of them would get him, no question. So could he hide up? Go upstairs? Impossible without getting up close and personal with the Spaniards. So where else would he go?* Yes, there was a small office behind the front desk but he would never make that with two trained marksmen so close. The only other alternative was the bar, in which...*Christ! I'm a sitting duck. If he comes in and sees the Taser, he'll know I'm a cop.*

Unless I get him first.

Jock wanted to report to London but there was no time. He switched off his phone. Couldn't have that ringing now. He left the window and moved as fast as his knees permitted. To cross the lobby to take cover behind the Spanish cops was impossible; Bardici would be there first. Quitting the bar now, he would be four-square in the line of fire between Bardici's gun and the Heckler & Koch rifles. There was no escape. He was trapped in the cosy but drab surroundings. He looked round for a hiding place but there was nowhere obvious to conceal his bulky frame.

Maybe if I stand opposite the door. If it opens, I let him have it with the Taser.

No. Not a good idea. The Spanish cops might let loose their Heckler & Koch rifles. I'd be shot—collateral damage, a small price to pay for killing Bardici in a flurry of bullets.

There was one chance and he took it. He dodged behind the curve of the bar counter and saw just sufficient space to duck under it and squeeze himself between two metal beer kegs and a sink. The near foetal position, his knees screaming for relief from being so badly bent, was distinctly preferable to doing nothing.

Surrounded by the smell of stale beer and pipework, Jock could no longer see what was happening in the car park but judging by the lack of gunfire, Botía's men must have been closing in on the dealers. Perhaps some of the gang were even surrendering in the face of the overwhelming odds. But there was no way of knowing from the shouts in frantic Spanish, his only impression of the conflict outside.

Jock's limited view was toward the door into the bar and then only if he craned his neck so that one eye could peer round the woodwork. *What is Bardici doing?* Two shots rang out from somewhere—had that been Bardici? Or had they come from a Beretta outside? Jock wasn't sure. Then from the lobby came shouting in Spanish followed by a burst of shots as the door to the bar was flung wide open. Jock pulled himself tighter into his hiding place, just able to glimpse a pair of feet—or more precisely, Bardici's Colorado-style leather CAT boots.

For barely a second, the feet were motionless as Bardici checked out the room. *Is he puzzled at finding the room empty?* Jock couldn't be sure. Then the feet turned away and he slammed the door shut. From the lobby came the sound of raised voices. Bardici's feet moved rapidly as first a table, one chair and then another were stacked to barricade the door. Just as quickly, Bardici pulled them away, dismissing them as too light. Instead, he placed his back against the door. Jock flinched as he saw and heard the door shudder as someone on the other side tried to force entry. At the second attempt, the door bulged open maybe half a metre before Bardici's weight once again slammed it shut.

Jock saw Bardici's feet swivel so that he was now sideways to the door, his back facing the Scot. This could be his best chance—his *only* chance. If Bardici retreated, Jock realised he would be in a hopeless position, trapped beneath the counter with no room to move, let alone to escape. This was no time to sit it out. It was a time for action.

The bar door was rammed partly open again but once more Bardici's heaving shoulder gradually forced it shut. Judging by the laboured breathing, Bardici would not be able to resist much longer. The Albanian would soon be forced to retreat and tuck beneath the bar was the obvious choice for Custer's Last Stand. Jock eased himself out from under the bar to give the Taser a clear shot. He felt exposed but knew he was okay so long as Bardici did not turn round.

As Jock leaned hard to his right, edging out to get a better balance, his left foot struck one of the casks with a dull metallic clang. Instantly, Bardici whirled around. Almost immediately, the Albanian saw the Taser and Jock's crouching figure. He looked shocked but only for a split second. The Albanian's gun was still clutched in his hand and as the two men's eyes met, Jock saw that hand pivot upward to shoot. But even as it did so, the door, no longer restrained by Bardici's weight, burst open and struck him, so that as he fired, his body was knocked off balance and the bullet flew harmlessly over the counter before embedding itself into a wall.

There was a loud crash as the door slammed into the discarded table. Jock heard more shouts from the lobby, followed by a burst of fire, the bullets smashing through the partly open door. Jock did not hesitate. Aiming at Bardici's chest as the Albanian struggled to regain his balance, Jock squeezed the trigger on the Taser and sent 50,000 volts searing across the four metres between them to hit Bardici square in the chest.

Bardici gasped and writhed as the powerful surge of electricity sent him toppling backward against the fallen furniture.

He twisted sideways, falling awkwardly to Jock's left, a quizzical look on his greasy features. Jock was puzzled too. He had seen a Taser used on a few occasions and usually the victim writhed and wriggled in spasm but Bardici lay still, sprawled beside the chairs. With another crash, the splintered remains of the door swung open, the corner slamming into Bardici's skull for good measure as he lay contorted on the floor. The two guards from the front door appeared. Instantly, one of them swung his rifle round to aim at Jock before recognizing him and lowering his weapon.

Slowly, Jock stood up. He was unable to move freely, his knees screaming for synovial fluid to get them moving again. He nodded to the officers, who now stood over Bardici's motionless body. Gingerly, Jock took a step forward, concerned about at the shit that would flow from him killing Bardici. But as he looked down, relief surged through him like a storm. There was blood trickling down Bardici's left cheek from a bullet hole close to his left ear. One of the shots fired through the door had slammed into the Albanian's skull. Death had been instantaneous.

It was quiet outside now, deathly quiet. Jock went to the window. A small group of policemen stood close to the corpses of the two gunmen. He could just see Botía in the other direction, standing beside a line of armed officers, their guns at the ready like a firing squad, all trained on the rear wall of the hotel. Jock could not see any of the gang but he assumed they were all standing with their hands pressed against the hotel wall, waiting to be frisked, handcuffed and taken away.

The two guards left the bar to return to their posts at the front exit, though it seemed superfluous now. Jock followed them, clambering over the fallen chairs. He turned left into the corridor leading to the car park. Once down the steps, he waved to Botía, receiving the signal to join him. Jock could see Adrian Fenwick, in handcuffs, being led toward one of several police vehicles. Foxy Boxy was being patted down, ready to be removed. Altogether, fourteen people had been arrested.

"The two gunmen over there are dead," Botía explained with a nod of satisfaction.

"Where did they appear from?"

"One of the vans with Malaga plates."

"Sounds like Foxy Boxy's men."

"They were English, yes. I heard them." He paused to watch another pair being led away. "And inside? I heard shooting."

"Erlis Bardici was shot dead resisting arrest."

"By you?"

Jock shook his head. "By one of your officers."

Botía nodded with satisfaction.

"I saw one of yer men go down. Is he okay?"

"He was hit in the chest and the force knocked him over but he will be okay. The chestplate did its job." Botía looked around at the scene. "Your colleague Inspector Holtom was right; we needed all these men." Jock nodded, thinking that but for him and Ratso, Botía might even now have been sitting at the wrong hotel, waiting for action. But he said nothing as Botía turned his attention to his ringing phone and issued more instructions in rapid-fire Spanish. His face creased into a broadening grin. "The entire crew of *Nomora* has been arrested. The ship is now being searched. The operation is over."

"The master, too? Micky Quigley?"

"Definitely—though he tried to escape."

"Congratulations, Comisario—a great job." Jock stretched out his hand and after a slight hesitation Botía clasped it and shook it warmly.

"We must have a drink before you go. We have much to celebrate, yes?"

Jock agreed but already his thoughts had turned to Ratso. How he would have loved seeing Bardici gunned down and Micky Quigley frogmarched away. But perhaps the boss was getting his own moment of satisfaction.

61

Biggin Hill, Southeast London

Just over twenty-seven minutes later, the Vauxhall Insignia pulled off the A233 between the blue signs announcing Biggin Hill Passenger Terminal. The famous wartime airbase had evolved over the years and was now home to executive jets and other pleasure craft, some of them not much bigger—and a few even smaller—than the Spitfires that had once dominated the runway. For about the hundredth time, Ratso checked his watch. Zandro could not be ahead of him—not after that gut-wrenchingly wild ride as Brian had skilfully scythed his way through the afternoon traffic like an F1 driver.

He tried Jock's number but it was still not ringing. *Forget it, Ratso!* Now, everything was about arresting Zandro. He checked with Central 3000 who linked him to Wensley Hughes. The news was good: the helicopter, India 99, had Zandro under observation just over four miles from the airport in heavy but moving traffic, closing from the northwest. The team from SCD11 were holding well back, leaving India 99 to make the running. "You'll have a team of covert armed officers," Hughes explained. "They are near Bromley."

"Something and nothing, sir. That could be just a few minutes away or too bloody late depending on traffic."

"There's also a people carrier full of uniforms scheduled deliberately to arrive soon after Zandro." Wensley Hughes wished him luck before adding a final comment. "Incidentally, how did you know Zandro would do a runner via Biggin Hill?"

"That's for later, sir, I'm arriving." Ratso had responded as the red and white barriers at the entrance appeared. The Insignia squealed to a halt t. The barriers were set about sixty metres back from the road and beside them was a small but solid-looking building that housed security. An efficient-looking woman in a navy blue uniform emerged almost at once. Ratso flashed his card.

Ratso leaned out of the window and flashed his I.D. "Are you alone? What's your name?"

"My colleague George is inside. I'm Moira Gardner."

"Right, Moira. Get George out here," Ratso ordered. "And quick. And then come with me."

The woman looked startled, her eyes narrowing as if to say she did not trust this clapped-out, unshaven bloke who looked more like a criminal than a detective from the Metropolitan Police. But after only briefly hesitating she hurried in to find her colleague. Seconds later she returned leading a rather older male.

"George, this is the start of a major police operation. We are going to arrest someone who will arrive in a black Mercedes in the next few minutes. He will give his name as Altin Vata but in fact it is Boris Zandro."

"Boris Zandro," the man echoed. "He's a regular!"

"Despite his false credentials, let him through but don't rush. He'll be in a black Mercedes saloon. On no account show any suspicion. He may be armed. He is certainly dangerous. Got it?" Ratso saw the man as a solid, safe pair of hands. "Good. Also arriving will be Assistant Commissioner Wensley Hughes and more police support. Don't waste a moment letting them through but only *after* Zandro is in the building. He must not see them arrive."

"Understood, sir." The guard half-saluted respectfully while Moira Gardner piled into the back seat beside him. "Move it," Ratso ordered Brian, who surged forward, the car heading straight for the squat red-brick control tower. At the last moment he lurched sharply right to pull up in front of the terminal entrance. Both passengers tumbled out and hurried through the glass door into the compact welcome zone. Straight ahead, Ratso saw two counters—one for reception, where a woman was talking on the phone and another on the right for what he assumed was a commercial company called Executive Handling. Had there been time, he would have briefed the woman sitting there in her smart tunic but there was not. Ratso could almost feel Zandro's breath on his neck. "Moira, take me to Special Branch and as we go, talk me through how Zandro will reach his jet."

Immediately, they turned away from the raised seating area to their right where a couple of passengers and a pilot were sipping coffee. They ignored the reception desk and turned toward the large glass windows that looked out to the apron. "That's Zandro's." Moira pointed outside to the rain swept tarmac. Just over forty metres away, gleaming white with a single line of red piping running along the fuselage, was a Gulfstream V, its twin Rolls Royce engines fitted just in front of the tail. The jet was certainly longer than a cricket pitch but not by that much. Along the fuselage were six windows. Behind the cockpit, the steps were down ready to receive passengers. Ratso felt a moment's envy thinking what he had to show for years of honest toil by comparison.

"Someone from Executive Handling will probably take him to UK Border Control," Moira explained. "He will pass through that after his passport has been checked. He will then pass through security and the woman from Executive Handling may walk him right through to the Departures Lounge. If ready, the pilot may cross the apron to meet the passenger or he may stay in the cockpit doing final checks. The Executive Handling woman will swipe her card at the secure door leading outside and may either just let him through or may help him with his baggage."

By this time, they had passed through an empty zone with the words UK Border Control just below the ceiling. It was unmanned and anything less like the queues and rows of desks for immigration officers at Heathrow or Gatwick was hard to imagine.

"Someone will check Zandro here?"

"Executive Handling will arrange for someone from Immigration to be here," Moira acknowledged, slightly more relaxed now. She led him a few steps farther. "The security checks are then done just there." She pointed to a small belt which fed the scanner, taking the typical Gucci, Hermes and other designer luggage of the rich and famous through to airside.

As Ratso took in the layout, a tall but well-built figure appeared. He was aged late thirties with Bradley Wiggins-style sideburns. There was an aggrieved look on his face at the intrusion. "What's going on here?" The man's strong Brummie accent made him sound as gloomy as a donkey with a sore throat.

The question was addressed to Moira Gardner but before she could answer, Ratso had shown his ID. "I'm conducting an operation that will take place in the next few minutes. And you are?"

"Rogerson. Mark Rogerson, Special Branch."

Before the man had a chance to say anything more, Ratso jumped in. "Excellent." He explained in headline terms what was happening to arrest Altin Vata and Rogerson's attitude changed instantly. Ratso judged that after months of nil excitement, Rogerson was pleased to be seeing some action.

"You're arresting him airside, then?"

Ratso had every reason neatly marshalled. "Once he's airside, he can't escape. He could be armed though."

Rogerson was dismissive. "We have the top specification scanners here."

Ratso gave a half smile. "That's one good reason for tackling him airside. It *reduces* the chance of him being armed. He's rich, well-connected but beneath that he's a bruiser, a street fighter. He will *not* go quietly. We can immediately hold him for using a false passport but we've years of shit to throw back at him." He saw Rogerson was in synch. "Will Zandro recognise you? Your colleagues?"

"There's two of us on duty. Me and Keith Groom. Yes, he'll have seen us both."

Ratso's phone vibrated. "Yes?"

"Target has just turned into the airport," reported Tosh. "He's approaching some type of security barrier now."

"Confirmed." Ratso turned to Rogerson. "He's arrived. Anyone in the departures lounge?"

"Quite a few city types. They're waiting for fog at Geneva to lift."

Ratso was pleased. "When Zandro enters the airside lounge, I want your colleague Keith to block the exit to landside so he cannot turn back. I want you to be mingling with the other waiting passengers. We'll nab him by the door leading to the apron.

Be armed and have the cuffs ready. Go now. Get your mate sorted." He paused. "Ah, Moira: tell the control tower that the flight must not, repeat not be cleared for take-off. In fact, no flight must be cleared for take-off. Understood?" As the listeners turned to hurry away, he added, "I'll be in the airside lounge. He doesn't know me."

Ratso walked through the body scanner, which was turned off—just as well, because the knuckleduster buckle on his belt would have triggered the alarm, as might his chunky steel cufflinks. For a moment he thought back to when he had unclipped the knuckleduster in the slums of Freeport. Then, it had been an unnecessary precaution; now he freed the buckle again and slipped the aggressively meaty device onto the fingers of his right hand. *Just in case.* He rolled up the belt and slipped it into his left pocket.

He glanced back but there was no sign of Zandro in his Altin Vata disguise. *You had to give it to the guy. He was well-prepared.* His escape plans must have been fine-tuned for an immediate departure—plans that clearly did not include his shopaholic young wife. Ratso entered the final departures lounge where there were about a dozen young executives of both sexes. Their body language shouted their frustration loud and clear over their delay. One or two nodded toward him in a friendly but remote manner, more acknowledging his presence than wanting to talk. *Sorry, guys. You'll just have to wait for your in-flight Romanée Conti and rare fillet steaks. Jealous, Ratso? After only a bacon buttie and a coffee on the incoming flight from Spain? You bet.*

Ratso now had a moment to think. He had only been in the terminal for four minutes and had achieved a great deal. *But what have I overlooked?* He could think of nothing yet a nagging doubt remained. So long as everybody else did their thing, surely nothing could go wrong. He tried to look like a billionaire awaiting his private flight as he strolled restlessly, pausing to gaze out at the five impressive jets that were parked at varying distances from the exit beside him.

In Zandro's waiting Gulfstream, he could see the pilot… and a co-pilot. *Shit! A co-pilot.* He had forgotten about him. Giles Mountford had someone seated next to him. *But who could it be? What does the co-pilot know, if anything? Nothing.* Giles would never have confided that he was a grass, a snout for an officer in SCD7. It was too risky to phone Giles now with someone seated beside him. *Sure, Giles would not take off without ATC clearance. That was a given. But the colleague? What would he do? Or what if Zandro kept a gun on board? What if Zandro got aboard and threatened the pilots with a gun? Forced them to take off? Shit!* He should have thought of this before. Too late now.

Zandro must never reach his jet.

He looked anxiously back toward the door leading to the security zone. Where the hell was Rogerson? Zandro would be here any moment and only Rogerson had the cuffs. And where was Wensley Hughes and the promised support? Surely they had arrived? He dialled and heard Hughes' gentle tone, calm and reassuring. "We are under a mile from the airport, well clear now of Bromley. Okay?"

"It might be." Ratso was looking anxiously over his shoulder. "Gotta go." He turned to look at the Gulfstream, imagining the tall, slim figure of Giles Mountford sitting in the cockpit. *God! I'm placing a load of trust in him. Under threat, who would he back? Too late to agonise now.*

Would Giles or the co-pilot personally be escorting him to the steps into the aircraft? Even as he looked, the light rain became a sharp shower that beat down harder, the raindrops bouncing off the tarmac. In these conditions, more likely someone from the terminal with an umbrella would escort any passenger across to the aircraft.

Once banged up, Zandro would be very suspicious of how he had been traced to Biggin Hill. *Maybe I should let Zandro think he was followed by a team on the ground.* Ratso felt an overwhelming duty to protect any informant like Giles. It was the feeling every copper had for someone who took risks to make a few quid. If Zandro ever discovered the truth, then somehow, someday, Zandro would have Mountford killed—that, or murder his wife and two kids.

With most snouts, the desire to protect them as a source was matched by contempt that someone would sell his mates down the river for money. Ratso occasionally felt like that with the lowlifes but Giles Mountford he saw very differently. The pilot had not wanted money. Worse still, he knew he would lose his job once Zandro was arrested. But he despised Zandro. Ratso thought back to that day, seven months back, when he had traced Mountford to the Coal Hole pub on the Strand in central London. He had cornered him, got chatting and then taken him to dinner up Wellington Street. There he had produced the before-and-after photos of young Freddie. The sight of them had turned him.

"I've two kids myself in a vulnerable age group. I despise the drug trade." Before dinner was over, he had agreed to do what little he could to destroy the man who paid him. *But is he to be trusted if Zandro reaches the plane and threatens him? Answer: don't let Zandro get near the Gulfstream.*

As he gazed round the room, he saw with relief that Rogerson had joined the throng of thwarted passengers. *Sorry, guys. Even if the fog lifts now in Geneva, you're not going.* Rogerson immediately immersed himself in conversation with a small group that were tapping their feet, standing close to the door to the tarmac as if their proximity would make the Swiss fog lift. Then Ratso saw him—a total stranger who appeared from the direction of the scanner. He knew it was Zandro but not from his appearance. He was being escorted by a woman with a large umbrella; she wheeled a small roll-along and he was carrying an executive case. *Good on you, Boris*, Ratso thought.

Altin Vata was nothing like Boris Zandro. He looked ten years older, his cheeks much fatter, his eyebrows much wilder and grey. In a Tyrolean hat and dark olive-green overcoat, he looked like a retired and prosperous Austrian banker, though the name still sounded Albanian. Ratso could not see the eyes but he was prepared to bet he was wearing coloured contacts. The stomach girth was the same—substantial but not obese. The shoes were more suitable for mountain walks than Zandro's usual crocodile loafers. The hair that circled the foot of his perky little hat was also greyer than normal. But the dead giveaway was the ubiquitous black leather attaché case with brass trimmings. Below the handle were the embossed initials *BKZ*. The roll-along was barely larger than an oversized briefcase of the type used by many pilots. He was travelling light but to where? Air Traffic would have known, if he had thought to check.

Ratso watched Zandro's eyes sweep the room. If he was inwardly nervous, it did not show. "I'm just checking that Mr Mountford is ready for you," the woman said to her passenger as she held the phone to her ear. Ratso was ready to make his move but was baulked by the passengers who had gathered closer to the exit, between him and Zandro. The woman smiled at her passenger. "They're ready, Mr. Vata. We can go across." The woman released the roll-along while she removed the swipe card from her tunic pocket. Ratso moved rapidly to circle the chattering group. *Damn them!* Rogerson had been better positioned and was closer to Zandro as the swipe card worked and the glass door opened. The sound of the thunderous rain filled the room.

Things were not going as planned. Where were the uniforms to make the arrest? It was now down to him and Rogerson. There were no regular police officers based at this small airport unlike the major ones where they patrolled with their weapons ready. *No time to blame yourself for this snafu. Play the ball where it lies, Ratso.*

He rushed toward Zandro's departing back. "Mr Boris Zandro. I'm Detective Inspector Holtom, Metropolitan Police and I'm arresting you for using a false passport." On hearing this, Rogerson made his move. As Zandro spun round on hearing his name, Rogerson grabbed Zandro's left arm, which held the attaché case. The startled look on Zandro's face was one to savour, one Ratso hoped he would remember long after his days in the force were over. The eyes seemed to be twice their normal size; his tongue flicked out and as quickly back in as the muscles of the solid jawline drooped just slightly.

Just as Ratso was almost in reach, he heard Rogerson let out an anguished howl of pain. It came from deep in his stomach and sounded almost primeval, to the horror of the nearest group. At first Ratso thought Zandro had stabbed him but as Rogerson reeled backward, releasing his grip, the detective could see what had happened.

In Zandro's right hand, he was holding what looked like a Mont Blanc pen, a symbol of wealth and status among pens. It was black, quite fat with the small white star on top of the cap. But Ratso knew instantly that Mont Blanc made no pens like this one. He guessed that a specialist in personal protection had created a fake that concealed a virulent pepper spray—ideal for passing undetected through airport security. The active ingredient of capsaicin had rendered Rogerson temporarily and painfully blind.

As Rogerson reeled back yelling, hands frantically rubbing his eyes, he was caught by one of the city types. Ratso faltered, uncertain what to do. *Zandro must not reach the jet.* As Ratso lunged forward, Zandro raised his arm to spray him but Ratso landed a fierce upward blow with the knuckleduster on Zandro's wrist. Zandro yelped and lost his grip on the spray which fell to the floor, hissing like an asp. The spray missed Ratso instead catching Zandro's escort full in the face. She too fell back screaming, leaving Ratso alone by the open door to the tarmac.

Ratso swung his right arm again and smashed it into the thickness of the overcoat below stomach level but other than a grunt, it had no effect. "Grab the bastard," Ratso called out to anybody around him just as Zandro's attaché case swung full tilt and caught him a mighty blow on his right cheek, the sharpness of the brass corner gouging out a chunk of flesh. Ratso rocked back, momentarily confused by the heavy impact and the blood already pouring down his face.

Zandro needed no prompting. Before anyone reacted to Ratso's cry for help, he had rushed out, slamming the door shut behind him.

"The swipe card! Where's the swipe card?" Ratso yelled as blood spattered to the floor. The woman's hands were empty—she had clasped them over her eyes. He finally spotted it lying on the floor by her side. A quick swipe and he dashed into the downpour out on the apron, his head throbbing, the blood from his cheek dripping copiously onto his windcheater.

Zandro was no longer built for speed and even though he had abandoned his roll-along, he was still only three-quarter way to the Gulfstream. Ignoring the pain, Ratso broke into a sprint, the lashing rain obscuring his vision. Ahead, Ratso saw Zandro signalling to a woman in a scarlet tunic on the aircraft's steps.

Ratso wondered what Mountford would do—and the co-pilot, too. *Zandro must think the pilot will take off. He knows nothing of the embargo by ATC. But under pressure, would Mountford refuse? Would he obey a scruff with a bleeding face and risk blowing his cover? Does Zandro have a gun on board? Would Mountford still refuse if threatened at gunpoint? And if he took off with me on board?* He didn't care to think that through too closely.

No time to worry about that, Ratso. Just get aboard, or you've lost everything.

A crash of thunder almost directly overhead filled the air as Ratso splashed the last few paces toward the shapely beauty of the Gulfstream. Zandro had reached the plane. Ratso could see he looked out of shape as he clasped the railing and then mounted the steps one at a time. Ratso heard him shout to the woman in the scarlet uniform, "Close the fucking door!" Ratso could see her just inside as Zandro stumbled in before turning right and out of sight.

The hostess looked startled on hearing Ratso's shouts of "Police! Stop!" but must have pressed whatever switch set the steps in motion. As Ratso grasped the rail, they started to pivot upward, heading for their final position flush with the plane, sealing the passengers inside. From the third step, Ratso launched himself horizontally into the cabin. He crashed to the floor in the galley area, the main cabin's plush leather seats and tables off to his right. In hurling himself aboard, he struck the hostess, who tottered backwards and crashed into a cupboard filled with what sounded like fine china. As he lay on the floor, struggling to orient himself, the door to the jet closed with a thud. He was trapped.

Ratso took in his surroundings. Neil Diamond's *Solitary Man* was playing quietly, filling the cabin. The interior smelled of new carpets, expensive leather and spicy air freshener. Right beside him, close to his head, were black stockings and a pair of expensive black leather shoes with high stiletto heels.

As he rose to his knees, he saw Zandro's hand fumbling under a table just a couple of metres away. Beyond the table were two thickly padded leather chairs in gunmetal grey. He could hear the crouching figure grunting with the effort, his breathing quite laboured from crossing the apron. Then came a crackle of sticky paper being ripped and Ratso knew it must have been holding some type of weapon to the table's underside.

Zandro still had his back turned, so it was impossible to see what he was reaching for but there was no time to find out. Pushing back the svelte stewardess to the sound of more crashing crockery, Ratso launched himself straight onto Zandro's back, pulling him from the table and wrapping his right arm around his neck in a throttling grip. The Tyrolean hat tumbled to the thick grey carpet.

Ratso needed help—the second Special Branch officer or Wensley Hughes' team. "Open the door," Ratso ordered the hostess, shooting her a sharp look over his shoulder. "I'm a police officer. Open the door now." He strained to keep a grip on the cumbersome figure, who was twisting and lurching as he tried to get a weapon into play. "Just do it!" Ratso shouted again but he heard no sound of the door being opened. He wondered what was happening in the terminal or on the wet tarmac outside.

Then the plane shuddered as the Rolls-Royce engines whined into life. *My God! Heaven help anyone too close to the jet now. You're on *your own, Ratso. You gotta win this struggle.* Was Giles Mountford obeying orders from the hostess who had done nothing about the door? Was the pilot bluffing—protecting his cover as Ratso had always advised him?

As he fought to maintain his fierce lock, he realised that while pounding the tarmac he'd lost his knuckleduster. He was now reliant on the strength of his arms and fists alone. *Just when I need it most*, he thought, swaying from side to side in time with Zandro, who was fighting to free himself from the bear hug and grab whatever was under the table.

Ratso heard a movement behind him. The next second he felt a sickening crack to his left shoulder as the hostess brought a fire extinguisher down in a vicious blow. No doubt she had hoped to crack open his head but with the two men's erratic movements, she had narrowly missed. Now the shiny silver cylinder tumbled to the floor close to his feet.

Ratso felt an immediate loss of power in his left arm. It fell away, momentarily useless. He tightened his grip on Zandro's neck, his clenched knuckle pushing deep into it. Both Zandro's hands were free to scrabble beneath the table if he could only get close enough. *Shit! Will the hostess try to reach whatever's under the table?* She had only to squeeze past the two men, who were locked together like copulating dogs. *She's bound to try.*

A single tactical mistake now and he was dead. Neither pilot seemed eager to intervene as the jet engines continued to warm up, ready to taxi away. Ratso dismissed any hope that Mountford would break cover now. The best hope was he would not taxi the plane in defiance of ATC orders.

The extinguisher lay close to Ratso's left foot. *That bitch could reach it. If she does, I won't be so lucky twice.* With just one arm, he knew he could not keep hold of the bucking and heaving

Albanian for much longer. It was time for a change of strategy. Instead of forcing Zandro's head downward with his full weight on the Albanian's back, he suddenly jerked his arm up, heaving Zandro's head back as far as he could. Then, when he could raise it no farther, he slammed it back down and smashed the Albanian's nose into the table top.

A howl of pain split the cabin and Ratso gleefully imagined the blood pouring down Zandro's face and his eyes flooding with tears. But still the brute wriggled and twisted, grappling to get his hands under the table. From the corner of his eye, Ratso saw the stewardess lean down beside him, seeking the extinguisher.

No way, no way. With his foot, he manoeuvred the cylinder out of her reach and then jerked Zandro's head upward again but this time instead of crashing it back down he heaved himself and his prisoner sideways, slamming Zandro's head into the fuselage to his right. The force stunned the Albanian enough to momentarily stop his heaving. Taking a huge gamble, Ratso released Zandro's neck and dived to the carpeted aisle, just in time to seize the extinguisher before the stewardess got it. He knew he had just a second or two before Zandro would gather his wits sufficiently to get hold of his weapon.

As he rose from the floor, he glimpsed both a large knife and a pistol under the table, the knife clinging precariously by thick brown tape, tantalisingly close to Zandro's hand. With a surge of power, Ratso rose to his full height and swung the extinguisher. It smashed into Zandro's temple with all the power of a cricketer's hook shot. Zandro's snarl died in his throat as he crashed onto the table, legs crumpling uselessly. A moment later his whole body slithered to the floor, blocking the aisle.

The hostess was now terrified for her own safety, no doubt mesmerised by the blood that covered the detective from ear to ear. "Out of my way, bitch," he commanded as he gave her an almighty shove, sending her reeling back toward the galley. She scrambled in the drawers and came up clutching a fork but before she could even attempt to use it, a short-arm jab to her midriff sent her tumbling to the floor. He wrenched the fork from her hand, stamped his foot into her stomach and banged loudly on the closed cockpit door.

Mountford must have looked through the spyhole and seen him looking badly injured. There was some hesitation as he debated what to do, or perhaps he was discussing it with his co-pilot. But after a short delay, the door opened and the languid figure of Giles Mountford appeared in his navy blue uniform and crisp white shirt with blue tie.

For a second, Ratso peered into the cockpit brimming with high-tech screens and dials, the sharpness of the colours starkly clear in the overall darkness. "Detective Inspector Holtom, Metropolitan Police." He flashed his card. "Switch off the engines. Then get the plane's door open at once." He barked out the orders for the benefit of both the co-pilot and the hostess, though he doubted she was in much shape to notice what was happening around her. Taking no chances and for good measure, he winded her again.

As Mountford squeezed past to open the door and release the steps, Ratso returned to the motionless figure of Zandro. From under the table he freed a Bowie knife with a six-inch blade and a loaded Glock. He checked the safety catch and trousered the gun but kept the nasty Bowie in his good hand in case of trouble. Seconds later, the whine of the engines died and a blast of cold air confirmed that the door was now open. Ratso welcomed the sound of the hail bouncing off the fuselage and all across the apron.

Still, there was nobody close to the plane but clustered by the terminal he saw a group of uniformed officers being briefed. Another posse of armed officers wearing the distinctive blue-and-white-checked baseball caps ran out to the tarmac to surround the plane, weapons at the ready and heads bowed against the fierce storm. He summoned the uniforms from the top of the steps with a shout and a wave, though with his bloodied face and fearsome knife he wondered what impression he was giving. Two officers bounded up the steps and crammed into the tiny galley area. "You okay, Ratso? Pity about the teeth." It was Inspector Harry Dunbar, an old mate from his early days in the force.

"Good to see you!" Ratso's grin was somewhat lopsided. "I'm in a better state than Zandro, that's for sure. Make sure he's still out cold." Ratso flicked his tongue round his swollen mouth and found that the blow from the attaché case had knocked out two front teeth and loosened another. He had never noticed during the fight but now he could feel blood trickling from his mouth to mix with the slowing flow from his cheek. "How's Rogerson and the woman? Zandro peppered them."

"Being treated." Dunbar looked at the hostess now lying in a foetal position on the floor.

"Cuff her. She's in deep shit. But secure Zandro first, even though he's out cold."

A young constable with a scar down his left cheek looked into the cockpit, where both pilots were now seated. They looked bemused by events. "Them?"

Ratso ordered the pilots to leave the cockpit and when they stood in front of him he challenged them in turn. "You. What's your name?"

"Mountford. Giles Mountford."

"And you?"

"Edward Sanders."

"I am arresting you both for obstructing the police and for assisting an offender." Ratso turned to the officer at the top of the steps. "Take them away for further questioning." For just long enough, Ratso was alone facing Mountford. He gave him a broad wink which the pilot ignored with a perfect poker face. Finally Ratso ordered the hostess removed. As she was lifted to her feet, she spat straight into Ratso's face before she was taken down the steps into the icy pellets of hail turning the tarmac white.

"Sir, I think you can put down that knife now," the constable grinned. Ratso laid it on the blood-spattered table along with the Glock.

"Careful of the gun. It's loaded."

Zandro only stirred after his hands had been secured behind his back by a couple of the support team. Then he was frogmarched like a drunk down the short stretch of the aisle and assisted down the steps to the tarmac. At that moment, the AC appeared from beneath an umbrella at the top of the steps. He saw the gun and knife and then spotted Ratso's bloodied face, his left arm hanging limply at his side. "Take a seat, that one near the back." He signalled that they were not to be disturbed. "Let's talk in headlines for a couple of minutes. Then you need to get yourself sorted. You better than you look?"

"Feeling great, sir! Feeling like *Christ! I've done it. I've got the bastard.*" There was a slight pause. "But Jock? He's okay?"

"He's fine. He got into a confrontation with Bardici – hence the loss of communication. The gang in Spain were all rounded up, including Micky Quigley." He stopped and turned to face Ratso. "Bardici is dead."

A look of enormous satisfaction nearly took over Ratso's lopsided and bloodied features. *RIP Neil.* Then he thought of Kirsty-Ann, who would whoop round her office at the news about Bardici. "Dead, eh? That saves Washington's neck. It was looking bad when Lance Ruthven's body turned up."

"With luck, a malleable pathologist and the Bahamas boys not being too interested, that corpse will become an unsolved crime statistic. I'm banking on you and Darren Roberts."

"Unless…"

"No, Todd." The AC smiled knowingly. "No *unless*. Adnan Shirafi remains off-limits. No way must his name come out. Bardici's death makes that far easier to achieve." The AC's words were spoken with finality. "Operation Clam is now a dead parrot."

Ratso was in no mood to let go of Shirafi. "Unless something comes out at Zandro's trial."

"Do you really believe Boris Zandro is going to name Shirafi? I think not. The words *the fat greedy bastard* on that recording apply to half the civilised world." Ratso felt constrained to agree, though he hated to do so.

"Terry Fenwick?"

"Fractured tib, fib and femur and now in hospital under twenty-four-hour supervision."

"And The cocaine? They found it?"

Hughes laughed. "But for your work in Freeport, Jock reckons it might never have been found. It was brilliantly concealed. There's been no time to remove it but the manhole cover into the water tank was cut open. Crammed full down there." The last words were said with real satisfaction.

Ratso was now lost for words, the energy that had driven him for so long suddenly draining away. He was running on empty.

Wensley Hughes motioned him off the comfy grey chair and put a fatherly arm over his shoulder. No words were needed as they walked slowly down the aisle between the maple tables. As they reached the galley, Ratso turned for a quiet moment, taking in the soft lights and opulent luxury that Zandro's crimes had bought. The sound of Neil Diamond's *Red, Red Wine* crooned from the wraparound sound system.

"This'll raise multimillions under the Proceeds of Crime Act." The AC's words reflected Ratso's thoughts.

"Hard to compare this with a night flight on Ryanair, isn't it, sir?"

Wensley Hughes stooped to exit and beckoned Ratso to follow. "Time you got cleaned up a bit. I'll get this sealed off as a crime scene."

Slowly Ratso descended the steps, holding onto the rail with his only working arm. The hail had stopped but the frozen chunks of ice crunched beneath their feet as they crossed to the bright lights of the terminal. The flight to Geneva was still grounded, fog or no fog and Ratso felt the curious stares from the delayed passengers. Then someone clapped, a solitary sound that quickly spread till everybody joined in as the figure with the torn jacket, dead arm and ripped and bloodied face walked slowly through. Several patted him on the shoulder. It was an extraordinary moment, quite surreal and something Ratso had never experienced before. He found it hard to cope with, this hero bit, so he continued walking with only a briefly raised hand in acknowledgment.

Hughes pointed to a men's room. "First, clean yourself up. Then let's grab a cup of tea before the ambulance picks you up."

"A cuppa and some biccies would be just great, if I've enough teeth left to bite with."

He followed the sign for the Gents' and wandered in, operating on autopilot. The obsession that had driven him for so long was over. No question, this had been the biggest moment of his career. And yet now he felt flat, limp, a sort of post-coital tryst without the sex.

He looked in the mirror and took in his swollen jaw and the gap where two teeth on the right side had been knocked out. Two others wiggled at his touch. *Need to get all this fixed before Kirsty-Ann arrives.* The dried blood covered most of his face; even his hairline was snagged with clotted lumps. He was shocked at the gaunt, unshaven features that stared back at him, the eyes sunk deep with dark rings.

At last, hot water filled the basin. He took a final look at the mess he was before sloshing the water over his face till it was pale crimson. He rinsed the last drops of blood from behind and inside his ears and then towelled himself down, gently dabbing the gouged cheek which was going to need some stitches. But he looked better and rather less like the loser after ten rounds with Mike Tyson.

His phone rang. It was Tosh. "Hey, boss! Congratulations. What a day! Coming back for a piss-up?"

"Thanks, Tosh. Let's wait for Jock. Maybe tomorrow."

"Sure, whatever. They nabbed three more in Leeds. By the way, the lads have already planned the first song for down the Nags Head."

Ratso knew some jibe was coming but was too exhausted to spot it. "Go on."

"*All I want for Christmas is my two front teeth, my two front teeth,*" sang Tosh with a chuckle in his voice.

Ratso laughed and felt better for it. "You'd better make the most of this party. Your 5:2 diet starts the next day. Wensley Hughes' orders. It'll be green tea and Ryvitas two days a week."

"I'll resign. Become a traffic warden. See you later, boss." He rang off, leaving Ratso in higher spirits. In the end, camaraderie was the glue; teamwork, team spirit and a shared sense of purpose made it all worthwhile. He'd have to ring Jock from the ambulance and congratulate him.

He looked in the mirror again. *Forget the swollen jaw, the lost teeth, the jagged rip down my cheek, the searing pain in my temple. This is life, the only life I really want. Living on the edge, sniffing out opportunities. That's for real. Now for the next Zandro to give me that rush. And until then? Well… it's Fulham at home on Saturday with the Stoke Mandeville lads. And then? Not too long till a week with a beautiful American blonde. Yes. That would do very nicely, thank you. Bring it on.*

THANKS!

Thanks for reading **Hard Place** and I hope you enjoyed it. If you did, it would be great to hear from you or you could put a review on Amazon or Goodreads.

Want to be kept informed of my new books? Contact me on email or by my website:

Email: Doug@douglasstewartbooks.com
Website: www.DouglasStewartBooks.com
Facebook: www.facebook.com/DouglasstewartBooks

COMING SOON
DEAD FIX
#2 in the Ratso series.

The opening chapters are below and I hope they will encourage you to enjoy another Ratso thriller

Dead Fix

1

London

The lean and fit looking man blinked as a tear splattered across the scrap of paper. Mark Rayner was seated alone on a comfy white leather sofa, a crudely scrawled message shaking in his hand. While parked at his local hospital, someone had tucked it under a wiper-blade of his Porsche Turbo. Of course, he had dreaded what *they* might do – somehow, some place, some time. Yet never in his lowest moments had he considered them stooping to this.

Mutilation.

After wiping away the worst of the tears, he glanced out as the sun set behind the silhouetted trees in his spacious garden. Of one thing, he was sure. Some bastard had been watching and waiting for him at the red brick hospital. Or had followed him there.

Maybe the evil bastard had even tailed him home.

Might now be lurking somewhere in the shadows.

At the front or round the back.

Perhaps be peering through a window.

Watching and waiting.

You were warned.

The words on the note haunted him. He let out an anguished howl as he relived what the surgeons had told him. The sound reverberated round walls lined with Impressionist artwork painted by his wife Yvonne. At the sight of them, guilt swept through him, making his body shake. For the third time since reaching home, he reached for the Grey Goose bottle and glugged down a generous swig. Then, as the note fell from his chinos, fluttering to the pinewood floor, he rolled sideways on the sofa, arms clenched around his knees, head tucked into the foetal position, shoulders heaving.

There was no choice now.

Not after this.

He had to go on.

Play their game.

Dance to their tune.

Unless…

2

New York City
Alex Anderson waved London's Daily Mail. "A hammer! That's what they used." He jabbed at the article. "Mark Rayner's baby was eight months old. Now, five weeks later, Rayner say she'll never walk, talk or do anything meaningful again." He glared at the placid features of the Indian before switching to the truculent face of the New Yorker.

For Enzo Pagano, Vijay Chetri and Alex Anderson, this was just another regular meeting - at least on the surface. Today though, the atmosphere was electric. Typically, they had worked well together, though they had never been friends. This was business, no more, no less.

The clipped sentences, the restless hands, the alcohol, the sideways glances and lowered eyes revealed the tensions. What never changed was the five-star opulence of their meeting-places like the Mandarin Oriental in Las Vegas, the George V in Paris, the Bel Air in Los Angeles and the Hermitage in Monaco.

Today, they were at the Pierre on East 61st Street with an elegant suite overlooking Central Park. Not that any of the trio gave a toss for the view. Sure, they liked the discreet ambience but they chose the luxury for the simple reason that they expected nothing less. Extravagance was their norm. Mainly they talked betting and money - horses, cricket, American football, baseball or basketball.

After neither listener showed any concern about the brutality, Anderson rose to his full height topping six feet. He advanced towards them, towering over them in their separate chairs. "His wife Yvonne – blinded for life. Acid thrown in her face." His dark eyes bored into each listener in turn. "Sure, Rayner did not deliver the fix." He leaned forward to smash his fist on the table. "Cost us a wad but does that make this okay?" Again he waved the pictures of mother and child. "Like hell it does!"

He went to the window. Down below, a horse towed a carriage of tourists into Central Park. Vijay spoke gently with a sing-song accent. "Alex, this was nothing to do with us." He sounded sincere but no way did Anderson believe him. The small but tubby Indian joined the Englishman looking down to the park entrance. He was too short to put a friendly hand on Anderson's shoulder but he clasped his elbow before continuing. "My guess? The heavy mob from Pakistan wanted Rayner, shall we say, *encouraged* never to fail again. They probably lost multi-millions."

Anderson said nothing. It was Pagano, sprawled sideways on the sofa who spoke. "See Alex? Nothing for us to feel bad about."

As Anderson looked round, he caught Pagano's condescending smile. He returned to stand over the corpulent figure, his voice raised. "Crap," retorted Anderson, stroking his hand over his thinning black hair, cut short and covering his ears. With the chiselled features and wide-set eyes, he looked both handsome and yet someone not to be messed with.

Pagano, though, had survived and thrived in the toughest parts of the Bronx and along the New Jersey shore. As if Anderson had not said a word, the New Yorker continued, rubbing his hand down his stubbled cheek, a chuckle in his voice. "Alex, Alex - we were *victims*. We trusted Rayner to fix Surrey Patriots to lose. Bigger fish than us lost so much more."

Anderson turned away to sit down with measured assurance, very aware that four eyes were staring at him. He was in no rush to contribute. He had not got rich without being calm under fire and cunning to a fault. "Whatever. Hammering a baby's brains, I mean that is fucking sick, so count me out - no more fixing cricket. I'm out of all that. I'll stick with HOSS." He brushed down the lapel of his grey suede jacket. "And Jupiter. I'm up for that."

It was just what Pagano wanted to hear. "Take a hike, Alex. You ain't picking and mixing in a candy store. You are in or out."

"Mark Rayner has got the message. He won't let us down again." Chetri sounded sincere but he addressed the words as much to his black tasselled loafers as to Anderson. "At his next televised match, he'll deliver the result we want."

Alex leaned back and clasped his hands behind his head but said nothing.

He knew it was better that way.

Play silent ... and deadly.

The long game.

3

London

Det. Inspector Todd "Ratso" Holtom was unsure just why he had received the call to meet the Assistant-Commissioner at New Scotland Yard. His last major investigation, *Operation Clam*, had been successful so he knew or *thought* he knew that he was not being carpeted.

He always walked when he could, his stride long and brisk, part of his desire to keep in shape for his remaining days as a club cricketer. Now pushing towards forty, it would not be long before clapped-out knees and weary muscles would prevent him from racing in to bowl at over 70mph.

After crossing the Thames, he passed the bell-tower of Big Ben. There, he quickened his pace with the intensity of the beat from Black Sabbath filling his ears. After passing through security at Scotland Yard, he took the elevator to the A-C's office where he was not kept waiting. As Big Ben struck eleven, Wensley Hughes offered him a coffee and a seat. "Prosecutions following *Clam* in good shape?"

"I believe so, sir. Both here and in Spain."

"Good. Excellent result." His fingers, touching as if in prayer, added to his monk-like appearance. "But you were lucky. Nailing Boris Zandro became an ego trip." He sucked in air through his narrowed mouth. "Not on. The risks you took – brave … but unacceptable." He fixed Ratso over his gold-rimmed glasses. "No room for glory, no need for heroes."

Hughes had been a loyal supporter and Ratso had no answer to the criticism, so he just nodded. It was pointless defending the indefensible.

"So, if you want further promotion, I want no repetition. Sticking your neck out on theories, I can live with. Results aren't achieved by blinkered thinking. Your enthusiasm serves you well. But becoming a maverick?" Hughes shook his placid features. "Not on. Not these days in the Met. Understood?"

"Understood, sir." Ratso waited for whatever else was coming.

The AC glanced at his monitor. "You've become an invaluable team-member in the drugs war." Ratso sensed an almighty *but* coming and his spirits drooped. He fought unsuccessfully to keep a poker face. He tilted his head sideways and tried to look away as Hughes nailed him with an unfaltering stare. "Relax, Todd. I can see what you're thinking. I'm not putting you out to grass." He placed his hands, palm down across the desk. "I think you'll like what I'm going to say." He topped up their coffees. "You like cricket."

"Love it, sir. Are you inviting me to captain the Met Police veterans?"

It was a facetious remark and Hughes smiled. "At your age? Get real. No. Let's talk match-fixing."

"It happens."

"Then your role will be to stop it. You read about Mark Rayner's wife and baby being attacked."

"Disgusting."

"The local police team are dealing with this as a personal matter. That or some local nutter."

"But you don't think so?"

"Rayner captains Surrey Patriots."

"You think this thug got at him by attacking his family? Something to do with fixing?"

COMING SOON

#2 in the Det. Inspector Todd "Ratso" Holtom series

DEAD FIX

Books by Douglas Stewart
Fiction
Hard Place
Undercurrent
The Dallas Dilemma
Cellars' Market
The Scaffold
Villa Plot, Counterplot
Case for Compensation

Contributions
M.O. – anthology
Capital Crimes – anthology

Nonfiction
Terror at Sea*
Piraten (German Language market)
Insult to Injury
A Family at Law

*An updated and re-released version of The Brutal Seas

WATCH OUT FOR

DEADLINE VEGAS

Ever wanted revenge against a casino? Bet you have! Dex does! After his sister is cheated playing roulette and then dies mysteriously, an obsession for revenge takes Dex from London to Panama and Las Vegas. Ignoring warnings, Dex takes on the casino bosses as he plans to destroy a London casino and to smash Space City, a glitzy Vegas mega-resort. But can Dex trust anyone in his dangerous mission? Can card-counting blackjack player Billy kick his addiction? Is TV presenter Tiffany too involved with her high-flying career? The action races towards its climax as Dex uses courage and cunning against the vile ruthlessness of the casino bosses.

ACKNOWLEDGEMENTS

Hard Place was inspired by a real-life successful operation by officers of London's Metropolitan Police but for a wide variety of reasons, the events in this fictional work are much changed—while remaining authentic.

As always, I am grateful to the many people who assisted on what proved to be a fascinating journey into the world of major international criminal activity. I love writing on a large canvas with my novels crossing borders and evoking images of different cultures, time-zones, climates and atmosphere. To all those who have enabled me to travel to distant lands and to support my research there, my sincere gratitude.

Old friends Rick and Sarah Heffernan in Northern Cyprus provided great hospitality whilst I researched the truth and fiction about the Turkish Republic of North Cyprus. Ray and Annie Foot also opened my eyes to the Bahamas during my time there and assisted with some useful input. My wife Bridget and daughter Lara have supported the quirks and foibles of an author at work. All deserve this named acknowledgement. Others, including serving police officers, must remain nameless. They provided true insight into their fight against hardened criminals and wealthy drug barons. They know of my gratitude and do not need public acknowledgement, although they deserve more public recognition for their long hours and work in dangerous circumstances.

As is evident from my previous books involving crime at sea - Undercurrent and *The Brutal Seas* (now updated and being re-released as Terror at Sea), I have always been fascinated by the significant role that ships play in underworld activity—without the wider public having any real insight into what goes on beyond our shores. *Hard Place*, while land-based, exposes how the sea and ships has been used. For this novel, besides advice from serving police officers, I am grateful to Graham Sowrey for his valuable insight about both ships and aviation. I hope I have interpreted all help correctly.

I am also indebted to the personnel at Biggin Hill Airport for granting me privileged access for part of my research. Thanks to Alison, Joanne and Michelle for their support and valuable advice in the design and editorial process.

HARD PLACE
First published 2015
This Edition 2017
Copyright © Chewton Limited, Douglas Stewart

The right of Douglas Stewart to be identified as the author of this work has been asserted by him in accordance with the Copyright, Designs and Patents Act 1988 and other current legislation.

You may not copy, store, distribute, transmit, reproduce or otherwise make available this publication (or any part of it) in any form or by any means (electronic, digital, optical, mechanical, photocopying, recording or by any other manner whatsoever) without the prior written consent of the author and of Chewton Limited. Any person or body who does any unauthorised act in relation to this publication may be liable to criminal prosecution and civil claims for damages.

All rights reserved.
ISBN: 1547169540
ISBN: 9781547169542

Chewton Publications, an imprint of Chewton Limited

ABOUT DOUGLAS STEWART

Born in Glasgow, Scotland, Douglas was brought
up in England and practised as an international lawyer in London and the USA. In tandem, he also developed a successful career as an internationally
widely-read author, with a chart-topper
and a WH Smith Paperback of the Week to his credit. He is married with 3 children.

Printed in Great Britain
by Amazon